Praise for Caroline Llewellyn's previous novels!

THE LADY OF THE LABYRINTH

"[*The Lady of the Labyrinth*] has Mary Stewart's decorative delight in the ancient world and Whitney's overlay of mystery."
—*Kirkus Reviews*

"An adventure tale of the first order, provides suspense, unexpected confrontations and danger galore."
—*The Chattanooga Times*

THE MASKS OF ROME

"A web of intrigue, deceit and danger . . . The action is fast-paced. . . . Enjoyable."
—*The New York Times Book Review*

"Compelling . . . With its rich atmosphere, deftness of plot and fully dimensioned characters, this accomplished debut delivers on its promise of romantic suspense and plenty more."
—*Publishers Weekly*

Also by Caroline Llewellyn
Published by Ivy Books:

THE MASKS OF ROME
THE LADY OF THE LABYRINTH

LIFE BLOOD

Caroline Llewellyn

IVY BOOKS • NEW YORK

Ivy Books
Published by Ballantine Books
Copyright © 1993 by Caroline Llewellyn Champlin

This is a work of fiction. Names, characters, places, and incidents either are the product of the author's imagination or are used fictitiously. Any resemblance to actual events or persons living or dead is entirely coincidental.

Library of Congress Catalog Card Number: 93-3953

ISBN 0-8041-1263-0

This edition published by arrangement with Charles Scribner's sons, an imprint of Macmillan Publishing Company.

Manufactured in the United States of America

First Ballantine Books Edition: November 1994

10 9 8 7 6 5 4 3 2 1

FOR KIT

I am grateful to Flora Davis, Emilie Jacobson, and Susanne Kirk for many things, but especially for their faith in my work; to the members of my writers' group for their encouragement and invaluable advice; and to Adrienne Mayor and Josh Ober for the fictional loan of Spike.

As always, I am grateful to Ted for more than I can say.

PROLOGUE

When Evelyn Allerton was killed, someone was watching. I know now who it must have been, just as I am certain of the murderer's identity, but in my drawings only the victim's face is visible. The other two are always turned away or hidden, for I have no proof.

I am a book illustrator. When I can afford to choose, I prefer to illustrate picture books for young children. Occasionally I write the text to accompany the pictures, but I rarely think of myself as a writer because the images come first and more easily than the words.

Drawing my nightmares has always helped to make them go away. When images of Evelyn Allerton's murder began to haunt me, I drew what I imagined had happened. At first, I simply wanted to be rid of those imaginings in order to live peacefully in a place I thought might be a home for my baby son, Max, and myself. Later, I drew to discover the truth.

There are over a dozen drawings, rough sketches most of them. They won't be used for any book of mine; this is hardly a story for very young children. I doubt, in fact, that anyone but me will see them. But I want to tell the story—my reasons will emerge as it unfolds—and the drawings can serve as a beginning.

They are only preliminary sketches now, pencil on paper. In their final form they ought to be woodcuts, blazing white lines on a deep black background. I want the boldness and the power of the woodcut, as well as its ability to evoke old illustrations from the earliest books.

For my story, which on the surface is a tale of murder and love, is really about a book.

1

This is how the story began, more than fifty years ago. Here are my pictures, in words.

Shipcote, 1938.

Snow is falling on the Cotswolds in thick, smothering flakes. It snuffs out the lights of the village, half a mile distant down the valley, and gives the darkness a deceptive bedtime peace. It blurs every outline, veiling the figure that struggles up the lane toward the cottage, obliterating the footprints left behind. The snow might easily be an accomplice.

Set back from the lane on a hillside, the cottage stands in a walled garden where boughs and vines droop under the weight of the snow. Its thick stone walls, which hold in the cold and the damp so well, muffle sounds; the casement windows are shut against the winter night; the front door is closed. However, something, some noise from inside perhaps, makes the figure that now stands on the doorstep pause with one gloved hand raised as though to knock.

The hand falls away from the door. A shaft of light piercing the milky darkness shows that the curtains of a downstairs window are not entirely drawn together. The figure at the door wades through the snow toward the window. Like spume tossed up by the wind, snowflakes swirl in the column of light, beating against the bent head, clinging to the wide-brimmed hat and the shoulders of the coat, as the figure peers through the narrow strip of mullioned glass.

A single large room runs the width of the cottage. It is lit only by two gas lamps and by the coal fire burning in the wide stone hearth set in the outer wall to the left. A coal scuttle with a shovel and a poker sits beside the grate. The dim light from the fire and the lamps barely penetrates the shadows that web the dingy wallpaper. A wing chair and a sofa, the armrests of their ill-fitting slipcovers worn and dirty, a round gate-legged dining table with three mismatched chairs, and a battered chest of drawers against one wall furnish the room. A heap of clothes lies cast off on the back of a chair, dirty dishes and empty milk bottles litter the top of the dining table. All that keeps the room from dreary squalor is the books that overflow the shelves of a bookcase.

Someone is pacing up and down the room, flickering back and forth in front of the window. She is an angular, big-boned woman in a shapeless black dress, a woman with a bitter, unhappy face who might be any age from twenty-five to forty. She is cradling something to her chest, her shoulders hunched as if she is in pain. Although she is shouting, her mouth ugly with the effort, only the sound of her anger, not the words themselves, reaches the watcher outside. Whoever is with her is out of sight, somewhere to the left of the window.

Perhaps the other's voice intervenes, for the woman abruptly stops before the fire and her head falls forward, wings of dark hair curtaining her face. For some moments she stands like that, as though listening.

But whatever the other says only enrages. The woman's head jerks up and the great dark eyes flame in her face, giving her a brief, gothic beauty. Her lips are moving again in soundless fury. Suddenly, she thrusts the object she is holding away from her body. It is a bundle of papers tied together with a dark ribbon, a manuscript. Then, in a swift, convulsive movement, as though casting out her own devil, the woman throws the manuscript onto the fire.

"No!" the watcher shouts, but the wind blows the cry away unheard.

The watcher runs toward the cottage door. Numb with the cold, the gloved hands grasp at the stiff, unyielding latch, slipping from the icy metal, then are raised to hammer on the wood. But again, some sound from within arrests the action. Pushing back through the snowdrifts to the window, the watcher looks in once more.

The woman lies sprawled on her right side in front of the fire, a dark mass of blood obscuring the upturned side of her face. In her right hand she clutches a single sheet of crumpled paper, splashed with crimson. Apart from the burning coal and the poker, which lies half in the hearth, the grate is empty.

Fear as sharp as an engraver's knife cuts this scene into the watcher's memory, deeply, indelibly.

Suddenly, the attacker appears, bends over the woman, and snatches the paper from her fingers, vanishing with equal swiftness from sight. Almost at once, the front door opens. The attacker, wrapped in a greatcoat, with a scarf hiding the head and most of the face, rushes out of the cottage and, without looking around, hurries down the path and through the gate, to disappear into the swirling snow.

The watcher stumbles slowly toward the door, hesitates on the threshold, as though afraid, then enters the front hall and turns slowly to the living room. To see the bloody scene beside the fireplace.

All that remains is the body. The manuscript is gone.

Blood hides the victim's left eye but the right bulges out from the shattered face. There is no pulse, no heartbeat, no ember of life glowing beneath the dulled flesh. The watcher refuses the final ritual to that staring eye and it remains open, fixed accusingly on the unseen.

A few feet away from the body lies the coal shovel, its blade edged with blood. Breathing hard, the watcher takes a handkerchief from a coat pocket and with trembling hands wipes the handle of the shovel.

After warming those gloved and shaking hands before the fire into a semblance of control, the water then proceeds deliberately to destroy the room, smashing the dirty plates and cups, knocking over chairs, throwing the heap of clothes to the floor. In front of the bookshelf, the watcher pauses for a moment, as though reluctant, then drags the books from the shelves. Upstairs, in the bedroom with its sagging double bed and tumbled sheets, the wardrobe is ransacked and the contents of drawers are dumped onto the floor. Only items of any value are taken, among them a gold pocket watch, a locket, and some coins from a purse on the nightstand by the bed. These the watcher places in a linen pillowcase, embroidered with the initials EBA, stripped from one of the pillows on the unmade bed.

The accomplice, for that is what the watcher has become, goes downstairs to the small kitchen, lights the candle that stands on a counter by the sink, and removes what little food there is from the icy larder shelves. Bread, cheese, carrots, some tins of soup are bundled into the pillowcase. Finally, the accomplice takes a small cast-iron frying pan from the stove, checks that the back door is bolted, and goes through the front door around to the back of the house. The pan smashes hard against the kitchen window, which breaks inward. A gloved hand reaches in and unhooks the catch, opening the window. Shards of glass and large clots of snow tumble onto the floor as the accomplice climbs in over the windowsill. The pan is carefully wiped and replaced on top of the stove.

The accomplice returns to the body to remove the gold wedding band from the woman's right hand. The ring, however, will not slide over the chapped and swollen flesh. Sweating with the effort, the accomplice forces the ring as far as it will go onto the knuckle, then gives up and, slinging the pillowcase over one shoulder, goes out through the front door, leaving it slightly ajar. On the path that leads to the gate, the footprints of the murderer are already half-filled with snow and will soon be invisible.

The accomplice, too, vanishes into the snowy night.

CHAPTER 1

A little more than fifty years after Evelyn Allerton's murder, I was in London to receive an annual award for "Best Children's Picture Book by a Commonwealth Illustrator," given by The British Society of Book Illustrators. It was my first trip to England. It was also my first time away from my son, Max. Five days of freedom from diaper-changing, bottle-warming, and interrupted sleep ought to have seemed an escape, and yet I missed him with a longing that took me by surprise.

London was a raucous, dirty, congested, glorious distraction. Everyone I met told me how lucky I was; this was not, they assured me, a typical English spring. Warmed by the unnatural sun, office workers on their lunch hour lay in the parks and squares like pale plants among the daisies. A few optimistic cafés had put tables outdoors and the markets were full of flowers: tulips, freesias, irises, and small pots of bright primroses.

The shapes of everyday things, cars, streetlights, the clothing people wore, were unfamiliar to me, or were juxtaposed in startling ways. Colors, especially green, took on new tones under the low blue English sky. I was overcome with a sudden consuming hunger to record details, the most insignificant, even the banal. I made dozens of sketches and if there was no time for drawing I took a photograph instead.

I was the compleat tourist, guidebook in hand, neck craned at the angle that so immediately distinguishes the sightseer from the native. Content to be alone, I wandered the streets unafraid of what I might find. London's past was not mine. When I turned a corner, there were no memories of my husband waiting for me. In Toronto, they were everywhere.

Apart from the awards dinner and meetings with several British publishers who were expressing a sudden interest in my work, I had only one obligation while I was in London—to get in touch with an elderly lady named May Armitage who had been a friend of my English grandmother.

I am my grandmother's namesake. She was Joanna Margaret Lorimer and I am Joanna Margaret Treleven, although she was always known as Nan and everyone calls me Jo. Nan had grown up near Gloucester, the only child of a country doctor and his wife. At eighteen, after her parents' deaths in an influenza epidemic, she went up to London to train as a nurse. Several years later, swept along in the tide of socialist fervor that carried so many to Spain, she joined the International Brigade, serving as a nurse in the Civil War. There she met and fell in love with a young Englishman named Charles Lorimer, an ambulance driver with the Brigade.

On their return to England, Nan and Charles had married and settled in a cottage near the Cotswold village of Shipcote. But only a few months later, apparently after a quarrel, Charles walked out the door of Longbarrow Cottage. Nan never saw him again. She was two months pregnant at the time. In her distress, Nan turned to May

Armitage, who was the village schoolteacher. The two women became friends, and Nan invited May to live with her. One night soon after my mother was born a fire broke out in the cottage. Nan, still weak from the difficult birth, was heavily asleep at the time and it was May who woke to the smell of smoke, got Nan and her baby out of bed and safely outdoors, then went back inside to put out the fire.

In the first years of World War II Nan and my mother emigrated to Canada, while May Armitage stayed on at Longbarrow Cottage. Nan died when I was ten years old, leaving Longbarrow Cottage to me. However, a provision in her will allowed May to remain in the cottage for as long as she liked, provided that she "keep the cottage in good repair" and pay the tax on it in lieu of rent. For the next seventeen years, May had complied with these terms.

I had never seen Longbarrow Cottage, nor had I met May. She corresponded with my mother at Christmas and usually sent me something unwearable that she had knitted herself. There was also the occasional letter over the years asking us to approve certain improvements she wanted to make at her own expense. These were always reasonable changes, new plumbing, new heating, rewiring, which my parents could not have afforded themselves. As well as her teacher's salary, May had, we knew, some sort of independent income. She had never married.

My parents had never expressed any annoyance at May's choosing to take advantage of the terms of Nan's will. We owed her a debt, they told me, that could never really be repaid.

I had intended to write to May before coming to England, to say that I would like to visit her, but somehow in the shuffle of preparations, work, and looking after Max, the letter remained unwritten. I did telephone twice, the day before I left, but there was no answer. There was no answer, either, to repeated calls to Longbarrow Cottage from London. On the afternoon of the fourth day of my visit, when I tried yet again, there was a recorded message saying that the number had been disconnected. No, the operator told me, when I asked, it had not been changed.

Disturbed, and feeling guilty over that unwritten letter, I sat on the edge of the bed in my hotel room, wondering what to do next. There was a firm of local solicitors, I remembered, who handled the minor legal transactions that cropped up from time to time concerning Longbarrow Cottage. Their office was in the town nearest to Shipcote, a place called Wychley. They might know if something had happened to May. After a moment, the name of the firm came to me: Munnings and Wooley. Directory Enquiries gave me its telephone number.

When I explained why I was calling, the secretary put me through to one of the partners. "Tony Munnings here, Miss Treleven. I'm very glad you called. I was about to write to you. You're in London, I gather."

"Only briefly." I told him about my attempts to get in touch with May.

"I'm afraid she's had a mild stroke." He went on to say that she had recently been discharged from the hospital and was living with a nephew and his family in a London suburb. "The cottage is empty now. Well, empty is perhaps the wrong word. Miss Armitage has left most of her furniture behind. She wants you to have it. I should add that while it's all very comfortable, there isn't anything of real value. It may prove more of a nuisance than a blessing."

"You don't think that when she's better she might like to come back?"

"I can't imagine that would be possible. Her left side is partly paralyzed, and apparently she'll need looking after. Her nephew and his wife seem happy to have her. I gather Miss Armitage has helped the family financially from time to time. No," he continued, his voice taking on a reassuring note, "you needn't worry. The cottage is yours now, in every sense."

My worry really had been more for May, who must be missing her home, than for myself. Longbarrow Cottage had always been more hers than mine. Only in childhood, while Nan was alive and telling stories of the place, had it seemed real to me. After Nan's death, I had rarely thought of it.

Still, there was an element of selfishness in my concern for May. The lack of rent apart, she had been the perfect tenant, sparing me all the responsibilities of ownership.

"Will you be able to come down and see the cottage?" Tony Munnings asked me.

"I wish I could. But I'm flying home tomorrow morning."

He then went on to say that I would have to make some decisions about the place fairly quickly, but in the meantime a couple named Ebborn, who lived close by, were keeping an eye on it. We agreed that he would write with all the business details.

"There is one other thing I should mention." The confident voice hesitated for a moment, as though searching for the right words. "I've been asked to inquire if you're interested in selling the cottage."

I was surprised. "So soon? What could make anyone think that I might be?"

"It's a local man. Nothing's a secret in a village, of course."

I hesitated, then said, "I'm willing to listen to his offer. If he wants to, he can call me here before I leave." I gave him the name and number of the hotel.

"Right, I'll tell him. His name's David Cornelius, by the way." He told me what the cottage might be worth, adding that of course I ought to have a proper appraisal made.

I did a quick conversion from pounds to Canadian dollars. And caught my breath. During Nan's lifetime, and at her death, unrenovated Cotswold cottages had sold for very little. That was bound to have changed, I knew—especially given the improvements May had made—but I was unprepared for just how much values had risen. Nan's gift to me was worth more than I had known.

Before we said good-bye, I asked Tony Munnings for the address and telephone number of May's nephew. When I called, the nephew's wife, Mrs. Mockridge, answered the phone. She had a warm, cheerful voice, and seemed pleased that I wanted to visit May. Yes, she said, May was up to having visitors.

"I don't want to tire her. . . ."

"Oh, you won't do that. Not if you talk about the past. It's the present that tires her, poor thing." She gave me directions for reaching their house on the Underground.

An hour later, I knocked at the front door of a small,

semidetached brick-and-stucco house in a long, straight
street of identical houses. Each had a rectangle of stained
glass above the door and a low-walled patch of front garden
with an ironwork gate. After a few moments, a plump,
middle-aged woman in a flour-streaked apron came to the
door. She had a round, friendly face and soft brown eyes.

"Mrs. Treleven? Come in, please." She stood back to let
me enter the narrow front hall. On the left, there was a
staircase carpeted in electric blue; to the right, through an
open door, was the living room. A painter's drop cloth covered much of the furniture.

Mrs. Mockridge apologized for the disorder as she took
my coat. "It was a bit of luck that Auntie May's room was
just painted before she came to us." She led me down the
hall into a small cluttered kitchen. One counter was covered
with mixing bowls and the raw ingredients for cookies that
were cooling on racks on the other counter. Through the
partly open door at the rear of the kitchen was a modern
addition that took up most of the narrow backyard. It had
been built for her mother, she told me, who had lived with
them until her death the year before. "Auntie May has her
own bedroom and bath, quite separate, as you can see. So
it's no trouble, really, to have her with us."

As we went into the little bedroom that lay beyond the
door, she said loudly, "Here's Miss Treleven to see you,
Auntie." To me, she added quietly, "You'll have to speak
up. Her hearing's not what it was."

May sat in an armchair beside the window. She was
dressed in a shapeless pale green wool dress with a blanket
of darker green over her lap. She looked like a mermaid
grown old, as frail and thin as some desiccated creature of
the sea washed up on the sand. Her face was that of an elderly, sweet-tempered child, and like a child she sat with
her hands resting in her lap, expectant. When she saw me
she gave a tremulous smile.

"My dear. How lovely to meet you at last."

"Now you sit here, dear," Mrs. Mockridge told me, dragging a straight-backed chair forward. "Nice and close to
Auntie. That's right. I'll just go and make the tea."

The bedroom was very warm and smelled, like the rest
of the house, of baking and paint, with a hint of something

medicinal. It was a prettily furnished, comfortable room with a window looking out onto the neighbor's strip of garden and beyond it to a series of narrow backyards with leafless trees or washing hung out to dry.

"Nan's grandchild." May leaned forward a little to peer at me through the gold-rimmed glasses perched on her nose. Her pale eyes had the glaucous look of old age, as though she were looking up through water. "Yes, I can see that you are. It's the mouth, I think, and perhaps the eyes." She sat back again, and a troubled look contracted the wrinkles of her face. "Your mother wrote to me not so very long ago. It was to tell me about your husband. . . . Such a terrible thing. He hasn't come back, has he?"

I could only stare at her. Peter, my husband, had died ten months ago, two months after Max's birth, in a sailing accident. He had taken his small sailboat out for an evening sail on the lake, despite warnings of rough weather. The capsized boat had been found early the next morning. Peter's body had washed up onshore several miles down the lake two days later.

While I fumbled or words, she continued, almost to herself, "No, no, how stupid of me. Do forgive me. I'm thinking of Nan's husband, of course." Her cloudy eyes met mine. "They had quarreled, you know. But she never believed that was why he left."

I said, "The police thought it was cowardice." My grandfather's call-up papers to officer training had arrived the day before his disappearance. When Nan had gone to the police about her missing husband, she had told them, naively, not only about their quarrel but also that his experiences in Spain had left him with a horror of war. Not unreasonably, the police assumed he had vanished to avoid both domestic unhappiness and combat.

A spasm of irritation crossed May's face. "The police knew nothing about it. It was simply an excuse not to look for him, that's what Nan always said. Your grandfather would have done his duty. He was no coward."

I was unconvinced. What else would you call a man who had abandoned his pregnant wife? I had never heard Nan say a word against him, however; but then, she had rarely spoken of him at all. I sometimes wondered if she had

hoped he would come back to her one day and it was for
that reason she had let May stay on in Longbarrow Cottage.
That way, someone would be there to tell him where she
had gone.

Curious, I asked May what she thought had happened to
my grandfather. "Oh, well"—she lifted her right hand
vaguely and let it fall again onto her lap—"I really couldn't
say. Men are such unfathomable creatures, aren't they?"
Before I could respond to this, she went on: "How did we
come to this unhappy subject?"

To distract her, I gave her the gift I had brought from
Canada. It was a small framed pen-and-ink drawing of
Longbarrow Cottage, which I had sketched from an old
black-and-white photograph. Obviously moved by this image of her former home, she insisted that I take down a
print of some country scene from the wall and hang the
drawing in its place. Without self-pity, she said quietly, "I
shall miss the garden in the spring. But I like to think of
your child playing there."

I could not bring myself to tell her that it was unlikely
Max and I would ever live in Longbarrow Cottage.

"Rafe is very fond of it," she went on. "The garden, I
mean. He was wonderful at picking slugs off the roses for
me. Took a joy in it that was quite ferocious. Curious
things, boys. Do you know what Lewis Carroll said? 'I am
fond of children, except boys.' I think that's too bad of him,
don't you? Boys aren't obviously lovely in the manner of
girls, of course, but if you bother to pick the slugs off them,
they've just as much charm."

It was the first gleam of humor I had seen on her face,
but almost at once it vanished, and she looked worried.
"Poor child, I don't think he's very happy."

Before I could ask her who the unhappy Rafe was, Mrs.
Mockridge came in with a folding tray-table on which were
two cups of tea and a plate of shortbread. As we drank our
tea, May asked about Max and my family, and I showed
her the pictures I carried in my purse. We talked about my
mother, who had remarried after my father's death, several
years earlier, and moved with my stepfather, Graham, to his
home in New Zealand. Then she began to speak of Nan.
She remembered her with obvious affection.

"Such a good friend. She always made me feel that Longbarrow Cottage was my home, as well as hers. Well, I used the word 'home,' but I don't believe she ever thought of it that way herself. She was very glad to leave it, you know, in the end."

"She used to tell me stories about the place," I said.

"Stories?" May looked puzzled.

"Yes, for children. She made them up out of a mix of local legends, fairy tales, and things she'd heard from villagers. Some took place in the cottage, some in the countryside around it. That's what she told me, anyway."

Nan's stories had entertained me throughout my early childhood, but I remembered best the stories she recounted during the dreary winter days of my recuperation from an appendix operation when I was ten years old. Although I hadn't known it at the time, Nan herself was dying of the cancer that would kill her six months later. A small graying figure in an old dressing gown, she had sat by my bed smoking cigarette after cigarette, forbidden fruit, telling her stories. While the overheated bedroom filled with smoke and the steam hissed in the radiator, I had lain on my pillows, listening. The ache from the incision, my friends, my life beyond the little room, all were forgotten.

The stories had poured out of Nan. Dark and powerful, they were stories of greed and hate, of secrets and violent death. At the heart of each of them, like the invisible worm, was a betrayal.

Most took the form of traditional fairy tales. Nan knew that I liked my fairy tales unexpurgated, their harsh details intact. My imagination fed on them in ways it never could with their paler, bowdlerized versions. I was a bloodthirsty child, and the rough justice of the red-hot dancing shoes and the nail-studded barrel for the cruel stepmother or the faithless servant was deeply satisfying to me. I was pleased, rather than upset, when the wicked characters in Nan's stories met deservedly horrible ends.

One story alone, however, had frustrated my desire for savage retribution. She told it more than once, with the intensity and emotion that make a tale seem a part of the teller. As though it were her own life she was unfolding.

There were three brothers, she said, who were bound to

one another by more than blood, for they shared a vision. They believed that all men were brothers, and they swore a great oath to work together to make their vision come true.

The oldest brother was steadfast and serious, with a loving heart. The middle brother, tall and golden, was clever and ambitious. The youngest was a brilliant artist.

This youngest brother created a treasure, which he vowed to share with mankind. But he fell in love with a witch in disguise. Under her spell, he gave her his treasure, whereupon she revealed her real nature to him. Ashamed and in despair, the youngest brother left the village in which they all lived and went out into the world.

When the steadfast oldest brother learned what had happened, he set off to search for the youngest brother. The middle brother, meanwhile, vowed to retrieve the treasure from the witch. At first, he attempted to persuade her with his charm and his beauty, but she only mocked him for his vanity. Then he threatened to expose her to the villagers, who feared witches and would have burned her if they had known who she really was. Angrily, she threatened to destroy the treasure. To save it, he killed her.

The steadfast oldest brother traveled far and wide looking for the youngest. In a country across the sea, he was told that his brother had died fighting in a war against a tyrant. With a grieving heart, he returned home to his village. But in the time that he had been away, the treasure had corrupted the middle brother. Fearful that his oldest brother might force him to share it, he killed him. The treasure brought him wealth and fame, and the love of a princess.

Here Nan had paused, crushing her cigarette in an ashtray overflowing with the stubs of many others, while I wondered what grisly form the middle brother's punishment would take. To my surprise, however, she told me that the story ended there. When I protested, outraged, Nan had said simply, "But I don't know what will happen to him."

Only her visible weariness, and a sadness that I had never seen before on her face, had stopped me from pressing her beyond this absurd and unsatisfactory answer.

May's voice came through my memories. "It wasn't stories for children she was writing," she was saying. "Not when I knew her. Mind you, she wasn't pleased when I found out." She shifted a little in her chair, with a slight look of pain on her face, as though her bones ached.

I was confused. "Found out about what?"

"Why, that she was writing a book. She was terribly secretive about it. Used to write in bed, with your mother asleep in the cot beside her. One night I caught her at it. She never heard my knock. When I came into her room, she was hunched over the paper, writing like someone possessed."

"I didn't know that she'd written a book."

"It was a mystery. Her book, I mean. Perhaps that was why she was so mysterious about it." May gave a thin little chuckle, like a cough, at her joke. "Everyone was writing mysteries in those days. They still are, aren't they? I never read them myself."

"Did you read Nan's?"

"She wouldn't let me. She said I could read it when it was published."

"Was it published?"

"Oh, yes, she found a publisher for it. She was very proud of that. I don't remember which one it was, I'm afraid."

"I wonder why she never mentioned it."

"I expect it was too painful. After what happened to it . . ." May's voice trailed off, and her eyes looked away from mine, fixing on some distant point beyond me. "Poor thing," she mused, "she never did have much luck. First her husband abandoning her in that dreadful manner. Then the fire in the cottage. And the war, of course. No wonder she wanted to leave this country."

"But the book," I asked her. "Wasn't it published after all?"

May's glance, suddenly acute, came back to me. "Oh, it was. Much good that it did. Her book was burned up along with a good many others when the bombs fell." She saw the surprise on my face. "But you must know about that?"

I shook my head, again confused. "Do you mean all the copies of the book were burned? How could that happen?"

"Why, when the Germans bombed London—was it New Year's Eve? After Christmas in 1941 . . . no, 1940 I believe it was. The bombs hit Paternoster Row, you see, where the publishers were. Thousands of books perished in the fires afterwards. I suppose books are nothing compared to lives. And yet . . ."

She sat for a moment without speaking, smoothing the blanket fringe with her right hand; the left remained immobile in her lap. Then, as though she had remembered my presence, she looked up at me again, blinking a little behind the glasses. "And so I never did read Nan's book. Copies were impossible to come by. A few might have survived, I suppose, but there were none for sale that I saw. Perhaps in London, but I never went up to London during the war."

No wonder Nan had never spoken of the book, I thought. She must have been devastated. I tried to imagine how I would feel if a book of mine were obliterated so completely, but could not.

"I wonder what the book was about."

I had been speaking half to myself, not really expecting May to know, but she replied promptly, "It was about a murder. Mysteries usually are, of course. That's all she would tell me. But I often wondered . . ."

"Yes?"

"You see, there was this dreadful murder we knew of. It was never solved. A woman named Evelyn . . ." She paused, and gave me a curious look. "Well, never mind, my dear. Best not to dwell on these things. Nan was quite right to go away. Much the wisest course. Nan had too much imagination. It's my belief she made herself unhappy with it. I have very little imagination myself and I must say I'm glad of it. Living on one's own, it's best that way."

When I was young my mother would tell me, often with pride but occasionally with a certain dismay, that I had inherited Nan's imagination. Like a fairy godmother's blessing, this was an equivocal legacy, the source both of violent nightmares and intense joy. As an adult, my imagination enabled me to earn my living at work that I loved, but it had also beguiled me into believing that I could make my husband happy.

"Do you remember the title of the book?" I asked May.

She frowned, her forehead pleating with tiny wrinkles. "I should. Let me think for a moment. I do remember very

clearly when she told me." In her quiet voice, she went on
to say that Nan had at first been uncertain what title to give
her book. "But one day she came to me with the baby, your
mother, in her arms. She said, 'May, I know now what I
shall call my book.' She was laughing but the tears were
streaming down her face. It upset me terribly to see her like
that."

We sat without speaking while May searched her memory. Then, with a triumphant smile, she looked at me and
said, "*Life Blood*. Yes, that was it. *Life Blood*."

CHAPTER 2

May sank back in her chair and closed her eyes, as if the
effort to recollect so much had exhausted her. "Nan," she
began tentatively, the pale eyes blinked open again, then
saw her mistake. "No, you're not Nan, are you?"

"I'm Jo," I said gently. "Nan's grandchild."

"Yes, of course. Foolish of me." With a trembling hand,
she brushed some biscuit crumbs from the blanket across
her knees. "We were talking about her, weren't we?"

"Yes, about her book. *Life Blood*."

Her look was suddenly puzzled. "You must want it very
badly, to offer so much for it. Far too much. I wish I could
make you a present of it." Before I could say anything, she
repeated, most querulously, "But I don't have a copy, you
know."

"I know. It's all right." I tried to make my voice reassuring. There was a logic to May's conversation, and if at
times it eluded me that was not her fault or mine but,
rather, a question of ellipses, words unexpressed but implied. In my work, I made pictures to fill the gaps left by

language; talking to May required something of the same effort of imagination.

"Someone thought you owned a copy of *Life Blood*," I said, "and wanted to buy it from you? Is that what happened?"

She considered this for a moment. "It was that man ... oh, what was his name?" She looked vaguely around her, as though the answer lay in the room, but this time her memory balked. "It's no use. Everything's going." The words were sad, but she seemed more resigned than upset. "I told him I never had a copy, but I don't think he believed me."

"When was this?"

"Not long ago. Before I came here. . . ." Her voice faded away as she gave up the effort to remember. She seemed to diminish before my eyes, shrinking into herself, inexpressibly frail. I had asked too many questions.

Guiltily, I stood up to leave. As we said good-bye, I took her right hand and bent to kiss her cheek. "It makes me very happy to think of Longbarrow Cottage in your hands," she said softly. There was a note of quiet conviction in her voice, as though some doubt or other had been resolved in her mind.

Mrs. Mockridge, who had left her baking and was standing beside me, overheard this. On our way to the front door together, she said with a confidential smile, "We'll just let her go on thinking that, shall we? It would be kinder that way." She handed me my coat. "I mean, I expect you'll want to sell the cottage, won't you?"

Probably, I agreed.

But as I walked away, I asked myself if I really did want to sell the cottage. Now that I had met May, now that I had heard about Nan's book and been reminded of Nan's stories, now that the place seemed more real to me, I was no longer so sure.

During the long return journey on the Underground, the strange story of Nan's book began to take hold of my imagination. Its images were stark and disturbing, and as the rush-hour crowds flowed around me, I saw a solitary figure hunched among the bedclothes late at night, writing "like someone possessed" while her baby slept beside her. And in the dark tunnels of the Underground, I could see her book burning with all the others in a vast crematorium of words that lit up the London night like an offering to some voracious god of war.

Other images were shifting, the images of my grandmother as I remembered her. Concealed within the loving, melancholy storyteller of my childhood had been someone unknown to me, a passionate and secretive young woman with a story she had never told her family. In the gallery of May's memories, that women had begun to emerge from her older self. But she was incomplete and colorless, a half-sketched female figure struggling to free herself from the gray husk of age. I could bring her to life again, perhaps, if I knew the details of her story.

When I got back to the hotel shortly after five, there was a message waiting for me. A Mr. Cornelius had telephoned, the desk clerk told me; he would ring again at five-thirty. I was startled to feel a twinge of dismay, almost a protective impulse of ownership, at the prospect of this stranger's interest in what, after all, belonged to me. As well as an uneasy, irrational sense that even to listen to an offer would be somehow a betrayal of both May and Nan.

I went upstairs to begin packing for the flight home. These few days alone and away from the familiar had given me back a part of myself that had almost ceased to exist, someone younger and freer, someone less dependent on the roles and routines that imperceptibly narrowed my sense of myself, someone happier. For a little while, I had shrugged off my responsibilities, forgotten, occasionally, that I was a mother, and slipped out of my hypothetical widow's weeds.

The telephone rang as I was transferring my clothes from the bureau drawers to the suitcase. I glanced at my watch—it was five-thirty. I went over to the nightstand by the bed and picked up the receiver.

"Hello?"

"Mrs. Treleven? My name is David Cornelius. Tony Munnings got in touch with me and suggested I call you." The pleasantly deep and unhurried voice on the other end of the line was, to my surprise, American. "I wondered if I could come and talk to you about Longbarrow Cottage."

"I'm flying back to Canada tomorrow morning, Mr. Cornelius. So we'll have to talk on the phone."

"Actually, I'm in London at the moment. Is there any possibility I could come to your hotel now? Or later this evening?" The note of inquiry was uninsistent. It seemed a polite request, nothing more.

Perhaps because I felt no sense of pressure from him I found myself saying that now would be fine. There was a sitting room off the lobby, I remembered; we could talk there. When I gave him directions, he told me that he knew the square and would be at the hotel by six o'clock.

Shortly before six, I went downstairs. As I left the elevator, a man in his mid-thirties wearing a brown leather jacket and jeans came through the front door. He was attractive, with long-limbed, dark-haired good looks. If he was David Cornelius, I thought, our conversation would at least have its aesthetic pleasures.

When he saw me, he raised an interrogative eyebrow and then, in response to my smile, crossed the floor toward me.

"Mrs. Treleven?" He looked straight at me, and his eyes belied the easygoing voice. Light gray flecked with brown, they shone like rain-washed stone, changeable and cool, glinting with an assessing intelligence.

"Miss. I use my maiden name."

"Thanks for agreeing to see me on such short notice." We shook hands. His grip was firm, the skin rough and slightly callused.

"I thought we could talk in there," I told him, pointing to the open doorway of the small sitting room off the lobby. The room turned out to be occupied, however, by a pair of formidable, tweedy women with tightly permed hair who were loudly differing about their next day's plans.

"There's a pub I know around the corner," David Cornelius suggested, with a slight smile. "It would be quieter."

There was time only for a polite exchange on the remarkable weather before we reached the pub, literally right around the corner from the hotel, down a short side street. It was called The Scholar's Arms—London University was nearby—and the sign out front showed a black mortarboard flanked by flagons.

Inside, the academic motif consisted mainly of college ties and scarves striping the wall behind the long wooden bar, and dozens of photographs of boating crews and cricket teams. Two men were just leaving a table near the door as we came in. David Cornelius quickly claimed it and pulled out a chair for me. "What can I get you?"

I asked for a lager, a half-pint. The Scholar's Arms reminded me that I had once enjoyed pubs. Although the wood-paneled, low-ceilinged room was crowded, with most tables filled and a number of people standing by the bar, no one had to raise his or her voice to be heard. Its atmosphere suggested that conversation mattered as much to its regulars as the stuff in their glasses.

David Cornelius came back with our drinks. He had a hard-looking, elegant body, lean and fit, and moved with the unselfconscious grace of a man at ease with his physical self. He handed my glass to me and sat down in the chair across the table, leaning back with one leg loosely crossed over the other.

"This probably seems premature," he began, with the hint of an apology in his voice. "After all, you haven't put the cottage on the market yet. But Tony Munnings said you were willing to listen to me."

"I'm not really sure yet what I'm going to do. I only found out today that May Armitage had left the cottage." I asked him if he knew May.

"A little. My son liked to visit her. I think Rafe considers her a friend, despite the difference in ages."

Rafe, I remembered, was the name of the boy May had mentioned that afternoon, the ferocious hunter of slugs, the child she had thought was unhappy. I asked him how old his son was.

"Eleven. In some ways, a very grown-up eleven. In others, not."

"Is he an American, too?" Perhaps, I thought, the boy was homesick.

He nodded. "Even more so, now that he's living here. It's brought out all his latent chauvinism. But sometimes I think that's because he's feeling disloyal. I'm willing to bet that somewhere inside him there's a little Anglophile struggling to get out." His smile was affectionate, and attractive; it broke up the classically smooth planes of his face, made him seem more approachable.

"Mr. Munnings told me that you were a local person," I began.

"But you're wondering how an American can be considered local. I might be, fifty years from now, if I live that long." His voice was dryly amused. "Tony Munnings was being generous. Right now I'm local only by association. My . . ." He paused, and seemed to change his mind about whatever it was he had been going to say. "Do you know the Mallabys?"

I shook my head. I could not remember my parents ever mentioning the names of people who lived in Shipcote; I doubted they knew of anyone but May.

"They're a local family, genuinely local. Friends of mine. They lent me a place to live when I first came to Shipcote, almost a year ago now. But I've been looking for a house of my own."

I noticed the pronouns: "I" and "me," rather than "we" and "our."

"Longbarrow Cottage struck me as a good choice for a couple of reasons," he went on. "Primarily, because Rafe likes it. Though I haven't mentioned the possibility of buying it to him yet—I don't want to get his hopes up. And then, of course, because of Shipcote Farm Park. I'm part owner." He would see that the name meant nothing to me. "Your land borders the farm for a few hundred feet," he said. "We share a fence."

I glanced at his hands as they cradled his glass. Like the rest of him, they were well shaped, with long, tapering fingers, but the skin was rough and the fingernails, though clean, were ragged. An old scab marked one knuckle. They were the hands of someone used to manual labor. Still, he seemed an unlikely farmer.

"You call it a farm park," I said, "rather than a farm. Why is that?"

"Because part of the place is open to the public. We run most of it as a straightforward working farm, part as an exhibition of our main purpose. Which is the preservation of rare breeds of farm animals. People come to see these animals and, with luck, go away realizing that it's important they survive."

I was surprised. "And that's going on right next door to Longbarrow Cottage? I hadn't realized . . ."

He misunderstood. "It really shouldn't be a problem. The farm itself is close to a thousand acres, but only twenty-five of them are used for the exhibition area. The public entrance is several miles from Longbarrow Cottage, on another road, and the land that borders yours is pasture."

"I wasn't thinking of it as a problem. The opposite, really. It sounds like a wonderful place."

"It is. I'm lucky to be involved with it. You don't often get a chance to help resurrect the past, and—if it doesn't sound too pious—protect the future at the same time. We need these animals. The bigger our genetic pool, the greater the chance of survival for everyone." The detached, slightly cool air had vanished. He was leaning forward now, enthusiasm for his subject plain on his face. Momentarily, I had a glimpse of someone much younger, a less sophisticated and more spontaneous self. That lost child is what I try to find in the grown-up features of adults when I draw them. It is always there, no matter how the years may have blurred or obscured it, if you look hard enough.

I liked the child I saw in David Cornelius's face. I was finding, too, that I liked the man.

"Proselytizing's part of our work," he added, with an apologetic smile as she leaned back again. "Persuading people that a pig is more than bacon, so to speak."

"You know, Mr. Cornelius—" I began.

"David, please."

"And I'm Jo. I was going to say that you're making it hard for me to listen to your offer for the cottage. I'm beginning to think I should see it for myself before I decide what to do about it."

He gave a rueful wince. "I had a feeling I might be talking myself out of the place. Is there any possibility you could change your flight? Come down to Shipcote tomorrow to take a look at the cottage?"

I shook my head. "I have to go home. I have a son, too. He's still a baby."

"I see." He smiled. "Your husband's probably desperate for your return, then. If he's been baby-sitting, I mean. Among other reasons, of course." His smile now was tinged with embarrassment, as though he realized how this might sound.

As it seemed impossible to respond without having to explain my circumstances, which could only complicate the issue and make us both uncomfortable, I simply smiled back and did not reply.

Simultaneously, we reached for our mugs. I finished the lager and set down my glass again. "I'd better go. I'm meeting someone for dinner." An English editor, interested in my work, had suggested we get together before I left. I found now that I was unaccountably grateful for the excuse to end the conversation. David Cornelius had a disturbing presence; he unsettled me for reasons I had no desire to understand.

He got up with me. "I'll walk back with you to the hotel."

"That's not necessary."

"My car's parked nearby." He picked up his jacket. As we went outside, he said, "I had been going to mention a figure. But I have the feeling you'd rather not hear it. Or am I wrong?"

"To be honest, it wouldn't mean much to me right now." This wasn't entirely true, but I was, in a sense, avoiding temptation. Unrealistic though it might seem, I wanted to keep money out of my decision. "If I do decide to sell, I'll ask Mr. Munnings to let you know. I just can't say when that will be."

"I'm in no hurry."

We had reached the hotel. "Thanks for the drink. I'm sorry if this was a waste of time."

"It wasn't."

There was nothing provocative in either his voice or his manner, and yet the words seemed open to interpretation. Then he said good-night and walked away across the square. Before I went into the hotel, I turned around, but he had already been swallowed up by the shadows of the plane trees.

The next day I flew back to Toronto. To my dismay, Max refused to look at me when I got home to our duplex apartment, turning his head away and clinging to my friend

Kasia as I tried to take him in my arms. Kasia, who had five small nephews and nieces, assured me this was perfectly normal behavior. Although he had been happy enough with her while I was away, she said, he was punishing me now for leaving him.

He would not allow me to give him his bottle, would accept it only from her. While she fed him on the sofa, I sat on the floor a few feet away with the Peter Rabbit I had brought him on my lap. As Kasia told me all that she and Max had done together, and I told her about London, Max eyed the toy with interest. Eventually, he pushed the bottle aside and twisted out of her lap, crawling across the rug to investigate more closely. For a little while he sat beside me, still refusing to look at me, fascinated by the shiny brass buttons sewn onto Peter Rabbit's blue jacket.

All at once, with a small grunt, he turned and clutched at me, burying his head against my arm. I was forgiven.

As Kasia was leaving, she remembered a letter that had arrived for me. "It's got a London address," she said. "It came just this morning. Otherwise I'd have phoned you in England, to see if you wanted me to open it." I thanked her again for all she had done, and then we hugged and said good-bye.

With Max on my hip, I went over to my desk. The air-mail letter from England lay on top of the small pile of mail, with my name and address typed on the envelope. The printed return address was a number on Sackville Street, Piccadilly, London.

When I opened the envelope, there was a single sheet of white paper. "Goddard Grant Ltd., Antiquarian Books," was printed at the top of the page, as well as the address already listed on the envelope. Below these were two short paragraphs of typing, and an illegible signature in black ink after the closing.

Dear Miss Treleven [I read]: We have been asked by a client to obtain a copy of *Life Blood* by J. M. Morrile, a novel published by Cobbet & Stewart in 1940. We understand that J. M. Morrile was your grandmother.

We are therefore writing to you, with the hope that you might have a copy of the book in your possession.

If you do, and are willing to part with it, our client would be interested in purchasing it from you. Realising that the book may have sentimental value to you, our client is prepared to pay fifty pounds for it. We would be most grateful for your reply.

My surprise at this letter was replaced almost at once by an intense curiosity.

Not once, in all the years of my growing up, had I ever heard anyone mention Nan's novel. Now, within the space of two days and from separate sources, I had learned not only that it existed, but that it was sought after by two people (unless Goddard Grant's client and May's "what's his name" were one and the same), who were willing to pay, by implication, more than it was really worth. Moreover, as Morrile was not Nan's maiden name, it seemed she had written under a pen name. I wondered why.

What I really wanted to know, however, was why *Life Blood* should suddenly be so valuable.

CHAPTER 3

When asked to describe my work, I am sometimes tempted to say that I fill in gaps. In essence, that is what an illustrator of picture books must do. I look for spaces in the story where my pictures will say what the words cannot.

As a very young child, I saw empty spaces as an invitation, spaces on walls, on sidewalks and smooth asphalt driveways, in the margins of books. The urge to fill them was irresistible, and I used whatever came to hand to satisfy it, a crayon, a piece of chalk, the sharp edge of a stone, or a lipstick dug out of my mother's purse. At first, it scarcely mattered to me what I drew on or with; all I cared about was filling that seductive emptiness. Eventually, however, I learned that blank spaces are important, too.

In the months after my husband's death, I had forgotten that lesson. My editor, Paulina Osnak, was the first to remind me of it.

We were in Paulina's office at the time, two days after my return to Toronto from London. A large, handsome woman with thick, graying hair coiled in an old-fashioned ring on the top of her head, she looks very much like Picasso's Gertrude Stein. She has an eye that rarely misses a superfluous word or a clumsy line, and a spirit in profound sympathy with those who create the words and the lines.

I had brought Paulina the fifth story in what, to my surprise, had become a successful series about a streetwise six-year-old named Geraldine, stories I both wrote and illustrated. Paulina was looking at my "dummy," the rough sketch of the book in miniature, one-quarter the size of the finished version, a model that avoided detail to concentrate on the main elements of the illustrations and the placing of the words on the page. The portfolio that contained the final, full-size pen-and-ink drawings for the story lay open on the desk between us. I had worked very hard on the illustrations, and they were good, I knew that, but I was still not satisfied with them. I counted on Paulina to define the problem for me.

Paulina turned the tiny pages of the dummy and sifted through the drawings without comment, in her fashion. Finally, she lifted her head and said quietly, "I'm astonished by how much you've accomplished, Jo. I had no idea you were working so hard. I had thought, well, after Peter's death you might not feel ... And then, you have Max to look after. When did you have time for all this?" She placed one hand on the drawings.

"I work when Max sleeps."

"Then when do you sleep?" Her dark eyes were worried. "As I remember it, babies never stay asleep for long."

I smiled. "They don't do anything for long." That sense of perpetual, inevitable change alternately saddens and exhilarates me as I watch Max grow. I draw him constantly, trying to capture the fleeting beauty of his infancy.

Paulina leafed through the dummy again. "I like this very much, Jo. The conception seems right. The story is good."

I could hear the "but" coming, and it did, in Paulina's gentle way. Closing the dummy, she placed it next to the portfolio with the illustrations. "But something happened on the way from this"—she touched the dummy first, and then the pile of drawings—"to these. They are wonderful drawings and the details in them are fascinating. But, you know, they aren't drawings for Geraldine's book. There's just too much detail.

"The really terrific thing about Geraldine has always been her energy. She's a child who tears through life, and the drawings have always moved with her. That's part of their appeal. There hasn't been a lot of detail in her other books, has there? Nothing to hold her back." She adjusted the shawl around her broad shoulders as she waited for me to think about what she had said.

I reached across her desk for the portfolio, took up each drawing in turn and stared at it, and saw what she meant. For me, drawing the myriad tiny parts of the pictures had been a way of escaping my thoughts, but those details weighed Geraldine down. She needed blank spaces to race across, bare ground to cover.

"I thought there was a problem," I said as I closed the portfolio, "but I couldn't see it. Everything in my life seems too close up right now for any kind of perspective."

Paulina looked at me without speaking, a long, shrewd look not without sympathy but mercifully free of pity. Briskly, she said, "The drawings shouldn't be difficult to fix. The ideas themselves don't need changing. They're good." She leaned forward, clasping her hands on her desk top. "Now, tell me something. You look after Max and you work. What else?"

"There isn't much time left over for anything else."

"You don't give yourself any time off?"

"Time off is time on my hands. I don't want that." Since Peter's death, I had been careful to fill every minute of my day and made sure that I went to bed each night exhausted.

"Anyway," I reminded her, "I've just had five days away." Paulina had been almost more excited than I was about the award, and had demanded to hear every detail of the professional side of my trip to London.

"I'm talking about making a real change."

I tied the black strings of the portfolio. "It's strange you say that now. Do you remember my telling you about my English grandmother?"

"Of course. The storyteller."

"I don't think I ever mentioned that she left me a house in England when she died." In brief, I told Paulina about Longbarrow Cottage and my visit to May Armitage.

"So you've come into your inheritance at last," Paulina said, when I finished.

I might have replied that it had come too late to matter. Once, the money from the sale of the cottage might have made a difference in our lives, Peter's and mine, but now it seemed unimportant. Geraldine's success, and Peter's life insurance, had given me the security I needed for Max's sake. Anything more was only an irony.

I confessed to Paulina that I did not really know what to do about the cottage. "In some ways, it's a nuisance."

"Nonsense," she replied vigorously. "It's a godsend. You admire Caldecott, Rackham, Beatrix Potter. Go and find out why they drew as they did. You need to make a space in your life—get away from some of the details, so to speak—this is your chance. A sabbatical." Spreading her hands wide, she gave a wry smile. "Forgive me. I can never resist giving advice, and you must have heard so much of it in these past months."

To distract her from pursuing this, and to tease her a little, because she loves mysteries almost as much as she loves children's books, I told her that in my grandmother's stories some very strange and unpleasant things had happened in and around Longbarrow Cottage.

Paulina rose to the bait. "What sorts of things?"

"The murder of a witch. Grave robbers turned into standing stones. There's a barrow, a Neolithic burial mound, in a field behind the cottage—it accounts for the name—and apparently there were a lot of local legends attached to the place. Some of them gruesome."

"These stories weren't for young children, then?"

"A few were." I told her one about a church mouse with an ear for bells, a hungry cat, and a lost treasure. When I finished, she said she liked it and we discussed the possibility of my illustrating it for a book.

"Any others?" she asked.

"Most of those I remember were for older children. Adventure stories, that sort of thing."

"A la Enid Blyton?"

"With a sharp twist of Roald Dahl."

As I described these stories to Paulina, I thought again about their parallels with the story of the three brothers: through each of them, like a black thread, ran the theme of betrayal. It seemed so striking that I found myself wondering what had compelled Nan to tell what was, essentially, the same story over and over again.

When I finished, Paulina's face wore that look of childish pleasure, a kind of innocent greed for more, that was the sign, to me, of success.

"Were any of these stories published?"

"Not that I know of. She did publish a book, but it wasn't for kids." I glanced at my watch and realized that there was no time to tell her about *Life Blood.* "I've got to go. I promised the baby-sitter I'd be home by four."

As Paulina walked to the door with me, I said that although she had called Longbarrow Cottage a godsend, I was not sure that my grandmother would have agreed with her.

"Why did she leave it to you, then?"

"Maybe that's the real reason I should see it. To find out."

That evening, when Max was asleep, I took out one of the drawings for Geraldine's book and, following Paulina's suggestion, began to pare down the details. While I worked, I reflected on all the good reasons there were to go to Shipcote.

The most obvious reason was to find out what I might be giving up if I did decide to sell the cottage. Another was to make the change of scene that, even if Max and I went over for only a few weeks, might allow me to think about the future in surroundings where the immediate past was absent.

Finally, and this I acknowledged to myself was the most compelling reason, I was curious to see a place that for a time in my childhood had filled my imagination.

In the end, however, it was another reason altogether that decided me.

Before I went to bed, I climbed the attic steps to look at my husband's paintings. After Peter's death, I had stacked his canvases carefully against the attic walls, covering them with dust sheets. I had not been able to bring myself to look at them since. Despite the greater space and the good north light in the attic, I still worked in the living room, just as I had while Peter was alive. I told myself, rightly, that I needed to be where I could see and hear Max, but I knew there was another reason why I avoided using the attic. In a sense, it still belonged to Peter; or, if not to the ghost of the man himself—for I was no believer in ghosts—to that of his unhappiness.

When I unveiled the paintings, setting each one in turn on the easel, I could see the anger and pain I had so steadfastly ignored while he was alive. The paintings then had merely seemed powerful and stark; now they were evidence of a desperation I had mistaken for the artistic intensity I myself lacked.

Most were abstracts, large oils predominantly in tones of blue and black with fierce slashes of bright color, vermilion, orange, chrome yellow, like streaks of lightning in a wide and turbulent prairie sky. There was also a portrait of his parents, both of whom had died when he was a teenager, painted from a photograph. It showed two unsmiling people portrayed in subtly different styles who seemed almost to occupy separate spaces. Theirs had not been a happy marriage; the painting made that clear.

In spite of his preference for nonrepresentational work, Peter had been a talented portrait painter. Portraits paid for the occasional luxury, such as his sailboat, but because he found portrait painting slow and uncongenial work, he had accepted only a few commissions. Although he sold paintings steadily, his bread-and-butter income had come from his teaching at the College of Art.

Peter and I had met in the classroom; I had been one of his students. He was a good teacher, perceptive, encourag-

ing, and, despite an essentially taciturn nature that was naturally inclined to silence rather than to discussion, able to
sum up in a few words the issues of a work. He reserved
his harshest criticisms for himself.

During the last year of his life, he had begun a series of
self-portraits in various styles. There were seven of them,
cruelly acute portrayals of character, unsparing in their de-
piction of his own weaknesses and discontent. He would
never have painted anyone else with such savagery. I had
been so upset by the first that he refused to show me the
others, and I saw them only after he died. The seventh in
the series was the one I found the most painful.

In that final self-portrait, Peter stands in three-quarter
profile in front of his easel, looking out from the painting,
over the viewer's shoulder, at something that seems a long
way off. His eyes are tired, abstracted, and his thin face has
a look of resignation, with none of the bitterness that so often consumed it in the months before he died. It was a bitterness rarely expressed in words but, rather, in a humorless
smile that I found hard to bear. Falling around him, like bi-
zarre snowflakes, are the severed wings of birds, painted in
such careful detail that an ornithologist would have no trouble identifying the birds from which the wings came. A
large mirror hangs on the wall behind Peter and in it is reflected the image of a pregnant woman, her head bowed so
that her light brown hair hides her face. Although the figure
is almost impressionistic, ghostlike and dimly seen through
the wings, I know that I am the woman. There are no colors in the painting, only shades of brown and gray. Silence
pervades the work, but it is not a peaceful silence.

If it were not for the self-portraits, I might have believed
along with everyone else that Peter's death was a tragic accident. But to me those paintings were his suicide note, and
the last, the one with the wings, a cruel postscript. At the
end, he had blamed me for his unhappiness. He had not really wanted marriage, he had not wanted children. For a little while, he had persuaded himself, and me, that family life
could give him the happiness that had always evaded him.
When he found that it could not, he simply gave up.

I was the only person who had seen the self-portraits.
Someone else might have been tempted to destroy them,

but while I was not so weak as that, I did not have the courage to let anyone else look at them.

As I lifted the painting from the easel and covered it back up, I was seized with a desperate wish to escape so much sorrow and guilt.

CHAPTER 4

Max and I arrived in England a week later. Our flight, delayed by a baggage handlers' strike, was late and it was midafternoon before I managed to maneuver Max in his stroller through Immigration, collect our luggage, file past Customs, feed and change Max, pick up our rental car, and drive onto the motorway, on the left-hand side of the road, and in the right direction. A minor sense of triumph at my achievement did not quite obscure the growing conviction that I was crazy to be doing this at all.

For the first two hours, as we approached, skirted, and left London behind, I concentrated on the driving. Traffic flowed relentlessly and at high speed around us, juggernauts, buses, other cars, even minis, passing us by. Tired and irritable, Max squirmed in his car seat, refusing for a time the solace of his bottle. I half-envied him his tears, and his faith that I would try to comfort them—the bliss, dubious thought it was, of being looked after.

We reached the outskirts of Oxford at rush hour. On the congested ring road around the city, dreaming spires and scholar gypsies were in short supply but businessmen with car phones abounded. When the A40 branched west off the ring road and narrowed to two lanes, they used the center line as a third lane, with their phones to their ears all the while. The adrenaline aroused by this display of nonchalance at sixty miles an hour routed the last of my jet lag. By now, mercifully, Max was asleep.

After Oxford, the countryside unrolled in wide fields bordered by newly green poplars, slowly rising to meet the eastern edge of the Cotswold hills. There, abruptly, the landscape changed.

The main road now ran along a ridge. To my right, small, well-tended farms bordered by stone walls dipped down into the wide river valley of the Windrush and rose again over smooth and rounded hills to a distant crest shadowed by moving clouds. The houses, farmhouses, and barns, old and new, were all built of the same stone, a stone that ranged in tone from creamy gold to a weathered gray. The layered drystone walls were everywhere, in good repair or, more often, crumbling away and covered with brambles. Against the dark brown of plowed earth, the pastureland was the brilliant green of shot silk, lit by shafts of sunlight, a green lush with the promise of life and growth. From the frantic high road, this countryside looked like the land of lost content, a fleeting vision of peace, past which the traffic was relentlessly bearing us.

Then, like a beckoning finger, a small white signpost appeared. SHIPCOTE, it read, 4 MILES. This was the turning I had been watching for.

The directions to Longbarrow Cottage that Tony Munnings, the lawyer, had sent me were clear and specific. "Twenty miles beyond Oxford," he wrote, "you must choose between two routes to Shipcote. Both are shown on the map enclosed. The first, marked in red, keeps to main roads for much of the way and will bring you to Longbarrow Cottage from the back, bypassing the village. If you take it you must go through Wychley, which is the local honeypot for tourists and day-trippers. This is a simple, direct route, but the traffic is heavy.

"The other, in yellow, avoids Wychley and follows the course of the Windrush. It will be slower and possibly muddier, but I think that the views and the absence of traffic are worth it. With this route, you approach the cottage through the village. A proper introduction, if first impressions weigh with you."

For reasons I barely understood, it seemed important that

Max and I should have, as Tony Munnings put it, a proper introduction to Longbarrow Cottage. And if I had needed another argument for the longer route, those words "absence of traffic" sufficed. I chose the second route to Shipcote, turning off the high main road down the winding lane blinkered by steep banks that led to the gentle valley of the Windrush.

Almost twenty years before, these patchworked fields and woods, the stone walls, and the river had been as familiar to me as the Toronto street with its squat, yellow-brick apartment buildings where I had lived. Nan had made the place real in words; I had drawn pictures from her descriptions. Those drawings were my first attempt to translate other people's words into images that were my own and yet faithful to the words themselves. Later, I learned that the best pictures conjure up ideas beyond that simple faithfulness.

After a mile or so, the road passed through a hamlet called Withyford, little more than a group of yellow-stone farm buildings with roofs of gray, lichen-covered tile. A square farmhouse sat at the corner where a dirt track off to my left ran down to a small bridge across the river. As I drove past, a big silver Jaguar approached from the opposite direction.

The driver of the Jaguar pulled into one of the passing places that came at intervals along the lane, a crescent cut into the hedgebank, and waited politely for me to go by. I waved to thank him, and in return he raised one gloved hand either in acknowledgment or greeting, a somewhat lordly but not unfriendly gesture. An elderly man with thinning hair brushed back in silver wings over his ears, he had the lean, pink-skinned look of someone with money. When our eyes met for an instant, the remote expression on his face suddenly sharpened into puzzled interest, almost as though he were trying to place me.

Immediately beyond Withyford was the tiny medieval church that Tony Munnings had described in his letter as the last landmark before Shipcote itself. The church sat alone across the river, with a miniature peaked bell tower in the center of its long, low roof, isolated among the pastures by some accident of history. Behind it, a broad band of woods rose to the crest of a ridge.

Driving slowly, I watched for my first sight of the village. When the hedge on my left was broken by the gated entrance to a field, I glimpsed a cluster of gabled roofs some distance downstream. Backing into the patch of muddy ground in front of the gate, I switched off the motor and loaded film into my camera; I wanted to record our arrival in Shipcote. Max grunted softly, shifted in his car seat, but slept on. His round little head was turned away from me, sunk down into the neck of his brown-and-yellow jacket with only his glossy auburn hair visible, like a chestnut in the leaves.

Before I got out of the car, I sat for a moment without moving, to listen to the sudden silence, a silence empty of traffic, empty of the dull roaring of jet engines, empty of the sound of the human voice. For the first time since Peter's death, I could not hear the echo of voices telling me how sorry they were, how life must go on. I heard only the wind and the birds.

Framed by the lone church a quarter of a mile upstream to my left, and by the village roughly the same distance downstream, the fields and hills lay bathed in the golden light of early evening. From the river's edge, the gray rooftops of Shipcote rose like uneven steps up a long, low hillside, following invisible roads in a vaguely cruciform pattern. I liked the way the meandering river and the undulating wave of green hill contrasted with the village's hard edges, the rectangular church tower, the flat pentagonal sides and sharply pointed gable ends of the houses, their steeply pitched roofs and oblong chimneys. I liked, too, the chameleon stone that changed with the light. For all that it seemed so plainly rooted in its setting, as natural a part of the landscape as the sheep that grazed the fields around it, Shipcote had, thanks to that ambiguous stone, a hint of the fantastical.

It was, for me, a landscape temporarily alive with images from a storied past, peopled by Nan's characters. And when the dog moved, I thought at first I had imagined it as well. Large and golden-brown, some sort of retriever perhaps, it must have been lying by the church door waiting for someone, for when the door opened it jumped up, and the sudden twist of its body caught my eye.

A woman with long, fair hair came out of the church and walked swiftly across the field, toward Shipcote. I expected the dog to follow, but it remained by the church. The woman did not turn to call it to her.

She was too far away for me to make out her features, but she moved with the confidence of a beautiful woman. Apart from a long white scarf, she was dressed all in green, with a knee-length unbuttoned green trench coat and tall green Wellingtons. The wind lifted and tossed her blond hair, the coat billowed around her, the scarf fluttered forward like a pennant. She moved across the grass like a dancer and only her shadow, long and black as it raced ahead of her, seemed earthbound. That buoyant, windblown energy contrasted so strikingly with the peaceful countryside that on impulse I took her picture.

As I lowered the camera, a man on a large black horse rode out of the woods behind the church and cantered quickly at an angle down the hillside toward the woman. I had an odd moment of déjà vu, a sense of the familiar, which I put down to a half-remembered tale of a highwayman, one of the local legends Nan had quarried for her stories, and a drawing I had made for it, heavily inspired by Noyes's Highwayman.

If the woman realized the horseman was approaching, she gave no sign of it. Even when he caught up to her she did not look around and her stride did not slacken. For a little way, he rode beside her and it was clear, from the way his body was turned in the saddle, his dark-haired head bent down, that he was speaking to her. At last, she stopped. He dismounted and the two of them stood together, facing each other. The horse lowered its neck to crop the grass.

To me, those small figures in profile were interesting chiefly for the long, slanting shadows that they cast against the sloping field and for the way in which the black of the shadows seemed to stain the vivid grass. Hoping that the film would register the exact shade of black in the green, I raised my camera again and snapped the scene.

As I did, the woman suddenly lifted her bent arm and pulled it back behind her head. I caught my breath, sure she was about to strike the man. But she only wanted to trap the hair that blew about her face. Still, that quick conviction of violence made me feel uneasy and oddly guilty, as though I had been spying.

There was something else. I knew now why the horse-man seemed familiar; I recognized him from the way in which he held himself. It was David Cornelius.

Abruptly, the woman turned and continued on her way. She came to a low wall dividing two fields and climbed over it, jumping down to the other side. She must have stumbled or lost her balance, for she fell onto one knee. David Cornelius called out a word that might have been her name. It sounded like "Mela."

Without looking back or answering, she got to her feet again and went swiftly on, almost running. Briefly, he stood watching her, then mounted his horse and galloped off up the hill. The evening breeze carried the rhythmical thudding of the horse's hoofbeats on the turf.

Only then, when he had vanished over the crest of the hill, did someone else emerge from the church. It was a man, a tall figure in a tweed jacket. He stood framed in the doorway, fitting a cap to his head, while the dog leaped about in front of him. Then he walked slowly away from the church in the opposite direction from Shipcote, with the dog trotting along at his side.

For a moment or two I speculated on what I had seen. Taken at face value, it appeared as if the woman had been meeting the man in the church surreptitiously, and that she and David Cornelius had been having some sort of argument, even a lovers' quarrel, which might have had something to do with the other man.

Then, conscious that there might well be any number of other reasons for the little drama I had witnessed, and conscious, too, of the time, I turned away from the gate and went back to the warmth of the car. It was time, I thought, to finish the last leg of our journey. Max would be waking soon and I wanted to be settled in before dark.

CHAPTER 5

Longbarrow Cottage lay on the far side of Shipcote, a quarter of a mile or so beyond the village, on a steep and narrow lane with high banks on either side topped by a thicket of trees and bushes. Daylight had already gone from the lane.

A stony dirty drive to the right led up to the cottage. The drive was so deeply rutted, the furrows filled with puddles left by some earlier rainfall, that I parked the car near the lane. Fifty yards away, on a hillside, sat the cottage, half-hidden in a large sloping garden enclosed by a crumbling stone wall. In the gathering dusk, shadows lay thick about the place, yet the promise of beauty remained, visible in the lines of the little house and in the way the surrounding countryside flowed and curved to embrace it.

"We're here," I said out loud to Max. "Home. Maybe." With these words came the first stirrings of hope, a sense of future I had not felt for a long time. All at once that prospect of a tangible inheritance for my son, something solid and enduring that I could pass on to him, held a promise of happiness.

From around his uptilted bottle, Max regarded me. His look was skeptical.

As I went to the other side of the car to unstrap him from his seat, I heard the sound of an engine coming from farther up the lane. In a moment, a truck appeared, the proverbial rattletrap, driven by a man slouching over the wheel. When he saw us, he slowed and stopped by the entrance to the drive. With one elbow resting on the open window, he called out a good evening. He looked about fifty or so, a coarsely handsome man with a pouchy face and gray hair

curling out from under a cloth cap pulled low on his forehead.

"You'll be the lady from America." It was a statement
rather than a question.

"Canada," I replied automatically.

"That's right," he said, as though the two were one and
the same. "I heard you were coming."

Max was fussing to be let out of the car seat. When I
straightened up again with him in my arms, the man was
standing by the open door of the truck. His descent from
the truck had been noiseless. A big, heavy figure in a bright
tweed jacket and matching trousers, he stood with his
thumbs hitched into his belt, arms akimbo, confident, almost knowing.

"Are you a neighbor of ours?" I asked him, trying to still
a small pang of unease.

"You might say so. You'll be living here now, will you?"
He spoke with what I took to be a country accent, his voice
deep and guttural, rolling his *r*'s, swallowing the *g*'s and *t*'s.

"For a while, yes."

"On your own, then?"

"Oh, no," I lied instinctively. "Friends will be staying
with us." I was beginning not to like his questions, or him.
"You'll have to excuse us, we're very tired." Opening the
back of the car, I retrieved Max's carryall from the seat.

"I dunno how the old lady stood it so long," he persisted,
stolidly ignoring my hint. "Alone in that house."

"What do you mean?" I said coldly. Max began to
squirm a little, and I jiggled him up and down gently in my
arms, rocking from one foot to the other.

"Her being so solitary. What with that murder and all."
His small eyes regarded me appraisingly. I did not like the
look.

I knew he expected me to ask him what murder, but I did
not want to give him the satisfaction. And I was in no
mood to listen to whatever grisly village horror he was obviously eager to shock me with. I opened my mouth to say
a curt good-bye but before I could utter a word he went
grimly on.

"Bashed in the head, she was. Blood all over. Never
caught him that done it. Lived alone up there, just like the

old lady." He nodded toward the house. "That's why I say I dunno how her stood it."

Unnerved by the location of this murder, confused by his pronouns and syntax, I began to feel angry. I was also dimly aware of a theatrical quality to the man's recitation that struck false. "Do you mean it happened in Longbarrow Cottage?" I asked him sharply. "Recently?"

He shrugged, and a sly look slid over his face. "Some time back." Abruptly, his tone changed, became ingratiating. He smiled, showing large and surprisingly white teeth with a glint of gold at the back of the mouth. "Well, good luck to you. If you need any work done round the place, let 'em know down at the pub. Name's Jope. They'll get word to me." He got back in his truck. Just before he drove off, I noticed a sign stuck to the back window: "It's a great day," it read. "Just watch some bastard spoil it."

Jope, and his ominous story, seemed to linger in the dusk where he had stood. The hope that I had felt on our arrival faded into dull weariness.

For some reason, I thought of that scene in *Kidnapped* where David Balfour meets the old crone in front of his wicked uncle's large and gloomy house. "Blood built it and blood shall bring it down," she tells him. "And I crack my thumb at it." The image had seemed so wonderfully powerful when I first read it as a child that for days afterward I had gone around muttering these words and cracking my thumb at anything that displeased me. Finally, my exasperated mother told me to stop, it would make my knuckle swell, she said.

But now I cracked my thumb at Jope's departing back. The ridiculous action did me good, made me smile. The man wasn't sinister, I reflected, just absurd. As for the murder, well, I didn't doubt that there would be other locals eager to tell me what had really happened. In the meantime, I would try not to think about it.

Only after Jope's truck had disappeared down the lane did it occur to me that I might have hired him on the spot to get our luggage up to the house. "Never mind," I said to Max. "I'd sooner have Norman Bates helping us with our suitcases."

With Max in one arm and his carryall over my shoulder,

I walked up the bumpy track to the house, picking my way around the puddles. The rain had brought out the scent of lilac and apple blossom, and the sweet smell of grass. At the top of the track, beneath the spreading branches of a beech, a barred wooden gate sagged open, partly torn from its hinges by a huge branch that had split off from the beech and fallen onto it. By the broken gate, I had a clear view of Longbarrow Cottage. Nan's house.

Built of stone the color of yellow-gray tweed, the cottage had the grace of all small, well-proportioned buildings. Its beauty lay in the harmony of stone and landscape, and in subtle details I only later learned to recognize. At first sight, it was a simple, flat-fronted, two-story house with a steeply pitched roof pierced by two gabled windows and flanked by tall chimneys at both ends. On the ground floor were two more windows in the front face, almost invisible behind the boxwood, on either side of the wooden front door. Dirty cream paint flaked from the door and window frames.

Green fields surrounded the cottage. On the western side, to my left as I faced it, they rose to meet a wood; on the east, they sloped down to the valley where the main road ran into Shipcote. This was now in darkness, but through the trees that fringed the road the rooftops of three or four other houses were just visible in the distance, smoke rising in thin, wavering lines from several chimneys.

A cluster of flowerpots stood forlornly on the front stoop, with the dried remnants of dead plants flopping over their sides. When I turned over the smallest of the pots, I found the key Tony Munnings had promised would be there. As I fitted it to the front-door lock, I felt the first small thrill of possession.

The door swung open at the push of my hand. Outside, the light was almost gone; indoors, it was already dark. I set the carryall down on the floor, shifted Max into both arms, and looked around. There was a lamp on a small table, and when I switched it on, the soft light revealed a short, narrow hall papered in pale yellow roses, with an uneven flagstone floor. Opposite the front door was a steep staircase to the second floor. To my right was a closed door. And to my left, down a single step under a low-beamed

doorway, was a large living room, which was furnished
with the things that May Armitage had left behind.

There were two armchairs and a sofa covered in a pretty
chintz, several wooden standing lamps with pleated shades,
a glass-fronted bookcase, and a large rug patterned in faded
flowers on the floor—simple, comfortable-looking furniture
that would be easy to live with. Between the two windows
in the west-facing wall was a large stone fireplace, whose
hearth was blocked off by a thick panel of black cast iron.
In front of it stood a wicker basket filled with yellowed
newspapers and old magazines.

Tony Munnings had promised the cottage would be
cleaned and heated, ready for us, and he had kept his word.
My first impression was of an enveloping, welcoming
warmth. And something more.

Longbarrow Cottage was one of those houses with a
presence, the resonance, perhaps, of other inhabitants, other
ages in its life. There was a spirit here, benign and peaceful, that seemed to reach out to me. I could feel the tension
from our journey dissolving, my weariness and doubts
eased, as I allowed the house to draw me into its embrace.

Abruptly, Max stiffened in my arms and wailed. He had
been patient, his outraged face seemed to say, but now he'd
had enough, he wanted food and my attention. Hurriedly, I
shucked off his jacket, letting it fall to the flagstones, and
went in search of the kitchen.

I tried the shut door first, but found only a cold, empty
room with the closed-off smell of long disuse. The kitchen,
it turned out, was off the living room. With walls distem-
pered in a watery blue spotted with damp, a tiny stove and
an even smaller refrigerator, and old, cracked linoleum on
the floor, it was not a sight to gladden the heart of a cook.
But I am no cook; I was merely relieved to find that the
stove worked, that hot water ran from the tap, and that
the fridge contained butter, milk, six eggs in a glass bowl,
and a wedge of cheese.

A square table topped with turquoise Formica stood
against one wall, with three ladder-backed chairs pulled up
to it. On the table, beside a loaf of bread and a pie, was an
envelope with my name handwritten on it. Reading it
would have to wait until Max's supper was ready—he was

howling in good earnest by now. No matter how often I
told myself that he was safe in my arms, unhurt, his crying
unerringly made every muscle in my stomach tighten. I cut
a slice from the loaf for Max, one from the pie—which
turned out to be a meat pie—for myself, then looked
around for something in which to heat up the jars of baby
food in the carryall. At last I found the pots and pans in a
tiny, chilly pantry by the back door.

There was no place to put Max while I fed him—his
stroller was still in the trunk of the car with the suitcases—so I sat him on my lap at the kitchen table as I
spooned vegetables into him at a furious rate. When he had
finished this, as well as some applesauce, I gave him a
plateful of cheese cubes to eat by himself, and opened the
note.

Dear Mrs. Treleven [it said]: Welcome to Longbarrow
Cottage. Tony Munnnings asked me to get the place
ready for you and your son. I have put a cot in one of
the bedrooms for him. You will find some provisions in
the fridge and on the table. The milkman calls very early
and will leave a list tomorrow of all he supplies. If you
want milk, etc., in the morning, just put a note out for
him on the front step tonight. If you need anything, or
have any questions, please call on me. Our farm is near
the top of the lane on the right. I will come by to see you
in a day or two.

It was signed "Pat Ebborn, Ashleaze Farm." She and her
husband were the couple who had been keeping an eye on
the cottage since May's departure. The thought that we had
at least one good neighbor to compensate for Jope cheered
me.

Afterward, as he sucked on his bottle, I carried Max upstairs. On the second floor, I found a bathroom and three
more rooms. The largest was almost filled by a double bed
and a crib, both made up with fresh sheets and blankets. Silently, I blessed Tony Munnings and Pat Ebborn. This bedroom and the room next to it, which was smaller and held
a single bed and a wardrobe, were at the front of the house.

The third room, next to the bathroom, at the back, was locked.

As I stood there, disconcerted, I thought I heard a faint scratching noise from the other side of the door. It sounded like mice. If we stayed, we would have to get a cat. I rattled the door handle to frighten them off, then took Max for his bath.

The bathroom was warm and reasonably modern. Inside a cupboard was the boiler that provided the heat and hot water for the house, and a shelf with a stack of clean sheets and towels. As I washed and changed Max into fresh diapers and his sleeper, I thought of Nan and May, and of all the others who had lived in Longbarrow Cottage since it was first built, sometime in the eighteenth century.

May had spent almost fifty years of her life here— perhaps that accounted for the sense I had of a presence in the place. In his letter, Tony Munnings had written that she had died of a second stroke a few days after my visit. It was not impossible to believe that her spirit had returned to the place she had loved. I found that I liked the idea of other people filling the house over the centuries, liked the knowledge that it was more than plaster and stone, that it was a building with a past.

Max's eyes began to close as I fed him the remains of his bottle. Lulled by the warmth of the bedroom, a full stomach, and the milk, which dribbled down his chin into the fat folds of his neck, he relaxed his grip on his blanket. One hand clenched and then opened, a spasm went through him, and he was asleep. As I laid him into the crib, tucking the blanket around him, I looked for Peter in the lines of his face, but I could not find him there. Perhaps there was no likeness yet, or perhaps it was simply that I could not remember Peter's face. It had vanished from my mind's eye when I learned of his death.

Quietly, I went downstairs for my own dinner. Then remembered, with a groan, that the luggage was still in the trunk of the car. Had I locked it? I couldn't remember. It seemed unlikely anyone would take our belongings, but I could not risk losing them.

When I opened the front door, the night was pitch-black and a thin rain was falling. The clouds that I had seen to the north, which had brought the rain, covered the moon. In the pantry, I found a flashlight, which still worked, and a fluorescent orange slicker hanging on a hook by the back door. It was a bit tight through the shoulders, made for someone smaller than me, someone May's size, although the color seemed an unlikely choice for an elderly lady.

Before I stepped outside, I stood listening for a moment. But there was only silence from upstairs. It wouldn't take me long to bring in the luggage, a few minutes at most. Closing the door behind me, I went out into the night.

CHAPTER 6

The flashlight's beam shone on the puddles as I picked my way down the track to the car. The rain brought out the rich branlike smell of earth and grass. It was a different rain than I was used to, a mist of fine drops soft against my face.

There were other differences as well. Apart from a gusting wind and the crunch of my footsteps on gravel, the silence was absolute, empty of the city sounds I was used to, of engines, horns, and the constant swish of tires on asphalt. And then there was the night itself, unfamiliar and filled with shadows. The darkness beyond the flashlight's range seemed impenetrable at first, unrelieved by the background glow that was always present at night in the city. I glanced back at the house, reassured by the lights shining from the windows. As the wind-shredded clouds thinned, allowing a pale moonlight to shine down, my eyes gradually began to adjust.

The wind moving through the moonlit trees made their shadows come alive. I thought of Nan, who had fashioned her stories from shadows of the past, from vanished Cotswold locals who lived on in legends. A gritty grain of truth lay at the heart of most legends, she had told me, and the slow accretion of fiction hardened in layers around it.

Nan's characters were vividly memorable. One, a highwayman named Dick the Handless, had played a major role in my nightmares for years. Intent on robbing a local nobleman's house, he had put his hand through the shutter on a window, to unbolt it. But the nobleman and his men, forewarned, were waiting inside for him. When the hand came through the shutter they pounced on it, tying it tightly with a curtain cord to the bolt on the window. Eagerly, they rushed out of the house to confront their captive. He, however, had vanished. They pursued distant hoofbeats, but these faded into silence in the depths of the nearby forest.

On their return to the house, the nobleman and his servants found the explanation for the highwayman's miraculous escape. Livid in the moonlight that filtered through the shutter, his severed hand dangled by its wrist from the bloodied yellow cord. The highwayman was never seen again but, according to Nan, his ghost, mounted on a horse, haunted the Cotswold lanes to her own day.

The image of that severed hand had obsessed me until I exorcised it with a drawing. It was then I began to realize I might have some power of my own, even though I was still a child.

I was remembering Dick the Handless as I unloaded the trunk of the car, not really paying attention when I set the canvas bag with Max's toys on a stony bit of ground. The bag fell over, spilling its contents into the mud. Cursing, I squatted down to pick them up again. When I shone the flashlight around, to make certain I had retrieved everything, the light picked up Max's red ball, which had rolled to the edge of the lane, a few feet away. Round and glistening, it bobbed in a puddle just out of reach.

The tight fit of the raincoat made it easier to move crabwise than to stand up again, and so I scuttled, ridiculously, toward the puddle. As I stretched my hand out for the ball, I heard the rhythmical clip-clop of a horse's hoofs coming quickly down the lane. Almost at once, the huge dark shadow of the horse loomed up in the road.

For one irrational instant, I was terrified. Like a fool, I panicked, tried to stand, and lost my balance. Desperately, I put one hand out to break my fall and as I did, the other, which held the flashlight, automatically lifted, shining the light straight through the rain into the horse's eyes. They blazed a momentary luminous yellow, then blinked out as the creature snorted and reared up.

Simultaneous with the horse's whinny came a startled oath in a man's voice. As I struggled to sit up, a dim shape jumped down from the horse and ran toward me.

"Rafe!" the man said, in a voice I knew at once. "Are you all right?" His hand gripped my arm, at first gently, then tightening as I straightened and looked up into his face. I had a confused impression of agonized dark eyes and rain-wet hair streaked across angular features. And of a desperate, angry anxiety so powerful it aroused in me an emotion that frightened me more than the man himself—an instinctive, involuntary yearning to comfort him.

"I'm not Rafe," I blurted out. It seemed essential David Cornelius should know this at once, for whatever reason.

He had seen his mistake before the words left my mouth. "You! I didn't realize ... Are you hurt?" He helped me struggle to my feet.

I shook my head, wiping the dirt and wet leaves from my hands. "I'm fine. But your horse—"

"Oh hell, Thatcher!" He turned around to look for the animal, which was standing, all but invisible, in the deep shadows cast by a clump of trees a little farther up the lane. At his approach, it suddenly shied, the bridle jingling as it danced nervously away. He gentled it, his words low and soothing, until it allowed him to come near enough to gather up the dangling reins. I picked up Max's ball and stuffed it back in the canvas bag after shaking off the worst of the muddy water.

"It was the raincoat, you see, the one you're wearing," David Cornelius said as he led the horse back toward me. "Rafe, my son, has one like it." his voice was quiet now, controlled, as though the business with the horse had forced him to calm himself, too. One hand was stroking the animal's neck. But when he came close enough, I could see that he looked exhausted and on edge, like a man who was nearing the end of his emotional rope. "Maybe you've seen him? An eleven-year-old, with brown hair and glasses? He was supposed to come home hours ago."

I thought, then, that I understood his desperation. Gently, I told him that I hadn't seen his son. "I just got here. The phone's not connected so I can't even offer to let you use it, to check—"

"Of course," he interrupted, looking around as though he were only now taking in my car and the suitcase sitting on the ground beside it. "I should have . . . I knew you were arriving today. Look, I didn't mean to grab you like that. I'm sorry if—"

"You must be very worried about your son."

The words seemed stiff and inadequate. Max had taught me what it meant to have my peace of mind utterly involved in the happiness and safety of another human creature. David Cornelius's anxieties about his child were contagious, and I was suddenly eager to get back to the cottage. "I wish I could offer to help you look for Rafe," I told him, "but I've left my own son alone in the house. He's asleep, but I'm afraid he might wake up." Stooping, I began to gather up the suitcases.

"Let me give you a hand with those." He was about to tie the horse's reins to a branch, but stopped when I said that I could manage alone.

"You go on looking for Rafe. I hope you find him soon."

He turned away, fitting his foot into a stirrup. The saddle leather creaked as he swung himself up onto the horse, and the two dark shapes merged into one. "Rafe likes to wander," he said, almost as though he were reassuring himself. "And he has no sense of time."

"Good night, then. And good luck." Over my shoulder, I thought I heard his own good-night but I was already halfway up the track to the cottage, stumbling as I hurried with the suitcases bumping against my legs. The sudden, violent apparition in the rainy night of a man searching for his son made me wish that I had never left Max alone. I wanted the reassurance of his small body in my arms.

When I reached the cottage, I set the suitcases down and opened the front door. Quietly, I stepped inside, straining to listen over the noise of my own panting. At first, there was a blessed silence. Max was still asleep.

Then I heard him laugh. Max's laugh always sounded comically like a creaky hinge. It was odd, that small noise in the stillness, like hearing someone chuckle in his sleep, yet reassuring. He was awake, but content.

I brought the suitcases inside and set them softly down on the floor. As I straightened I heard something else, something that stopped my breath. It was the sound of a voice talking.

Without pausing to think, I went quietly into the kitchen and found the long-bladed knife that lay beside the loaf of bread. The steel felt cold to my touch, as cold as my own flesh. I was trembling, but some desperate compulsion impelled me silently through the house and up the stairs toward the small sounds coming from Max's room. When I reached the top of the stairs, however, the voice had stopped.

Our bedroom, the one with the crib and double bed, was at the end of the hall, farthest away from the stairs. The door to the third room which had been locked, was open now. A glance into the room as I passed told me that, apart from two trunks placed side by side against one wall, it was empty. Edging along the hall to our bedroom, I peered through the crack left by the partly open door. Only the double bed was visible. Not Max, not whoever was with him.

Abruptly, Max began gurgling so loudly that I moved cautiously to the left, inch by inch, until I was standing at the opening of the door. When I saw who it was with my son, all the tension drained away from my body and I felt slack and weak. I ought to have known, I told myself dully.

I looked down at the knife in my hand, at my fingers curled so tightly around the handle. The sight made me feel sick. Carefully, I laid the knife down on the small chest of drawers in the hallway and pushed the bedroom door wide open.

A boy of about eleven years old, with spiky brown hair and glasses, stood beside the crib, sideways to me. He was cradling something, some sort of animal about the size of a cat—but too short-legged to be a cat—which turned and twisted in his arms. It looked a bit like a mink, its thick grayish-white fur masked like a raccoon with black around its eyes. The boy was dressed in jeans and an oversize army jacket, with a grubby sheepskin pouch hanging from his right shoulder. When he grinned at Max, I could see the light glinting off the braces on his teeth.

As for Max, who was standing in his crib with both hands clutching the rail, he was obviously delighted with the entertainment, crowing with pleasure as he watched the pair in front of him.

At the creak of the opening door, the boy whipped around toward me, causing the creature in his arms to run up onto his shoulder, where it perched, making a rapid, chittering noise. The look on the boy's thin face was abashed, but not surprised. "He was crying," he said quickly, in an American accent, pointing to Max. "I couldn't just let him cry."

"No. Of course not." I was too exhausted to be angry. "Does that animal bite?"

He shook his head so violently that the glasses slipped down his hose. With both hands on the temples, he pushed them up again.

"Good," I said. Then, "You must be Rafe."

This did surprise him. He blinked rapidly. "How come you know my name?"

"Your father told me. He's looking for you."

"Oh." He glanced away from me then, toward the creature on his shoulder. Deftly, he detached its claws from his jacket and placed it in the pouch hanging by his side. With its short front paws resting on the sheepskin, the animal looked out at us, its round, snub-nosed little face alert and curious.

"He thought I was you, outside just now," I went on. "This belongs to you, doesn't it?" Wearily, I pulled off the slicker and held it out to him.

He mumbled a thank-you as he took the raincoat and bunched it up, holding it against his shirtfront. I stifled an impulse to tell him that the coat would make the shirt wet. He was not my child, after all. I also repressed the urge to shout at him that he had just given me the worst fright of my life. Perhaps, if he had been tougher-looking, I might have; but there was something vulnerable about him, a fragility that prevented my anger. Besides, I told myself, there was probably some sort of punishment waiting for him at home.

Now that the boy's attention was elsewhere, Max was growing restless. He sat down heavily on his diapered bottom and whimpered, holding his arms out to me. As I picked him up, I asked the boy how he had managed to get into the cottage.

"I have a key. Miss Armitage gave it to me. I didn't mean to trespass." From behind the glasses, his brown eyes looked earnestly into mine. Fringed with thick, dark lashes, the eyes, like the tortoiseshell glasses, seemed too large for the pale, freckled face. "I only wanted to get my coat. I left it here the last time I visited her. But I . . . I fell asleep, and when I heard you come in I got scared. I figured you'd be angry with me, so I hid."

"May I have the key, please?" He fished it out from a front pocket and gave it to me, muttering that he meant to leave it for me on the kitchen table. "You were in the locked room, weren't you?" I said. The noise I had taken for mice must have been his pet.

He nodded. "There's a bolt on the other side. I wanted to come out, but . . ." His voice trailed off.

There were other questions I ought to have asked him, but I was too tired to listen to his explanations, and I wasn't sure they would be the truth anyway. "Come on," I told him, "I'll drive you back to your house. You ought to call your father but the phone's not connected yet."

"It's not far," he said, following me downstairs. "I can walk."

I was tempted to let him. By now, I was so tired and hungry that the simple act of driving Rafe Cornelius home seemed almost impossible. But I had only to put Max in his place, or to recall his father's face, to know that I had to see him safely to his own door.

Distracted by the boy's pet, Max forgot to complain at being bundled into his jacket, twisting his head to get a better look at the creature in the pouch. "What kind of animal is your friend there?" I asked.

"He's a ferret. His name is Spike."

"A ferret. You mean like Sredni Vashtar?" Nervously, I stared at Spike. Saki's cautionary tale, with its sinister, aunt-murdering ferret, had made a deep impression on me—although that bloodthirsty beast was hard to reconcile with this small, lively animal. The impudent little face that peered over the edge of the pouch had a peculiar charm, and the bright eyes seemed full of curiosity, not malice.

Rafe Cornelius scowled. "That story," he said contemptuously. "Ferrets aren't really like that, you know. They don't go around eating people and stuff."

"I'm relieved to hear it." I opened the front door and ushered the boy forward, then followed with Max, locking the door behind us.

"What's your baby's name?" he asked, as we went down the path together to the car. When I told him, he said that his mother had a baby, too.

"A girl or a boy?" I wondered why David Cornelius had omitted mention of another child.

"A girl. I wish it was a boy like Max. She's useless. She just lies there." After a moment's unease, I thought to ask how old his sister was. "Half sister," he corrected. "My mom and dad are divorced. She got married again and had this baby last month."

"I see." It explained why David Cornelius had used the singular in speaking of his plans when we met in London, but I wondered why it had never occurred to me that the woman I had seen him with earlier might be his wife, or former wife. As I started the car, I asked Rafe where his mother was and he replied that she lived in London.

Not his wife, then.

Rafe's directions to his father's house came rote-fashion, almost chanted. "Down Blacksmith's Lane, right at Hangman's Stone, and left by Shaking Charlotte."

" 'Right here, left there' as we go will have to do. I'm a stranger in town."

"Sorry. I forgot." Blacksmith's Lane, he added, was the road we were on, the one that ran past the cottage.

"What's Shaking Charlotte?"

"It's a tree near the church. An oak. Well, what's left of it anyway. Most of it fell down in a snowstorm a long time ago. People thought it was a witch who was turned into a tree." His voice held a mixture of scoffing disbelief and wistfulness, the hint that he would like to believe but thought himself too old for such foolishness.

"Does everything here have a name?"

"Yeah. You do, too."

"Me? What am I called?"

"May's Canadian. That's what they call you in the village anyway."

It wasn't so bad, I reflected; I had been called worse. I was driving slowly, with extreme care, for I did not have much faith in my ability to remember to keep to the left side of the road. At the bottom of the lane was the wider road that led into the village, and here the boy told me to turn right. He leaned forward and pointed out a large object next to a clump of trees. "That's Hangman's Stone. Do you want to know why it's called that?"

"Can I guess?"

"Sure, but I bet you won't get it right."

"Well, how's this? A man was carrying a stolen sheep over his shoulders. He tied the front legs and back legs around his neck with a rope, but the sheep was heavy and he got tired. So when he saw the stone, he rested the sheep on top of it. But the sheep slipped off the other side and then—" I made a choking, gurgling noise. "The sheep hanged him."

There was a momentary silence in the backseat. Then, accusingly, "You already knew."

I laughed. "My grandmother told me that story years ago. She used to live in Longbarrow Cottage."

"I know. Miss Armitage told me."

"May said you used to visit her."

"Yes." There was a small pause. "I miss her." I wondered if Rafe's visit to the cottage tonight had anything to do with his missing his friend. "There's the church," he said suddenly. "Now you turn left."

He guided me down a drive overhung with trees that ran between the church and a cottage on the corner, half-hidden by the curve of a high stone wall. It ended in a broad sweep of gravel in front of a long, low, gabled house with lights burning in the windows. Even in the dark, the house looked old and handsome.

"So you're lord of the manor," I said, as I stopped the car in front of the walk that led up to the house.

"That's Summerhays. Benedict and Clarissa's house," he replied. "We live behind it, in Oldbarn."

"In the barn?"

"Well, it used to be the barn, until they fixed it up. Now it's a house."

I was too tired to ask him who Benedict and Clarissa were. He opened his door, said good-bye to Max, then began a guilty-sounding thank-you to me. I was about to tell him that I intended to see him safely to his father when the front door of the house opened and a woman came out onto the step. "Rafe," she called, "is that you?"

"Yes, coming," he shouted back. As he scrambled out of the car, he said to me, "It's okay. That's Mela." With the ferret and the raincoat in his arms, he went slowly toward the woman who had run from his father in the field by the ancient church.

CHAPTER 7

By the time I got back to the cottage, hauling the stroller up from the car with Max on my hip, I was so tired that the ground seemed to be rolling under my feet. To conserve my energy for dealing with Max, I opened the suitcases in the front hall, rather than dragging them upstairs, digging through my clothes until I found a nightgown and the makeup bag with my toothbrush. While Max sat on the bath mat hurling toys about the room, I took a quick, scalding bath, then warmed up another bottle of milk, and settled us both into the double bed with a collection of plastic cars and trucks. After an endless number of traffic pileups staged by me for his amusement, he closed his eyes at last.

For all my exhaustion, I kept waking up. Max in my room did not disturb me—he was not a restless sleeper; it was the silence. A silence so palpable it seemed almost a physical presence. I put this queer sensation down to my overstrained nerves and jet lag, and drew comfort from the sound of Max's breathing. When sleep did come, it was full of dreams of murdered women and bloody hands, the images all tumbled together like an untidy sheaf of drawings.

Max woke at dawn, grumpy with hunger. In the kitchen, I warmed a bottle, feeling the cracks of the cold linoleum under my bare feet while I jiggled Max up and down in my arms and stared, bleary-eyed, out the window.

The first sunlight lay slanting on the long grass, shimmering with the night's rain. In the midst of the wide expanse of back garden were the remains of what must once have been May's vegetable patch, now a hillocky rectangle of weedy earth with an upended plastic bottle on a stick, presumably to frighten away the birds. There was a small stone shed abutting the house by the back door, a lean-to with a rusting corrugated iron roof and a heap of broken flowerpots stacked up against one wall. Beyond the garden wall was a sloping field grazed by sheep and their bleating lambs, tufts of white wool that drifted like clouds through the early-morning haze.

The long barrow rose from the far edge of the field. Last night I had taken it for a low hill crowned with trees, amorphous in the dusk. Now I saw that its long swelling shape had the form of a green dune, a smoothly rounded mound with the stand of thin trees on top and what seemed to be a thicket of bushes at its base. As far as I could judge, the barrow appeared to be about a hundred feet long and ten feet high.

Then, through the pearly light, I saw something moving about on it, a figure that might have been a person crouching, or an animal. I was peering at it, trying to make it out, when Max reminded me of his bottle.

"Buh," he shouted, aggrieved, his hand stretched out and pointing. "Buh!"

While Max sucked on his milk, I changed him and put him into his crib with the bottle—guiltily, because it was an indulgence forbidden by every book on babies I had ever read—then climbed once more under the heap of bedcovers as though they were a refuge. I sank into a deep, and this time dreamless, sleep.

A determined thudding noise came dimly through the fog of sleep. Startled, I sat up. It took me a moment to realize that the thudding was being made by someone knocking on the front door, and that, judging by the narrow line of bright morning light shining into the room between the curtains, Max and I had slept for a long time. My alarm clock read nine-thirty.

When I went to the window to pull aside the curtains, I was half-blinded by the sudden brightness. Unfastening the casement, I called down that I was coming. A woman's voice, light and attractive, replied that I should take my time. From the open window, I could see the distant roofs of Shipcote through the light green canopy of trees. The birds were singing, and the air smelled sweet and clean with the new day.

Wrapping Max in his blanket, I went downstairs to open the front door. Standing outside, a large basket in her arms, was the woman who had greeted Rafe Cornelius on his return home the night before. Slim and fair-haired, with the silvery sheen of the truly blond, she shimmered, or so it seemed to me, in the daze of sunlight that shone around her. I blinked, dazzled, while Max turned his head away, burying it on my shoulder.

"Oh, I'm so sorry, I've waked you," she said ruefully. "I came to thank you for bringing Rafe home last night. I'm Mela Mallaby."

She had the short upper lip and small nose of a certain type of delicate English beauty, eyes that were a true cornflower blue, and clear, almost transparent, skin. The mass of shining hair was caught with combs over her ears, waving thickly to the shoulders of her green velvet jacket. It was a pleasure to look at her, as though Arthur Rackham's Alice in Wonderland had suddenly appeared, grown-up and on my doorstep.

I realized I was staring, and asked her to come inside, flipping a blouse back into an open suitcase with one foot before she could step on it. As she entered, the scent of her perfume was carried in on the current of cool outdoor air, a subtle mixture of violets and lily of the valley, and some other grassy, ferny element.

I hoisted Max around to my chest, to hide my crumpled nightgown, catching a faint whiff of wet diaper, and ran a hand through my unbrushed hair. "I enjoyed meeting Rafe," I said, as I led her through into the living room, "even if the circumstances were a little unconventional."

She smiled, a charming smile that disclosed small white teeth. "You're very forgiving. He told us that you caught him trespassing. Rafe's like Spike that way—he loves to go where he shouldn't."

"Sounds like any self-respecting boy and ferret to me."

"What you have to look forward to. The boy, I mean." She gestured at Max. He was still unusually shy, pushing himself against me, refusing to look at her. "They're so sweet at this age, aren't they? Almost edible. Speaking of which," she went on, "I've brought you some groceries. In case you haven't had time to shop." She lifted the basket lid so that I could see the contents—glass jars, foil-wrapped packages, and some sort of large leafy vegetable that looked like spinach with a permanent.

I thanked her, touched by the trouble she had taken for a stranger.

"Rafe wanted to bring it over. But I thought you might have had enough of him for a while. Shall I put it in the kitchen?"

"Yes, thanks. It's over there." I turned to show her, but she told me that she knew the way.

"May and I were old friends," she explained, setting the basket down in the midst of the litter of dirty dishes on the kitchen table. "She was my teacher in infant school. The most wonderful teacher. Never a cross word."

"Rafe obviously misses her," I said, a little dryly.

"She had a way with children. Always saw their good side. I'm afraid that meant one could get round her, pull the wool over her eyes a bit. Still, she was a darling."

Light and musical, Mela Mallaby's voice had an odd catch in it from time to time, a small breath between words like a sigh, that made certain phrases come out in a little rush of air. It gave an intimacy to what she said, as though it were a confidence shared only with the listener. She began to unpack the basket. "David—Rafe's father—would have come himself to thank you, but he had to go up to London at some horrible hour this morning."

The way she said his name, with an intimate possessiveness, made a subtle but explicit claim to him. As I carried the dirty dishes over to the sink and filled the kettle with water for tea, I wondered what their relationship was. A glance at her left hand revealed nothing; her ring finger was bare.

When I asked her if she would like a cup of tea, she shook her head, picking up the empty basket. "I know you must be too jet-lagged to want to entertain, and anyway, I have a thousand things to do this morning. But you must come to Sunday lunch at Summerhays tomorrow. Bring your son, too. Blackie—Mrs. Blackwell, the housekeeper—is mad about babies. She'll look after him while we eat." This was said over her shoulder to me as she went back through the living room on her way to the front door. She walked with the swift grace I'd noticed the day before, all her movements fluid as water, implicit with energy.

"It's really kind of you," I began, as she opened the door.

"Oh no, it's not kind at all," she replied, before I could say more. She had turned toward me, her face smooth and smiling. "Cousins should look after each other, don't you think?"

I must have looked as blankly nonplussed as I felt, for she continued, less confidently, "Well, we are cousins, after all, no matter how many times removed it might be."

"You must be confusing me with someone else."

"I don't think so. Your grandfather was Charles Lorimer, wasn't he?"

"Yes, that was his name."

"There you are, then. He and Benedict were first cousins, and Benedict is my grandfather." She tilted her head to one side, eyes slightly narrowed. "Didn't you know?"

"No, I had no idea," I said slowly. "It's a complete surprise."

She smiled. "A pleasant one, I hope."

"Oh, of course." I tried to inject some warmth into my voice. "It's just that I'm, well ... surprised," I finished lamely. "Is your grandfather's last name Mallaby, too?"

"It is. So you really didn't know? How extraordinary. And here we thought . . ." She did not finish whatever it was she had been going to say, but for a moment there was a look of almost malicious amusement on her face. "I gather they grew up together, were both at Oxford. They were great friends, before your grandfather did his vanishing act.

Benedict Mallaby. I said the name to myself, but there were no reverberations from the past. I had never heard it before.

"I'll inflict the family tree on you later, if you like," Mela Mallaby was saying. "It's respectable enough, by and large. Though there are a few horrors on it, mostly of the sacred monster variety." Mock thoughtfully, she continued, "I wonder how many people emigrate to escape their dreadful relatives? No more awful Aunt Agnes, good-bye to Great-uncle Andrew and his boring stories of the war. Perhaps that's why your grandmother left."

I laughed. "The relativity theory of mass migration? Maybe you're right. Though I don't remember Nan ever complaining about relatives she'd left behind." Or talking about them at all, for that matter.

"Well, I don't know why we should have been hidden from you, but I promise that Benedict and Clarissa aren't the least bit dreadful. I can't say as much for the rest of us, I'm afraid. Although my brother, Robin, has his moments. But come and judge for yourself tomorrow."

I said, not altogether truthfully, that I would look forward to it.

"Twelve-thirty suit you? Good. See you then."

I watched her Range Rover back down the drive before I suddenly remembered the kettle boiling away in the kitchen. While Max sat in his stroller, I prepared our breakfast and thought about Mela Mallaby's revelation.

It seemed strange to me that, in a village as small as Shipcote, the existence of my grandfather's relatives should have been ignored by Nan. Perhaps they hadn't approved of the marriage; perhaps they hadn't lived in the village when Nan did, but moved there later; or perhaps the bitterness she must have felt at her husband's desertion had tainted her feelings about his cousin as well. Speculation was

pointless. I would try to find a way to ask Benedict
Mallaby himself at lunch tomorrow.

A shaft of sunlight falling through the kitchen window
struck the round glass jar of marmalade on the table. On the
paper label stuck to the lid, someone had written: "Ginger
marmalade, Summerhays." Everything in the village was la-
beled, I reflected, spooning some of the marmalade onto
bread for Max—the houses, a bit of ground, even a jar of
marmalade. Everything belonged.

Curious as I was to meet the Mallabys, I felt ambivalent
about the unexpected connection. I had come to Shipcote
secure in my anonymity. If questions became too personal,
I was free to reinvent the recent past, revise my own history, and who was to know or care? But already I had acquired labels of my own: "the lady from America," "May's
Canadian," the owner of Longbarrow Cottage. And now,
the cousin of Mela Mallaby.

CHAPTER 8

Midmorning, I pushed Max in his stroller up the lane to
Ashleaze Farm. I wanted to thank Pat Ebborn for her part
in preparing Longbarrow Cottage, and to ask her where
Shipcote did its grocery shopping.

The first signs of the farm were two rounded roofs of
corrugated metal, humped and gray like the backs of elephants, rising behind a line of young poplars on the right
whose sharp, peppery smell filled the air. The roofs covered
open-sided farm sheds filled with enormous circular bales
of hay wrapped up in black plastic sheeting. Beyond the
sheds, across a tidy, concrete yard, was a massive stone
barn. The rows of narrow slits that pierced its sides like arrow loops in a castle wall gave the barn the look of some

ancient fortification. Its huge wooden doors were shut; from behind them came the mournful lowing of a cow.

The large, gabled farmhouse of honey-colored stone sat directly across the lane from the barn, behind a protective wing of steep-roofed stone outbuildings that met the house at an angle, like a crooked arm protecting its face. Immediately behind the house rose a low, wooded hill. The site and the plan of the buildings combined to give the subtle effect of an embrace—the hill flowed down to enfold the farm, while the wing of outbuildings cradled the farmhouse and the people who lived there.

The gate stood open, but planted in the grass verge beside it was a small sign. It read: BEWARE GOOSE.

As I hesitated, debating whether or not to lift Max out of the stroller, safely beyond the reach of a goose's beak, a woman came out of a doorway, carrying a bucket. She looked about sixty or so and was dressed in a waterproof jacket, a pair of overalls, and green rubber boots, with oversize leather gloves like gauntlets on her hands. She was tall, with a male ranginess and stride. I might have mistaken her for a man but for the stylish cut of her hair. When she saw us, she called out a friendly hello.

"Mrs. Ebborn?" I asked as she approached. She nodded, peeling off the leather gloves. "I'm Jo Treleven. And this is Max."

"I thought you must be." The smile on her shrewd, weather-beaten face was welcoming. "How was your first night in the cottage?"

"Very comfortable, thanks to you." When I tried to tell her how grateful I was for all she'd done to get the place ready, she brushed aside my words.

"My daily, Mrs. Kyte, did the cleaning, and Tony Munnings paid her for it," she said matter-of-factly. "As for the food, that's just being a neighbor. I often cook for ten here, so there's always enough and to spare in my deep freeze. Now, come inside, why don't you, and have a cup of tea." She smiled down at Max. "You'd like a biscuit, wouldn't you, my love?"

As I accepted for the two of us, a large white goose came rushing toward us, honking loudly. Quickly, I scooped Max up out of reach.

"The little one's quite safe," Pat Ebborn told me. "Stanley's just an early warning system, not at all dangerous. He likes to make a fuss, but he'd never hurt you. Go on, be off with you, old fraud!" This, in affectionate tones to the goose as she flapped her arms at it.

The goose retreated a few paces, but followed behind, chivying us along with its honking. Enchanted, Max twisted himself around in my arms, trying to keep it in sight. Pat Ebborn led us into a gabled porch jutting out from the facade of the house. She took our coats, then pulled off her boots and overalls, revealing lilac tweed trousers and a pale lavender cashmere sweater. When she ran her hands through her short hair, tucking the ends behind her ears, I saw that there were small pearl studs in her earlobes. The transformation from farmhand to casually elegant lady was disconcertingly swift and complete.

She then took us into the oldest kitchen I had ever seen. A long, tile-topped counter ran down the center of the room, dividing it into utterly different halves. To the left, with a window overlooking the courtyard, was an ultramodern kitchen with sleek, restaurant-size appliances—stove, fridge, dishwasher, microwave—in burnished steel and gleaming chocolate enamel, backed up by a battery of gadgets hanging from wire racks on the wall. Nothing in it looked more than a year old. The other side, to the right of the counter, was a comfortably shabby country kitchen complete with a cat sleeping in a rocking chair beside an old woodstove, six assorted chairs pulled up to a wooden trestle table, and a floor-to-ceiling, open-fronted dresser crammed with knickknacks. Everything on this side, apart from the cat, looked at least fifty years old.

Used, perhaps, to the reactions of those seeing the room for the first time, Pat Ebborn explained good-humoredly, "I wanted to cook in the new kitchen, but eat in the old one. I let the decorators loose on one half, wouldn't let them touch the other. I'm not one for clean sweeps of the past."

"I can see that it might not be so terrible to cook for ten in this kitchen," I told her.

"Actually, it's just William and myself at the moment. But in the season I take in bed-and-breakfasters, now that our two boys are grown up and gone." She went to one of the cupboards and took down a tin decorated with a picture of the Queen Mother. "An oatmeal biscuit or a rusk, poppet?" she asked Max, holding out one in each hand. He reached out for the rusk and crammed it into his mouth.

While we sat at the wooden table drinking cups of strong, milky tea, Pat Ebborn told me where the shops were, that diapers—or nappies, as she called them—could be found at the chemist's—the drugstore—in Wychley, and how to go about getting the phone hooked up. In the meantime, she said, I was welcome to use theirs. She insisted that Max borrow the high chair her own children had sat in. "William will bring it round later," she told me firmly. A fund of practical information and help, she was clearly pleased to pass it on, and yet seemed the least pushy of women. I liked her dryly humorous manner, and her way with Max, not forcing herself on him but making a connection by slow degrees until he lost his shyness and smiled easily at her. She was brisk and forthright, but asked no personal questions, allowing me to volunteer what I would. When I mentioned the kind of work I did, she told me that Oxford or Cirencester would be my best bet for supplies.

About Max's father she did not inquire.

Max squirmed off my lap, eager to visit the cat. While I squatted beside him, keeping him from reaching out for the tempting tail, I thought to ask Pat Ebborn about Jope. I said that I had met him in passing the day before and that he'd offered to do odd jobs around the cottage. "Is he reliable?" What I really wanted to know was, Was he as ominous as he seemed?

Patt Ebborn seemed surprised. "Odd jobs? Is that what he said? I'd have thought he had enough of those at his own place." She lifted the teapot lid, peered inside, then rose and carried the pot over to the stove. It was a moment before she continued, and when she did she said simply, "William will find you someone else to give you a hand."

This seemed to confirm my suspicions, but before I could go on to ask her about Jope's story of the murder in the cottage, the kitchen door opened and a big, red-faced man came stamping through into the room. His first words were furious.

"Some fool's gone and cut the bloody fence again! Can

you credit it?" Bafflement was mixed with the rage. He had turned his broad back to Max and me in our corner near the woodstove, never having noticed us in his anger.

"In the same place?" Pat Ebborn asked him quietly as she poured boiling water from the kettle into the teapot.

He shook his head. "By the tump." At least, that's what I thought he said. It sounded like some arcane oath, although I assumed it referred to a place. "It's just lucky we spotted it before the lambs got into the brambles. D'you know, I wouldn't like to say it to Cornelius without proof, but I'd almost swear it was that—"

"William," Pat Ebborn said quickly, "we have visitors." She glanced past him at Max and me.

"Ah," he said, and turned around to us with a startled look. He had a high-colored, blue-eyed face, large and square, with thick, sandy eyebrows and fair hair, graying like his wife's. "Sorry. Didn't see you there."

"This is Mrs. Treleven and her baby. The lady who owns Longbarrow Cottage. My husband, William."

His greeting was as friendly as his wife's had been, but with a trace of shyness. He told me he had seen the car as he passed by Longbarrow Cottage early that morning, and asked how we were settling in. He seemed pleased when I gave him much the same answer as I had given his wife, praising her generosity and her meat pie. His eyes rarely met mine when he spoke to me, but the occasional piercing glance confirmed my impression that he was assessing me all the same. He smelled pleasantly of the farm, and of a mixture of fresh outdoor air and tobacco.

Pat Ebborn handed her husband a cup of tea, which he drank off at one gulp. "That's better," he said, holding the cup out to her for a refill. He happened to glance down, and saw that he was still wearing his boots, which were thick with mud. "Sorry, love," he said to her in a mild voice. "Forgot about the boots." The earlier anger appeared to have vanished. He sat down heavily in a chair near us and began to pull off the boots, wiping his hands afterward on the cloth she gave him.

We talked a little about May Armitage. Like Mela Mallaby, William and Pat Ebborn remembered her with obvious affection as a teacher of their sons, as well as a neighbor. William Ebborn told me, with patent approval, that she had kept Longbarrow Cottage up. "You'll not find much wrong there, apart from it needing some paint. The garden's not what it was, of course. It was a picture once, before her arthritis got to be too much for her."

"Pity about the beech," Pat Ebborn said. "It was the winds we had in January that did it. Brought down a lot of trees round here. Probably brought us this odd weather we're having as well." The unseasonable warmth had played havoc with the growing season, she told me, and would surely bring out the pests. Her husband nodded his agreement. From this, if for no other reason, I would have known they were farmers and was glad I had not waxed lyrical about the beauties of the early spring.

She went on to say that May had always spoken fondly of my grandmother. "People thought May was mad, spending her own money on the cottage the way she did. Putting in proper plumbing and heating, and so forth. Even though it made sense for her to be comfortable in the place. But she told me once that your grandmother had been so kind to her she wanted to leave the place in good order for you."

Had they known my grandmother? I asked.

Pat Ebborn shook her head. "I only came to Shipcote in the fifties, after William and I married. But you met her, didn't you, William?"

"He said that he had. "I don't remember her well—I was only a lad of ten or so at the time. But I went with my father once to do some work at the cottage when she lived there. There was a fire, I believe. A wall was damaged. I remember she was particular about the way the stone was relaid."

"William's father was a stonemason," his wife told me. "The Ebborns all were masons, back to the building of St. Paul's. The stone for it came from quarries the family owned near here."

William Ebborn gave a small smile. "I was the black sheep of the family. A farmer instead of a mason. As to your grandmother—I seem to remember she left Shipcote soon after the fire. She must have been a kind woman, to let May Armitage stay on like that." He set his teacup down in its saucer and turned to his wife. "I've got to tell

Cornelius about that business with the fence. He won't be pleased. It may mean someone'll have to patrol at night."

As he pulled on his boots, Pat Ebborn said, "Mrs. Treleven was asking about Carl Jope. He offered to do odd jobs for her. I told her you might be able to find someone else for her." Her voice was flat, without inflection.

"Ah. Yes." He looked back at her for a moment, then turned to me. "Do you need someone this minute?"

"No, I don't think so. It's just that Mr. Jope offered, and he seemed to me, well, someone I might not be comfortable with." Another look passed between husband and wife. "For instance, he said that a murder happened in Longbarrow Cottage. But he wouldn't tell me—"

"That man," Pat Ebborn interrupted, her face disgusted. "So he welcomed you with that bit of old news, did he? You mustn't be put off by anything he says. He likes to stir things up."

"Anyway, it happened more than fifty years ago," William Ebborn continued. "Before your grandmother's time. A tramp killed a woman living in the cottage. It's nothing for you to fret yourself over." To his wife, he said, "I'm going to the farm park, to find Cornelius." As he said good-bye to me, he reached out one large callused hand to touch Max gently on the head. He paused at the doorway, then turned around to me. "Your property borders ours and the farm park's for a bit. Around the tump. You might have a look at your fence."

"The tump?"

"The barrow," his wife explained. "Tump's what the local people call it, Goody Ridler's Tump, after some poor old creature the credulous thought was a witch."

I said, "There was someone climbing on it this morning."

"Was there?" William Ebborn replied, annoyed. "There shouldn't have been. It's fenced in all the way round, to keep people out. Did you get a good look at them?"

I shook my head. "They were too far away, and there was too much mist. It was just a shape moving around. I'm fairly sure it was a person, though, not an animal."

He looked thoughtful, but only nodded good-bye and

went outside. Pat Ebborn said, "The Mallabys will be furious if someone's been digging at the tump."

"They own it?" I distracted Max from the allure of the cat with another biscuit from the tin she held out to me.

She replied that they were part owners of the farm park, along with David Cornelius, but had kept clear ownership of the land on which the long barrow stood. "They're very particular about preserving it. Too many amateur diggers in the past, I suppose, trying their luck."

"For what?"

"Treasure," she said dryly. "What sort depends on the treasure seeker." Witches and a murdered woman, burial mounds and treasure—it was as if, by taking possession of Longbarrow Cottage, I had walked into the middle of one of Nan's stories. "Heaven knows what they'll be digging us up for, two thousand years from now. Pocket calculators, I expect." She gestured to the teapot, but I shook my head. From the small restless noises Max was making as he strained against my hold, I knew we should leave.

As we stood up, I told Pat Ebborn that I had met Mela Mallaby earlier this morning, and had learned from her that we were distant cousins. "And you'd not known that?" she asked me, looking surprised. "Well, now I come to think of it, I do remember May saying there'd been some sort of falling out."

Perhaps that explained Nan's silence on the subject of the Mallabys, I thought as I bundled Max into his jacket. "Did May say what sort exactly?"

"If she did, I don't remember. I rather think she didn't. May wasn't one for gossiping." She held the door open for me, and we went outdoors together. "She was the least inquisitive woman I have ever known. I imagine that's why children liked her. She listened to them, never cross-questioned them."

As she walked with us to the gate, accompanied by Stanley, who was less vociferous with departing guests, I thanked her again for making us so welcome. She told me she was very glad that Max and I had come to Shipcote, and that she hoped we would stay. She said it as though she meant it.

An odd feeling began to possess me as I pushed Max's

stroller back down the lane to the cottage. It was the same unsettled sensation I always felt at the beginning of an interesting project, the urge to know more, to see more. Among all the various details slowly gathering around the kernel of an as yet unformed idea, the conviction was growing that one particular story waited to be told.

But which? Or whose?

CHAPTER 9

As Max and I were going back up the drive to Longbarrow Cottage, a small red sports car, its top down, drove in behind us. The lanky young man who extracted himself from behind the wheel had fair, schoolboyish good looks and a hesitant smile. Or perhaps the smile only seemed uncertain in contrast with the confidence expressed by the car and the well-tailored way he was dressed, all moss-green tweed and cashmere.

"Jo Treleven? Welcome to Shipcote." He extended one hand and introduced himself as Robin Mallaby. "I gather my sister dropped our bombshell on you earlier."

"Do I look shell-shocked?" I said as we shook hands. "It's only jet lag."

"Oh, I didn't mean . . ." Flushing and stumbling a little over his words, he began to explain that he only meant to say it must have come as a surprise, an unknown cousin turning up on the doorstep, and as for the jet lag, why, I looked amazingly well for someone fresh off a transatlantic flight. . . . Something in my face brought the flow of words to a halt. He laughed, abashed. "Let me start again. If it's not a bad time, I was wondering if I might have a word with you. But if it's at all inconvenient . . . ?"

I took pity on him. "Would you like a cup of coffee?"

"Thanks awfully," he said eagerly. "I promise not to stay too long."

Stay as long as you like, I was tempted to tell him. The ease with which he blushed suggested he was not entirely sure of himself, and this diffidence in a man as obviously presentable as Robin Mallaby was, in my experience anyway, rare enough to make him interesting.

"It seems we're cousins, you and I," he said to Max as we went up the path together. Max grinned back at him. "Glad you're pleased about it. So am I." In the kitchen, he offered to hold Max while I put the kettle on. "If you wouldn't mind, that is?"

"I don't mind at all. It's up to Max and he'll let you know how he feels about it. I'm only surprised you want to." Especially, I thought, in those clothes. "But maybe you have kids of your own." He seemed too young, however, not much more than twenty-two or -three.

He sat down on a kitchen chair and settled an unprotesting Max on his knee. "I'm not married, but I do like babies. They have such charming smiles."

No more charming than yours, I wanted to say, but merely handed him a tea towel. "Protect yourself." While I made the coffee, he bounced Max on his knee to a version of "This is the way the gentlemen ride." He looked like someone who would know how gentlemen rode. Once the coffee was ready, I relieved him of Max and led him into the living room, where I put Max on the rug with the small bag of toys I'd brought from Toronto. When I straightened up, I found Robin Mallaby's eyes on me.

He flushed again, his skin turning pink as the blood rose to his cheeks "Sorry. It's just that I imagined someone different."

"Different?" I wondered why he would have any preconception of me at all. "How do you mean?"

"Oh, more like our side of the family, I suppose."

"I'm told I take after my grandmother. She was the other side."

"I'm somewhat vague on family history, I'm afraid. My own grandmother, Clarissa, is always on at me about it, trying to educate me. Family's terribly important to her. But I suppose at her age there's not a lot else to ... Anyway, I should tell you why I'm here. Apart from wanting to say hello, I mean." He swallowed some coffee and set the mug down, too hard, slopping coffee over the rim onto the table-top. Apologizing, he looked helplessly around. I gave him a tissue and as he wiped up the liquid he said that he had heard I might be selling Longbarrow Cottage.

"It's one of the reasons I've come here," I replied warily as I kept an eye on Max, who had abandoned his toys and was preparing to cruise the furniture. "To decide what to do about it."

"I see. Well, it would be a shame to lose a cousin so soon after finding her. But," he went on hurriedly, as though eager to get the next few sentences over with quickly, "if you do decide against staying, I hope you'll sell the cottage to me. I realize it's a bit much, coming straight to you like this when you've only just arrived. But it's not often that a house here comes on the market and I thought I'd better not delay. And," he added, with the air of making a small confession, "I do tend to act on impulse, I'm afraid."

I was disconcerted but not, on the whole, offended, per-haps because he seemed so young and unsure of himself, a little like Max in his clumsiness, both verbal and physical. "I don't know if you've had other offers," he was saying. His voice trailed off on a rising inflection.

Apparently he was ignorant of David Cornelius's interest in the cottage, which struck me as odd, given that the other man was a friend of his family. However, if David Cornelius hadn't mentioned it to him I didn't see why I should. All I said now was that he would certainly have the opportunity to respond to any offers I might get.

"I'm prepared to make a substantial offer for the cot-tage." He mentioned a sum that seemed enormous by any standard. It confirmed what the car and the clothes had al-ready suggested, that Robin Mallaby must have substantial means. "And it might influence your thinking to know I would be willing to pay in Canadian dollars, rather than pounds. I imagine, too, that I would be able to arrange the sale in a way that would save you a considerable amount in British taxes. Through the family firm, you know." The manner in which he said all this, sucking in his cheeks and leaning forward a little toward me with his hands on his knees, almost as if he were imitating someone much older, all the while hinting at something slightly questionable but lucrative for me, seemed faintly ridiculous, coming as it did from a man who still looked so much like a boy. On the other hand, it might have been part of his appeal, that sense of someone playing at being grown-up.

"The family firm?"

"Mallaby's. The publishers. You haven't heard of us?" I shook my head. "We're a small firm but I think it's fair to say our reputation is greater than our size. And we're one of the few publishers left who are still independent. Benedict founded the firm before the Second World War. He had a tremendous success with the first book he published, a novel called *This Sad Ceremonial.* It's quite famous."

I said that I had read it long ago in high school, where it was an assigned text. I did not tell him that the story of a young man's struggle to reconcile his socialist idealism with a conservative upbringing and a disastrous marriage had failed to grip me, despite its classic status and Lawrencian trappings.

"It was written by my great-uncle, Stephen Allerton, Clarissa's brother. An amazing fellow. One of those thirties writers who actually went to Spain and fought, instead of just gassing on about wanting to. Died a hero. He lived here for a time."

"Here? You mean in Longbarrow Cottage?"

"Yes. That's partly why I'd like to buy the cottage." He watched as Max carefully transferred his grip from the chair to the arm of the sofa. "I suppose Clarissa's efforts to get me interested in family history haven't been completely wasted," he added with a laugh. "But more important, I want a place of my own in the village. I generally come down from London on the weekends. There's always room at Summerhays, but not much privacy. If you see what I mean."

"You wouldn't mind the house being empty during the week?"

His expression was blank. "Why should I?"

"It's just that Tony Munnings told me there were problems with a couple of weekend places in Shipcote."

"Oh, right. You're referring to the arson. But the owners weren't locals. That would make a difference."

"I see." I wondered how he could be so sure of that. I also wondered if there was a subtle threat in the observation; I was not, after all, a local. Before I could ask him, however, Max, who had been studying the back of Robin Mallaby's head from his vantage point behind the sofa, lost his grip and with a sudden aggrieved wail disappeared from view. When I murmured something about lunch as I went to pick him up, Robin Mallaby took the hint.

"Well, then, until tomorrow," he said, standing up. "At Summerhays."

"Yes. I'm looking forward to it."

"You'll enjoy the food, if nothing else. Benedict and Clarissa have a first-rate cook." He glanced away briefly, then back at me. "About tomorrow ... The thing is, I'd rather my family didn't know that I'm interested in the cottage. Not just now anyway. Would you mind not mentioning it to them?" His light brown eyes gazed earnestly down into mine. "There's a very good reason, I promise you."

Reluctant to commit myself without knowing more, I compromised. "I won't tell a lie if anyone asks me directly. But I won't volunteer anything, either."

This seemed to content him. "Fair enough. Thanks for being such a good sport about it." As Max and I walked with him to the front door, he asked if he could give me a tour around the neighborhood someday soon. "To see the lie of the land, so to speak." When I said that I would like that, he proposed the following Saturday. "Maybe by then you'll have thought over my offer." Conscious, perhaps, that this might sound too insistent, he added, "I don't mean to rush you. . . . Well, of course, that's just what I would like to do. But it won't happen again, I promise."

Another promise, I thought. Offers and promises seemed to slip easily off Robin Mallaby's tongue. All the same, disarmed despite myself, I smiled back at him.

As I closed the front door, it occurred to me that everything I'd ever read about the insularity of English villages was proving to be untrue. In Shipcote, at least, the inhabitants seemed only too willing to welcome the newcomer.

With one exception, I amended, remembering that unknown arsonist.

CHAPTER 10

Wychley lay on a steep hillside, a small market town
neatly bordered by the river and the main road, which ran
past it along the crest of the hill. The High Street swooped
down through the center, narrowed to cross the Windrush
over a single-lane hump-backed bridge, and vanished
abruptly into the green hills that rose on the opposite side
of the river. At the upper end of the town, the street was
lined on either hand by a row of pollarded lime trees,
which screened the ancient houses that paraded downhill to
meet the shops.

On a Saturday afternoon, the place was swarming with
life. An endless line of cars, trucks, and buses moved
slowly up and down the High Street. There was a sharp
smell of diesel in the air and a clamor of engines and clash-
ing gears as heavy vehicles climbed the hill. In the lower
part of the town, where the shops were, the sidewalks were
thick with people.

I had been warned by Pat Ebborn that I might have trouble parking and should use the public car park, which was
only a short distance from the High Street, just behind the
church. Crowded with cars, it was at the river's edge,
bounded by the high wall of the churchyard and a tributary
stream fringed with willows. A black-and-white water bird
with yellow legs swam among their trailing, spidery
branches.

The silent back streets smelled of wood smoke and cre-
osote. Old stone houses lined the way, flush with the sidewalk, the windows of their lower stories just at eye level.

Every so often a narrow alleyway led into a small, cobble-stone courtyard surrounded by tiny cottages, where tubs of tulips and primroses marked the narrow stoops. There was an appealingly private air to these gray little back streets.

But the High Street, which was for several steep and curving blocks a window-shopper's dream of English charm, clearly wanted attention. Medieval merchants' houses had become tearooms, art galleries, antiques shops, gift shops, shops selling woolens, shops selling horse brasses and rush baskets filled with dried flowers, shops whose stone fronts were decorated with china plates and racks of postcards, with doors and trim freshly painted in olive green or lavender or oxblood and neat gilt lettering above the entrance.

I was too weary, and Max's patience too uncertain, for either sightseeing or a major shopping; they would have to wait until Monday. Dinner could be the remains of the meat pie, and Sunday lunch would be taken care of by the Mallabys. For the time being, I only needed a few groceries and some diapers.

On our way to the small supermarket halfway up the street, we passed a shop selling garden statuary. Max cried out with pleasure at the sight of a pair of life-size hunting dogs that sat on their haunches among the fauns and sundi-als littering the sidewalk. As I leaned forward to help him pat their rough noses, a man hurrying along bumped into me. It was David Cornelius.

"Excuse me," he said automatically. Then, on recogniz-ing me, he laughed and said that this time, at least, he hadn't actually knocked me over. "I'm not sure where to begin, with apologies or thanks," he went on in a rueful voice. "I owe you an embarrassing number of each."

"There's no need for either. It isn't every day Max and I get to know a ferret. And I can understand why May Armitage was so taken with Rafe." I was surprised to find I had to make an effort to meet his gaze; I was used to feel-ing reasonably comfortable with men. There was an awk-ward pause while the crowds flowed around us on either side, with the occasional disgruntled look cast our way for blocking the sidewalk.

He squatted down in front of Max. "Rafe told me you

were the kind of fellow who gives babies a good name. I see what he meant." Max grinned back at him.

Like Robin Mallaby, he had a way with children, but there the resemblance ended. Compared to this man, I thought, Robin Mallaby was little more than a child himself. As he straightened up, someone in a passing Land Rover called out to him and he raised a hand in greeting. "Be right there," he called back, then turned to me. "Look, I've got to go, but I wish—" He hesitated. "What I mean to say is, I feel like you must think—" At that moment, a woman pulling a small wicker shopping buggy announced curtly that we were in her way.

While I maneuvered the stroller to one side, David Cornelius abandoned whatever it was he'd wanted to say and merely told me he looked forward to seeing me at Summerhays the next day. As we said good-bye, it occurred to me that Sunday lunch with the Mallabys might have its attractions after all.

Before we reached the supermarket, Max and I passed a bow-fronted window with a display of books and pamphlets on Wychley. "Check out your past," said a sign on top of a pile of books. It was the local library. On impulse, I went inside.

It was a small warren of a library, three oddly shaped rooms opening off each other, low-ceilinged, lined with book-filled shelves, with chairs and tables scattered in corners. A small, dark-haired woman with glasses and an eager manner sat behind a desk near the front door, dealing with the people who were waiting in a short line, books in their arms. The system was slow and old-fashioned, with small cardboard tickets handed in or given out, but no one appeared to be impatient with it. The librarian had a friendly word for everyone, wanting to know if they had liked a book, recommending something different or more of the same.

While Max and I waited, I looked for Nan's novel in the card catalog, and felt a small pang of disappointment at its absence, although I hadn't really expected to find it there.

When the librarian was free, I told her that I was interested in tracing a novel published in England fifty years ago. "I checked your card catalog, and you don't have it. But I thought maybe another library might."

"Is it well-known, this book?" she asked me. When I shook my head, and explained the circumstances of its printing, she looked doubtful. "I expect you'd have difficulty finding it in all but the largest libraries. If you're a member, we could try to borrow it for you." As I filled out a registration form, she added that there was one type of library that was sure to have the book. She explained that the copyright law required publishers to give one copy of every book they published to certain designated libraries. "The closest is the Bodleian, the university library in Oxford."

"And this law existed fifty years ago?"

"As far as I know. It's your best chance. Unfortunately, the books in the Bodleian don't circulate. You'd have to read it in the library."

"Would I be allowed in?"

"You'd have to inquire there."

When I returned my registration card, the librarian looked at it and smiled. "Longbarrow Cottage. That's the one by Goody Ridler's Tump, isn't it? We used to picnic nearby when I was a child. Liked to frighten ourselves with stories of what was buried below it. An old witch, standing upright—that was a favorite. And then all those poor little—" She stopped suddenly, as though aware that someone who lived so close to the barrow might not be eager to know these things. Quickly, she added, "Old wives' tales. You should hear some of the stories my granny told. Made me afraid to go out after dark."

"As you're new here," she continued, "you ought to take a look at what we have on local history. Have you seen our display? Some of the material is rather fascinating." When I asked if there was anything specifically on Shipcote, she picked out several books and gave them to me. "These each have a chapter or two."

Max began to squirm restlessly in his seat. Hurriedly, I thanked the librarian, collected my books, and continued on up the street to the supermarket and Boots, the chemist, where I left my film for developing.

By now, Max was crying furiously and nothing I could do would console him. He rejected every attempt at distraction—it only incited him to greater fury. Finally, I gave up trying to comfort him and pushed the stroller as quickly as I could back to the car park, doing my best to ignore the sympathetic, amused, or disapproving looks on the faces of the people we passed.

In the parking lot, a man and woman were standing beside a Range Rover not far from my car, talking intently. When their heads turned at our noisy approach, I recognized Mela Mallaby but not the man with her, who looked less than delighted by the sight of a woman with a yelling baby. Mela, however, called out a friendly hello. Laughing, she gestured at the churchyard across the wall. "He's going to wake them up over there, you know."

"Maybe I could find a baby-sitter among them," I said grimly.

"Are you that desperate?"

"Only when he screams like this." As we spoke I took Max out of his stroller and gently jogged him up and down in my arms. This time the screaming stopped. The man with Mela looked distinctly relieved.

Mela made introductions. "Jo, this is Gerald Fenton. Gerald's a neighbor. Jo's the long-lost cousin I've been telling you about, Gerald."

In his mid-to-early forties, with disconcertingly pale eyes, Gerald Fenton had chilly good looks and the reserved manner of a man who found frequent opportunities for looking down his long, bony nose. Or perhaps it was simply that I didn't like the way he looked at Max.

He said, "Mela tells me you're testing the waters here, so to speak." I understood him to mean that I was undecided about staying, but as I did not think that it was something I had discussed with Mela, I wondered how she had learned this. Not from her brother, at any rate.

"Gerald is hoping you'll find the waters too cold for your taste," Mela said. "He covets Longbarrow Cottage, you see."

"Mela, for God's sake." He sounded mildly exasperated rather than angry. "I'm simply on the lookout for opportunities, Mrs. Treleven."

"Gerald would like to gobble up all of Shipcote if he could. All in a good cause, of course. Keep the bloody foreigners out, eh, Gerald?" She had dropped her chin and deepened her voice, mimicking his stiff tones perfectly. "You and Carl Jope together."

"Mela exaggerates," he told me evenly. "I'm on the local preservation committee. I assure you we have nothing against people like yourself coming into the village." With a heavily humorous voice, he added, "Unless, of course, you plan to turn Longbarrow Cottage into a nightclub."

"Just a drop-in center for troubled teens. Wasn't that what you told me, Jo?" Mela's expression was innocently questioning.

A shadow crossed Fenton's face, as though he believed her, until he saw that she was teasing him. "Oh, ha ha. Very good." The laugh was not convincing.

"At the moment I have no plans at all for the cottage, Mr. Fenton," I said. "But it looks like there's a growing list of people who want me to sell." It was beginning to make me uneasy, this interest in what seemed so newly mine.

"You mustn't take Mela too seriously. I have acquired one or two properties in Shipcote lately, but I promise you I have no designs on Longbarrow Cottage. Unless . . . ?"

"Yes, yes, Gerald. Jo understand perfectly." Mela turned to me. "Real estate is the subtext of every conversation these days. Very boring." She went on to tell Fenton that I was having lunch with the Mallabys the next day. "Why don't you come, Gerald? Susan, too, of course."

It seemed a perfectly innocuous invitation, but for some reason Fenton looked annoyed. "No can do, I'm afraid. Susan's parents are coming down from London for lunch."

"All of you together for the day? What fun."

"As you say." Fenton's voice was curt.

She was teasing him again, that was plain, and it was equally plain he didn't like it, but there was something else implicit in their words to each other, a subtext I was sure had nothing to do with real estate. The undercurrents made me uncomfortable. Max was falling asleep on my shoulder, so I said good-bye, adding to Mela that I was looking forward to lunch the next day.

She and Gerald Fenton must have separated soon afterward themselves, for as I drove out of the lot I saw Fenton opening the door of a station wagon parked by the river. A dog jumped down onto the asphalt from the front seat. When I saw his dog, I recognized Gerald Fenton at last. It was the same golden-brown Labrador, I was sure, that had waited at the door of Withyford church.

On the drive back to Shipcote, I thought about the pairing of Gerald Fenton and Mela Mallaby. That they were somehow a couple seemed indisputable; the tension between them had been palpable. But if they were illicit lovers—he had a wife named Susan, apparently—then how did David Cornelius fit into the picture? With some dismay, I acknowledged to myself the hope that he would prove to have no place at all in any picture that included Mela Mallaby.

At the cottage, Max slept on as I took him out of the car and carried him upstairs to his crib. Exhausted myself, I stretched out for a moment on the living room sofa with the books the librarian in Wychley had given me. As I flipped through the pages of one that included a chapter on Shipcote, the words "Goody Ridler's Tump" caught my eye. The passage on the barrow was grimly fascinating.

The long barrow was Neolithic, I read, built four to five thousand years ago using the same techniques of drystone, or mortarless, walling still practiced in the Cotswolds today. Almost nothing seemed to be known about the people who had constructed it, for they left no written records, but that did not stop antiquarians and archaeologists from theorizing about their intentions. According to various lights, the barrow was a burial chamber for their royal dead, a monument to their gods, who required human sacrifice, or some sort of astronomical tool used by their priests for observing the phases of the sun and the moon. Or any or all of these together.

Popular legends about the place tended to picture it as a sacred site for the practice of bloody Druid rites, the grave of a giant interred upright, and a fairies' hill thick with their hidden gold. The nastiest of these tales was the source of its name.

In the seventeenth century, Goody Ridler, a Shipcote woman, had been a "baby-farmer." Merchants' daughters and servant girls who became pregnant out of wedlock went to live with her while waiting for the birth of their babies. After the babies arrived, the mothers gave the old woman money to raise the children and to apprentice them when they became old enough. According to the writer, Goody Ridler accepted the money but killed the babies and buried their bodies in the barrow, which was subsequently named for her when her grisly deeds were discovered.

I couldn't bear to read any more and shut the book. As I put it back on the pile with the others, there was a knock on the front door. It was William Ebborn, with the high chair.

Obviously an antique, it was the prettiest high chair I had ever seen, made of pale oak with spool carving on its four legs and crosspieces, and a woven cane seat and back framed in bentwood. William Ebborn told me that it had been his as a child, and his father's and grandfather's before that. "Our boys used it, too. And I expect theirs will, when they have 'em."

The Ebborns' willingness to lend a stranger a possession that surely had material as well as sentimental value was more evidence, if I had needed it, that I was lucky in my neighbors. Then, from his coat pocket, William Ebborn produced a small aluminum container. "The wife's made dumplings for tea. She sent you down some, to try. Mind now, it's hot."

His visit had cheered me up, I told him, and went on to describe what I had been reading before his arrival. From the window over the sink, we could see the barrow's long, dark hump in the evening light. "I almost don't want to look at it now," I added.

He did not make fun of my distress. "Yes, it's a terrible story. Never liked it myself. A lot of nonsense, of course. There was some old widow who kept a cottage school. Her daughter got in the family way with no husband in sight. The child died at birth and the two women buried it out near the barrow. People started talking, as they will. And romancing. If I had a pound for every tale told in this place, I'd be the richest man in England."

His matter-of-factness was comforting, or would have been if he had not gone on to say that he would be grateful if I would let him know if I saw anyone on the barrow again. "This trouble with the fences, you see. We'd like to catch whoever's responsible."

"Of course. Though at the moment the telephone's not connected. So it would have to be after the fact."

"No matter. As soon as you're able." On his way through the living room he showed me where he and his father had repaired the stonework about the fireplace. "Pity to block it off like that. It was a real Cotswold hearth, big enough to bake in."

"Could it be reopened easily, do you think? It would be nice to have a fireplace we could use."

He smoothed his chin with one hand as he considered the fireplace. "Depends on what shape the flue's in. The chimney's bound to need cleaning, too. I know someone who could have a look at it for you. Shall I send him over?"

"Can I let you know? I'm not even sure yet that we're staying."

"Take your time. It's best to get to know a place properly. And it's not everyone who can live in the country, especially on their own."

"I've been a city person all my life. People all around. I guess it's going to take a while to get used to feeling alone." As soon as I said it, I was sorry—it sounded so self-pitying. The effect of the long day, weariness, and the simple fact that William Ebborn had a kind face. "I mean, not having houses on either side."

He gave me a shrewd look. "It's easy enough to ignore your neighbors in a city. Even if they're only across the wall from you. It's different in the country."

I told him that, as far as I was concerned, he and his wife had already set a high standard for country neighborliness. But he was as modestly reluctant as she had been to see anything special about their kindness to me.

After he had gone, Max woke up from his nap. While he tried out his new high chair, I warmed the jars of baby food that I had bought in Wychley, but as I had feared, he took one suspicious swallow of the new brand and then refused the rest. Pat Ebborn's dumplings, however, were another matter; those, he devoured. Light and delicious under a coating of fried bread crumbs, they were flecked with a tangy yellow cheese. When they were all eaten, he cried for more.

"All right," I promised him with my fingers crossed, "I'll get the recipe. Maybe I'll even learn to cook." It was not a prospect that filled me with pleasure.

As I put Max to bed, I noticed how silent it was when the birds stopped singing. The lingering evening light had suddenly gone, and it was dark. Once or twice a car passed by in the lane, a brief glow of headlights against the curtains, the rumble of an engine. Then the silence returned, deeper than before. Too tired to mind, I went to bed at the same time as Max, letting the silence take me to sleep.

Late that night, I woke again with bad dreams. The wind had risen. It sounded like the sea, surf crashing on the shore. Max was sleeping soundly, his breathing loud in the room. The same sense of pressure that I had felt the night before seemed to be weighing on me, as though the heavy covers were stifling me. As I flung off the quilt, I realized that I had forgotten to turn down the central heating before going to bed. Perhaps it was simply that the room was stuffy with heat.

As quietly as I could, in order not to disturb Max, I swung my feet over the bed, feeling the floor for my slippers. When my toes pressed down on something softly squishy that made a faint squeak it was all I could do not to cry out, but it was only Max's toy pig. Eventually, my heart settled back into its normal rhythm and I found my slippers.

Downstairs, I adjusted the thermostat, then went into the kitchen for a glass of water for my parched throat. Fogged with sleep, I bent over the kitchen sink, drinking thirstily. Setting the empty glass down on the drain board, I rubbed at my eyes to clear them of the gritty weariness that blurred my vision. For a moment, an aurora borealis shimmered behind my eyelids. When I opened my eyes, staring straight into the darkness beyond the window, I saw a pinprick of light, minuscule, wavering, like a firefly's glow. I blinked, and it was gone.

A trick played by my eyes, I decided. The light had been the residual image of the fireworks behind my lids. Remembering William Ebborn's request, however, I stood

watching the darkness for some minutes. The light did not
reappear.

CHAPTER 11

Sunday began with a cool gray rain. The fields and woods
were hazed by mist, and the green of the swelling hills was
like the green of the ocean, undulating under the low sky.
Behind the cottage, Goody Ridler's Tump rose against the
horizon, humped and mysterious as the long back of Jo-
nah's whale. I wondered again about that brief flicker of
light. Had it really been a trick of my weary eyes, or had
someone been out on the barrow last night?

During the morning, the clouds broke up, drifting eastward across an increasingly blue sky. While Max played
and napped, I unpacked and put away our belongings. Lack
of a good night's sleep was beginning to take its toll; when
Max pulled a tidy drawerful of clothes apart while my back
was turned and draped himself in panty hose and bras, I
was too tired even to reach for my sketch pad. Wishing
now that I had refused the Mallabys' invitation, I gave him
some lunch, then dressed him in the plum-colored playsuit
that made him look like a ripe damson, stuffed the carryall
with various supplies, and locked up the cottage. On the
way to the car, laden with Max and his paraphernalia, I
tried to remember what it was like to go places with my
arms free.

Shipcote had a sleepy Sunday peace, the quiet of green
gardens and age. The only dramatic note was the wave of
some small purple flower that spilled over a wall, drowning
the spent blossoms of faded daffodils.

I drove down the yew-lined drive to Summerhays and
parked beside several other cars on the wide expanse of

gravel. With its gables and dormers in pointed contrast to the smooth flat facade and oblong mullioned windows, the old house seemed its own geometric territory within the softer curvilinear landscape. Scarlet tulips lined the walk up to the front door, the shining globes of their full-blown petals like broken goblets spilling blood.

A plump, grandmotherly woman answered my knock. With her round gold-framed glasses, small beaky nose, and the layered cut of her ruffled gray-brown hair, she had the look of a friendly owl. "Mrs. Treleven? Come in, please. Lovely to see the sun, isn't it?" She stepped back into a wide, light-filled entrance hall hung with paintings. To the left and right, passages led away to other parts of the house, and behind her, a wide staircase mounted to a landing with a row of tall mullioned windows and a life-size portrait of some massive, whiskery Victorian worthy.

"That's old Josiah Allerton, Mrs. Mallaby's great-uncle," the woman told me, seeing my glance. "Looks a proper terror, doesn't he?" She took the carryall from me and held out her arms for Max. "Shall I hold the little fellow while you take off your coat? Just leave it on the chair there."

This, I assumed, must be the Mrs. Blackwell who Mela had said was mad about babies. As Max made no objection to her overtures, I handed him to her. She settled him comfortably into the crook of one round arm and asked his name. When I told her, she beamed down at him. "Well, you're a handsome lad, aren't you, Max?" He smiled back at her, recognizing a soft touch at once.

"The family are in the drawing room," she told me, leading the way along a short passageway that branched off the main hall. Small landscapes hung on walls the color of creamy tomato soup and the wide, dark floorboards gleamed with polishing. At the end of the little passage there was a pair of double doors with brass handles. Mrs. Blackwell opened one of the doors, standing aside with Max to let me enter ahead of her. A babble of voices flowed out to meet us.

No one noticed us at first. For a few brief moments I was free to observe, unobserved.

Dazzling in the sunlight, the Mallabys' drawing room was a feast for all the senses. Rich with color and opulent

fabrics, scented by applewood and the cold, sharp fragrance
of freesias, alive with a chatter of voices, it was a room
where the past and the present, luxury and simple comfort,
and the stamp of personality combined to produce great
beauty. The walls were paneled in pale carved oak and
hung with billowy-clouded seascapes and eighteenth-
century portraits of bosomy ladies in blue satin. Plump, tas-
seled sofas and chairs slipcovered in yellow damask were
heaped with embroidered pillows; an oriental shawl was
draped over a large chair in ivory brocade as though over
a woman's creamy shoulders; beautiful Persian rugs in
tones of blue and red lay underfoot. Overhead, a white plas-
terwork ceiling covered the room like an elaborate icing on
a fruitcake.

Four of five people stood at the far end of the room near
some French doors framed with heavy blue damask curtains
that fell in pooling folds to the floor. Their attention seemed
to be focused on the doors, but they were looking up, not
out at the walled garden bright with flowers visible through
the glass. As I looked up, too, I saw what had transfixed
them all.

Undulating like a gray-and-white Slinky toy across the
round brass curtain rod was Rafe Cornelius's ferret, Spike.

The babble of voices rose, expostulating, laughing, encouraging, offering advice to Rafe, who had climbed onto
a chair and was holding something up to the ferret in one
outstretched hand. Mela Mallaby and David Cornelius were
steadying the chair for Rafe. Nearby, a young man with a
lively, likable face sat down at a grand piano and began
playing, with exaggerated flourishes of his hands, the kind
of music that accompanies Keystone Kops movies. A large
middle-aged woman in a tentlike Indian-print dress was
steadily eating canapés from a plate on top of the piano.
Her eyes, too, were fixed on Spike, and the look on her
face suggested that the Society for the Protection of Ferrets
would find no friend in her.

In that suspended moment while the ferret balanced, chittering, on the round knob at one end of the rod, I noticed
three other people. They were down the room to my right,
grouped near the fire that was burning beneath a white mar-
ble mantelpiece, an elegant, elderly woman sitting in a

wing chair, flanked by two equally aged men. Dressed in a rose-pink wool suit, the old lady held herself so erect that her back did not touch the chair. Pure white hair waved back from a sharply cut profile. She might have been in her early seventies, the men perhaps a little older. They stood on either side of her, like the two large brown-spotted china dogs that bracketed the fireplace—and yet unlike, too, for whereas the dogs were a matched pair, the men could not have been more dissimilar in their looks. Caught up by the little drama at the end of the room, they hadn't noticed our arrival either.

I looked around, but Robin Mallaby was nowhere to be seen.

All at once, Rafe succeeded in luring Spike down from his perch, and Max, who was still in Mrs. Blackwell's arms, crowed loudly, delighted by the sight of his two friends. The scene broke up, everyone turning their faces now to us. The man at the piano ran his fingers briskly up the keys, and then began to play a gentle classical piece.

Mela came quickly down the length of the room to welcome us. She was wearing a very short, very tight bright green wool skirt over stockings of a paler green and a green-and-white striped silk shirt with the collar turned up. Her hair fell like bright gilt ribbons around her face, which was alight with such welcome that I felt guilty for my unfriendly thoughts about her.

"Here are Jo and Max," she announced in her clear, musical voice to the room at large. As she took my arm, she added, too softly for the others to hear, "Do you feel as if you're being thrown to the lions? Don't worry. Only one of us here bites."

I pretended alarm. "Which one is that?"

She opened her cornflower eyes very wide. "Why, Spike, of course."

"Then I'm safe. We're friends already."

With a formality that verged on ceremony, Mela led us at an angle across the room, past the others as they gathered around the fire, to the old lady sitting in the wing chair. I smiled at Rafe, who was standing with his father beside Mrs. Blackwell, showing Spike to Max, and got a small shy wave of the hand in return.

"Grandmother," Mela was saying, "this is Jo Treleven."

Clarissa Mallaby must have been very beautiful once. Traces of that beauty remained in the high-browed, oval face and in her extraordinary eyes, which were the color of dried violets and so heavily lidded that they had a sensuality I rarely saw in women of her age. Above all, it was the way she carried herself, erect and with the hint of arrogance in the tilt of her head, that spoke of confidence bred from a long conviction of her powers. She was like a lily fading on its slim and graceful stem, a faint, seductive perfume still rising from shriveled petals.

"Welcome to Summerhays, my dear." Her voice was pleasantly weary, with a slight drawl in it. It was somehow at odds with that erect carriage, as though the effort made to hold the body so upright could not extend to the voice. "You must be thinking you've acquired some very peculiar relatives. But I promise you that we don't usually entertain ferrets in our drawing room."

"I understand ferrets have virtues I wasn't aware of before," I replied. "Rafe enlightened me the other evening."

"You have a charitable spirit," she said dryly. "I am afraid that I still find them rather sinister." She lifted one long thin hand, heavy with rings, from the white shawl that lay over the armrest of her chair, indicating the man who stood at her right side. "This is my husband, Benedict."

My grandfather's cousin was the man in the Jaguar I had seen the day Max and I arrived. He was as impressive in his way as his wife, tall, lean, assured-looking, his skin that healthy pink I had noticed before. He wore a well-cut tweed suit and a cream tattersall shirt, with the gold chain of a pocket watch curving from his waistcoat pocket. His back was not so erect as his wife's, however, and he stooped a little over her, almost as if protecting her. And there was a faintly melancholy cast to his features that made him seem somehow less formidable than he might otherwise have been.

"Mela tells me we have the advantage of you," he said as we shook hands. He had a crisp, genial voice that sounded as though it belonged to a much younger man. "It must seem a little hard, having such a covey of relatives sprung on you like this."

I murmured some platitude about how delighted I was to meet them all.

"Oh, I'm afraid this isn't all of us," he replied, smiling pleasantly. "There are one or two others lurking in the undergrowth. But we won't inflict them on you just yet."

"Goodness, Benedict," his wife said in her slow, deliberate drawl, "you make us sound as if we have Mrs. Rochester in the attic. We're all of us quite harmless, my dear," she added, to me. "Even dear Willoughby has mellowed." She turned her head slightly to look up at the other man who stood by her side. He smiled down at her in return, his face mottling with sudden color. She introduced him as Willoughby Webb Springer, an old friend of the family, adding that he was a retired English don at Oxford.

In contrast to Benedict Mallaby, his companion piece on the other side of the chair, Willoughby Webb Springer seemed at first glance insignificant, a dapper little man in a well-cut suit with the pale, long-nosed face of an aged and intelligent sheep. He had been snuffling into a cloth handkerchief while Clarissa Mallaby talked, and now a fit of sneezing interrupted whatever greeting he might have given me.

"Poor Willoughby. Such a tiresome cold," Mela said sympathetically. In a lowered voice, she whispered to me as the others waited for the series of noisy sneezes to end, "Poor Grandmother, too. He insists on attending her like some antique courtier. We call him The Constant Nymph." Her eyes were bright with malice.

"It's not a cold, I tell you," Willoughby Webb Springer was protesting in a high-pitched voice between sneezes. "I'm sure I'm allergic to that wretched creature." He gave a baleful look in the direction of Spike, who was cradled in Rafe's arms, entertaining Max.

Meanwhile, the senior Mallabys made welcoming noises at Max, gratified me by recognizing that he seemed superior to most babies his age, and told me that Mrs. Blackwell had assembled some old baby toys for his pleasure in the conservatory. "It's lovely and warm there," Clarissa Mallaby assured me. "He can't possibly take a chill. And Mrs. Blackwell will see that he comes to no harm."

So Max was borne off in the arms of Mrs. Blackwell,

looking cheerful enough. As Rafe stowed Spike away in his shoulder pouch, David Cornelius bent his head to his son and murmured in his ear. The boy turned and slipped out into the garden through the French doors, closing them again behind him. Willoughby Webb Springer muttered something about the importance of knowing the difference between pets and savage beasts.

Mela touched my arm. "Jo, let me introduce my aunt, Cecilia Breakspear. Everyone calls her Cece." It seemed an improbably playful nickname for the large, matronly woman in the Indian-print dress. She was very overweight, with a face that seemed to spread beyond its bones, but her skin was firm and pink and there was something impressive about so much smoothly solid flesh. With her graying flaxen hair, tip-tilted nose, and violet eyes, which were her mother's eyes although smaller and less expressive, and her general air of massive solidity, she looked like an aging doll on steroids. She nodded to me, then moved away to join her mother, one hand holding a glass of what looked like sherry, the other clutching some sort of canapé.

"Aunt Cece's married to an Oxford philosopher," Mela told me; the ambiguous way she said it made it sound as though this were a dubious distinction. "Uncle George is quite terrifyingly brilliant." And again sotto voce, "Or so I'm told. He's the most silent man in England. And when he does speak, I can never understand a word he says."

Mela paused to call down the room to the man playing the piano, who had come to the end of his piece. As they debated what he should play next, I looked around, wondering if Cece Breakspear had heard Mela's brief sketch of her husband. But she was speaking to Clarissa Mallaby and seemed oblivious. The two women, mother and daughter, shared the beautiful color of their eyes, but were otherwise a study in contrasts. Cece Breakspear loomed over her delicately made parent like a cuckoo's chick in the nest of a tiny lark. The expression on her broad face was petulant, and I heard her say loudly, "Well, it's time a decision was made."

Clarissa Mallaby bowed her head, smoothing the fringe on her shawl. I thought she murmured her husband's name. Benedict Mallaby's response was immediate and firm.

"We'll discuss that some other time, shall we, Cece? Willoughby here was just telling me—"

I did not hear the rest. "David has been patiently waiting for his chance to say hello to you, Jo," Mela said, turning back to me.

David Cornelius was putting another log of wood on the fire as we approached. When he straightened, Mela placed her hand on his arm. It was, I thought, a deliberate gesture—she had touched no one else—as though she wanted to mark him out as hers. They made a very handsome couple, his dark good looks a foil for her silvery fairness. Each had that long-limbed elegance that was so striking, although his was somehow lazily solid-looking, almost earthy, whereas hers was like quicksilver, all fluid, sparkling movement. "You two have already met, of course," Mela said to me.

As we said hello, his smile was sardonic. "I doubt that you remember my welcome to Shipcote with much pleasure." To the others, in explanation, he added, "Thatcher and I almost ran her over in the dark when she first arrived."

When I said that it was an unforgettable welcome at least, his mouth twitched with amusement. "And as it meant that Max and I met Rafe and Spike, I do remember it with pleasure."

This was as much for Rafe's benefit as his father's. The boy had come back into the room, without Spike, and was standing at David Cornelius's side. He gave me a grateful look. No one had scolded him for the ferret's behavior but from the hunch of his shoulders it seemed obvious that he felt himself to be in disgrace. He tugged at his father's elbow and I could hear him quietly asking if he really had to eat lunch with us. His father nodded, his face stern. "Then I want to sit beside her," Rafe said firmly, indicating with his head that he meant me.

"Even if Miss Treleven was saint enough to say yes, it's Clarissa who decides where we sit," his father replied, with a slanting, amused glance at me. "Now, why don't you go and help Mrs. Blackwell entertain Max? To make up for your crimes."

Rafe's face was chagrined. "You don't have to tell me to

do it. I like Max. He's not a pain like Christine." This was
said in a mutter as he took himself off. I assumed Christine
was his baby sister.

A look passed between his father and Mela. "Spike's influence, no doubt," she said with a little shrug of dismay.

"You've won Rafe over," David Cornelius told me. "He
says you didn't scream when you saw Spike. The acid test
of character, as far as Rafe's concerned."

"I'm flattered. To be honest, though, it was jet lag, not
strength of character. I was too tired to scream."

"You're being modest. I don't remember your screaming
when I knocked you over, either."

"Why, David," Mela said lightly, "this encounter of
yours sounds much more exciting than the description you
gave me the other night." She linked her arm through his,
and as she did he gave her a look that seemed more speculative than affectionate. "I'm astonished you dared to
come here today, Jo," she continued. "After David's rough
welcome. It's very adventurous of you."

"Isn't that what travel's all about? Adventure. I ought to
be grateful I've found it so quickly."

I said it facetiously, but Mela pretended to take the words
seriously. "Is that why you're here? For adventure? I'm
afraid you're going to be disappointed. Shipcote's terribly
dull, you know."

"That's hard to believe. So far I've heard of at least four
mysteries, all set in the village." I was thinking of the murder in the cottage, the tumulus and its various legends, the
Ebborns' fence cutter, and, the one that I was really interested in, the mystery of Nan's book. I might have added another to the list—that strange little scene by the ancient
church that I had witnessed on the day of my arrival and in
which both she and David Cornelius had played a part.

Mela stared at me. Slowly, with a drawl that made her
sound very much like her grandmother, she said, "I'm not
sure I like mysteries myself. I'm a great believer in letting
sleeping dogs lie. Much safer. David darling, we're not being good hosts. Jo doesn't have a drink. What would you
like, Jo? Sherry, whiskey?"

"Sherry, please." I almost never drank sherry, but it
seemed appropriate to the occasion. For whatever reason—

Mela's asides and her brittle, stagy humor, the somewhat studied formality that seemed to have seized everyone in the room at my appearance, and a slight air of tension, which might have been of my own making or purely imaginary—I felt as if I had walked into a drawing room comedy. And I was the only one, apart perhaps from Rafe, who did not know her lines.

"There is another reason people travel, isn't there?" Mela continued when David Cornelius had gone off to get our drinks, her voice suddenly serious. We were standing alone together near the windows that looked out on the beautiful walled garden. "To escape. To leave something behind."

I gave a guarded reply. "I suppose that's true, in some cases."

Mela fingered a broad silver bracelet that circled her slim wrist like a shackle, turning it back and forth as though the weight of it hurt. "It was, in my case. When my older brother died last year, I felt I had to escape. So I went to Africa, and for three months left behind every reminder of Phil. And in your case," she continued, before I had a chance to say a word, "Max's father has been left behind."

This was outrageous, and yet she said it in such a way, gravely, without malice, that I was not outraged, or even offended. But I was confused. I knew I was being asked to meet her revelation with one of my own, and this seemed somehow a challenge, almost a test.

She was watching me as she played with the bracelet, her blue eyes opaque. It struck me that at times she combined both the deviousness and the directness of a child. That might even have been part of her appeal.

"Perhaps I like to travel light," I said, conscious as I spoke of how lame my reply was. Yet it was no business of hers where my husband was. That drop of shared familial blood did not give her the right to my privacy.

"Men can be so heavy, can't they? Filled with all those unspoken emotions. They do tend to drag at one." She was mocking me, lumping me with lumpish men who kept too much to themselves.

Suddenly it seemed important to be honest with her. I heard myself saying flatly, almost against my will, "My

husband died in a sailing accident. I don't mean to be secretive about it. It's just that it's still painful to talk about."

She made none of the conventional responses. Instead,
she said quietly, "Then you know what loss is."

She said it with that peculiar, idiosyncratic hiccup of air
before the penultimate word, and I could have sworn there
was relief in her voice. It made me feel that I was hearing
Mela herself, the real self, for the first time. Momentarily,
a cord tightened between us; an intimacy, of a kind, had
been established. I wasn't sure, however, that I welcomed
it.

Before I could do more than register that subtle shift in
our relationship, the piano player came up to us. He looked
about twenty-five or -six, had a snub-nosed face, freckled
and boyish, with thick brown hair that flopped forward over
his forehead, and a disarming smile that transformed his
otherwise plain features. "I'm Val Lenthall," he told me.
"There'll be a quiz later. If you fail to remember all our
names, you win Spike."

I laughed. "I'll start memorizing them now."

"I'm sure you know them already," Mela said. She had
reassumed her playful, almost artificial manner. "North
Americans are generally so good about that sort of thing.
Whereas we English are absolutely hopeless with names.
We don't like to give our own and we never remember
anyone else's. So we simply avoid using names whenever
possible. Old thing, old chap, my dear . . ."

This started a discussion of names as totems and the various forms of power a name could have. Each of us had a
list of favorite names, hated names, ridiculous names. Inevitably, the conversation turned to the American custom of
using first names so freely.

The others, the senior Mallabys and Willoughby Webb
Springer, were drawn into the discussion, but Cece
Breakspear refused to take part. By now, she had finished
off the canapés and was well into another large glass of
sherry. She drank the last of the sherry, set the glass down
with such vehemence that it seemed only good luck it did
not shatter, and moved with a kind of elephantine swaying
across the room. Picking up the Sunday papers from the top
of an end table, she sank heavily into a sofa. Her response

was so bad-tempered that I was taken aback, but everyone else seemed not to mind, or else they were used to her behavior.

On the issue of American usage, the group split along generational rather than national lines. "Although I'm a great admirer of many things American," Willoughby Webb Springer said gravely, with a nod of his narrow head to David Cornelius, "I do take exception to that particular import. Nowadays, people use given names much as if they were clubs. They try to bludgeon one into friendship through the repeated use of one's Christian name. I believe a man's name should be given the respect one would accord any other of his possessions."

Unseen by Webb Springer, Mela rolled her eyes. I stifled an impulse to giggle. A name like Willoughby, I reflected, would make a fairly hefty club. But from then on, as though in perverse reaction to his pronouncement, I always thought of him by his first name alone.

"Mind you, it's all right for a man to swallow up a woman's name," Val Lenthall was saying bravely.

Willoughby took offense. "I was under the impression we were discussing Christian names," he replied tartly.

"Val has a distinguished local name," Clarissa said in a smooth interjection, lifting her head on its long neck and turning to smile up at him. He looked pleased to be singled out by her. She was a woman, I thought, who still had power over men. "There have been Lenthalls in Wychley for three hundred years, haven't there, Val?"

"I'm afraid the place is riddled with us." He gave a self-deprecating smile. "My most famous ancestor was called The Great Braggart and Liar of his Age. Some of us are still trying to live that down."

"And does that mean you always tell the truth?" Mela asked him.

"But of course. Although if I were a liar I would say that anyway, wouldn't I?"

"Ah. Now I shall have to wonder about all those compliments you've paid me."

Val Lenthall flushed, the color rising in a scarlet tide until it covered his freckles. Shifting uneasily from one foot to the other, he gave a quick half-glance at David Cornelius, who was standing beside him. Mela laughed. "Oh, don't worry, Val. David knows I'm teasing you. Besides, he's the least jealous of men. Aren't you, my love?"

David Cornelius did not answer her question directly. Instead, he said quietly, his eyes on hers, " 'O, beware, my lord, of jealousy. It is the green-eyed monster which doth mock the meat it feeds on.' "

"Quite delicious advice, I always thought, coming as it does from Iago." Willoughby punctuated his remark with three quick sneezes into the handkerchief. "Damn that animal." Clarissa Mallaby raised one hand and patted him gently on the arm.

"How very literary of you, David," Mela said over the sneezes. "Fancy your being able to quote Shakespeare." Her voice was playful, without apparent sarcasm, and yet the comment seemed hostile, perhaps because there was clearly some sort of subtle tension between the two of them. It vibrated at a pitch that made it only intermittently detectable, like the tiny whine of a mosquito, inaudible until it nears the ear.

Benedict Mallaby observed that the name Treleven must mean I had Cornish blood. I nodded. "My father's family were miners who came to Canada to work in the mines around Sudbury. But even Cornish tin miners found winters in the north hard to take. So they moved to Toronto and went to work building the city sewer systems. My father was the family rebel, the first to work above ground."

"What at?" David Cornelius asked me. His face held an amused interest.

"He was a teacher."

"And what's the Jo short for?" he continued. "Josepha, Jocanda, Joelly?"

"Nothing so exotic. It's Joanna. I'm named for my grandmother." Grateful for the excuse to mention Nan, I turned to Clarissa and Benedict Mallaby. "You knew her, didn't you?" Remembering Pat Ebborn's comment that there had been some sort of falling out, I was curious to hear their response.

"Not well, I'm afraid," Benedict replied, fingering the gold chain of his pocket watch. The expression on his face revealed only polite regret. "She and Charles were together so short a time, of course. And when she lived here in the village, we were living in London. We rarely had the opportunity to meet."

I said that as I had never known my grandfather, I hoped that sometime he might tell me a little about him.

He merely nodded and looked away, then began a sibilant, tuneless whistling between his teeth.

In her slow, attractive drawl, Clarissa Mallaby answered for her husband. "Whatever we can tell you, we will. But you know, my dear, he was a bit of a puzzle, your grandfather. We thought we knew him well, Benedict and I. You were more like brothers than cousins, weren't you, darling?" Her husband gave a grunt of assent, his face opaque. "And yet, we found later we hardly knew him at all.

"But now," she continued, rising from the chair, "we must go in to luncheon."

CHAPTER 12

With one hand on her husband's arm, Clarissa Mallaby slowly stood up. Willoughby Webb Springer picked up her shawl from the armrest of her chair, folded it neatly in half, and smoothed it almost lovingly over his arm. Then he gave her the ivory-handled cane that had lain against the chair, hidden underneath the shawl. Upright, she held herself just as erectly, but she moved with a fragile deliberation that forced the rest of us to the same stately pace.

Willoughby offered his free arm to Cece Breakspear. With a rustling of falling newspapers, she heaved herself up from the sofa. They made an odd couple, he such a tidy little man, she so blowsy and large, but the look they exchanged was surprisingly affectionate. He whispered something in her ear, at which she gave a bark of laughter.

David Cornelius and Val Lenthall left the fireside to join the little procession as it moved slowly toward the double doors. They were discussing Shipcote Farm Park, weighing the success of some sort of rare breed of sheep recently acquired, and it seemed clear from their conversation that Val Lenthall was the manager or overseer of the farm.

Benedict Mallaby turned around to the two men. "Any sign of the scoundrel who's been cutting the fences?"

David Cornelius shook his head. "We didn't find any damage today. Not yet, anyway. But we've got a man on night patrol now." Perhaps that accounted for the light I thought I had seen last night.

"It's very odd that no one else has had their fences cut," Clarissa said. "This must be someone with a grudge against the farm park."

While they stood discussing the problem, I mentioned to Mela that I wanted to check on Max before we all sat down to lunch. When I asked her how to find the conservatory, she replied that she would take me there herself. With a word of explanation to her grandparents, we left the drawing room together.

A telephone on a small table near the front door began to ring as we came out into the entrance hall. Mela crossed over to it and picked up the receiver. "Summerhays." She listened to the voice on the other end of the line, then frowned and said, "Oh, Robin, you're impossible." Shaking her sleeve back from her wrist, she glanced at her watch. "Look, the plane leaves in two hours. You'll never make it if you don't stir yourself."

Robin Mallaby clearly was not going to show up for lunch. On the whole, I was relieved to be spared the pretense that we had never met.

"Jo," Mela called to me, "this is going to take a moment. Could you find your own way to the conservatory? Go down there"—she pointed to the passageway on the other side of the front hall—"and around the corner. You can't miss it." I nodded, and as I moved away, she began to speak again into the phone. "Well, you haven't much choice, have you?"

The conservatory was an octagonal Victorian addition of glass and ironwork grafted onto the southern end of the house. Rafe and Max were playing on the rush matting that covered the floor while Mrs. Blackwell looked on from a wicker rocking chair, crocheting. Max was pleased to see me when I knelt beside him, grabbing at my arm to pull himself up against me and lean his head into my neck. Once he had reassured himself with this contact, he let go again and plumped himself back down among the litter of toys spread across the matting. There was a wooden zoo with dozens of painted animals that Rafe was arranging in pairs, a family of three stuffed bears and a pigtailed Goldilocks doll, and a set of handmade painted blocks carved with different insects. They all had the battered look—worn paint, missing button eyes, and chipped edges—of much-loved toys.

When I admired them, Mrs. Blackwell told me that they had once belonged to Mela and her brothers, and to Mallaby children in the generation before them. Mela and Robin, she said, had been hard on their playthings. "They loved to fling them about. Well, children do, of course. Mela treated that doll of hers something shocking. I must have mended it a score of times. Philip now, he always played with his toys beautifully. Even when he was just a scrap of a thing, like your Max."

"Was Philip the oldest?"

"By five years. But he always seemed much older than the other two. He was a serious little fellow, with a lovely smile to him that could melt your heart." Her own smile faded as she told me that he had died the previous year.

"Was it an accident of some sort?"

"Cancer." Her face crumpled as she said the word and the crochet hook paused for a moment. She bent over her work, unwinding more wool from the ball, before she continued. "Mela took it hard, poor girl. He was more like a father than a brother to her and Robin. Their father died, you see, when they were still kiddies."

I asked her if their mother was still alive.

"Not so's you'd notice."

Hearing a change in the tone of the housekeeper's voice, Max looked up at her with curiosity, then crawled over to Rafe's side.

"Right after Robin was born, the younger Mrs. Mallaby

ran off with an Italian gentleman." Mrs. Blackwell pronounced the word "Eye-tal-ian." "Had herself two more
children and hasn't been back since." There was a small
clatter as Rafe suddenly ran one hand down the line of animals, knocking them over like dominoes.

Death and desertion, then, explained the generational gap
in the drawing room, where only Cece Breakspear repre-
sented the middle-aged. Mrs. Blackwell went on to say that
Clarissa and Benedict had taken the children in after their
father had died. "They all grew up here. But Philip, he was
the one who stayed on. Mela and Robin always had their
hearts set on London. Mind you, since Mr. Cornelius has
been here, we see more of Mela. He's partial to country
life, just like Philip was."

"Are you taking my name in vain, Mrs. Blackwell?" Unnoticed by us as we talked, David Cornelius had come into
the conservatory. Smiling at the housekeeper, he crossed the
room to stand above his son. "Lunchtime, Rafe." Rafe nodded and quickly began to pick up the animals, placing them
neatly back in their box. His father then turned to me as I
took Max's bottle from the diaper bag. "I've been asked to
fetch you as well as Rafe. Clarissa has arrived in the dining
room." He made it a mock formal announcement, as though
reporting a royal progress. "So has the roast beef."

When I asked Mrs. Blackwell if she would mind looking
after Max a little longer, she made it seem as though I were
doing her a favor by allowing her to have more time with
Max. "You go and have your dinner. I'll just give him his
milk, and then we'll have a little visit round the house." As
we left the conservatory, I said that I wished I could take
Mrs. Blackwell home with me.

"You'd hear more about the Mallabys than even a rela-
tive should have to listen to," David Cornelius warned me.
"Mrs. Boswell, Mela calls her. It's a good thing for them
she doesn't see herself as their biographer."

"You think she'd write an exposé?"

He laughed. "If anyone knows their secrets, she does.
But no, she's very loyal. It's just that she doesn't make any
distinctions. Everything about the Mallabys is equally interesting to her." But not, by implication, to him? Or was I

misinterpreting that trace of exasperated humor in his voice?

Rafe, who had been listening to this exchange, wanted to know if a story that Mrs. Blackwell had told him was true. "She says Clarissa's family was so poor they had to sell Summerhays when she was a little girl. And that Benedict made a lot of money and bought it back for her when they got married. Mrs. Blackwell says it was his wedding present to her."

His father replied that the story was true. "The Allertons were landowners in Shipcote for centuries. They'd lived in Summerhays since the place was built in the early 1700s. So it was pretty tough on Clarissa and her family when they couldn't afford to keep it."

"Some present. I guess if you give your wife a present like that she'll stay married to you." Rafe flashed a quick, sidelong look at his father; behind his glasses his eyes were unreadable. "Maybe the present you gave Mom was too small," he said in a toneless voice.

Quietly, his father replied, "That's not fair to your mothers, Rafe. Or to me."

There was an open doorway just ahead on our left. Without another word, Rafe disappeared through it. David Cornelius's eyes met mine, and he gave a small shrug as he stood back to let me follow Rafe into the dining room.

The room smelled of roast beef and gravy. Long and low-ceilinged, its dark wood paneling lit partially by the sunlight filtering through latticed glass and partially by electric sconces, it seemed older than the drawing room, with a flagstone floor partly covered by a wine-red carpet and small casement windows placed deeply into the thick walls.

Clarissa Mallaby and Cece Breakspear were already seated, but the men were standing, waiting for us. From her place at one end of the table, Clarissa called to Rafe to sit on her left. "I want to hear about this school of yours," she told him. Interpreting this, perhaps, as a sign of her forgiveness for Spike's behavior, Rafe gave his father a half-smile of relief as he went to her side. She then motioned to Willoughby to sit down at her right, beside Cece. Mela and I sat on either side of Benedict Mallaby, with David

Cornelius beside Mela and Val Lenthall between Rafe and me.

As we took our places, Clarissa asked me if Max was happy with Mrs. Blackwell. When I replied that he couldn't help but be, Mela said with a laugh, "That's because he's male. Blackie is a man's woman."

"Now, Mela," Clarissa said, "she was very good to you when you were a child."

"Yes, but she preferred the boys. She never really approved of me—I was too naughty. But David's put me in her good books. Virtue by association." Her glance at him was ambiguous, something more than flirtatious but not precisely intimate either. He raised an eyebrow but made no comment.

"And why should that make a difference?" her aunt inquired. It was not an altogether friendly question.

"Because David was Phil's friend," Mela said simply. For the first time, I heard a genuinely loving note in her voice. "That qualifies him as an apostle, in Blackie's book."

Benedict Mallaby turned to me and asked if our arrival, Max's and mine, had gone smoothly. When I replied that it had, he wanted to know if I'd had time to meet any of the villagers yet.

"Just the Ebborns, who've been very kind to me. And a man named Jope."

"Then," he replied with a small smile, "you've met the best and the worst that the village has to offer." He began to carve the roast beef, placing two slices on each plate and adding a small golden Yorkshire pudding and some juice from beside the roast before passing the plates to Mela.

"Pat and William are lovely people," Mela told me. She uncovered the two silver serving dishes in front of her, which were filled with young broccoli and roast potatoes. "But Carl Jope . . ." Her nose wrinkled with distaste. "Gerald Fenton claims Jope can lower the value of a house simply by standing in front of it."

"Or raise its fire insurance premiums," Val Lenthall said wryly.

Benedict paused in the carving to look at him with mock severity. "Are you implying Carl Jope had something to do with those fires, Val?"

"It's difficult not to make certain assumptions. Given his expressed opinion about outsiders buying up cottages, and the fact that he'd had run-ins with the owners of both the cottages that were torched."

"Surely you know that the long-suffering Mrs. Jope swears he was at home with her when they occurred?" Benedict's voice was heavily ironical.

"That poor woman," Clarissa said. "Why she ever married the man is beyond me. Her first husband was perfectly charming."

"And, like many charming men," Benedict observed dryly, "perfectly incompetent about money. Perhaps she thought herself lucky that Jope was willing to take on a widow with debts and a child. Perhaps the question should be, Why did Jope marry her?"

"I should have thought that was obvious," Cece Breakspear said. "You only had to look at the daughter to know why Carl Jope was willing to have her in his house."

"Really, Cece," Clarissa said reprovingly. "There's never been any suggestion of impropriety there. If anything, he coveted the farm. One has to admit he saved it from her creditors."

An unconvinced "Umph" was Cece Breakspear's only reply.

Willoughby said that the daughter had been a student at his college several years before. He glanced around the table with a malicious smile. "Very promising, I understand. Before she—"

"Yes. Quite." Benedict Mallaby's voice was repressive. Whatever Jope's stepdaughter had done remained unexplained. As Benedict handed another plate to Mela, he asked me how I had come to meet Jope.

"He was passing by when Max and I arrived. He welcomed me with a gruesome story about some poor woman murdered in Longbarrow Cottage."

There was a short silence, just long enough to make me uncomfortably aware that I had said something wrong. Mela and Benedict exchanged glances, while Cece Breakspear stared down the table at me as if I had suddenly metamorphosed into Spike. Into the silence, Clarissa Mallaby drawled, "That poor woman was my sister-in-law.

My brother Stephen's widow. Stephen and Evelyn had the cottage before your grandmother."

I could feel myself flushing. "I'm so sorry, I didn't realize—"

She waved a hand. "You weren't to know. And she was an impossible woman, wasn't she, Willoughby?"

"Oh, quite impossible. If anyone ever asked to be murdered, it was Evelyn." In the middle of ladling gravy over his meat, Webb Springer paused with a pained expression on his long sheep's face, as though the memory of the dead woman still had the power to annoy him. "Such a temper, I remember. Made poor Stephen's life a perfect misery. I often thought that war must have seemed to him marvelously restful after life with Evelyn." For my benefit, he added in explanation, "Clarissa's brother fought in the Spanish Civil War. For the Republican cause, of course."

"Evelyn's death is very ancient history now, my dear," Clarissa said to me. "Quite without significance."

This almost shockingly brisk dismissal of sentiment allowed Rafe to indulge his curiosity. "Who killed her?"

"A tramp," Benedict replied succinctly, as though to close the subject. "Or so the police conjectured. Now, if everyone has a plate, shall we say grace?"

As we bowed our heads, I was remembering some words May Armitage had spoken. Speculating on the plot of *Life Blood*, she had said, "There was this terrible murder we knew of. A woman named Evelyn . . ." Evidently, she had thought that Nan's mystery might have been inspired by Evelyn Allerton's death.

"Didn't they ever catch the murderer?" Rafe persisted as we began to eat.

"No," Clarissa sipped a little of her wine. "I wish I could regret that fact, Rafe, but I find that I cannot." Momentarily, some dark emotion clouded her violet eyes, at odds with the tranquil voice and manner. The heavy lids closed, as though she were weary. When she opened them again, the serenity of her gaze was restored.

Loyally, Willoughby said, "One would be hard put to find anyone outside the police who lamented the escape of Evelyn's murderer. It's my belief that some crimes are best left unsolved. When they result in a general good."

I wondered what Evelyn Allerton had done to make herself so detested.

Undeflected, Rafe continued to probe. "But how did they know it was a tramp?"

"By deduction," Willoughby replied. "A piece of Evelyn's jewelry turned up in a pawnbroker's shop in Liverpool. Brought in, apparently, by a man who looked like a tramp. To the pawnbroker, at any rate."

"That doesn't sound like proof to me," Rafe said reasonably. "It could have been someone pretending to be a tramp."

Equably, his father ordered him to give it a rest. To the table at large, he added, "Unsolved mysteries are Rafe's favorite reading these days. That, and books on prehistoric burial mounds." He looked across at me, one eyebrow lifted in amused apology. "I'm afraid this means Rafe's going to find Longbarrow Cottage even more appealing. A burial mound in the backyard and a murder indoors."

I could see how attractive that must make it, I said. Turning to Rafe, I told him that the next time he came to visit I hoped he would educate me about barrows. "I'd like to hear the history, not just the horrible legends." As his mouth was full of food, he had to be contented with energetically nodding his approval of this proposal.

"You know about charming Goody Ridler, then," Val Lenthall asked me, "and her murderous little ways?"

Mela mimed disgust. Her slim fingers held the knife and fork near their ends, delicately cutting up her food. She had given herself the smallest helpings. "Rafe's convinced that treasure's buried in the long barrow, not babies' bodies. He'd be digging there if we'd let him."

Rafe gave her a slanting look; it was not friendly. I had noticed that he seemed uneasy with her, almost resentful, refusing to meet her eyes when she spoke to him.

"As a boy," Val Lenthall was saying, "I heard the barrow was so full of gold that when the sheep lay down on it their fleece turned yellow."

Willoughby wiped his mouth carefully with his napkin. "I deplore these amateurish assaults on our prehistoric sites. Most of them are no better than grave robbery. The barrow has suffered so many that I very much doubt if anything of interest remains to be found, even by proper archaeologists. Let alone by a boy with a spade."

Benedict, who was pouring wine into my glass, said, "There are some lines from Ossian I think of when I see the long barrow. You'll know them, Willoughby, I'm sure." With his eyes fixed on some point above our heads, he recited slowly, " 'We shall pass away like a dream. Our tombs will be lost on the heath and the hunter shall not know the place of our rest. Give us the song of other years. Let the night pass away on the sound, and morning return with joy.' " He gave the words a melancholy beauty, and in the silence that followed looked down the table at his wife. His smile seemed tinged with a strange compassion. She looked back at him, unsmiling, her eyes grave.

Then, briskly, he began to tell Willoughby about a book Mallaby's was planning to publish, a novel set in prehistoric Britain. "Not our usual sort of thing. But the chap who wrote it is extremely promising. He's one of Mela's finds. Tell Willoughby why you think he's a good bet, Mela."

As Mela complied, giving her reasons with assurance and a certain casual authority, I realized that she must be directly involved in running the family publishing house. The teasing, provocative manner dropped away, revealing a straightforwardness that was somehow different from the deliberate intimacy she had established with me when she told me about her brother's death. A vein of tough intelligence, it appeared, ran through that shimmering personality. She seemed all at once older, and more substantial.

I was struck by something else, that I had no sense of who Mela Mallaby really was. It was easy to see, however, why David Cornelius, or any man, would find her so attractive. She had the allure of all beautiful and essentially elusive creatures.

When I glanced away from her, I found David Cornelius's eyes on me. His gaze was speculative, as if he had been assessing me in turn. The look wasn't unfriendly, but it seemed puzzled, almost at a loss. If he was embarrassed to be caught staring, it didn't show, but I found it impossible not to shift my eyes away from his.

"This book is a gamble," Mela was saying. "Some people feel we ought to play it safe until the economy settles down. And it is true that larger publishing houses than Mallaby's are in trouble."

"But Mela's judgment has always been good," Benedict said to the table at large. He looked fondly at his grand-daughter.

"I like taking a risk. When I know it's a sure thing." There was the faintest trace of complacency on her face as she smiled at the contradiction.

"Well, I do remember Philip saying that if anyone had inherited your publishing genes, Benedict," Willoughby observed, "it was Mela." He gazed benignly at her. "I'm sure that Mallaby's will weather these difficult times so long as you are at your grandfather's right hand, my dear. And I'm sure you're right about this book. It sounds intriguing."

She thanked him, adding, "To make assurance doubly sure, I'll ask you to review it when it's out."

"I'm afraid, my dear, that my reviewing days are over. Perhaps this is as good a moment as any to tell everyone my news. . . ." He paused, gazing around the table, then added with the air of someone who knows he is dropping a small but highly satisfying bombshell, "You see, I'm writing my memoirs now."

"For publication?" Cece Breakspear asked him when the general exclamations of surprise had died down. "That should ruffle a few feathers."

"Precisely the object of the exercise." Although he ducked his head modestly, he looked slyly pleased with himself. Then he noticed a blob of gravy on his silk tie. Irritably, he reached for his napkin.

Before he could deal with the offending spot, Clarissa dipped the end of her own napkin in her water glass and leaned forward to rub gently at the tie. Her hand was trembling slightly.

"Mallaby's will publish them, of course," Cece continued, turning to her father. She had a remarkable knack for making everything she said sound somehow pugnacious.

Benedict replied smoothly, "Of course. I should be very offended if Willoughby took his memoirs anywhere else."

"We'll make sure you get a healthy promotion budget," Mela said to Willoughby. "It's only your due, after all." She turned to me, to add in explanation, "You see, Willoughby was really the founder of the Mallaby family fortunes. My great-uncle Stephen wrote a novel—perhaps you've heard of it, *This Sad Ceremonial*?"

I repeated pretty much what I had said when Robin Mallaby asked me the same question, that the book had been required reading when I was at school.

"Well, Willoughby's was the review that made the book famous," Mela went on. "And the book made Benedict's new publishing house very successful. So we really have Willoughby to thank for everything." Her voice was serious enough, but the blue eyes were amused as they met mine, as though inviting me to share some private joke that lay beneath the words, a joke that seemed to be at his expense.

"Now, Mela. Such an exaggeration. You embarrass me." He visibly preened himself, however, smoothing the silk tie back into place.

"Nonsense, Willoughby. Mela's quite right. Here's to you, and to the memoirs." As Benedict raised his glass to the other man, Clarissa murmured, "Dear Willoughby. Such a staunch friend for so many years."

He took her hand and made a graceful little speech about what their friendship had meant to him.

While attention was focused on Willoughby and Clarissa, I happened to glance at Benedict. He was staring at his wife and friend. The expression of urbane good humor that seemed habitual to his face had vanished. If the idea hadn't seemed so absurd, I might almost have said that he looked afraid.

During the dessert, apple pie with custard sauce, the conversation at my end of the table turned to Shipcote Farm Park, which would shortly open to the public. David Cornelius was saying that if the vandalism continued they would have to hire more workers. "We're short staffed as it is. And now with a man on night patrol . . ."

Rafe paused with the spoon halfway to his mouth. "There's someone patrolling? Does he carry a gun?" His eyes were wide.

Val Lenthall laughed. "This is a vandal we're after, Rafe, not a murderer. If we catch him we'll just break his legs for him, to teach him to mend his ways." When he saw Rafe's horrified expression he quickly dropped the teasing. "Joke, Rafe. No guns, no violence. We're peaceable folks. We'll just warn him off."

Cece Breakspear, who had been eating steadily and with concentration, looked up from her plate. "I hear that Gerald Fenton's made the farm park an offer. Doesn't it make sense to accept? This was Phil's project, after all, not ours. Now that he's gone I simply don't see the point of continuing on with it. Not when the land is so valuable." She gazed around the table, and in the silence inquired if there was any more tart.

"You're forgetting that it's David's project now," Mela said as she cut her aunt a large slice of apple pie, pouring custard around it until the sugared crust was swimming in a deep pool of the thick yellow sauce. It was so blatantly too much that it seemed almost insulting, but Cece Breakspear accepted it without comment and immediately began to spoon it up.

"I hadn't forgotten," she replied between mouthfuls. "But we have a share in it. And I for one am no longer willing to be a sleeping partner."

"Silent partner, Aunt Cece," Mela told her, pressing a grin out of the corners of her mouth. "That's what the Americans say. You wouldn't want to be misunderstood."

Cece gave her niece a dangerous look but before she could speak, Clarissa said firmly, "I don't see any reason why this issue should be discussed now." With a little grunt, Cece returned her attention to her food and for the rest of the meal said nothing more.

Val Lenthall turned to me. "This is always a tricky question and I never know quite how to phrase it so as not to offend women with children but—"

"What do I do?" I finished for him.

"Well, exactly. Although I was going to ask whether there was any special field that interested you. Apart from being a mother, I mean. Which of course is a full-time job in itself." He blushed, looking anxious. "You aren't offended, I hope?"

I told him I wasn't. "I illustrate children's books. Sometimes I write them as well."

Rafe, who had overheard this exchange, wanted to know

the titles of my books. When I mentioned two I'd illustrated for older children, thinking he might have come across them, he said, "I know them! They're great. Especially *Shape-shifter*. Remember, Dad? The one about the Indian boy and the shaman?"

"I remember." David Cornelius smiled. "It really was a favorite of Rafe's," he told me. "He asked for it over and over again. Which was fine with me, because your illustrations were so interesting—"

"They were amazing!" Rafe broke in. "In one picture you could see the shaman be three different creatures, each on top of the other. Like layers. It depended on how you held the book," he explained to the others. "He starts as a snake and ends as the thunderbird, with a salmon in between. It was my favorite."

"Mine, too," I told him. Technically, it had been the most difficult to pull off. I had spent hours with transparencies in various combinations before finding a way to hide the serpent in the curving line of the fish's tail as it flowed into the eagle's wing. After I had chosen the arrangement of the creatures, their evolution from one to the next was achieved with layers of watercolor.

"Have you been published over here?" Benedict asked me. When I said no, only in Canada and the United States, he asked if I had brought copies of my books with me. Two or three of them, I replied. "Then you must bring them round," he said. "I'd be very interested in having a look."

Pleased, I said that I would like that.

"I seem to remember that your grandfather was something of an artist," Clarissa told me. She looked at her husband for confirmation. "Isn't that right, dear?"

He nodded. "Charles always carried a sketchbook on our walks together. As I remember, he was quite good." Something about the memory seemed to make him uncomfortable. He pushed away his dessert plate. "Where shall we take coffee, Clarissa?"

"In the library, I think. Then Max can join us," she told me as we rose from the table. "There's very little there that he can pull over on himself. He'll be free to crawl about in safety." She asked Mela to find Mrs. Blackwell and Max.

The library, which was across the little hallway from the

dining room, looked out on the same expanse of green lawn as the conservatory. With its grille-fronted bookshelves, leather-topped desk, and smell of tobacco, wood smoke, and dog—an elegant Irish setter lay stretched out on the rug—it seemed a man's room. But it was dominated by a woman. Her portrait, a full-length oil by an artist instantly recognizable for the ebullient virtuosity with which he had painted fashionable women in the mid-century, hung on the wall at the far end of the room.

While the others gathered around Clarissa as she poured the coffee, I walked over to the portrait.

In bright yellow tones softened with blues and lavenders, it showed a beautiful woman standing in a garden with a basket of flowers in her arms. She was the still center of a swirling movement of children and pets, the calm at the eye of the storm. Three boys grappled together on the grass, a plump little girl, arms outstretched, tried to coax a dove down from its perch on the branch of a tree, and a pair of spaniels leaped up at a cat arched on the stone wall behind the woman. Delicate and palely blond, she seemed at once too finely made to be the source of so much boisterous life and yet indisputably a part of it, the fulcrum around which everything pivoted. The unclouded violet gaze of her eyes identified her at once as a young Clarissa.

David Cornelius came up beside me. "Considine painted that in 1949, just before he died. Of apoplexy, Benedict always says, brought on by shouting at the children to shut up."

"Are they all Clarissa's and Benedict's?"

"Were. Only Cece is still alive. The two middle boys died in a sailing accident when they were teenagers. The oldest—Mela's father—died in his late twenties."

"It must be a terrible thing, to outlive your children."

"And a grandchild. In some ways, Phil's death might have been harder for them. He was so obviously the one who was going to carry everything on. The family business, Summerhays, Shipcote Farm Park. Clarissa had a heart attack just after his death. It aged Benedict, too."

I wanted to ask him how he, an American, had come to be involved with the farm park, but just then Mela came into the library with Mrs. Blackwell, who was carrying Max.

"He made a great fuss when I tried to take him from Blackie," Mela said as I gathered Max into my arms. "Didn't I tell you that she has a way with young men?"

After I had thanked Mrs. Blackwell, who protested once again that it had been her pleasure, Max and I settled onto the end of the sofa farthest from the fire, where Max could watch the setter. Rafe was sitting on the floor beside the dog. Holding a cup of coffee in one hand, Benedict Mallaby came over to us. The coffee was for me, he said, placing it beside me on an end table. He sat down at the other end of the sofa.

"Family occasions can be wearing at the best of times," he said, as though he had read my mind—or face. I was exhausted, my head swirling with all I had heard. "I hope meeting so many of us at once hasn't tired you."

"Not at all. You've made me feel very welcome here. If I look weary, it's only jet lag."

"I gather your grandmother never mentioned us to you."

"She might have. I was only ten when she died."

"I see."

Max was trying to pull himself up against the back of the sofa, but the slippery leather was making it difficult. Benedict placed one hand under his bottom and gave him a gentle push up.

There was a little pause, while I drank some of the coffee, trying to keep it from being spilled by Max's bouncing. Benedict began whistling tunelessly between his teeth, almost inaudibly. Max, who had been fascinated by the gold watch chain curving across his waistcoat, reached out to touch it.

"You like that, do you, young fellow?" Unfastening the chain, Benedict took the watch from his pocket and dangled it in front of Max, who watched, covetous, as the gold disk gently swung back and forth, glinting in the light from the fire. Then, in a lucky sweep of one arm, Max caught hold of the chain and pulled the watch toward him. Laughing at his strength, Benedict allowed him to have it.

At that moment, Willoughby called out to Benedict, asking him a question about a book he had taken down from the shelf. While Benedict's attention was momentarily distracted, Max lifted the tempting object toward his mouth. I intercepted it just before his lips closed on the smooth golden curve, trading his pacifier for it.

The pocket watch had a hinged gold cover protecting the glass, which wasn't quite fastened. Curious, I opened it. On the reverse side of the cover, in a flowing, delicate script, was an inscription that read, "A good book is the precious life blood of a master spirit." It was an apt sentiment to find engraved in a publisher's watch, but its suitability was not what made me stare at the inscription. Two words, of course, leaped out from the rest.

Life blood.

CHAPTER 13

Benedict Mallaby turned around on the sofa and saw that I was holding the watch. A spasm of mingled anger and anxiety fleetingly crossed his face. Assuming he was worried about the watch, I held it out to him. "Max was about to eat it, but I rescued it in time."

Closing the book he was holding, Willoughby Webb Springer gave a dry little laugh, somewhere between a cough and a chuckle. " 'Time devours everything,' Ovid wrote. Perhaps he ought to have said that babies devour everything, including time."

"Time most of all," I said. We smiled at each other. Despite his finicky manner and the malicious edge to his humor, I was inclined to like him, perhaps simply because he had shown an interest in my work during lunch, asking intelligent questions, listening carefully to my answers. But once or twice, I had looked up to find his eyes on me with a curiosity in them that made me uneasy.

At the other end of the sofa, Benedict was fumbling with the watch chain as he struggled to fit the small gold bar at the end of the chain into the narrow buttonhole of his waistcoat. When I mentioned the inscription and asked him if it was a quotation, he stared vaguely up at me as though he hadn't quite heard my question.

Beside me, Willoughby made a curious snorting sound, like stifled laughter. When I glanced at him, he was staring at his friend with amusement on his face, as though at some shared, private joke.

"A quotation?" Benedict replied slowly. The faded blue eyes moved thoughtfully from Willoughby back to me. "Why, yes. Rather an important one for those of us in the book trade. From a famous seventeenth-century defense of the freedom to print without a license."

"Such comforting words—" Willoughby began.

"It's a coincidence—" I said at the same time, meaning to tell them about Nan's book.

We both stopped and made polite noises about who was to proceed, but before either of us could go on, Max lost his balance and slid off the slippery leather cushions onto the floor. He wailed loudly, more from shock and tiredness than from any hurt; the rug and his diaper had cushioned his landing. It was time, I said, that I took him home for his nap.

Willoughby became almost disconcertingly genial. I really must come to Oxford to visit him, he told me as I stood up with Max in my arms. "A friend of mine writes children's books. You might enjoy meeting him." He named a famous writer-illustrator. When I replied that I would like very much to meet him, he took a slim leather-bound notebook from the breast pocket of his jacket. A miniature gold pen was attached. "I'll ring you up about it in a day or two," he said as he opened the notebook. "Perhaps we can have lunch together."

I gave him my telephone number, adding that the phone might not be connected until later in the week.

"Aren't you nervous at night?" Mela asked me. "On your own in such an isolated place without a telephone? I'd be absolutely terrified."

Before I could respond, Clarissa said firmly, "Nonsense,

Mela. Whyever should she be? This isn't London after all. A woman on her own is much safer living here. When I think of you alone in that flat . . ."

Mela slipped one arm around her grandmother's waist. "Knightsbridge is hardly the combat zone, darling. And I simply meant that anyone with a small child worries about illness and accidents."

"If anything should happen, Jo must come to us, of course." Clarissa took my hand and gave it a gentle squeeze. Under the paperthin skin, her hand had a surprising strength. "It's lovely to have you as part of our family, my dear."

Behind her, Cece Breakspear's face made it plain she had her own opinion on the subject.

At that moment, Mrs. Blackwell appeared in the doorway of the library to say that Mela had a telephone call. Before she left the room, Mela told me that she would be up in London for most of the week but would come by Longbarrow Cottage when she returned on Friday. "But do let me know if you're in London. We could have lunch."

Val Lenthall, David Cornelius, and Rafe walked out to my rental car with me. They were going on to the farm park. "Come and have a look at the place sometime this week," Val Lenthall told me. "You can get a jump on the public opening that way. Have your own private tour." David Cornelius seconded the invitation, saying that Max would enjoy it. We settled on Tuesday morning.

Rafe was making funny faces through the window at Max in his car seat, who laughed excitedly before turning his head away, overcome. I invited him to visit us after school the following day. "Bring Spike, too."

"Can I?" he asked his father.

"If you don't have too much homework," David Cornelius replied. "And if you're home by six this time." Rafe promised, waved good-bye to us, and went off across the gravel with the two men, his father's arm around his shoulders.

I got into the car, winding down the window to let in the mild afternoon air, then searched in my purse for the keys. Footsteps crunched on the gravel, approaching the car from behind. I lifted my head to the windowsill as I turned slightly in the seat to see who it was. Simultaneously, David Cornelius leaned down to speak to me and placed his own hand on the windowsill. For a moment, it rested on mine.

The simple touch of his warm flesh and the unexpected nearness of his face, so close to mine that to any onlooker we might have seemed about to kiss, startled me. Unthinkingly, I flinched back and pulled my hand away. Painfully aware that my reaction must have seemed rude, I said awkwardly that he had surprised me.

"A bad habit of mine." He seemed disconcerted rather than offended. "Look, I wanted to say that I could get the man on night patrol to keep an eye on your place as well."

"That's not necessary."

"No, of course it's not necessary. But since it's on his route, anyway . . ."

"All right." Embarrassment made me curt; my response sounded ungracious even to my own ears. "Thanks."

He seemed about to say something else, thought better of it, nodded, and turned away again.

The keys, I suddenly remembered, were in my coat pocket.

It was after three when we got back to the cottage. I was exhausted. For all their charm, the Mallabys were a strenuous family. They exacted the tribute of attention; even, in Mela's case, demanded it. And the swirl of subterranean currents—or subtexts, to use Mela's word—beneath the relatively smooth surface of their conversation had made for an uneasy footing, the sense that I was constantly being drawn out of my depth.

As I prepared a bottle for Max, I slopped milk on my dress. I sponged it off and then hung the dress to dry on the clothesline that ran from a hook by the back door to a post. Afterward, Max and I fell asleep beside each other on my bed. When we woke up, sometime shortly after four-thirty, I set out, pushing Max in his stroller, for a walk up the lane to clear my head of sleep and the sluggish heaviness that comes with eating too much rich food.

It was a greenly golden afternoon, smelling of apple blossoms and sun-warmed grass. By the gate, the wounded copper beech unfurled its tiny russet leaves. They shimmered like small brown stars against the sky, each one fuzzed with down, translucent as a membrane and soft, almost rubbery, to the touch.

At Summerhays, a temporarily heightened sensibility had sharpened my perceptions; nothing was familiar, therefore everything was, for the moment, equally interesting. Now, as I went up the lane with Max, snippets of lunchtime conversation replayed themselves in my mind. Emotions lingered like static, joining apparently disparate incidents in a tangle that seemed at once random and yet meaningful.

Somehow, Mela's mercurial changes in mood, David Cornelius's unreadable reserve, and the bad temper that smoldered behind Cece Breakspear's eyes were linked. Somehow, despite Clarissa Mallaby's blithe dismissal of it, the murder of Evelyn Allerton still mattered. As did Willoughby Webb Springer's memoirs, and the words engraved on Benedict Mallaby's watch. They were all connected. Somehow.

There had been a curiously dark cast to much of the conversation. The subject of death, had never seemed very far from people's lips: murder, infanticide, death by cancer, by accident, by natural causes. Hints at other, only slightly less unpleasant themes—abandonment, incest, arson, grave robbery—had run like thin black threads through the talk. But there had been too many vivid impressions at Summerhays that day for a clear image to emerge.

We passed by Ashleaze Farm. Smoke curled lazily up from a chimney, but even the guard goose, Stanley, was nowhere in sight. Beyond the farm and the woods, where the lane rose onto the uplands, the wolds were bathed in the brilliant western light of late afternoon. They spread out in wide billows of green and brown, striped with stone walls, furrowed by the plow, rolling on to the horizon. Only the occasional clump of trees and a cluster of rooftops in a valley interrupted their smooth expanse. A thin line of cloud to the southwest was flushed with an apricot glow; overhead the sky was a clear, deep blue. Birds sang, the wind blew crisp yet mild against the skin, and I was suddenly filled with an intoxicating sense of freedom.

Here on the wolds the steep banks of hedgerow gave way to drystone walls on either side of the road. To my right, the wall was interrupted by a rutted farm track wide enough for a tractor. It lay in a shallow dip between a flowering hawthorn hedge and a drystone wall as high as my waist. A few hundred feet ahead, its destination was hidden by the thick white blossoms of the hedge. I pushed the stroller off the road onto the track, curious to see where it led. So long as my pace was leisurely, the jolting of the wheels on the bumpy ground didn't seem to bother Max.

After a few minutes, we came to the crest of a little hill. Here, the track split in two. The main branch, lined by the hawthorn, continued gently downhill toward the distant cluster of rooftops, another farm perhaps. To my right, a narrower spur, a footpath, crossed the wall at a stile, keeping to the high ground. A wooden sign painted with the symbol of a hiker, which I assumed indicated a public right-of-way, pointed eastward across a wide, fallow field of close-cropped turf. Several hundred yards to the south, the field was edged by the woods that rose behind Ashleaze Farm.

I hesitated, debating whether the effort required to get Max and the stroller over the stile was worth it. The sight and sound of a lark caroling high over the field decided me.

With Max in my arms, I climbed over the stile, then went back for the stroller while he sampled the tiny blue and yellow wildflowers studding the short grass. I once had illustrated the story of the old woman, her pig, and a stile for a collection of nursery rhymes. As I removed the wildflower salad from Max's mouth, I had a certain fellow feeling for her.

The footpath ran along the crest of a steep rise, above a small, shallow valley partly filled with bramble bushes. A movement in the valley caught my eye. It was followed by another, and another. The brambles were alive with rabbits. I squatted down beside Max, pointing to the creatures as they hopped about in the slanting rays of sunlight. The light picked out hillocks dotting the low hillside on the opposite bank, which must have been the openings to the rabbits' burrows. There seemed to be hundreds of them, a warren.

Max began to rock forward in the stroller, his signal that he wanted us to be moving on. In the distance he had seen something more interesting that the rabbits—a flock of sheep and their lambs.

A barbed-wire fence, which topped the crumbled remains of a stone wall, separated the woods from the field. A lone wild apple tree grew up through the barbed wire from a break in the wall, with blossoms thick as clotted snow on its branches. The solitary splash of white against the green grove made the darkness of the woods seem more impenetrable. With the western sun behind them, the trees were shadowy and cloudlike.

I hoped that once we were clear of the woods there would be a view of Longbarrow Cottage, but I had forgotten Goody Ridler's Tump. Its massive green bulk swelled out from the edge of the woods, effectively blocking any sight of the cottage. From this side, the barrow looked like a deep-bellied ark carved out of the earth, floating in the wave of greenery that lapped at its flanks.

The footpath now turned left, descending into the valley. With the stroller, it was impossible to go forward, and as the barbed-wire fence separated the field in which the long barrow lay from the one with the footpath, impossible, too, to go around Goody Ridler's Tump and down to the cottage. We would have to go back the way we had come.

Before we turned around, I took Max out of the stroller to let him stretch his legs a little. The padding of turf made it a good place for him to tumble about. While he practiced standing up, clinging to the stroller for balance, I sat on my folded jacket and opened my sketchbook to draw the barrow.

Four thousand years ago, Neolithic men and women had labored with antler picks and wooden shovels to build this tomb for their dead. The slow encroachment of the earth had long since blurred any distinction between the manmade and the natural. Now the long barrow seemed an organic ambiguity, bred from the bone of the land and yet alien to it.

As I sat in the sunshine it was easy enough to people the barrow with those ghosts of the prehistoric past. A blink erased the barbed wire, the only sign of modern life. Easy enough, too, to sketch in a woman standing where the entrance to the mound might once have been. She was holding a baby in her arms, watching as the body of the man who had fathered her child was carried inside the tomb.

But it was impossible, I knew, ever to enter her mind or to understand what she had felt.

Peter and I had never talked about death, even when thoughts of death must have consumed him. Not knowing what he himself would have wanted, I had taken his ashes out on the lake in a friend's sailboat and scattered them over the water. As the wind swirled the ashes away from me, I had felt obscurely guilty, as if the act, overtly that of a grieving wife, were instead a covert effort to rid myself of the last traces of his physical presence. The absence of a grave had spared me a symbol that could only remind me of my own failure. But would Max someday reproach me for the lack of a place where he could mourn his father?

A cloud moved across the sun. The sheep lifted their heads from the grass, sniffed the air, then began to trot quickly away down the hill, bleating for their lambs. Something had disturbed them. Rooks broke from the woods with a loud beating of wings and circled above the hill in a dark swarm, cawing their distress. Suddenly, the air was cooler, the wind sharper, and the lonely hillside no longer such a pleasant place to linger. The barrow, bright with sunshine a moment ago, looked sullen now, shadowed by the woods. It might have been that ancient memorial to death, or simply the shift in atmosphere, a sinking of mercury, that made me long for the warmth of another human being. I felt islanded, bereft. The parallels between my life and Nan's frightened me. They seemed to augur a fate like hers, a lifelong wound of loss and sorrow that bitterness would not allow to heal. Turning to Max for comfort, I touched the soft rounded flesh of his cheek.

I knew, however, that I had to protect my child from my own loneliness.

There was a sudden grating cry from the woods, so harsh that it made me jump up and stare with fear at the trees. The shocking sound had to have been made by some bird or animal, but was like none that I had ever heard before, a staccato screech of terror. As I stood there, scanning the woods for a movement or sign of the creature, I had the uncanny sense that someone was looking back at me. Quickly,

I put the sketchbook in my shoulder bag, fastened Max into his stroller, and hurried back along the footpath.

Max at once began to fret. When I pushed the stroller faster, he cried in earnest, protesting the jouncing. I stopped to lift him onto my hip. Breathless with the effort, I half-jogged up the path, bouncing the stroller ahead of me over the ruts and stones. In the crook of my arm, Max was laughing now, pleased with the new game.

As we skirted the perimeter of the woods, I could feel that watchful, inimical gaze fastened to us as tangibly as if something unspeakable had dropped onto my shoulder and was clinging to my coat. The urge to shake myself free of it was overwhelming.

At last, sweating and exhausted, I reached the stile.

I had to catch my breath. I leaned against a wooden post, gazing back the way we had come. The wind moved through the wild apple blossoms. The rocks descended into the trees, settling like flakes of soot into the soft dark mass of leaf. A solitary lamb came ambling up the hillside, its wool silvered by the angled light.

Whatever predator had provoked that screech of terror—a fox, a hawk, one of Spike's untamed cousins, perhaps—it was gone. My imagination had made me as much its prey as the silly startled sheep. Too much talk of murder at lunch, too many thoughts of death, too little sleep.

When Max and I got back, Longbarrow Cottage had a quite air of welcome in the late-afternoon light. It glowed, as though the sun's imprint lingered, diffused throughout the golden stone. Once again, I felt that I was coming home. Warm, secure, with the settled endurance of a building made to last through centuries rather than decades, the house seemed to offer its thick walls as a refuge from fear.

While Max played, I blu-tacked the drawings and sketches I had brought with me from Toronto to the living room walls, and stuck branches of lilac and apple blossom from the garden in some china jugs I found in the pantry. Many of the drawings were of Max, a few were studies of mice, preliminary sketches for Nan's story of the church mouse, which I had promised Paulina, my editor. The drawings, flowers, and Max's toys made the room seem more our own.

All the same, the fear lingered. Like a chill, it was easily caught, less easy to shake off. All through supper, bathtime, Max's bedtime story, the gradually darkening night outside reminded me that I would spend another night alone with my child in a place where no one was near enough to hear me if I called out for help. Mela's question echoed in my head: "Aren't you afraid, on your own . . . ?"

Before I went to bed, I checked that the doors and windows were securely latched. Then I got out of bed and checked again.

Finally, too tired even to worry, I fell asleep with the bedside lamp alight. As I drifted off, I remembered, too late, my dress hanging on the line outside.

CHAPTER 14

The dream that woke me was a nightmare.

In the dream, I was the watcher in the woods. It was night, and a full moon shone with cold radiance above the long barrow. There were no colors, only shades of black polished by the white brilliance of the moon to a metallic sheen. Around the high mound of the tumulus, dark shapes moved in a silent procession, human shadows without definition, hunched and sexless. Gradually, these faded; the barrow seemed to suck them in.

A solitary figure remained standing in the moonlight. Although her face was turned away from me, I knew that it was the woman of my drawing. But her arms were empty now; her child was gone. With a sudden convulsive shudder, she threw herself at the barrow, clawing at it, digging into it with a bone, tearing away the grass. Her violent breathing filled the deep silence of the night. It made a sound like the wind. At last, she hurled the bone away and flung herself facedown against the earth, arms outstretched in despair.

An ache of pity for her, like a bruise, hurt my side. I would have gone to her, but I was powerless to leave the grove. Then, as I watched, the woman rose to all fours like an animal, with her head lifted to the moon, and howled. Her cry was the same desolate scream of fear that I had heard from the woods that afternoon. My own mouth opened, but I could make no sound.

Still crouching, the woman turned slowly toward me. The harsh glare of the moon picked out every feature of her face, blanched and dreadful.

It was my face.

With a violent start of terror, I sat up in bed. At first, the vision of the woman and the barrow blurred the details of the room, as though it were a scene painted on an overlay and placed across reality. As it dissolved, the dreadful white face lingered, bodiless, and in my head the scream echoed, far off. Then I was alone with Max in the silent bedroom.

By the light from the bedside lamp, I could see the outline of his body under the blankets in his crib. I could hear his breathing, rhythmical, heavy. But I got out of bed and went over to the crib to place my hand on his chest, to feel the steady rise and fall of his rib cage, to make sure that he was simply asleep.

His head lay in profile against the sheet. It emphasized the tender curve of his forehead, the small, pronounced bump of his nose. A mauve shadow stained the eyelid above the delicate feathering of dark lashes; light bloomed on his unmarked, translucent skin. No other form of beauty, no other being, had such power to move me. As I gazed down at him, I could feel the dream's hold on me weaken, as though his flesh and blood were a sufficient amulet against its desolation.

I turned away from the crib and looked at my alarm clock. It was only eleven-thirty. Sleep, for a while at least, was impossible. I put on my dressing gown and slippers, and went downstairs to the kitchen, switching on every light along the way.

The wind had risen in the night. It whispered about the house, brushing against the stone with faint scratchings of bush and branch. I filled the kettle and measured coffee into a filter. With my back to the uncurtained kitchen window, I stood watching the flame that flickered blue and yellow under the kettle. The sight gave me an atavistic sense of comfort.

While the coffee filtered through into the cup, I heated milk in a little saucepan. I was just tipping out the hot milk, mixing it half and half with the coffee, when a loud knocking hammered against the front door. My hand jerked, spilling hot milk over the counter and onto the floor. Cursing, I grabbed some paper towel and dropped it onto the milk, then went to the door.

"Who is it?" I called through the wood. My voice sounded thin in my ears.

"David Cornelius."

Startled, I unlocked and opened the door. He was standing a little distance from the entrance, his face averted as if he were looking at something, or someone, behind him in the night. Momentarily, he seemed indistinct, a figure obscured by shadow. When he turned toward me, the light from the hall splashed across his face like a revelation.

"Is everything all right?" he asked me. He was breathing hard, as though he had been running, and above the rolled collar of his thick white sweater his neck and face were flushed. In one hand he held a large flashlight, its beam pointed to the ground.

"Yes, fine. Why? What's wrong?"

"I was walking along the fence, up by the barrow. I saw your lights come on." He hesitated a moment, then slowly, almost uncertainly, said, "I could have sworn there was someone in back of the cottage. I ran down as quickly as I could, but when I got here they were gone. Did you hear or see someone? Is that why you turned on the lights?"

"No, no, I didn't hear anything until you knocked. I . . . it was just that I couldn't sleep, so I came downstairs." Uneasily, I stared past him at the massed shapes of trees and bushes that stood against the dark line of the garden wall. It would be simple enough to slip away from the cottage under their cover, one more shadow among their shadows.

Beyond the wall, the darkness was broken only by the pin-pricks of light from houses down in Shipcote.

Quickly, as though to reassure me, he said, "There's no one there now—I gave a good look around. Maybe there never was anybody. It might have been just a trick of the light."

The night air gusted about us, cold bursts of wind pushing past me into the hall. Shivering, I asked him to come in. "I was just making some coffee. Would you like a cup?"

"Coffee sounds wonderful." He smiled and for a moment looked younger and less formidable, and very like Rafe. He leaned against the doorjamb to pull off his muddy boots, then followed me through to the kitchen.

"Why are you patrolling yourself?" I asked him as I put the kettle on to boil again and took another cup down from the shelf. "I thought someone else was doing it tonight."

"His wife is ill. He couldn't leave her." He stood with his back against the kitchen counter, his jacket hanging from one hand, but immediately moved forward when he saw me begin to mop up the spilled milk. "Can I help with that?"

"No, but you can measure the amount of coffee you like. The filter's over there, beside your cup."

He laid his jacket over the back of a chair; a rough work jacket of a dull waxy green, it was very like the one worn by William Ebborn on his visit to the cottage the evening before. Like William Ebborn's, too, his presence was comforting. But there was a difference in my response to the two men; whatever I felt for David Cornelius, it was not the easy, uncomplicated liking that the older man had instinctively aroused in me.

We took our coffee into the living room. As he sat down on the sofa, facing the blocked-up hearth, he told me that he had come to the cottage once before with Rafe to visit May Armitage. "It's a beautiful place. It hasn't been spoiled by charm."

I knew what he meant. Several houses in the village looked at though their renovations had been carried out by a Kate Greenaway fanatic. They had the static period charm of her illustrations, an unreal perfection of detail, down to the placing of the last rosebush. Still, it struck me that this was a curious statement from a man involved with Mela Mallaby.

There was a silence. "You're working long hours," I said, to make conversation.

He gave a small shrug. "I'm used to it. The lambing season's just over. On a busy night, you're like a polygamist with a dozen wives who've all gone into labor at the same time. You end up playing midwife to some, then bottle-feeding the babies whose mothers reject them."

"You've just cured me of any desire to raise sheep. But how did you get involved with Shipcote Farm Park? Were you a farmer in the States?"

I was a broker on Wall Street. But I grew up on a farm in Connecticut." He swallowed some coffee. "Mela's brother Phil was a friend of mind. He knew I was looking for something interesting to invest in, and suggested the farm park. I learned a lot from Phil, and Val Lenthall, who's really the expert. After Phil's death, I got more involved." He went on to say that he had come to England to be near Rafe. "Rafe's mother married an Englishman after our divorce two years ago."

"She had custody of Rafe?"

"We share custody. The divorce was comparatively friendly." He sat forward, resting his elbows on his knees, the cup held in both hands. After a pause in which he seemed to hesitate, as though wondering how much to tell me, he said, "The split was my fault, not Jennifer's. I was a workaholic in those days and she finally got tired of it. When she married again, I suppose I could have insisted that Rafe stay in the States, but by then I understood things a little better." His smile was ironic. "Luckily, I'd made enough money to act on that understanding."

"Rafe mentioned a baby sister—"

"That's why he's living with me for the moment, and goes to London for visits. It's his decision. Jennifer's not happy about it, but at least she can concentrate on the baby without worrying about the effect it's having on Rafe. He's jealous, I'm afraid. The divorce has been very tough for him. I regret that most of all." He was looking into his cup as he spoke, gently swirling the liquid around. Only the words themselves betrayed emotion: his eyes were invisible, his voice quietly matter-of-fact.

"What about you?" he continued. The cool, gray-brown eyes looked across at me and in them, and in his voice, was something that made his question seem more than a polite conversational return of service. "Will you stay here?"

"Actually, at this moment, I'm fairly certain I'll sell and go back." If he was pleased that his chances of acquiring Longbarrow Cottage had grown stronger, his face did not reveal it. "If Max were older," I said slowly, "or if there were other cottages close by, I might be tempted to stay. But I really only left Toronto because I wanted to get away from the familiar for a while." I told him then that my husband had died the year before.

"I didn't know. I'm sorry." He said this with a quiet sympathy free of the curiosity I had often heard in other voices, seen in other faces.

"This seemed like a chance to try a new direction. Not that I was dissatisfied. Just that I was becoming too insular, narrow. I thought I should take the blinkers off."

"I suppose I could say that those were my reasons for getting involved in the farm park. And something else. There's a line that used to haunt me when I worked on the Street. Maybe because it seemed to sum up what was missing in my life. 'A green thought in a green shade.' " He gave a faint, embarrassed smile, as though confessing to some more aberrant preoccupation. "The first time I saw Shipcote Farm, I remembered those words. If green thoughts are possible anywhere these days, it's here." He leaned forward to set his cup down on the table between the sofa and the chair, and as he did the light from the lamp flowed down over him.

I studied his face as though he presented some troubling problem of composition. The elements that made up his good looks were straightforward enough, a classical shapeliness to his head, the long smooth line of cheek and jaw, but it was a certain asymmetry in the planes of his face, an unevenness, that gave the looks their distinction. That, and an easy, unaggressive masculinity, implicit in the way he moved his body, which managed to be simultaneously reassuring and unsettling.

He caught my gaze and raised an eyebrow.

I flushed. "I have a bad habit of staring. I don't mean to be rude. But I'm always trying to figure out what makes a particular face individual. I have sketchbooks full of faces. They fascinate me." I knew I was explaining too much.

What he said next surprised me. "At lunch today, I found myself wondering what you were thinking. You seemed so detached, observing us." He smiled, to soften the words, and looked around at the sketches on the walls. "But when you told us about your work, I realized you would look at things—at us, maybe—differently."

"Mostly I'm trying to catch people unawares. When people pose, something freezes in them, and in me."

His gaze was grave, considering. "You're good at paying attention. But I'd say you don't like it much when it's paid to you. Not the visual kind, anyway."

This was acute of him, and I wondered how he had known it. "For my kind of work, it's better if I efface myself. Especially drawing children. They should forget you're there."

"And adults? How do you make them forget you're there?" He was smiling now, but underneath the smile was the shadow of a seriousness I did not know how to interpret.

I tried to keep my voice light. "Make them work. When they concentrate on what they're doing, they don't see you anymore. It's not hard."

"Really? You don't strike me as someone who'd become invisible so easily."

Once again, I could not sustain his gaze; I looked down at my hands as they lay in my lap. There was a profound nocturnal stillness, around the house and within the room. Within myself. I felt as though I were straining to hear some words spoken in a whisper, words that mattered.

This time the silence went on a little too long.

"I'd better get back," he said, almost awkwardly. He stood up. Before I could tell him to leave the cup on the table, he took it into the kitchen and set it in the sink. With a glance at the pantry door, he said, too casually, "Why don't I take a quick look out back while I'm here?" When I agreed, he unlocked and opened both the pantry and the back doors. For a moment, he stood on the back stoop, looking out. Then, astonishingly, he laughed.

"I think I've just found our prowler. Come and take a look at this."

"This" was my forgotten dress, hanging on the clothesline. When the wind twisted the hanger and lifted the long sleeves, the dress flapped and danced in the light from the window. A sudden gust pushed the hanger away into the darkness at the other end of the line, where the dress became invisible. In a moment, another shove from the wind sent the hanger sliding back again into the light. As the dress blew back toward me, I caught it and took it down from the line. The wool was cold and damp between my fingers.

"I think relief has the edge on embarrassment," he said as I locked the back door. "But only just." His face showed his chagrin.

"There *could* have been someone. I'm glad you were there. Really."

He made a vague sound of polite disbelief. "You must be fed up with Cornelius males disturbing your privacy."

I denied it, naturally, and said something about being grateful to him for keeping an eye on the cottage, which was true enough. But he was right, although not in the way he meant. For reasons of his own, he seemed equally uncomfortable and the few words we spoke walking back to the front door were stilted. As I watched him put on his boots, I was suddenly impatient for him to be gone.

Afterward, on my way up to bed, I told myself that I hadn't been completely honest with David Cornelius. I had come to Shipcote to escape the familiar, to try a new direction, that was true enough, but I was also in search of something else, a peace that would heal the wounds of the past year. For all its gentle beauty, Longbarrow Cottage seemed unlikely now to offer that peace. It was too lonely for me. Or perhaps I was too lonely for it, too much a prey to my own imagination.

Already, I could see that imagination beginning to work—on the Mallabys, on David Cornelius, and on the cottage itself—could feel the strong temptation to make something out of them, to create stories and images that might have nothing at all to do with reality.

CHAPTER 15

I woke to the bleating of lambs. They called their mothers with the same peremptory note as Max, who stirred and sat up in his crib, demanding his breakfast. Sunlight poured onto the bed as I changed and dressed him. He kicked his fat legs in its warmth, laughing with the pleasure in life that comes from a good night's sleep.

The milkman had come and gone, leaving three pints on the front doorstep. The bottles had several inches of cream at the top and caps of silver foil. They clinked against each other as I carried them into the kitchen, where Max was eating scrambled egg and strips of toast with marmalade. "Look, Max." I held up a bottle. "Milk the way cows used to make it."

In the morning light the emotions of the night before, like the dream, now seemed merely the products of too little sleep and a too vivid imagination. All that remained were the dirty coffee cups, David Cornelius's and mine, in the sink. And the memory of his face as he had talked of his son.

When Max finished his breakfast, I put him down on the living room rug with his toys and books, sitting cross-legged beside him with a cup of coffee and an omelet into which I had grated the last of the cheese. Gradually, as I ate, a surreptitious pleasure in the pride of ownership began to creep over me. I knew I should resist it, in order to have the strength of mind to sell the cottage, but the butter-yellow curtains beside the windows hung like banners heralding the view, inviting me to admire the sharply focused image of curved green against the low blue sky.

The wide strength of the stone fireplace, despite the cast-iron plate sheathing the hearth, appealed to me. It seemed to echo the strength of the cottage itself. Seductive images of domesticity began to take shape: the fallen apple boughs in the orchard burning in the fireplace, fresh paint gleaming on the wood trim, the wide wooden floorboards sanded and polished. Almost unconsciously, I found myself debating the possibilities of the small, north-facing bedroom as a studio, wondering how much work would be required to resurrect May's garden. If I had a radio or a television, I thought, the evenings might seem less lonely; if I had a dog, I might feel less vulnerable.

Then, like a fragment from the dream, an image flashed into my mind. A woman sprawled out, like the woman on the barrow, but in death, not mourning. Among all those who had lived peacefully here, there was one who had been unhappy and who had died violently. Evelyn Allerton's imprint lingered, too, it seemed.

Later that morning we went to Wychley. I had an appointment to see Tony Munnings. Although I was no longer quite so determined to sell Longbarrow Cottage, I wanted to discuss the various options I might have.

Midmorning on a Monday, the little town was busy, but I found a parking space on the High Street in front of a bakery. The offices of Munnings and Wooley were on Sheep Street, which ran westward from the High Street about halfway up the hill. At the corner where the two met, there was a tiny open markeplace, a pillared space below an overhanging half-timbered house with room for a single fruit-and-vegetable stand. I stopped to buy some apples. One of the customers, a girl with spiky dark hair hennaed crimson at the ends and a heavy-looking knapsack on her back, had a child of about two years old, but not much bigger than Max, in a stroller beside her.

The apples were unfamiliar to me. Pointing to a pile of small yellowish ones with pale red streaks, I asked the woman behind the stall what they were called. "Cox's Orange Pippins," she told me. "They've a lovely flavor." I took a bag and began to fill it.

"Here, you don't want to eat that!" Squatting down beside Max, the girl gently removed a small green worm from his grip before he could carry it to his mouth. She grinned up at me with dark eyes fiercely outlined in kohl; the pointed features of her small face had an odd, foxy appeal. She looked about twenty-one or -two, older than my first impression of her. "I thought kids hated greens," she said with a grin.

"If it moves, Max will eat it, no matter the color." I thanked her for stopping him in time.

"It must've come off these cabbages." She stood up, shaking out her long black coat. Oversized, with sleeves cut very wide, it hung loosely on her small frame, giving her a waifish look that was emphasized by the large, dramatic eyes. A single extraordinary earring dangled from her right ear, a green galleon in full sail.

The stallholder took an apple and gave it a vigorous wipe on her apron. "Here, love, try this instead." She held it out to Max. "No charge for the worm and none for the apple," she told me with a cheerful grin. She took a second apple and gave it to the child in the other stroller.

"Say thank you, Annie," the young woman told the little girl while I similarly instructed Max. Silently, the two children stared gravely up at the stallholder, then turned and scrutinized each other with the same comical look of doubt.

Tony Munnings had told me to look for an old hotel called The Pear Tree. Four doors beyond it, a highly polished brass sign fixed to the stone discreetly announced the offices of Munnings and Wooley, Solicitors, est. 1886. The small, two-story building was considerably older than the law firm; the date above the door was 1743. Inside, the ground-floor reception room did its best to persuade you that the late twentieth century had added little more than certain conveniences of current technology—a telephone, a word processor, a fax machine—without affecting the solid tradition implied by the Edwardian furnishings and the portraits of the two original partners. The only other modern touch was the girl who sat typing on the word processor. She looked up and smiled as Max and I came into the room.

"Oh, yes," she said when I gave my name. "Mr.

Munnings's expecting you." I took Max in my arms and followed her along a short, paneled corridor to a closed door. She tapped lightly and opened it. "Miss Treleven is here."

"Come in, come in," a voice said cheerfully.

Tony Munnings was older than I had judged him to be from his voice, a tall man in his mid-forties with thinning dark hair and smooth, pleasant features. He wore reading glasses, which he removed and laid on the desk. Between his eyebrows ran a deep, vertical groove, the only noticable line on his face, giving him a faintly worried air. His office was furnished in the same style as the reception area, with the addition of a tiny, elegant fireplace and a wide desk covered with papers and files. The window behind the desk looked out onto the street but was veiled in net curtains.

His welcome was friendly enough, with the offer of tea, which I declined, and a biscuit for Max, which he accepted, but I sensed a slight constraint, as though he were not entirely at his ease with me.

After I had thanked him for all he had done to get the cottage ready, and for the directions he had sent me, we discussed various bits of business relating to the cottage: the taxes—or rates, as he called them—and my obligations as a property owner. Then he inquired if I had given any more thought to what I would do with the place. I replied that although I was still undecided, my inclination was to sell. "I'm just not comfortable there at night."

"I can see it might be difficult. Although there are times when a place to one's self, no matter how isolated, has its attractions." He smiled a little ruefully. "My wife's parents live with us. A mixed blessing." More seriously, he went on to say that he hoped I wasn't worried by the two recent incidents of arson in the village. "In each case, there's a chance that the fires began accidentally." That was not, I reflected, what the Mallabys had implied yesterday at lunch.

I asked if it would be possible to rent the cottage. He looked doubtful. "Well, yes, you could do. But if a time came when you wanted to sell, a tenant might make difficulties about leaving. And the law is decidedly in the tenant's favor."

At my request, he gave me a list of the various expenses

incurred on my behalf, in addition to his fee. While I settled the account, I said, "This firm handled the sale of the cottage when my grandmother bought it, isn't that right?"

"It was your grandfather, not your grandmother, who originally purchased the cottage. My own grandfather handled the transaction."

I was surprised; for some reason, I had always assumed that Nan had bought the place. "Do you have the original deed?"

He nodded. A faint flush of red discolored the thin skin across his cheekbones.

"I thought that maybe Munnings and Wooley might have acted on her behalf on other occasions, that you might still have papers of hers. Or his."

He hesitated briefly, then said with visible reluctance. "This is very awkward, Miss Treleven. You see, after our telephone conversation, the same thought occurred to me. This is an old family firm, and we've kept all our back files. I'm afraid they were somewhat in disarray until several years ago, when we computerized. At that point we transferred those files that were not fed into the data base to cabinets in our storage room.

"When I asked Gail, our secretary, to check the files in storage, she found one under your grandfather's name." He picked up his reading glasses, opening and closing the temples as he spoke. "Gail put the file in my in-tray along with some others I'd requested that day. There were two or three papers in the file, but I only looked at the copy of the deed. I meant to go through the others later, to examine them for anything that might be of interest to you. However, I'm afraid the file was buried . . ." With a small embarrassed smile, he indicated the desk top. "When I remembered to look for it this morning, knowing you'd be coming in, I couldn't find it.

"Gail checked to see if it had been refiled. Or misfiled. Unfortunately, she hasn't been able to locate it yet." The vertical line between his eyebrows deepened. "I'm very sorry. Ordinarily, we take every precaution to ensure that all papers relating to our clients are treated with care. I can only hope that it may yet turn up. It may have somehow become mixed with another file." He did not sound convinced of either possibility, however.

"Did your secretary notice what was in the file?"

"I asked her. She never looked inside." He leaned forward, his hands resting on the desk, clasping the pair of glasses. "I feel very bad about this. We'll do our best to find it." He seemed genuinely conscience-stricken, perhaps more disturbed by the loss of the file than I was. I was annoyed but tried not to show it and said that I assumed that the file would turn up eventually.

Shifting Max from my lap to my shoulder, I stood up. Tony Munnings and I agreed that I would let him know about the sale of the cottage as soon as I had made up my mind. As I pushed the stroller back toward the High Street, I wondered whether the lawyer would have told me about the missing file unasked. On the whole, I was inclined to believe that he would have, if not at once, then later, when he was sure it could not be found. He struck me as an honest person, although I recognized that this impression was based purely on instinct. As for his air of constraint, I put that down to embarrassment.

On the High Street beyond the supermarket there was a public telephone. Talking intently into the receiver, her shoulders hunched forward, was the young woman in the long black coat. Behind her, the little girl in the stroller was crying, stretching her arm down to her apple, which lay on the pavement out of reach.

I pushed Max over and picked up the apple. As I did, I heard the young woman say loudly, "Look, I didn't come for the money!" There was a pause. "Well, you tell him from me he's a bloody coward!" Then, more softly, "And you're a bitch." She slammed the receiver down. When she turned around, the fierce black eyes were furious.

Embarrassed to have heard so much, I said, "Your little girl was crying." I held up the apple in explanation. "Can I give her another?"

"Thanks." The anger had faded, but something lingered, a sort of weary disgust that made her face seem older than the twenty or so years of her age.

"Oh, Annie, don't make such a fuss," she told the child. Her voice was tired now, rather than angry or impatient.

She took a crumpled tissue from her coat pocket and gently wiped the little girl's nose. I offered the fresh apple. With a shy smile, the child accepted it. She had light hair and pretty, delicate features, with milky skin so fair that the blue veins underneath were visible.

The young woman picked up the pack from the pavement and swung it onto her back. She winked at Max, lifted her hand to me and, checking for a break in the traffic, pushed the stroller quickly across the road.

Max and I continued down the street. The librarian was arranging some books in the window of the library as we passed by and when she looked up and saw us, I waved. Smiling, she beckoned me inside.

"I thought you might like to know that there'll be a secondhand book dealers' fair in Oxford this weekend," she told me while she held the door open for the stroller. "At the Randolph Hotel. You might be able to find the book you're after there." She gave me a leaflet with the details.

While we were in the library, it occurred to me to look for Stephen Allerton's novel, *This Sad Ceremonial*, to read it again in light of what I had learned about the man. Perhaps now that I was older I would understand its appeal. There was a copy on the shelf, with the dog-eared, grimyedged look of a book that has been much read. When I came to check it out, the librarian mentioned that the author had been a local man. "Perhaps you know that?" she asked me. I replied that someone had told me Allerton had once lived in Longbarrow Cottage. "In that case," she said, "you must read his biography. We have a copy. I'll just see if it's in."

She returned with the book in her hand. When she gave it to me I saw with surprise that the author was Willoughby Webb Springer. Less surprising, perhaps, was the publisher. Like Allerton's novel, his biography had been published by Mallaby's.

"It's rather a sad life, considering his talents," she said. "Of course, he died much too young. And apparently he had a shrew of a wife, poor man. She was murdered. . . ." She stopped and looked flustered, as though she had just remembered where I lived.

"Yes, I know. In Longbarrow Cottage." I smiled, to show

how little the grim fact bothered me. "I haven't met her ghost on the stairs yet."

Intending to take Max to the river to watch the ducks, I stopped at the car to drop off the books and the apples, but the smell of fresh bread from the bakery made me pause. A notice by the door announced that there was a tearoom upstairs. The sights of the cakes in the window, and my curiosity about the biography, persuaded me that it was time to indulge in an English tradition. I left the stroller in the car and went inside with Max.

The tearoom was a long, light room with large stone fireplaces at either end, a row of windows overlooking the street, and exposed wooden beams running across the ceiling. There were flowers on the tables and a rack of newspapers by the cashier's desk for patrons to read while they ate. A trolley stood in the center of the room, its tiers filled with meringues, chocolate eclairs, cakes, and scones. I sat down at a table for two by a window.

The waitress brought a high chair for Max and took my order for tea and scones. While Max chewed on his apple, I opened the biography of Stephen Allerton.

The back flap, which had been cut from the discarded jacket and pasted onto the inside front cover, described Willoughby Webb Springer as "the respected literary critic and Oxford scholar" and gave a list of his publications. Most of these seemed to be collections of essays and books of criticism. The biography, published in 1958, had a preface, an index and bibliography at the end, and in the middle two pages of black-and-white photographs, mostly snapshots of Stephen Allerton at various periods of his relatively short life.

The first was a family photograph taken when Stephen and Clarissa Allerton were small. It was an Edwardian summer scene posed on the lawn in front of Summerhays, with two solemn and very beautiful children in pinafores, clasping hands. Their mother wore a wide hat and flowing white dress, and had a clever, serious face. Their father was a handsome man with finely drawn features, a drooping mustache, and an indolent curve to his long, thin body.

Later photographs showed Stephen Allerton as an equally beautiful adult, with his father's features and his mother's grave, intelligent air. In the last photograph, taken in Spain, he stood gesturing with a cigarette between his fingers, obviously caught in mid-sentence. It was the only one in which he was smiling.

There was also a photograph of Evelyn Allerton. She was leaning against a doorway with her arms clasped in front of her, almost expressionless. Dark wings of short hair framed a high, round forehead, high-bridged nose, and large, staring, almost exophthalmic, eyes. It was an arresting, rather than a beautiful, face, with a discontented look about the mouth.

One photograph was of a group of six young people sitting on some terrace steps; among them only Allerton, Clarissa, and Benedict were identified. Startled, I looked more closely at it. Half-hidden behind Benedict's head was a young man with dark hair and slightly blurred features. He was hardly noticeable. Most eyes looking at the picture would probably focus on the brother and sister, both so striking, who faced the camera with the same air of confident ease. But I was certain that the young man was Charles Lorimer, my grandfather. I knew his face from a photograph my mother had.

I turned to the index. There were entries for Clarissa and Benedict Mallaby, for Evelyn Allerton, and for Longbarrow Cottage. None, however, for Charles Lorimer.

I scanned the brief preface. In it, Willoughby described how, as an eighteen-year-old student at Oxford, he had met Stephen Allerton and Benedict Mallaby at an exhibition of antique printing presses. Stephen Allerton, who had been a keen amateur printer, had kept his own small press at Longbarrow Cottage. Willoughby had come to Shipcote on occasional weekends in the mid-thirties to visit Stephen, lending a hand with whatever project he and Benedict were currently involved in printing, often poems by their circle of friends, or by Stephen himself. Then in 1937, Allerton left England to fight in the Spanish Civil War.

From Willoughby's introduction, it was evident that Stephen Allerton had been one of the "golden lads" of the thirties, poet, novelist, idealist, soldier, and finally, tragically, dust. His admiration for his subject undisguised, Willoughby wrote in glowing terms of Stephen's brilliance, beauty, and heroic commitment to his ideals. There was no sign here in the introduction of the dry, acerbic personality on display at Summerhays.

By chance, while I was flipping back and forth among the various entries for Longbarrow Cottage cited in the index, I came across a description of Evelyn Allerton's death. Or rather, an account of the police theory of how she had died.

Someone had broken into the cottage during a blizzard and killed her with a poker, then ransacked the place. Because of the snow, her body had not been found for several days. In curious contrast to much of the rest of the prose, which was serious and at times almost academical, this passage had a lurid touch, with chilling details about the position and state of the body.

The tea in my cup grew cold as I read on. Finally, Max began to squirm. I took him onto my knee so that he could look out the window at the people and traffic passing below, and managed to read for another five minutes before he refused to be further distracted. Gulping down my cold tea, I wrapped the scone in a paper napkin and paid my bill. As a reward for his good behavior, I took Max down to the river to commune with the ducks for a quarter of an hour, then retraced my steps to Munnings and Wooley. There was another question I wanted to ask Tony Munnings: whether he knew when my grandfather had purchased Longbarrow Cottage.

As I approached the building that housed the law firm, a man came out of the doorway. It was Benedict Mallaby. He looked preoccupied, frowning slightly, but when he glanced up and saw us, his expression shifted into a genial warmth. "Tony Munnings told me he'd just seen you," he said after we'd greeted each other and I had thanked him for Sunday's hospitality.

"You're a client of his?"

"And his father's before him. We inherited the firm, so to speak, from the Allertons. Clarissa's family."

"My grandmother was their client. And my grandfather. You know, I've just been reading about Mrs. Mallaby's brother—"

"You mustn't be so formal with us," he interrupted, his

voice lightly teasing. "After all, you're part of the family.
Despite that little conversation about names yesterday,
we're not so stuffy as it might appear."

I smiled and said that no one who entertained babies and
ferrets could possibly be considered stuffy. Then, determined to keep to the subject of the book, I went on. "Mr.
Webb Springer's—I mean, Willoughby's—biography im-
plies that your brother-in-law owned Longbarrow Cottage. I
was just wondering how and when my grandfather came to
buy it."

Rubbing the bridge of his nose, he gazed away from me,
into the distance. "Ah, yes. Well, actually, Charles was the
owner. It was rather a complicated business. I'm afraid I
have an appointment just now, otherwise . . ." His voice
drifted off, vague, leaving the politely accommodating response to me.

Suddenly, however, I wanted to be direct, to push him to
some sort of answer. He could put my persistence down to
a North American lack of subtlety. "There doesn't appear
to be any mention of him in the biography. That seems
strange."

His glance came back to me. He hesitated, and then, as
if making up his mind to something, said quickly, "Look,
there's a pub just along here. I have a few minutes. If you
like, I'll tell you a bit about it."

I glanced down and saw that Max had fallen asleep in
the stroller. As it was near his naptime, it seemed likely he
would sleep long enough for me to hear what Benedict had
to say. We walked along to The Bull, an old and rambling
pub with black beams running across its low ceilings and a
comfortable, almost luxurious atmosphere compounded of
log fires, polished brass, and plush-covered cushions.

We found a small round table near one of the fireplaces
and sat down with our glasses. In his stroller next to my
chair, Max slept on. Benedict crossed one long, tweed-
covered leg over the other, jiggling an elegant leather-shod
foot up and down. He was whistling almost silently between his teeth, a habit he seemed to have. I waited. After
a moment, he said, "Well, where to begin? I suppose you
know the sad ending already? Charles's disappearance, I
mean."

I nodded. "But that's all I know."

"Really? How extraordinary. I should have thought . . ." He did not finish the sentence but seemed struck by something and hesitated for a moment before he went on. At last, he said in a careful voice, "But of course you only found out about us the other day, didn't you? Curious, that. How do you account for your grandmother's silence on the subject?" Over the rim of his glass, the faded blue eyes considered me as he drank his beer.

"I can't. I was hoping you might give me some idea."

"Ah." He set the glass down on the table. And again left a little silence.

Feeling that we were not making much headway, I asked if he would mind telling me what he remembered about my grandfather. He inclined his head in acquiescence, but the way he began was surprising. Reflectively, he said, "You know, the thirties were a remarkable time. In some ways, they were rather like the sixties. That communal sense, the naive belief in brotherhood.

"Charles and I met Stephen at Oxford. The three of us were sure we could change the world. Through literature, of all misguided notions. We were going to live together, publish great work, make a new order of society. Needless to say, we were very young." He gave a snort of laughter, not precisely contemptuous, more pitying. "Charles had just come into a small inheritance. He bought Longbarrow Cottage and a printing press. An Albion. Lovely piece of work. Charles always had an eye for beauty." He took another sip from his beer. "William Morris said something about 'the hallowing of labour by art.' That was pretty much our credo. The three of us lived and worked together in the cottage. And for six months or so, it seemed that we really might accomplish something.

"Then Evelyn came along." His reminiscent smile gave way to a somber look. "She was a waitress in a café in Oxford. She'd had an unhappy life. Stephen found that very attractive. He had rather a tendency to see himself as a Sir Galahad. It was his weakness." His voice was very dry. "As you heard yesterday, she was a difficult woman. Charles couldn't abide her. Neither, for that matter, could I. Naturally, that made her all the more appealing to

Stephen. When he married her, Charles simply turned the cottage over to them and we left. The understanding was they would look for a place of their own. But then Stephen went off to fight in Spain, and under the circumstances your grandfather could hardly ask Evelyn to leave. Not that she was likely to if he had. She was an obstinate woman." Dryly, he added, 'If she hadn't been killed, she might be living there still."

All this was interesting, but it only made my initial question more pointed. "If my grandfather was that close to you all," I said, "then why wasn't he mentioned in the biography?"

Benedict looked around the room with a vague air. "I think you'll find there are one or two references to Charles. But it's true, he is somewhat slighted. You see, he rather let us down. And I'm afraid feelings were still quite strong when Willoughby wrote the biography."

"Because he disappeared like that, you mean? Without a word to anyone."

"Umm. Among other things."

I waited, but he did not elaborate. I decided then to ask him about the title of Nan's book, to see if he had any idea why she might have used the words engraved on his watch.

He looked at me almost suspiciously. For the first time, his voice held a trace of annoyance. "The watch was Stephen's. A gift from Charles. The words refer to Stephen's novel, *This Sad Ceremonial*. They were extravagant, I suppose, but Charles could be generous, particularly with praise." As if he had heard the curtness in his voice, he said more gently, "Your grandmother misunderstood many things about Charles's relationship with Stephen and myself. I believe it's not uncommon for a wife to feel a certain amount of jealousy of her husband's old friends. To see them as a rather questionable influence. I can only speculate, but I would say there was an ironical intent to her choice of title. Charles believed in Stephen's genius—to a fault, perhaps. Your grandmother may have wearied of hearing about the book."

I was surprised. "Was *her* novel about *his* novel, then?"

This time his glance was so acute that it seemed to rip through the amiably vague air that had accompanied his words. "But surely you've read her book?" His voice was bluntly incredulous.

I shook my head. "I only just found out about it. I'm beginning to realize there's a lot I didn't know."

He seemed bemused by this admission, shaking his head slowly. "Curiouser and curiouser."

That should be my line, I felt like saying. Instead, I returned his own question to him. No, he replied, he had not read *Life Blood*. It was said so firmly, repressively, that although I wanted to ask him if he at least knew what the book was about, I hesitated. He set his empty glass down on the table and glanced at the pocket watch. "I really ought to be going. If you're ready . . . ?"

As we parted company outside, he said in a kindly if somewhat remote voice that he hoped the complications of the past would not affect my own stay here. The mild blue gaze rested on me for a moment and then he said good-bye and walked away.

CHAPTER 16

Before Max and I left Wychley, I picked up the film I had left for developing at Boots. The photographs had turned out well, with sharp, distinct colors, especially those of Shipcote and Withyford Church. As I flicked quickly through them, one caught my attention. It was the photograph of David Cornelius and Mela Mallaby, the one I'd taken for their shadows on the grass. It was not the shadows that struck me now, however, but the small figure standing at the edge of the trees on the hill beyond the church. A boy's figure.

If Rafe Cornelius had witnessed that scene between his father and Mela, it might explain his obvious antipathy to

her. And if he, like myself, suspected her of meeting Gerald
Fenton on the sly, he would have a reason to distrust her as
well.

Rafe had implied that he'd spent that afternoon in
Longbarrow Cottage, falling asleep there and waking only
on our arrival, Max's and mine. Perhaps, instead, he had
run back to the cottage to think over what he had just seen,
unable to face his father or Mela. The cottage had been a
refuge of sorts for him, after all, while May was alive.

As Max and I drove back to Shipcote along the river
road, I saw a familiar figure with a knapsack pushing a
stroller on the road ahead, just beyond Withyford. It was
the young woman from Wychley and her child.

As the car approached, she maneuvered the stroller closer
to the verge, but did not look around. I slowed, and pulled
over to the side of the road a little way beyond, opening my
window. When they came level with us, her glance was
guarded at first, warming only when she recognized me.

"Can I give you a lift somewhere?"

She nodded. "We're going to Shipcote, to the pub. Do
you know it?"

"The Mason's Arms? By the bridge?"

"That's it."

While she folded up the stroller and put it and the back-
pack in the trunk among the groceries, I held the little girl.
After Max's solid bulk, the child seemed barely a weight in
my arms. Her fine, pale hair floated like milkweed silk
around the soft pink curve of her ears. She turned her head
to gaze up at me, the unblinking blue eyes grave but unafraid.

The young woman climbed into the backseat, settling the
child on her lap, then leaned forward to greet Max, who
was twisting around in his car seat trying to get a look at
our passengers. He was making the small noises deep in his
throat that meant he was excited. When she made noises
back at him, his eyes widened and he smiled, putting his
head on one side, flirting with her.

I introduced Max, and then myself. In return, she told me
that she was Sophie Dymock and her daughter was Anna.
Anna, she said, was two years old; Max was half her

daughter's age, but he must have weighed twice as much. She asked if I was living locally.

"In Longbarrow Cottage. Do you know it?"

"Sure. But where's Miss Armitage gone?"

When I explained, she said, "I didn't know. I've been away for the last couple of years."

"Do you come from Shipcote?"

"Yeah. Unfortunately." There was an implicit, half-humorous shrug in her voice, which sounded resigned rather than bitter. I glanced in the rearview mirror, but her head was bent over the child as she pointed out a swan on the river. The noon sun shone down on the curving line of the leafless willows along the river, the soft green fields, the cluster of creamy houses on the hillside. There was nothing visible in the pretty scene to account for Sophie Dymock's dislike of the place.

On the other side of the little bridge, I pulled up by The Mason's Arms. Stretching my arm out along the seat back, I turned and asked her if she was sure she wanted me to drop her here. "It's no trouble to take you right to wherever you're going."

"I'm going to visit my mum. At Crookfield Farm?" When I said that I hadn't been in Shipcote long enough to recognize place-names, she explained that the farm lay on the outskirts of the village to the east. "It's not far, but I thought I'd ring first from the pub, to see if she's in. If she's not, Anna and I'll get something to eat while we wait."

"Why don't you come and have lunch with Max and me?" I was prompted partly by an instinctive liking and partly by a curiosity about her that was as much visual as personal. She was not strictly beautiful, or even pretty, but her face had a mobility and a kind of sweet-and-sour appeal that gave it an interest straightforward good looks often lack.

There was another reason, which I only half-admitted to myself: returning to Longbarrow Cottage might be easier if I had company.

Willoughby Webb Springer's portrayal of Evelyn Allerton's murder had been powerfully disturbing. The scenes he had described flashed in and out of my thoughts, as if I had stared too long at his words, turning them into afterimages that lingered like an optical illusion on the retina of my mind. Part of their power lay in the juxtaposition of that bloody violence with the gentle peace of the cottage. The murder seemed to violate not only the victim but the place.

"There's plenty to eat," I told Sophie Dymock as she hesitated. "I've just done the shopping."

"Well, then, thanks, that'd be great. But I'll ring from here anyway. It'd be easier than going up to the farm." That might be true, but as she went into the pub with Anna on her hip I wondered if she was reluctant to confront her mother before an onlooker. If she had been speaking to her mother during that telephone conversation I had overhead in Wychley, her homecoming seemed likely to be stormy.

In a few minutes, she and Anna came back to the car. There had been no answer to her call, she told me as they got in. "It's odd. She's usually there at midday, cooking dinner."

I was amused to hear, like an echo, my own assumptions about my mother's availability when I had lived at home. "Isn't she expecting you?"

"No. I didn't phone ahead." Her voice was suddenly cool, closed off. It must have been some other woman, then, who had provoked that expletive in Wychley.

When we got to the cottage, Max struggled to be put down on the grass in the garden, so Sophie kept an eye on the children while I unloaded the groceries and carried them inside. Something, a vague disquiet and the need to take a preparatory mental breath, stopped me on the threshold with my arms full of packages.

When I was five or six years old, someone had given me the edition of *Grimm's Fairy Tales* illustrated by Arthur Rackham. His pictures were so terrifying that it took all my courage to open the book and look inside, and I often slammed it shut again at once, frightened off by a giant or a pair of quarreling gnomes. But the power of his drawings never failed to tempt me to another look. Now, about to step into my own living room, I remembered that childish dread and the irresistible temptation.

I walked quickly through the living room into the kitchen

and dumped the packages on the table, then went back to stand in front of the fireplace. Deliberately, one by one, I called up the images of Evelyn Allerton's murder. I tried to make them a problem of composition or materials, a difficult and unsympathetic assignment, as though the murder were a fiction and I its illustrator. But they refused to be so neatly framed.

Unhappily, I looked down at the long slab of hearthstone where Evelyn Allerton's blood had splashed. A country superstition, Nan had told me once, held that blood shed in violence could never be washed away. Some trace of it would remain, indelible, as the evidence of a brutal death. Mercifully, there were too many stains on the stone, grease stains, smoke stains, and unidentifiable others, to be able to distinguish that grotesque sign, if it was there, from the rest.

"Hallo?" It was Sophie calling from the front door. I went to help her with the children. As we took off their outdoor clothes, she told me she had been taught by May Armitage when she was a little girl. Like Mela, she remembered the old lady with affection. "She was a bit of a softy. Not much on discipline."

The dangling earring snagged on her collar as she slipped out of her coat. I helped to free it, and admired the details of the tiny papier-mâché ship, its gilded rigging and billowing sails. Earrings were her fetish, Sophie said. "I'd feel naked without one."

Underneath her coat, Sophie wore layers of clothing, all of them black: a man's pin-striped vest over a long cotton shirt that reached to mid-thigh and whose sleeves almost covered her hands, a skirt skimming her knees, thick stockings with a silver thread woven through them, and ankle boots with rolled tops. Anna was dressed conventionally in a pale yellow sweater embroidered with butterflies and a grass-green corduroy pinafore dress. For all her palely delicate air, she had the look of a child who was well taken care of. I tended to lug Max about like a stuffed bolster, he seemed so sturdy and well padded, but Sophie handled Anna with great gentleness, as if she were something fragile and very precious.

Sophie saw the drawings on the walls in the living room and asked if I was an artist. When I told her what I did for a living, she went on to say that she had known an illustrator once. "A Welshman. We did a project together. This was his contribution." Her eyes were mischievous as she rolled up one long black sleeve of her shirt. Wreathed around her lower arm, its tail circling her wrist like a bracelet, was the elaborate tattoo of a red dragon.

It was a beautiful, unsettling piece of work. Savagely expressive, the dragon's face was plumed with thin lines of smoke, and every scale on its writhing, undulating body was sharply defined. But each squirm of its coils as Sophie twisted her arm was a reminder of the medium in which its creator had worked. The effect was macabre, as it was undoubtedly meant to be.

After admiring it, I said I hoped her part of the project was more than serving as a living canvas.

She looked mildly offended. "Course it was. Words usually come before the illustration, don't they? I supplied the words." She explained that this was several years ago, when she had been a university student. "The lecturer told us to try our hand at writing part of an epic poem. My Welsh friend had the daft idea that he would illustrate my work."

We went into the kitchen, where Sophie helped me get the children's lunch ready. As we heated up the sausage rolls and cut cheese into cubes, then made a mixed salad for ourselves, I said, "I wish I'd been there when you turned in your assignment."

"The lecturer thought it was brilliant. Not my poem so much—it really wasn't very good—but the illustration. She asked for my Welsh friend's address. He told me later she wanted him to tattoo Grendel on her left shoulder. You know, the monster in *Beowulf*."

"Was it painful, your tattoo, I mean?"

She looked up from quartering oranges, and grimaced. "Yeah, it was. Enough so I can say I've suffered for literature. But it's a great way to meet men. Makes 'em think maybe I've got others in more interesting places."

"I'll remember that."

"You on your own, too?" When I nodded, she added, "Aren't we lucky, then? Men can be such shits." She paused, as though considering this, before adding, "Some men." With a smile, she amended further. "Well, one or two anyway."

Listening to her, looking at her, I found it impossible to gauge her background or her age. Sometimes she spoke with a teenager's loose, offhand slanginess, swallowing syllables in an exaggerated fashion, a way of speaking that went with her slightly tough air of independence. At other times, the university education surfaced and she switched into a precise, almost elegant, diction, using the voice of someone much older, or at least with a certain experience of the world. Like her speech, there was a contrariness to her manner as well. It alternated between an impulsive warmth and sudden coolness, as though she needed to remind herself not to give too much away.

Max was sitting in his high chair and Anna on several cushions piled on a kitchen chair. He grabbed fistfuls of the cheese cubes and crammed them into his mouth, but she picked up each cube delicately between thumb and forefinger. They eyed one another from time to time, each clearly fascinated by the other. As Sophie and I ate our sausage rolls and salad, I asked her if she would mind my sketching Anna. Go ahead, she replied. I would have preferred to sketch Sophie herself, but something, that occasional reserve of hers, perhaps, made me hesitate.

While I worked with the sketchbook across my knee, I asked her if she had come to Shipcote for long. She shook her head. "Just for the night. I've chucked in my job, so this seemed a good time for a visit." She had been working for an English family in Paris as a nanny, she explained, but the father of the baby she'd been taking care of had made one too many passes at her. "I fended him off—I didn't want to leave 'cause I had Anna to consider. Most people don't want a nanny with a kid of her own. Anyway, I liked his wife and their baby was lovely. But she figured out what he was up to, and they had a big row on Saturday. So I got out."

I glanced up at her from the sketch. The expression on her face was no more troubled than her voice; she did not seem angry or even annoyed, merely resigned, as though her departure was the inevitable result of circumstances she had tried without success to control.

"What will you do now?"

"Look for a job. I've got a bit of money saved up. And there's a squat in London where Anna and I can stay for a couple of days 'til I find something." She didn't seem particularly worried by the prospect.

She glanced over my shoulder at the sketch of Anna. The little girl had a characteristic look, a shy gravity, which with her delicate prettiness gave her the aspect of a child from some earlier age. That was what I had tried to catch. Sophie seemed so pleased with it that I rolled it up tightly, slipped on an elastic band, and handed it to her. "As thanks for rescuing the worm from Max."

She did not thank me but instead reached up to her right ear and unscrewed the green galleon. "A swap," she said firmly as she gave it to me, ignoring my protests. "It'll go with your eyes." Then she picked up Anna and said it was time they were going. She refused the offer of a lift to her mother's house, saying she wanted to walk through the village. "It's good to take a look at your roots every now and then, isn't it? Reminds you why you left in the first place."

We said good-bye. If they came back to Shipcote again, she told me, she and Anna would look us up. We had never discussed how long Max and I would be staying, and as there seemed no point in telling her now, I simply said that I hoped to see her again. Still, when she walked down the drive to the lane, pushing Anna ahead in the stroller, I found myself wanting to call her back.

I carried Max upstairs for his nap. When he was asleep, I picked up Willoughby's biography of Stephen Allerton and stretched out on my bed.

Although my grandfather's name had not turned up in the index, I remembered Benedict's assertion that he was mentioned once or twice. Searching back and forth through the book for passages that seemed promising, I skimmed over the words, and as I did, Stephen Allerton's life began to take shape. In the process, I also learned a certain amount about Benedict Mallaby. The young man who emerged from the book seemed very different from the affluent businessman with the silver Jaguar.

Stephen and Benedict had been idealistic socialists committed to left-wing causes, like many others in the thirties.

In 1936, they had founded Longbarrow Press to print the writings of a small circle of "like-minded friends," in particular Stephen's poems and his novel when it was completed. Neither man had had much money, and what little extra they had was spent on the press. I remembered that in the pub Benedict had said that it was my grandfather who actually bought the printing press.

But it seemed that Charles Lorimer had been banished from the text as thoroughly as he had disappeared from life. He was absent, simply absent from lives and from memories, a man as insubstantial as a ghost, his pale shadow to be found somewhere between the lines, if one knew where to look. For the first time, I could feel sorry for him.

In 1938, Stephen had gone off to Spain to join the international volunteer effort against Franco's forces. He was presumed killed there in a battle, although his body was never found. Among the effects sent back to his widow was the completed manuscript of *This Sad Ceremonial*. Evelyn, who was still living in Longbarrow Cottage, resisted appeals to permit its publication. Just before her death, however, she had a change of heart and sent the manuscript to Benedict. *This Sad Ceremonial* was the first book to appear from Benedict's new publishing house, Mallaby & Co. It achieved immediately critical and financial success.

Willoughby described Evelyn in circumspect terms. That Stephen's wife had been a difficult woman who resented his writing and his allegiances came through clearly nonetheless. Although Willoughby touched only lightly on the Allertons' sexual relationship, describing it as "troubled," he implied that the lack of a child intensified Evelyn's bitterness.

The two had met and married young, and too quickly to discover their incompatibilities beforehand. Evelyn was an orphan, and working class. Willoughby hinted at pity rather than love on Stephen's part, and the desire, perhaps, to practice his ideals of universal brotherhood. She had not shared his beliefs or his interest in literature. All they had in common, Willoughby said in one passage, was her unhappiness and his need, at first, to assuage it.

At one point, with reference to Stephen's tortured rela-

tionship with Evelyn and to his self-immolation in the
Spanish Civil War, Willoughby wrote: "Allerton's life was
dominated by the myth of Prometheus. To create, the artist
must subject himself to intense suffering; only out of that
suffering will he produce work of lasting value." It was an
interesting concept, I thought with grim amusement, the deliberate choice of an inappropriate spouse with an eye to
productive misery.

Subtly, through his description of the ideals of
Longbarrow Press and its creators and their eventual destruction by Evelyn Allerton's jealousy and her temper,
Willoughby made me feel that it was not so much the murder that had violated the spirit of Longbarrow Cottage as
Evelyn Allerton herself. He left me with the distinct impression that she had deserved what she got.

As I read on, still searching without success for Charles
Lorimer's name, a paragraph leaped out at me.

After Stephen left for Spain, Evelyn acquired an unfortunate reputation among some of the country people. Her
appearance, which became increasingly unkempt, and her
manner, always aloof and now reclusive, alienated them.
Her outbreaks of irrational anger frightened them. The
ignorant called her a witch.

A witch.

In Nan's story, a witch was killed for the treasure she
possessed, a treasure created by the idealistic youngest
brother. When I was ten years old, I had drawn the treasure
with the Grail in mind, as a golden cup blazing with jewels,
but in fact Nan had never explicitly described it, saying
only that it was something precious. There was no reason,
I realized now, why the treasure could not have been a
book.

I began to make connections between the story and reality. If Nan had used what she knew about the Allertons, the
witch was surely Evelyn, the artist suffering and dying for
his beliefs was Stephen, and the treasure was his novel.
Who, then, was the golden-haired middle brother, the one
who had killed the witch to save the treasure from destruction, the one who, corrupted by its possession, had also

murdered the "steadfast" eldest brother? And who was that eldest brother?

I turned to the group photograph taken in Longbarrow Cottage. There sat Benedict, fair and handsome, half-obscuring his cousin Charles. Two men who, in Clarissa's words, had been "as close as brothers." I closed the biography and dropped it onto the bed beside me.

The answers to my questions were obvious and inescapable. The murderous middle brother was Benedict Mallaby. The eldest brother was my grandfather, Charles Lorimer. Beneath its fairy-tale trappings, Nan's story was saying that Benedict had killed Evelyn to get Stephen's manuscript and had killed Charles to keep it.

Nan might be saying that and more, I told myself sternly, but merely saying it did not make it true. Idly, as an occupation for my fingers while I thought, I took my sketch pad and a pencil from the bedside table and began to draw.

Nan's stories were fiction, I reminded myself. They had been created by an imagination working on isolated details of fact. She might have made her stories, perhaps even her novel, out of Evelyn Allerton's death, but that did not necessarily mean they were any more factual than the stories she had fashioned from Shipcote legends. The parallels with reality gave the illusion of fact, made the stories appear biographical, even autobiographical, but all fiction transmuted the writer's own experience and knowledge. Readers or listeners made assumptions about literal truth at their peril.

A story did not make Benedict a murderer any more than it absolved Charles from abandoning his pregnant wife. According to Willoughby, Evelyn had sent Benedict the manuscript of her own free will; there had been no need to kill her for it. Benedict had no reason to kill her, or to kill his cousin Charles.

Nan, however, might have needed to believe that Charles was murdered. The alternatives, that he was a coward, that she had somehow failed him, that he had left her for someone else, or that he simply didn't want her anymore, might have been too painful for her to accept. His disappearance left her with more than the coming child; it also undoubtedly left her with despair and anger, even guilt. She might have found it easier to live with the belief that he had died. But murdered, and by someone who had been like a brother to him? What had made her choose a violent death for her husband, at Benedict's hands?

May's words, her description of Nan writing "like someone possessed," came back to me. I might never understand her compulsion to make a murderer out of Benedict and a victim out of my grandfather, but I thought I understood the compulsion that had resulted in *Life Blood*. She had been possessed by grief, and by anger. If she had not transformed those emotions in some fashion, made something concrete from them, they might have destroyed her and damaged her child. I understood that easily enough. The act of writing *Life Blood*, as much as the story it told, was surely a form of catharsis for her, and a way of protecting my mother. And I was willing to bet that, even if Evelyn Allerton's death figured in it in some manner, the novel offered an explanation for Charles's disappearance. When the book was finished, Nan had felt no need to tell the story again.

Until she knew she was dying.

Then, at the end of her life, the story came back to possess her once more. The tales she told me with such passion were variations on themes that must have retained their hold over her for more than thirty years: theft, betrayal, and violent death. These obsessions—that did not seem to me to be too strong a word for them—could only have sprung from Charles's disappearance. What other source could they have had?

I glanced down again at my sketch. I had been drawing the cottage living room, using Willoughby's description of the way it had looked on the night of Evelyn Allerton's murder. The details were in place, the open hearth with the coal fire burning, the sad clutter of old newspapers and dirty dishes, the snow falling outside the uncurtained window, but it was like an empty set waiting for the actors, Evelyn Allerton and her murderer, to appear.

CHAPTER 17

Later that afternoon, Rafe came by after school with Spike. He held the end of an extendable nylon dog leash on a reel, which was attached to the ferret's collar. Spike sniffed about the living room, examining every cranny, trying to squeeze himself through every opening, no matter how narrow. He looked like a large and speedy inchworm humping along, as though his long arched back, rather than his short legs, were doing most of the work.

For some reason, the fireplace in particular fascinated the ferret. "He knows there's a tunnel behind that," Rafe told me, pointing to the panel that blocked off the opening. There was a crumbling bit of masonry on the right side of the hearth, where the stone seemed loose. The ferret stood on his hind legs and nosed aside some small pieces of the mortar, which fell in a shower to the hearthstone below.

"Stop that!" Rafe scolded the animal as he picked him up. "If you wreck the place we won't be invited back." He detached the leash from the collar and tucked Spike into the shoulder bag, then fished in his pocket.

"I brought something to show you." When he held out his hand, there was a triangular piece of whitish stone on his palm. "Go ahead. You can hold it."

I put Max down to play with his toys on the rug and took the stone from Rafe. It fit neatly into my own palm, a smooth piece of what might have been limestone that was shaped almost exactly like a map of Africa, bulging out on the left side, curving deeply inward on the right below a sharp protrusion that looked like the Horn of Africa, and smoothly rounded at the bottom, at the Cape of Good Hope. A blunt ridge of stone ran across its upper third. I turned it over. The reverse was flat and very smooth, and held the perfect fossil of a tiny white shell, a miniature scallop shell, embedded in the center.

Rafe watched me, bright-eyed behind his glasses. "You know what it is?" I shook my head. "It's a tool. Neolithic. Maybe as much as four thousand years old. Look," he said, reaching for the stone, "I'll show you how it was used."

He grasped it with his thumb placed in the indentation on the right side, below the Horn, his forefinger curved across the broad top, and the other three fingers curled around the narrower bottom. "If you hold it this way it can be a hammer. See how it's flattened here?" He showed me the thickest part of the left side, where the edge was smooth and flat. "Then, if you turn it upside down, you can use it for scraping animal skins or something. This end is worn down and rounded, see?" He pointed to the long end of the stone, shaped like the toe of Africa. "Here, try it yourself."

When I placed my hand as he had done, my fingers fit the smooth grooves on the stone so perfectly, whichever way I held it, that I knew he must be right. My thumb settled into the concave groove where, millennia ago, the constant pressure of another thumb had left its mark, like a maker's mark, in the stone. I turned the tool over again and with the tip of my forefinger I traced the delicate ribbed fan of the shell. Each of its tiny radials was a distinct, dark line against the white limestone.

Someone had chosen this piece of stone, I was certain, not only because its shape suited their purpose but because of the shell. A judgment had been made, a discrimination, which had been inspired by more than simple pragmatism, which could even be described as aesthetic. Four thousand years ago someone had found the stone with its shell set like a jewel in the center, and had thought it beautiful.

With the stone's cool weight on my palm, I felt as though I held a life in my hand, a life whose imprint remained and to which I was somehow connected. For an instant, that ages-old past seemed real to me. I could feel my spirit yearn toward it. It was the more recent past, measured in months rather than in millennia, from which I turned away, found so ungraspable.

Rafe began to speak about the fossil shell. "I was thinking that maybe it made the stone seem like a good-luck charm. You know, magical." Behind the glasses, his eyes widened with excitement. "It makes sense, doesn't it? Especially considering where I found it. Like they'd put it there just because it was special, sort of a treasure—" He stopped abruptly and flushed, his gaze dropping away from mine.

"Where *did* you find it?" I thought I knew, however. That guilty blush signified a trespass of some sort, and given what he had just said about treasure, the most likely forbidden ground was Goody Ridler's Tump.

He was looking down at Spike, caressing the creature's smooth head with one finger, his face almost invisible under the long thatch of brown hair falling across his forehead. After a moment, he raised his eyes. "You won't tell, will you?"

"I can't promise that. So maybe you shouldn't say."

"You've probably guessed."

"Probably."

"Don't you see, if I found it there, there might be other stuff?" His voice was pleading. "We should be looking."

"I would be. If it were my property." For all the sympathy I felt, I could not meet his appeal.

His eyes slid away from mine, and he nodded, acknowledging that he understood. But the set of his jaw testified to a mute resistance.

I handed the stone tool back. It was real treasure, I told him. "As good as finding gold."

He nodded solemnly, tucking it away in his pocket again. "I thought you'd like it." Then, mumbled as though it were a confession of sorts, he added, "I'm not going to show anyone else."

"Not even your father?"

"He'd only ask where I found it. I don't want to have to lie to him."

Max was restless now that Spike was tucked away out of sight. He crawled over to us and stood against my leg, clutching at my trousers. When I suggested we all take a walk together, Rafe seemed happy to agree. We could walk part of an ancient pathway, he said, if I liked. It was a track older than the stone tool, made by the first people on the

Cotswolds, the nomadic hunter-gatherers, and used by all those who had come after them.

"Look, I'll show you where it is." He pulled a map out of the side pocket of his shoulder bag. His father made him carry it with him, he told me, so he would always be able to find his way home again from his wanderings in the countryside around Shipcote.

Spreading the map out on the floor, Rafe located Shipcote, a small, pale pink rectangle along the wriggling yellow line of road, with the church designated by a cross and even The Mason's Arms marked by the word "inn" printed in tiny letters beside the blue ribbon of the Windrush.

"Here's Longbarrow Cottage. And here's Goody Ridler's Tump." He pointed to a minuscule square of pink outside the village to the northwest. Directly north of it was the tumulus, with the words "long barrow" in a vaguely archaic-looking script beside a star.

"And this is the track." Rafe's finger traced out a faint line of red dots. It came from the north and ran past the long barrow, jogged west for a short distance along Blacksmith's Lane, then turned south down a valley between two parallel fingers of pale green that signified woods to cross the Windrush at the ford near Withyford church. There it turned west again to follow the old Wychley road, which had been the main road before the modern one was built, up on the crest of the hill, to accommodate traffic unaffected by the winds that blew across the wolds.

I told Rafe that I had walked part of it, the section that included the long barrow, yesterday afternoon with Max. "But I'd like to see the stretch that runs down to Withyford church." He warned me that some of it might prove too bumpy for the stroller, so I put Max in a carrier that I could wear on my back. We went up Blacksmith's Lane, Rafe and I, with Spike's head sticking out of the pouch and Max riding high on my back, each comically like some small patrol on the alert.

The lane was lacy with cowparsley and the starry heads of wildflowers spreading through the green tangle of its steep banks. As we walked along, Rafe described his theory about the long barrow and the track. Like many only children, he seemed perfectly comfortable talking to a grown-up. He spoke with the slightly pedantic air of a child who knows his subject almost too well, and with the eager conviction that what he is saying must be as fascinating to his listener as it is to himself.

His theory involved Dick the Handless. He told me that the highwayman was known to have used the track to reach the old Wychley road, to prey on the coaches that traveled its route, then to retreat with his takings back along the track to safety in Wychwood Forest, a vast wood that once had covered much of this part of the Cotswolds. Legend held that some of his hoard had remained hidden in the forest after his death.

"I think he hid stuff in the barrow," Rafe said. "It makes sense. People were superstitious about the place, so they left it alone. That made it safe. Plus he could get to it easily along the track. Besides, in those days, Wychwood Forest came right down to Shipcote. The barrow would have been in the forest."

"But haven't there been excavations?"

"Sure, a hundred years ago. But they didn't excavate the whole barrow. Only where they found an entrance and a burial chamber. But sometimes barrows had more than one entrance, and false entrances to trick grave robbers. Maybe he found one of those and used it."

"I'd have thought the Mallabys would be curious to know what's underneath. I wonder why they don't let archaeologists dig."

"Maybe because it's theirs." Rafe's voice was suddenly harsh. "I think they like to keep things to themselves. They're always going on about outsiders and how the family's got to stick together. I don't know why anybody'd want to join their stupid family anyway."

The outburst caught me by surprise, and perhaps Rafe as well, for he at once looked shamefaced. "Well, Clarissa's okay. She understands about the barrow. She said she used to try to find treasure there, too—even wanted to be buried there—when she was a kid." He stopped to tug a long stalk of bearded grass from the verge, chewing on it as we walked along. "But sometimes she seems different," he added reflectively, "like someone else. More like the rest of them, I guess."

I was uncertain how I ought to respond, or whether I should say anything at all. There was no reason why I should defend the Mallabys to him when he undoubtedly knew them better than I did, and yet I suspected his judgment of them was colored by the belief that his father was involved with Mela.

As we passed Ashleaze Farm, Pat Ebborn was in the courtyard planting out geraniums in a big wooden tub by the gate. She called out a hello, and Rafe and I stopped to chat. At the sight of us, Stanley, who was patrolling the area, came rushing up, honking and hissing, to defend his territory. After she shooed the goose off, I thanked her for the high chair her husband had brought for Max.

"Just be sure you strap the little one in properly," she told me as she firmed the earth around a geranium. "My oldest was always wriggling out." She inquired after Spike with a genuine interest that patently pleased Rafe. After we'd said good-bye and walked on, he observed that she was a nice lady. "She told me I could go anywhere on the farm, as long as I didn't bother the animals."

"Do you go in there?" I motioned with my head at the dense thicket of trees rising up on our right behind the farm. When he replied that it was a great place for finding salamanders and bugs if you turned over enough rocks, I felt foolish, remembering how I had hurried past it the previous afternoon. Perhaps the presence I had felt there had only been that of a boy in search of salamanders.

In a few minutes, we had passed the entrance to the track that led to the barrow and had come to a thick stand of larch and pine on the left. Here the road dipped sharply down into a little valley before rising up onto the wolds again past a second wood. At the bottom of the valley was a gate opening into a fallow pasture that ran like a green river between the pair of wooded hills. The pale line of the footpath creased the grass, leading gently downhill, away from the lane.

A sign marked the track as both footpath and bridle path. Below it, another sign, hand-painted, stated that as the land was private property all visitors should keep to the track. When I asked Rafe who the owner was, he scowled. "Mr. Fenton. He lives in Withyford Manor. If he had his way, nobody'd be allowed to walk here. I hope we don't run into him."

Gerald Fenton was a land-hungry man, Mela had implied when we met in Wychley, and one reluctant to let outsiders into the village. It was no surprise to learn that he resented this right-of-way across his property.

Rafe shut the gate behind us, carefully looping the rope over the post to hold it in place, and then we set off down the sloping track through lush grass thick with buttercups. The lane was soon out of sight. We were enclosed in a place apart, serene, inviolate, the only sound the liquid notes of birdsong spilling from the woods. Yet it seemed to throb with the invisible life of the past, a green force carried through the narrow vein that ran beneath our feet. As though the primal physical energy of the first wayfarers and all who had followed in their footsteps, Neolithic farmers, Roman soldiers, medieval shepherds, modern hikers, had somehow infused the ground with their spirit.

"There's a place I saw once back home, sort of like this," Rafe said. "A track used by the Indians with a burial mound at the end of it. We went there once, my mom and dad and me. Before."

I asked Rafe if he missed the United States. Sometimes, he replied. Then, almost grudgingly, he added that he liked England, that there were a lot of interesting things to think about, like barrows, for instance. "It's not the States I miss so much," he continued after a moment. "I miss the way things used to be."

Carefully, I said, "My father died a couple of years ago, and then my mother remarried and went to live in New Zealand. She's very happy, I know that, but still . . ."

He looked up at me. "Do grown-ups mind that sort of thing, too?"

"Sometimes. I like Graham, my stepfather, a lot, but I miss my father. And I wish my mother weren't living so far away."

"At least you didn't get a new sister."

"No, but I did get four stepbrothers, four stepsisters-in-law, if that's the right word for them, and so many

stepnieces and -nephews that I'm still not sure of all their
names. On the whole, I'm glad to have more family, even
though they're on the other side of the world. I was an only
child, and it was hard sometimes."

"Not for me." He said this with a kind of defiant bravado. "There were lots of good things about being the only
one."

I smiled at him. "Yes, I suppose there were. Still, I hope
Max'll have brothers and sisters someday."

"You mean, you want to get married again?" He looked
at me thoughtfully; perhaps he found it hard to believe that
anyone would ever want to marry.

"Someday."

We walked on in silence. Once, he squatted down to examine a large beetle on its back in the middle of the path,
struggling with waving legs to right itself. Frowning, he
gave it some gentle assistance with a twig, then watched it
hurry off into the grass. When he stood up again, he said,
"Grown-ups always talk about how kids my age are too
young to make important decisions by themselves. But I
see grown-ups all around me doing stuff no kid would be
dumb enough to do. And they wouldn't even listen to a kid
if he tried to tell them."

"Are you sure?"

Slowly, he said, "Sometimes the truth is hard to tell so
that someone will listen. They don't want to know bad
things about people they like."

I wondered if these oblique references were to the
Mallabys in general or to Mela in particular. I was inclined
to believe it was the latter. But what "bad things" did Rafe
suspect Mela of? An affair with Gerald Fenton, which was,
after all, what I myself suspected? That might explain his
anger and his confusion. Loyalty to his father might make
him feel he should tell him the truth, yet equally Rafe
might be reluctant to hurt him with that truth.

A pair of small blue butterflies danced by, flitting low
over the grass. They settled together on the broad white
head of a stalk of Queen Anne's lace, joined in the oldest
dance of all, the almost invisible trembling of their wings
the only sign of whatever frail sensation possessed them.
Their brief union consummated, they fluttered away on sep-

arate currents of air, wisps of pale blue gauze against the green.

Cautiously, I said, "I think most parents would want to be told if something's worrying their child. But you know, grown-ups are usually responsible for their own happiness or unhappiness. If we love them, it hurts us to see them making mistakes, but sometimes we have to let them work things out for themselves. All we can do is go on loving them." Then, because I was conscious of my own failings in this regard, I added, "I agree, though—it's hard not to feel we should tell them what to do."

Rafe was about to speak when we heard hoofbeats behind us. We turned around to see David Cornelius, mounted on Thatcher, cantering toward us down the little valley. "Don't tell him, please," Rafe pleaded, suddenly anxious, "what we've been talking about."

"Of course I won't."

Reassured, he ran back along the track to meet his father.

CHAPTER 18

David Cornelius dismounted. With Rafe beside him, he walked toward me, leading Thatcher by the reins. He was wearing jeans and riding boots, with an open-necked tattersall shirt whose sleeves were rolled up to his elbows. His leather jacket hung from the pommel of the saddle. He looked like a man who spent all day in the open air, burnished by the sun and the wind; like the horse, he had an elegant, hard-muscled energy, a powerfully physical presence.

"I saw Pat Ebborn in the lane just now," he called out to me as they approached. "She told me you three had come this way. Mind if I walk along with you?"

"Of course not." But the memory of his visit to Longbarrow Cottage the previous night weighed on me just enough to keep me from feeling wholly at ease.

Some of Rafe's worries seemed to evaporate in his father's company. He danced along at our side, eager to talk, wanting me to notice that the hillsides were ridged in parallel furrows, like green corrugated cardboard. Medieval plowing had done it, he said, a team of oxen yoked to a heavy plow year after year turning over the same patch of ground had scored the earth indelibly. "Later this land was turned into pasture and never farmed again. So it stayed like this."

At that moment, the ferret stuck its head out of Rafe's pouch and Thatcher shied away, whinnying. "Spike's making her nervous," David told Rafe. "You'd better go on ahead of us." Obligingly, Rafe ran down the track, and as soon as the ferret's scent had lessened, the horse paced quietly at David's side. When Rafe was out of hearing, David said, "Rafe came into the world telling the doctor the various techniques for cutting the umbilical cord. He hasn't stopped talking since."

"There's a line my father used to quote: 'Silence is the virtue of fools.' Rafe's no fool. I like listening to him."

He glanced at me, amused, and reached out to touch Max's cheek. "Then you'll be prepared when this one starts to talk."

Without Rafe, however, a constraint seemed to settle on us. When the silence threatened to go on too long, I asked him why his horse was called Thatcher.

"Because she always takes her fences. And because she can be as stubborn as hell." He gave a small smile. "Benedict's explanation, not mine. He sold her to me when he decided his riding days were over."

"He was a fan of Mrs. Thatcher, then?"

He nodded. "And a party stalwart. I'm surprised he's never run for office."

I wasn't; not if what Nan believed was true and lay waiting for an enterprising reporter to uncover. "He was a socialist once," I said, "in the thirties. An idealist. I wonder what happened."

David shrugged. "Ideals can age as badly as idealists.

Most of us are idealists when we're young. The trick is staying that way."

"You seem to have managed it. Because of the work you do at the farm park, I mean."

He gave me a sideways, self-deprecating smile. "That's not idealism. That's simple pragmatism."

The right carrier strap was rubbing into my shoulder; carefully, I eased it over a little. Behind me, Max was crooning happily to himself. Curious, I asked David if he liked Benedict Mallaby.

"Yes, on the whole I do. But he isn't someone you can easily get to know. I always have the feeling he's holding something back. Himself, perhaps. He gives the impression there's a tremendous reserve underneath all that smooth, landed-gentry courtesy. Maybe, in his case, manners masketh man. But he's been generous to me. More than." He asked me what my own impression was.

"What you said just now, that he's holding something back." On impulse, I added, "But it's more than that. That he's hiding something." As soon as the words were out, I wished them back again, unsure of his reaction.

He seemed surprised, but said he thought I might be right. "I'd say, at a guess, that it's a deep unhappiness. But then, three of their four children dying . . ."

Rafe called out to us. He wanted to show us some mounds in an earthy bank on the hillside to our left, partially hidden by stunted bushes just below the barbed-wire fence that separated the field from the pine woods. David tied Thatcher's reins to the low branch of a flowering cherry. When we climbed up the gentle incline to investigate, we found Rafe holding on tightly to Spike, who was making low-pitched chuckling noises as he struggled to get out of the pouch.

"Rabbits," Rafe explained. "He can smell them." The rabbits' small black pellets were everywhere through the grass. Low mounds of earth surrounded the entrances to their burrows, which made swiss cheese of this part of the hillside. In their midst was a much bigger hole, the earth in front of its entrance worn smooth and hard, which must have belonged to some large animal. There was a rank smell in the air. Spike could barely contain himself, baring his sharp little teeth and chittering fiercely. He looked and sounded as ferocious as his wild cousins.

"It's a fox's earth," David said, squatting down to examine it.

"Right in the middle of the rabbits' homes?" I was amazed. "And they go on living in them?"

"Rabbits aren't noted for their intelligence," he replied dryly. "The fox leaves them alone at first. They get used to him coming and going, begin to trust him. Then one day, when the hunt has gone badly and his belly is empty . . ."

Rafe had walked a little way off in an attempt to calm Spike. He seemed slightly cast down by this evidence of the rabbits' credulity.

"Hey!" The sudden angry cry broke against the peaceful stillness. Gerald Fenton was striding along the track with the tan Labrador by his side. "Can't you read, boy?" he shouted at Rafe, who was standing uncertainly halfway down the hillside.

David stood up and turned around. "Hello, Fenton," he called out pleasantly. "Sorry if we were trespassing." He joined Rafe, putting one arm over his shoulder as we all walked down the hill to the track.

"Oh, it's you, Cornelius." Gerald Fenton's voice was a shade less furious, but as we approached him I could see that the skin around the nostrils of his long nose was pinched white and his eyes were icy. The dog sat quietly on its haunches at his side.

"You know my son, Rafe, of course," David said when we all met up on the track. "Have you met Miss Treleven and her son?"

"Yes. How do you do." A grudging warmth began to creep into his voice.

"Fine, thank you." Although it had not been a question, something compelled me to answer him as though it were. The scene was stilted, and more than a little ridiculous. He was clearly outraged that we had left the track, as he had every right to be, and I felt as guilty and resentful as any child caught trespassing by the neighborhood grouch. Something, perhaps the simple desire to remain on good terms with his neighbors, was checking his temper, however.

"You breed pheasants, don't you?" David asked him.

He looked startled, and somewhat suspicious of this seeming non sequitur. "Yes. Why?"

David turned and pointed out the fox's earth up on the hillside, half-hidden by the blackthorn bushes. "You might want to do something about that."

"Oh, I see. Decent of you to let me know." The anger had faded away and his long, pale face took on a peculiar expression, as though an effort to be friendly were doing battle with a more customary hauteur. It was the expression of a man who believes himself your superior but needs something from you. "Sorry about just now. Didn't mean to let fly at your boy like that." Abruptly, he said, "I was going to drop by the farm park later this afternoon to see you. Did they tell you?"

David nodded. "I thought I'd ride over and save you the trouble."

The frosty eyes considered this for a moment, almost assessingly, as if it might be a ploy of some sort on David's part. Curtly, he said, "Kind of you. Shall we?" With one arm, rather like a host showing us into his living room, he indicated that we should all continue on together.

While the two men followed, talking desultorily about farming, I walked ahead with Rafe, who kept a glum silence. Max began to fret a little. I handed him the small bottle of juice I had brought.

Soon we came to another gate, where the valley opened up into broad, grazed fields that rolled down past Withyford church to the river. It occurred to me that, with one exception—the most important one, perhaps—all the participants of the little scene I had witnessed the afternoon of my arrival were here now. Gerald Fenton and his dog; David and Thatcher. Only Mela was absent. Yet, subtly, she made her presence felt. We had all fallen silent, and I wondered if the others were also thinking of her, remembering.

Rafe announced that he wanted to show me something inside the church, something interesting. We could go inside, the door was never locked. While the two men stood talking outside the low stone wall that enclosed the churchyard, Rafe and Max and I walked through a rusting iron gate and up the beaten path to a small wooden door in the south side.

Turning the iron ring set into the door, we entered a simple whitewashed space, airy and silent. There were plain, shoulder-high box pews, a pulpit of worm-eaten oak, and an old stone font. Daylight shone in through narrow lancet windows set with faintly colored diamond panes of glass. The interior had the purity of all small and simple sanctuaries, a sense of holiness lingering in the cool, clear light.

What made the place remarkable, however, was the wall painting. Facing the door through which we had entered, it filled one section of the north wall: three crowned men in knee-length robes with an earth-red, skeletal figure lurking off to their right. Behind this emblem of death was the outline of a long, low hill.

"Is that what you wanted me to see?" I asked Rafe.

He nodded. "The barrow. It's Goody Ridler's Tump."

There were handouts on a table by the door, a printed sheet of information about the church. The wall painting was medieval, I read, thought to be based on a cautionary tale of three kings and a specter, whose grim message was, "As you are, so once was I; and as I am, so will you be." The drawing of the hill, the handout stated, was open to interpretation. It made no mention of the long barrow.

When I asked Rafe how he knew it was Goody Ridler's Tump, he shrugged and replied with the sublime assurance of an eleven-year-old, "I just know. What else could it be?"

When Rafe and I came outside again, David was alone, sitting on the wall, while Thatcher cropped the grass nearby. Gerald Fenton and his dog were walking rapidly away westward along the track in the direction of Withyford Manor. Max began to grumble, and I asked David to help me off with the carrier, then took Max out and put him down on the soft, clean grass of the churchyard to stretch his legs.

"Mr. Fenton wants to buy Shipcote Farm Park, doesn't he?" Rafe asked his father while I stooped over Max, guiding his steps over the bumpy turf.

"He's made an offer. I just told him that I'm not interested in selling my share."

"Good. I don't like Mr. Fenton."

"Neither do I. But I'd like to stay on good terms with him."

"He's very rich, isn't he?" Very, his father replied. "Does he have more money than you?"

David laughed. "A lot more."

"Where did he get it?"

"His wife is rich. Unkind people say that's why he married her. But he's making her richer."

"I wouldn't marry for money," Rafe said decidedly. Then, "Would you?"

"No."

"What would you marry for?"

"Happiness," David replied lightly. He reached over and tousled his son's hair. "Have you got marriage on your mind, Rafe?"

But Rafe would not look up at him. "Sort of," he muttered. He plucked a blade of grass and began to chew on it. "Not for me. Someone else."

"I don't know anyone who's planning to get married," David told him firmly. "Okay?"

"Okay." This time Rafe's eyes met his father's, and he smiled.

When we left the churchyard, Max refused to go back in the carrier, drawing up his legs and twisting away in my arms. David suggested Max might like to ride with him, promising to keep a good grip on him. When I said that it was worth a try, David mounted Thatcher and I handed Max up to him, where he sat tucked against David's front, with David's left arm securely around his stomach. For a moment, Max seemed about to protest, but then something made him change his mind. He looked around at David, then down at me, and gave a broad smile of pleasure. "Guh," he said happily, "guh." And when David urged Thatcher forward to a gentle walk, he laughed.

When we reached Blacksmith's Lane, David handed Max back down to me, explaining that he would cross the fields to the farm park. I said I would give Rafe a lift home. Twenty minutes later, as we pulled into the wide gravel drive at Summerhays, Mela was just getting out of her Range Rover.

"What's she doing here?" Rafe muttered from the back-seat. "She's supposed to be in London."

Mela crossed the gravel to my car. She was very lovely, with the sunlight on her hair and that brilliant smile of hers, almost irresistible. Yet Rafe plainly resisted her. I could see his determination to do so in the set of his jaw as he got out of the car.

"Surprised to see me?" she asked him. He nodded, his eyes sullen. "Painters at the office. You never know when they'll deign to appear, do you?" she commented to me with a laugh. "I've come back to escape them. Fax machines make offices practically obsolete anyway. Besides, there are so many interesting things happening here."

Abruptly, Rafe muttered something about needing to do his homework and jogged away across the gravel to the wooden gate set in the high wall. As we watched him go, Mela gave an amused, helpless-seeming shrug of her pretty shoulders. "Boys are such a mystery to me. But you and Rafe seem to have become great friends."

I looked up at her through the open window. "I hope so. He's very likable and very bright. More interesting than many adults I've met."

"He has a remarkable imagination, doesn't he? Quite extraordinary." She gave me a slanting look. "But one can't help wishing he kept it under better control. He does rather tend to get carried away. Makes mysteries out of very little."

Which, I thought, was a polite way of calling him a liar. I said, "You told me you didn't like mysteries. At lunch the other day."

"Did I? I suppose it's not so much the mystery itself as people poking their noses in where they don't belong. Unhealthy curiosity." If she had said this differently it might have seemed some sort of warning, but her tone was light. "I've suggested to David he ought to think about a boarding school for Rafe. My brothers and I all went off when we were nine. We adored it. There really isn't much to do in the country for a child of Rafe's age, except get into trouble."

It seemed to me, although I did not say so, that for a boy with Rafe's interests there was plenty to do. I could see why Mela would be interested in sending him off to school, however.

As I pulled out of the drive, I saw Sophie and Anna coming along the road toward us. From the grim set of Sophie's face, I assumed that the visit to her mother had not gone well.

CHAPTER 19

"Has something happened?" I asked Sophie as we drew up beside her. Nothing good, that much was plain. Even Anna seemed to droop in her stroller, her small face wan and unhappy. Mother and child, each in her own way, looked near some limit or other.

Sophie only shrugged in answer to my question, then said flatly, "I won't stop here tonight. Anna and I are going to London." How? I asked her. "There's a coach to Oxford that comes through Wychley at seven. I'll get the train from there."

I glanced at Anna. She looked so weary that on impulse I invited Sophie to stay at Longbarrow Cottage for the night. Seeing her hesitate, I told her that she would be doing me a favor. "I've been finding it hard to be on my own there after dark. I'd be grateful for your company."

She made a sound of mild disbelief. "Sure. I know who'd be doing who a favor. But thanks, I'll say yes." She put the stroller in the trunk and got into the backseat with Anna. We had not driven more than a few hundred yards, however, before she rested one hand on my shoulder and asked me in an urgent voice to stop. Ahead, a small green Ford was turning cautiously into the road from the lane that Sophie had told me led to Crookfield Farm, where her mother lived.

Leaving Anna with us, she got out and walked toward the other car, which slowed and drew up next to her. At the wheel was an older woman who leaned out of her open window to speak to Sophie. Strands of unkempt, graying dark hair fell beside her face, which was reddened and puffy as though from crying.

The two of them talked intently together for several minutes, once or twice glancing back at me. At last the older woman reached up with one hand to touch Sophie's cheek. Sophie bent down and kissed her, then walked back toward us as the other car turned around and drove off in the direction from which it had come.

"That was my mother," Sophie said as she got in beside Anna. "She was coming to look for us, to drive us to Wychley. I told her I was stopping with you."

"Is everything okay?"

"No. But it's better now." That was all she would say. The tone of her voice discouraged questions.

When we got back to the cottage we agreed that I would sort out bedding and bathe the children while she got dinner ready. The single bed in the middle room was big enough for Anna and herself, she said; she would push it against one wall to keep Anna from falling out. As the children splashed together in the bath, the smell of frying onions and herbs drifted up the stairs.

Max, generally so conservative about his food, ate two helpings of the meal Sophie had prepared. Although it was difficult to see the color come back to the cheeks of a child as naturally pale as Anna, an air of quiet well-being returned to her face as she sat at the table. Sophie had given them a simple stew of vegetables with chunks of bean curd added for protein. She had bought the bean curd and spices in a delicatessen in Wychley that morning, she told me wistfully, in order to make dinner for her mother.

Our dinner was an adult version of the stew she had given the children, with wine and stronger spices added. I was prepared to swallow the bean curd in polite silence but its blandly chewy texture went perfectly with the spicy sauce and the mixture of soft and crunchy vegetables. It was delicious, and she looked pleased when I said so. She told me that she had discovered she liked to cook some years ago.

"I used to help out at dinner parties round here, to earn a bit extra. Do the puddings, that sort of thing. Sometimes I'd be asked to serve at table, too, but after doing it once I always said no. I didn't like the way some men look at you. Like you're there for the afters." She made a small grimace of distaste. "One or two of the women, though, were the worst. Ordering you about like Lady Muck."

Sophie did not tell me her reasons for refusing to stay with her mother, and I did not ask. Given that she had left home before Anna was born and had returned for the first time today, I thought it was likely her mother had been unhappy about her pregnancy and remained unreconciled to Anna's existence.

After the stew, we finished the bottle of wine with a wedge of Camembert. Eventually the wine made me so sleepy I began to yawn. "I've got to go bed," I told Sophie. "Leave the dishes. They can wait 'til the morning."

"I'll just rinse them off. You go on up."

I was too tired to argue. Effortlessly, I fell asleep, and for the first time since our arrival at Longbarrow Cottage, my sleep was undisturbed and dreamless. When I woke up at five and went downstairs to fix Max his early-morning bottle, the kitchen was spotless, the dishes washed and stacked in the drying rack. Just before Max and I dozed off again, a thought occurred to me.

The next time I woke up, it was eight-thirty and Max's crib was empty, but through the open bedroom door I could hear children's noises, happy ones. Anna seemed to be responsible for most of them. Cinching the sash on my dressing gown, I wandered down the hall. Max and Anna were in the bathroom with Sophie. Sophie was sitting on the closed lid of the toilet with Max on her lap, trying to wipe Anna's face with a washcloth, while Anna turned her head away, intently explaining her resistance to her mother. "No soap, Mama. Anna no like soap." The loquaciousness halted as soon as she noticed me.

Sophie looked up. "Max here was standing in his cot when Anna and I went past your room. I figured you might like a lie-in so I gave him some breakfast with us. I hope that was okay?"

"Wonderful." I stretched. I felt normal again, not shell-shocked the way I had for the past three mornings.

Sophie said that there was a pot of tea waiting for me, keeping warm on the stove, which she called "the cooker." As I drank a cup of the strong, dark liquid, I made toast and boiled an egg, which I carried into the living room to eat with the others. In her quiet way, Anna had already begun to mother Max. When he pulled off his sock and tried to put it into his mouth, she gently took it away from him and gave it to Sophie. He did not seem to mind.

"Sophie," I began, "I have a proposal to put to you." This was the product of the idea that had crossed my mind as I fell asleep after giving Max his early bottle. The more I had considered it, the more attractive it had become. It was time, I thought, to establish some sort of schedule for my work.

"Oh, yes?" Her voice was neutral.

I explained why Max and I had come to Shipcote. "This was to be a vacation as much as anything else. Though I'd like to get some work done, too. I thought we'd stay for at least three weeks, but I'm finding the nights here alone difficult. I thought maybe you'd be interested in staying and helping me with Max while you looked for something permanent. We could work out some sort of fair payment for you. I'm flexible about times. I'd just like some free time for my work, and another grown-up here at night."

Briefly, she thought this over, then said matter-of-factly that my proposal suited her. "As long as we're agreed that either of us can say if it isn't working out."

"That's fine with me."

"Right, then."

And so it was settled between us with the minimum of fuss. She would have to go up to London the next day to get the rest of their belongings, which she had left with a friend. I had to go to London as well, I said; we could travel together. I wanted to visit Goddard Grant, the antiquarian bookstore that had sent me the letter containing the offer from its unnamed client to purchase *Life Blood*.

As we tidied away the breakfast things, I remembered

Val Lenthall's invitation to Shipcote Farm Park that morning. When I mentioned it to Sophie and asked if she and Anna would like to come along, she said she would.

When children and strollers were loaded into the car, we drove down Blacksmith's Lane, turning left onto the narrow road that led away from Shipcote. Joined to one another by a line of low stone wall thick with ivy and moss, pretty stone cottages sat behind small front gardens. A contractor's van was parked in front of one that was under renovation. The sound of hammering and workmen's shouts came from the cottage windows that were open to the warm air. Two men stood talking in the front garden. I recognized the taller of the two, with his cold good looks and long nose. So did Sophie.

"Gerald Fenton," she said without enthusiasm. "The parents of a friend of mine used to own that cottage. And her grandparents before them, and so on for at least three more generations. But Fenton offered her parents so much for the place they sold up. They live in Bournemouth now."

"I was warned that he was after Longbarrow Cottage. Do you know him well?"

She made a noncommittal sound. "Well enough. I helped his wife with two or three dinner parties at Withyford Manor. She writes books on famous gardens, talks about 'Vita' this and 'Gertrude' that as if she knew them. She spent a fortune having a medieval garden made at the manor. It was fantastic, I'll give her that. All sorts of herbs I'd never heard of laid out in beautiful patterns. But do you know what Gerald Fenton did? Put an enormous dish antenna smack in one corner of it. He said it was the only place the reception was any good. Susan Fenton would bring people out on the terrace to admire her garden and all they'd talk about was how you could get cricket from India on the hideous thing."

"And he's on the local preservation committee?"

"Only because he likes to tell other people what they can't do. He has the aesthetics of a newt." She giggled. "Someone once said he has an edifice complex. Buying buildings in his sex life."

The road began to climb gently, bordered on the left by a thick beech hedge. A pheasant flew out from the dried coppery leaves, whirring up into the woods on the other side. "I suppose you must know most of the people in Shipcote," I said.

"I used to. Living in a village, everyone knows everyone else. At least they think they do." Her voice was dry.

"Meaning?"

"Meaning you're used to seeing someone about the place, you never bother to take a second look."

When she asked which of the locals I had met so far, I mentioned the Ebborns, who were favorites of hers, and the Mallabys. I told her that Benedict and my grandfather had been cousins. Briefly, I described my lunch at Summerhays, keeping my opinions neutral. "They're an interesting family," I concluded. "I'm not quite sure what to make of them."

As she was in the backseat I could not see her face, but when she spoke her voice slipped into what sounded to my untrained ear like a mock-cockney accent. "You want to be careful with that lot. They'll have you on toast."

I laughed. "Translation, please."

Straight-voiced this time, she said simply, "Don't trust them."

When I glanced quickly at her over my shoulder, her face made it plain she was not joking. I turned back to the road. "Why not?"

"Because they look at everything, and everyone, to see what's in it for them. Mela Mallaby especially." Her voice was stiff with dislike, and something else, a shading of anger. Then, as Rafe had, she qualified her remarks. "The old lady's not so bad. But as for the rest of them . . . Watch," she said suddenly, "the turn's just ahead."

The road crested the hill and brought us out onto the uplands, wide and windswept and empty. A lane forked off to the left, with a sign marking it as the entrance to Shipcote Farm Park. It doubled back down into the valley and then turned west up over several small hills before reaching a plateau where there was a cluster of stone buildings. The largest of these, according to a sign, was a welcome center that housed a gift shop, cafeteria, lecture hall, and office. Beyond was a large modern barn and, stretching across five or so acres of rolling ground, fenced enclosures filled with animals.

A stiff breeze was blowing, fresh with the smell of grass, that carried the babylike cries of lambs and the bass of a cow's complaint. As we crossed the grassy parking area, Val Lenthall was just coming out of one of the smaller sheds. He waved when he caught sight of us, and started over with a small black-and-white Shetland sheepdog trotting at his heels.

"You see we've accepted your invitation, and brought friends," I said when we met up. I introduced Sophie and Anna. "I hope this is a convenient time?"

"Absolutely. Come see our babies." He led the way through a gate to a path running between the wide grassy enclosures. These penned in a variety of animals, goats, pigs, sheep, cows, and horses, many of which had young. The air was loud with the cries of lambs and kids.

We paused to admire a goat with a shaggy golden coat, a long, patriarchal beard, and extraordinary horns that looked like a pair of wings springing from its forehead. It was a Golden Guernsey, he told us. The goat stood on its hind legs with its forelegs resting on the top bar of the fence, peering down at Max, who stood clutching the bottom bar looking up. Goat and child considered each other. Then the goat stretched out its neck and neatly removed Max's hat from his head. Surprised, Max let go of the rail and plopped down on his bottom.

"Here, you've already had breakfast!" Val retrieved the hat before the goat could do more than sample the bobble on top. He took us over to look at twin lambs in a small pen next to the barn. Still tiny, each had the look of a toy, spraddle-legged and fluffy, with bright black eyes set like buttons deep in their curly white fleece. The ewe, who lay in the grass beside them, had some of the charm of her children, with long waving fleece and a calm, contemplative manner.

From across the farmyard, one of the farm workers called to Val. He would be right back, he told us; in the meantime, we should have a look around. The dog hesitated, obviously uncertain whether to go with its master or stay with us. Sophie knelt down and scratched it around the ears. Anna, meanwhile, had noticed that the barn door was slightly ajar. Before we could stop her, she slipped inside. We followed her, and the dog followed us.

The barn was warm and light, and smelled of hay and animal. A man was standing at the far end with his back to us, leaning over the side of a pen. When the dog went bounding up to him, he whipped around, looking angry. It was David Cornelius. Then he saw us and his face relaxed. He grabbed the dog's collar and came down the length of the barn.

"*Quel casserole!*" Sophie whispered, next to me. I gave her a puzzled look. "What a dish," she translated, indicating with her head that she meant David.

"You shouldn't be in here," he said to me when he reached us. "We've got a very nervous ewe who's just given birth. And she's got a bad habit of trampling her offspring to death if she's disturbed." Although his voice was mild enough, there was a shade of annoyance in his face. Sophie glanced at me and mimicked the face of a scolded schoolgirl. He kept his grip on the dog as he escorted us back outside and closed the barn door, tightly this time. Val Lenthall hurried over. "Sorry," he said to David, "I should have warned them."

"It's okay," David replied, setting the dog free. "I think Medea's decided to let this one live." He looked weary, his skin pale, leached of the color glowing in it the previous day. But he made an effort to be welcoming to Sophie as I introduced them to each other, and managed a smile for Anna and Max.

The two men took us around the pens, describing the various breeds, although it was Val who did most of the talking. At one point, riveted by three white kids frisking near the fence, Max refused to budge. While Val took Sophie and Anna off to another enclosure to let Anna see some piglets, David stayed with Max and me. He seemed abstracted, saying very little. I left it up to him to make conversation or not, as he wished; after all, I told myself, a single working parent was entitled to his moods. Instead, I concentrated on the kids, studying the way they pranced across the grass with a knobbly-kneed, long-legged grace, like baby ballerinas.

Val and Sophie were laughing together as they came back with Anna. Sophie looked very pretty, her cheeks pinked by the wind and her dark eyes sparkling. Val seemed taken with her, although the reason for this might have had less to do with her looks than with certain other qualities, for he said to David as they joined us, "She knows as much about pigs as we do." There was admiration in his voice.

"I should," she replied. "I grew up on a farm."

"Around here?" Val asked her. She nodded. "Which one?"

"Crookfield Farm." She watched the two men as she said this. David's face was unreadable, but Val flushed and glanced at Anna. It was clear he had heard some, at least, of Sophie's story. There was a moment's uncomfortable silence, broken by a woman calling out to David from the gate that he was wanted on the telephone in the office. He excused himself and strode away.

Val asked if we would like something to eat. "We haven't much, as the place isn't officially open yet. But the scones are fresh." As we walked toward the main building together, he offered an oblique apology for David's subdued welcome.

"David had the bad luck to be on last night when Medea lambed. She usually tries to live up to her name. Her lambs are always beauties—if they survive their mother's attentions. Then Mela turned up, earlier this morning, upset about something. So he's had a rough start to the day."

Inside, the main building had a broad central lobby, with the cafeteria on one side and the gift shop and a small lecture hall on the other. In the cafeteria, chairs were upended on tables, but the small kitchen behind the counter had two big, steaming urns, one of tea and one of coffee, as well as a heaping plateful of scones. We helped ourselves, pouring milk from a jug for the children, and sat down with Val at the long kitchen table.

I let Sophie and Val do most of the talking while I fed bits of scone and honey to Max and helped Anna with her cup of milk. Val and Sophie shared the same slightly skewed sense of humor and, it emerged, a taste for jazz piano. For Sophie's benefit, I described Val's funny riff in the

Mallabys' drawing room, his musical accompaniment to Spike's capture. When she said she hoped to hear him play sometime, he looked pleased. Finally, after the last sticky patches of honey were swabbed from the children's cheeks, we pushed back our chairs to leave.

As we stood in the lobby, thanking Val for the tour, David came out from the office. He had a small toy for each of the children, a miniature black lamb with a bell on a ribbon around its neck. It was a Soay, he said, a sheep very much like the first sheep domesticated by Neolithic man. "Sheep get a bad press," he added. "Some breeds, like this one, are actually very smart."

"Yeah, but we don't want intelligent lamb chops, do we?" Sophie said shrewdly. "I mean, nobody wants to eat meat that's smarter than they are."

As we were laughing, one of the farm workers came through the main door and beckoned to David. Sophie and I said good-bye then, and went outside with the children.

"Now there's a man who could persuade me to like pigs again," Sophie said.

"Which one?"

"I'm not choosy. Pigs in general."

"No, I mean which man."

"Ah. Well, yours is attractive, but I'm no poacher. I mean the other one. Val."

"Mine? What makes you think—?"

"From the way you were so careful not to look at him—" She broke off, her attention distracted by something in the distance. "Oh, God," she muttered softly.

She was staring at the parking area, where two men appeared to be in some sort of heated discussion. The younger, dressed in rough work clothes and Wellingtons, stood with his hands shoved into his jacket pockets, his elbows tight against his body. The other, a stocky man in a loud checked jacket with matching cap pulled low over curling gray hair, was gesticulating furiously with both arms. In the back of a Land Rover nearby, a dog began to bark. The two men turned and walked toward us, silent now but obviously angry. The one in the cap was Carl Jope. When he saw us, his face shifted into an unpleasant smile.

He nodded to me, then looked at Sophie. "Well, well. Going in for farming after all, are we, Soph'?"

She picked Anna up and made no reply. The realization came to me with a small shock that Carl Jope was her stepfather.

Meanwhile, David and Val had come outside and crossed over to us. "What can we do for you, Mr. Jope?" David said, carefully polite.

"Now that's for you to say. Seeing as your man's pinched my dog."

"That's it in the back of the Land Rover," the other man said. "I found it just now worrying the sheep again, down by Barrowacre. So I collared it and brought it back here."

Offensively slowly and with a mock show of reasonableness, Carl Jope said, "Those sheep of yours were on the wrong side of the fence. If you can't take care to keep your fences in good repair, you can't expect others to look after strays for you. Now can you?"

The young farm worker gave David a worried look. "The fence was cut. We didn't find it 'til now—it was hidden by the hedgerow. Half a dozen had got out. His dog was scattering them."

Val and David glanced at each other. "Did you get them all?" Val asked him.

The other man nodded. "They were in a bit of a state. But the dog hadn't actually attacked them."

"Attack them!" Jope said with disgust. "Course he wouldn't attack them! That dog has more sense than most people."

Quietly, David told the farm worker to let Jope have his dog. "But this is twice we've had trouble from that dog of yours, Mr. Jope. And it strikes me as a strange coincidence that you just happened to be in the area where the fence was cut."

Jope became indignant. "Are you saying I had something to do with that? There are slander laws in this country, Cornelius. Maybe foreigners like you should read them." But his blustering outrage rang false. It reminded me of the theatrical element to his account of Evelyn Allerton's death on the evening of my arrival at Longbarrow Cottage.

"There are laws about destruction of property as well," Val was saying hotly. "And arson."

Jope's face changed, became suffused with dark blood and a genuine anger. The pouchy eyes looked dangerous. He seemed about to reply, then changed his mind and shrugged. Before he followed the other man to retrieve his dog, he gave Sophie a sour smile. "Watch it, Soph'. Some of these breeds don't look so rare to me. You want to be careful about mixing bloodlines." She simply stared at him, her face expressionless. He grinned and went off to get his dog, whistling loudly.

We said an awkward good-bye to the two men. After we had driven in silence for a mile or so, Sophie said, "That's why I don't come back very often."

"It must be difficult," I said awkwardly, "having someone like Carl Jope as a stepfather."

" 'Father' isn't a word I'd ever use about Carl." She was silent for a moment, then told me that her mother had married him when she, Sophie, was fifteen. "I had two years of him, then got out."

"Does he have any redeeming features?"

"Maybe if you're his bank manager. Carl's never been short of cash. Where it comes from is anyone's guess."

She went on to say that she had come to Shipcote only because she had expected Jope to be away. Her mother had written that he was going to a livestock show in Bristol and would stay there overnight. It seemed providential, Sophie said, when she realized she would have to leave Paris. But she had arrived at Crookfield Farm with Anna to discover that he had changed his mind and come home early, in a raging fury because his truck had given him trouble on the way. After a violent quarrel, Sophie had taken Anna and left.

"Why did your mother marry him?"

"I used to wonder that, when I was younger. I thought maybe it was because he saved our farm after my dad died. Now I know it's more basic than that." She paused and then said succinctly, "Bed. Then, anyway. Now I hear he has a woman in Cirencester."

"I see."

"I try not to. That's one of the reasons I left."

There wasn't much I could say to that. As we turned into the drive at Longbarrow Cottage, she asked me why Val had said what he did about arson laws. When I explained, she said surprisingly, "That doesn't sound like something Carl would do. Small meannesses, yes. But arson's a risk in all sorts of ways."

After a pause, she added, less comfortingly, "Still, Carl's probably capable of anything.

CHAPTER 20

The next morning we drove under chilly gray skies to the nearest train station, in a small town not far from Wychley. The uncertain pleasures of traveling with children had the blessing of British Rail; it was cheaper to travel with Max than alone, provided that we took designated trains. At the magazine kiosk, Sophie bought juices and croissants for all of us, while I picked up a pocket guide to London. When the train drew in, we found seats facing each other, with a table between us where we could deposit the snacks and the small toys we had brought along to amuse the children. We stowed the strollers under the seats and sat down. All around us, newspapers went up like barricades.

"So what will you and Max do in London?" Sophie asked me as the train gathered speed.

"Visit secondhand bookstores. And maybe the British Museum." The British Museum Reading Room was a copyright library, according to the librarian in Wychley. Briefly, I told Sophie about my search for Nan's book. When I mentioned that a German air raid had destroyed much of the printing before the book could reach bookstores, she was sympathetically interested; she had read about the bombings.

"I think it was George Bernard Shaw who said the Germans had done what his publishers never could," she said. "Disposed of an entire printing of his book in less than twenty-four hours."

My smile was a bit forced. "He could afford to joke about it. He knew his work would be reprinted. Nan's wasn't."

"So your best hope is libraries?"

"And maybe finding some surviving copy in a second-hand bookstore somewhere. But I have competition." I told her about May's mysterious gentleman, and about the letter from Goddard Grant Ltd. "I'm hoping the bookshop will give me the name of their client. That way I might at least be able to learn what it is that makes the book so valuable."

Sophie's sharp little face was alight with interest. "It sounds like a mystery."

"Literally," I replied. "I mean, the book itself may be a mystery, a murder mystery. That's what May Armitage thought. But I don't know the details." I was reluctant to tell Sophie about Evelyn Allerton's death and my suspicion that Nan had used it in her book, afraid it might put her off staying with us in the cottage.

Sophie brushed croissant crumbs from Anna's face and clothes. "Do you happen to know where your grandmother's book was set?" she asked me.

"Shipcote, I think."

She glanced at me. "I've forgotten if you said when it was your grandmother lived in Longbarrow Cottage."

"I didn't say, but it was 1939 and 1940. She emigrated with my mother in the fall of 1940."

"I see." In a casual voice, she asked if I had ever heard of a woman named Evelyn Allerton.

I gave a wry smile. "Yes, I have. I suspect the book's about her death." I ought to have guessed that Sophie was hardly the type to be spooked by a fifty-year-old murder.

When I confessed my qualms to her, she laughed and said she'd had the same concern about my reaction. "If you'd never heard of Evelyn Allerton, I'd have kept quiet. Nobody wants to know that sort of thing happened in their house. But I did wonder, seeing as your grandmother had lived in Longbarrow Cottage."

"What do you know about the murder?"

"My mum's dad was the local constable at the time. So I used to hear stories. Granddad liked to tell me about his old cases."

"Is he still alive?"

She shook her head. "He died six years ago, just before my father. I'm glad he never knew about my mum marrying Carl. He would have hated it." At that moment, Anna spilled her apple juice all over the table and we had to snatch up the books and toys in its widening path. Cleaning up the sticky juice, changing Max's diaper, and taking Anna to the bathroom kept us too busy to talk until the train reached London.

Sophie refused my offer to treat her to a taxi to her friend's house; the Underground was no problem for her, and she was sure her friend would drive them and their belongings back to the station afterward. Before separating, we agreed on a return train and a meeting place.

Max and I took a taxi to Goddard Grant. The antiquarian bookshop was housed in a narrow, bow-fronted brown-brick building just off Piccadilly. Inside, the shop was narrow and deep, widening at the back into a second, larger room where a fat young man in a suit that was too tight across his back stood on library steps, arranging a row of books. Halfway down the shop another man, rather sleek and vulpine-looking, was talking with a fur-coated woman with lacquered black hair. A book in one hand, he was about to usher her through an office door when he saw us come in. He called out to the assistant, who came to the front desk, where I waited with Max.

The assistant had a plump, egg-shaped face and mild brown eyes. When he asked how he could help me, I told him about the letter I'd received. "The signature was difficult to read, so I'm not sure who I should be talking to. I don't have the letter with me, I'm afraid."

"That's no problem. I should be able to find the information in the computer. *Life Blood*, you said, by J. M. Morrile?"

"That's right."

There was a computer terminal on the desk behind the counter. As he went around to it, the shop door opened and an extremely elderly man came in with slow, uncertain steps, carrying a string bag over one arm. When the assistant called out good-morning to him, he turned and nodded to us before tottering his way over to a table marked "Modern First Editions." The young man asked me how to spell the author's name and then tapped in some letters on the keyboard. After a moment, he said, "There it is. It was Miss Fitch who wrote to you on behalf of our client. I'm afraid she's not in today, however."

I explained that as I was only in London for the day I hoped he could tell me who it was that wanted to buy the book. "I don't have a copy myself. But the author was my grandmother, and I'm pleased someone is interested in her work. I'd like to get in touch with them. They might know more about the book than I do."

His plump face expressed regret. "I'm sorry. We're not allowed to give out the names of our clients. To be honest," he leaned forward and added, more quietly, "it's a question of commission. You do see what I mean?"

I nodded. "But I don't have the book to sell, so it's not as if I'd go behind your back."

He shrugged. "I'm sorry. Perhaps if you spoke with Mr. Grant when he's free—" There was a crash of falling books behind me. I turned around to see the old man with the string bag looking mournfully down at a litter of books on the floor at his feet.

"Oh, dear," the young man muttered, and hurried out from behind the desk. "That's quite all right, sir. No, no, let me do it. . . ." The old man was leaning forward precariously as he attempted to pick up the books. It seemed more than likely he would topple over after them.

On the other side of the counter, the computer hummed softly to itself. I glanced around. The assistant was turned away from me, stooping over the books on the floor, the old man was preoccupied with his apologies, and Max in his stroller was my sole observer. Quickly, I leaned forward across the counter, craning my neck. The green letters glowed brightly on the screen. I scanned the entry: author, title, publisher, and below, client.

Goddard Grant's client was Willoughby Webb Springer. Hastily, I stepped back again. The assistant had been too busy checking the books for damage and rearranging them on the tabletop to notice me. In a moment, after reassuring the apologetic old man with a kind "Quite all right, no harm done," he came back to the counter. He glanced at the computer terminal and then at me, and in the mild brown eyes was a hint of a suspicion. This was probably confirmed when I told him I would not wait for Mr. Grant but would return some other day to discuss the matter with him. "In the meantime," I added, "please tell Miss Fitch that I don't own a copy of the book."

As I left the shop with Max, I felt a mixture of guilt and triumph. And an uneasy confusion. Why had Willoughby felt it necessary to contact me through the bookshop rather than writing to me himself? And why hadn't he mentioned his interest in *Life Blood* when we met at Summerhays?

On the pavement outside, I consulted the index of my guidebook under bookshops and discovered that a number of secondhand book dealers were clustered together on Charing Cross Road. I hailed another taxi. While Max drank his bottle and the West Indian driver talked without requiring any response from me, I pondered the implications of my discovery.

For some reason, Willoughby did not want me to know that he was interested in *Life Blood*. I thought about his casual invitation to meet his famous illustrator friend in Oxford. It might be nothing more than a decoy, a way of getting us together, ostensibly to discuss book illustration, without letting on to anyone, including myself, his real purpose in wanting to see me. But why?

The taxi driver deposited us at the end of Charing Cross Road where the secondhand bookstores were thickest. One by one, Max and I visited each, and in each I asked the same question and received the same negative reply. We came to one whose sign out front claimed that it specialized in, among a long list of other subjects, mysteries. With revived hope, I pushed Max's stroller through the front door.

It was a small, rather seedy-looking shop that smelled of old carpeting, dusty books, and other people's bodies. A girl in makeup so heavy it looked rollered on stood behind the counter drinking coffee from a Styrofoam cup. She glanced up incuriously as I maneuvered the stroller between the tables. When I repeated my request, she told me in flat nasal vowels to try the Valley of Forgotten Novels. "Downstairs, in the long corridor."

I unstrapped Max from the stroller and carried him down the steep steps that led to a low-ceilinged basement with a strong smell of mildew. The Valley of Forgotten Novels was as dismal as it sounded, a cheerless hallway of flaking paint and shelf upon shelf of books alphabetized by author, with curved spines, worn covers, and the look of the unloved upon them. It was the place where books went to die. I was almost relieved not to find Nan's book among them.

When Max and I came back upstairs, the girl was sorting through books with a sudden air of efficiency and a middleaged man with a face as worn as the shapeless gray sweater that hung from his bony shoulders was tossing a Styrofoam cup into a wastebasket. As he seemed marginally more businesslike than the girl, I asked him if the bookstore had a search service. He nodded and gave me a form to fill out, shaking his head in the discouraging fashion I had grown used to when he read the title and author. "Can't hold out much hope, I'm afraid. Still, you never know."

"Do you know how much it might be worth?" I asked him. I explained the circumstances of its printing.

He shrugged. "I've no idea. But I can check." He turned and took down from the shelf behind him a book that, he told me, listed recent prices paid for secondhand and rare books. He paged through the book, pausing once, then shaking his head, before closing it with a little bang. "It isn't there. That doesn't mean it couldn't fetch something. Just that a copy hasn't come up for sale."

I thanked him and left. But my luck was no better in the other bookshops. At last, discouraged and hungry, I took Max into a café for some lunch. We ate fish and chips and then, while he sucked on his bottle, I consulted the map and decided that we would walk to the British Museum. Max fell asleep on the way, perhaps as a form of self-defense against the noise and the sea of legs that swarmed past him.

In the vast entrance hall of the museum, thronged by tourists and schoolchildren, a guard gave me directions to the admissions office for the Reading Room. There I was told that my passport and a photo, which would be taken on the spot without charge, were sufficient identification for a temporary pass. Because Max was asleep I was allowed to take him in with me; if he woke up and began to cry, however, we would have to leave.

The Reading Room was a vast circular space, a well of silence under a high dome, disturbed only by rustling pages and shuffled feet and the occasional scraping of chair legs on the floor. The cupola was painted a cool sky blue, and it rose, like the higher reaches of human thought, from the warm earth tones of the bindings on the books that lined the shelves around the room. Beneath it, enclosed behind a curving desk, sat the librarians. Like spokes in a wheel, the desks for the readers fanned out from this central hub.

I checked the book catalog, found an entry for Nan's book without difficulty, filled out a request form and handed it in. While I waited, I sat beside Max, who slept on, and sketched the room. When the librarian returned, she had the book in her hand. I took it eagerly and opened it up in front of her.

It had been neatly gutted.

Someone had cut away the central portion of the pages, leaving a frame of yellowed paper, so that when the book was closed it appeared intact. But the vandal had scooped out the words from the book like the flesh of a melon, leaving only the rind.

The librarian saw my reaction and asked what the trouble was. As wordless as the book itself, I held it out to her. She was angry, and sympathetic to my distress, but she told me with a weary resignation that she had seen similar acts of vandalism before and was no longer surprised by them. I asked if there was any way of finding out who might have requested the book before me.

She shook her head ruefully. "I'd say this was done some time ago. You can see how yellowed the cut edges are. I doubt that we'll still have the request slip. But of course we'll look into it."

Frustrated, furious with the unknown vandal, and very tired, I left the museum with Max. At Paddington Station, we found Sophie and Anna standing beside their luggage. Fortunately, the two large suitcases had wheels so that Sophie and I were able to drag one each behind us while we pushed the strollers down the platform to our train. We were in good time and easily claimed an empty compartment in an old-fashioned, second-class nonsmoking carriage. Cursing their weight, Sophie and I hoisted the suitcases into the overhead racks.

After the children were settled, Sophie sank down on the seat. "So, did you find a copy of your grandmother's book?"

"What was left of one." Dismay grew on her face as I described the mutilated copy. Before I could tell her that I had, as a small compensation, discovered the name of Goddard Grant's secretive client, Max put his head back and wailed. I checked his diapers, offered him his bottle, a cracker, and finally, to give Sophie and Anna a break from the cacophony, took him out into the corridor. As soon as I was up and moving, he stopped howling, but started up immediately when I tried to sit back down. Sophie and I took turns marching him up and down the corridor while the train swayed along.

The drive to Shipcote was not much better. Max fell asleep in his car seat at once, but Anna took up his lament. By the time we reached the cottage, Sophie and I were exhausted. A single coherent thought pierced through my weariness: that it was lovely to be home.

As we struggled indoors with children, suitcases, and various odds and ends, I saw a white envelope on the mat. I threw it onto the hall table, too preoccupied with getting us all settled and the children's dinner under way to bother with it for the moment. Later, when I remembered it as Sophie and I were about to sit down to our own dinner, the children asleep at last, I found an invitation from Willoughby Webb Springer to lunch at his college the following Monday at noon.

Sophie saw the look on my face. "Bad news?"

"An invitation to lunch. At Martyrs Hall College."

"One just says Martyrs Hall, my dear." Her voice was exaggeratedly plummy, mocking her own stricture. "It's also called The Hall. But one only gets to call it that if one's been there oneself."

I looked across the table at her, suddenly remembering

that Willoughby had called her a promising student. "One has, hasn't one?"

"Umm. Briefly. Until Anna came along. I'm the classic example," she said wryly, spreading butter on her bread, "the girl who thought it couldn't happen to her." Marriage was not an option, she added, without elaborating; neither was going home. "But I wanted the baby. That was the one thing I was sure of. I didn't know why, I just knew I did. Strange."

It did not seem strange to me, however. Sophie struck me as someone who would always know at once what she wanted or did not want, even if the reasons themselves were not always apparent to her.

Little by little, her story came out, or as much of it as she was willing to tell. Four months pregnant, she had dropped out of university to take a job as a nanny in Paris with the married sister of a friend. The couple were in the diplomatic service and had older children. Because they led a strenuous social life, they needed someone living in to see to their children. For this reason, and because they were kind people, they were happy to have Sophie with them despite the coming baby. And they were delighted to discover that they had in Sophie a good cook as well. But two years later the couple were posted to the United States. They arranged another job for her as a nanny with friends of friends, the people whom she'd left four days ago.

"They didn't know the husband was an MTF," Sophie explained as we carried the dirty dishes through into the kitchen.

"MTF?"

"The diplomatic service puts that on the files of men who like to feel up the secretaries. 'Must Touch Flesh.' "

I looked up from the plates I was scraping, amused. "Like the black spot? Death to their careers?"

Sophie gave a short laugh. "Hardly. More a recommendation of what sort of secretary they should have. If they're married, they get an ugly one. If not, not." She turned on the taps and shot a squirt of green detergent into the dishpan. "That's only a guess, mind you."

Sophie's cynicism might be softened with jokes, but it and certain sweeping unfavorable comments about men that she made from time to time must have had their origins in that last employer, the MTF, as well as in Carl Jope. Probably in Anna's nameless father, as well.

After the dishes were finished, we took our coffee into the living room. Half seriously, while I considered whether or not to tell Sophie about Willoughby Webb Springer, I said that I was a little dubious about lunch at an Oxford college. "Maybe you should give me a lesson in passing the port."

"You don't want to take lessons from me. I disgraced myself, remember?"

"Is the place *that* Victorian?"

"Morality wasn't the issue. Intelligence was. Getting pregnant was a stupid thing to do. Having the baby was even stupider. You've no idea how often I was told that. As if I'd failed some sort of intelligence test." She deepened her voice. " 'A poor Third, Miss Dymock. We expected better things of you.' " Then she shrugged. "In my opinion, Anna's a First.

"As for Martyrs Hall, it's out of this world. Literally. You'll see what I mean. It's very rich and beautiful. That can make you feel rich and beautiful, too. Like you have some sort of divine right to the goodies and don't have to pay for them." Her voice was tinged with enough bitterness to make me wonder if Anna's father had been a fellow student. "Henry the Eighth founded the place," she added, with a humorous twist to her mouth, "and his spirit lives on."

She sipped a little of the hot coffee. "On the other hand, it can also make you wonder how you got there and why they let you stay. You keep waiting for someone to tap you on the shoulder. 'Excuse me, but there's been a mistake. You're not the right Sophie Dymock. You'll have to leave now.' It was almost a relief when I found out Anna was on the way."

I was surprised. She seemed the last person to lack self-confidence. It was another oxymoron, that contradictory element to her character. All I said, however, was that she made the place sound formidable.

"I didn't mean to scare you off. Actually, it's a remarkable place—you should see it. You aren't thinking of saying no, are you? I'll be here to look after Max, after all."

"I'm just wondering why the man who invited me is being so friendly. It's not what you're thinking," I was quick to add when she began to smile. "He's well over seventy."

"So? What's age got to do with it? Who is he anyway?"

"Willoughby Webb Springer."

"Oh, in that case . . ." She giggled, and curled her legs up underneath her on the sofa. "Old Webbed Sphincter. Yeah, you're safe enough with him." She saw my look. "That's what we called him, the students, I mean."

"Mela Mallaby called him The Constant Nymph."

"I like that. There *is* something larval about the man. Undeveloped. Where did you meet him?"

At the Mallabys' house, I replied, during that Sunday lunch. I told her what he had said about her, that she had been a promising student. Her dark eyes narrowed. "How did my name come up?"

"Well, actually, it was your step- . . . it was Carl Jope's name that came up. Yours sort of followed." To turn the subject a little, and because I was interested in her opinion of him, I asked her what she thought of Willoughby.

"Bit of a relic from the way Martyrs Hall used to be. Most dons like him have died off." She gave a mischievous smile. "They should stuff him when he goes. Put him in the university museum along with the dodo." Her expression changed, became serious. "He's a collector, rare books, that sort of thing. But I've heard he has an invisible collection as well."

"What of?"

"Little-known facts about people."

"He *is* a biographer," I pointed out.

"These facts aren't for publication. They're so he has something on you."

"That makes him sound like a blackmailer."

"It's not that. More like power."

I thought about the dapper little sheep-faced man I had met at lunch. Maybe, I thought. There had been something unsettling about him. When I told Sophie that he was writing his memoirs, she grinned. "Make sure you don't tell him anything you wouldn't want to see in print, then."

"There's something else, something I mean to tell you when Max threw his fit in the train. It turns out he's the one trying to get hold of Nan's book."

Plainly intrigued, she suggested that he might have vandalized the British Museum Reading Room's copy of *Life Blood*.

"That seems so farfetched, Sophie. He collects books, you said."

"Collectors can be pretty ruthless. After all, the fewer copies there are of a rare book, the more valuable the others become."

"But the book's not valuable to begin with."

"Maybe he knows something you don't."

Later, as I got ready for bed, I took this line of reasoning one step further. The letter from Goddard Grant Ltd. was bound to make me wonder why someone else should want the book, perhaps even make me curious enough to read the book, if I hadn't already. For some reason, I remembered what Mela had said about letting sleeping dogs lie. There was another interpretation that could be given to Willoughby Webb Springer's interest in Nan's book. Rather than letting those sleeping dogs alone, he might, for some reason of his own, be interested in stirring them up.

CHAPTER 21

The following day's mail brought a large manila envelope from my mother. Before leaving Toronto, I had called and told her about my visit to May. Surprised to hear of the existence of Nan's book, which Nan had never mentioned, she promised to look through Nan's belongings and forward to me anything that might be relevant.

Inside the envelope was a letter clipped to four sheets of

photocopying and several newspaper articles. "What a jumble!" my mother wrote, describing her search through Nan's papers. "No wonder I couldn't face it before. Graham egged me on, and mopped up the tears afterwards. There was no sign of her novel, but I'm sending three reviews of it I found. Heaven knows why she kept two of them. They're awful! But they do explain why she never talked about the book.

"Thought you'd like to see your grandfather's letter, too. I'm only sending a photocopy—I would hate to lose the original. It shows how complicated we humans are, that a man who wrote such a letter could go off without a word. Nan must have suffered so, believing at one moment he'd come back someday, then sure that only death could account for his disappearance. Cold comfort either way.

"I don't think the rest of her things would interest you— her nursing diplomas, letters from May (dear, but so boring!), that sort of thing. Won't throw anything out, though."

The photocopy of my grandfather's letter followed, written in a careful, flowing script that was easy to read. It was dated November 8, 1938.

My darling,
Saying goodbye to you last week was the most difficult thing I have done in a very long time. But I am happy to know that you are safely in London now, away from this chaos and misery. You must not feel, as you say you do in your letter, like a deserter. Your work here was courageous and compassionate. If I told you how you are missed, you would only feel worse, but take some comfort from the knowledge you made a difference to many, not just to me.

I had a letter from my old friend Benedict Mallaby the other day, written months ago but held up somewhere along the line. I was overjoyed to hear from him, for when I saw him he was very bitter towards me. He wrote to tell me of the murder of Stephen Allerton's wife, killed last March, soon after I left England. I have seen too much death here and she was too unlikeable a woman for me to feel anything more than a resurrection of pity for Stephen, who died before he was free of her.

Benedict tells me that before she died, she sent him the manuscript of Stephen's book. Benedict's powers of persuasion are formidable, I know, but all the same I am astonished. She had seemed so determined to prevent its being published, so filled with hatred toward Stephen's work and his friends. No matter that she was living rent-free in Longbarrow Cottage. Evelyn never had a sense of obligation to anyone. She was a woman who took what was offered without thanks, only to complain subsequently that it wasn't good enough.

Benedict and I had planned to visit her the night before I left England, to plead with her yet again. I was on my way to Liverpool, to say goodbye to Mother. We drove to Shipcote together in my car, Benedict and I, intending to spend the night with Clarissa Allerton, Stephen's sister. But a blizzard came down suddenly and, fearful the snow might make it impossible to leave the next morning, I dropped Benedict on the high road to make his own way down to the village. The blizzard grew worse, Benedict tells me, and he abandoned the idea of seeing Evelyn that night. She was killed soon afterwards, by a passing tramp it seems.

I confess I was relieved to avoid Evelyn, and to part from Benedict. He and I had argued all the way from London. He believed that I was making a terrible mistake, coming to Spain. Stephen's death had been pointless, he told me, and I was risking my own life fruitlessly. He accused me, as well, of letting him down with regard to the plans we had made to move Longbarrow Press to London. I could have a greater influence on events through the press, he argued, than by driving an ambulance in a foreign war. Obstinate as I am, his arguments only strengthened my resolve. I accused him of abandoning all we had once believed in. That was how we parted, each of us angry and disappointed with the other.

That night seems emblematic somehow of all that has followed in this terrible war. Anger that divides brother from brother, the confusion of motives so that truth is lost, and the sublime indifference of the natural world to our petty plans and desires. But Benedict writes in a spirit of reconciliation. He says we will publish Stephen's book on my return. So perhaps the dreams we had are not quite dead.

Benedict has a set of keys to Longbarrow Cottage. I gave them to him before I left. You must ask him for them if you would like to move to the cottage while you wait for me to return. It stands empty now; Clarissa and Benedict have removed Evelyn's possessions. You and I have seen so much death here; that of one unhappy woman should haunt us no more than any other.

The nights here are very cold now and we lie in the open covered only in our coats. There are no blankets. As I wait for sleep to come, I think of the dead. How often, I wonder, did I fail to save a man who might have lived in someone else's care? Our ambulance is ill-equipped, the roads riddled with holes that add to the torment of the wounded as we transport them, and I lack the necessary skills and medicines that might have eased their pain. You have heard all this before, but such thoughts haunt me now that I am about to leave.

Tomorrow we will drive the ambulance to Ripoll, to see that it reaches the right people. The worst failure would be to let it fall into the hands of the enemy. I still think of them as the enemy, but this war has made me into something of a pacifist, or perhaps it's simply that I no longer am able to see the truth as clearly as I once thought I did. I long for peace, and to be with you again. I miss you more than I can say.

I laid the pages down on my lap and rested my head against the sofa back. Several days after my grandfather had written this letter, he was captured and thrown into a Nationalist prison. Beaten and half-starved, he had remained there for five months. Released at last when the civil war ended in Franco's victory, he was able to make his way slowly back across the Pyrenees through France to England. But apparently his experiences in Spain had damaged him beyond repair.

Tears came into my eyes. A man who all my life had been merely an unhappy shade now had substance, seemed to stand before me vivid and human, speaking to me. This was not someone who would knowingly abandon his wife and coming child; this was a man whose principles would rule his private life as well as his political convictions. I was certain of it.

Turning to Nan's reviews, I found three long strips of yellowing newsprint, each attached to a square of faded green paper on which was printed the name of the clipping service, The General Press Cutting Association. As Nan had emigrated to Canada before *Life Blood* was published, she must have paid the clipping service to send her any reviews of the book. The name of the newspaper or journal from which the review had been taken, *The Sunday Times*, *The Manchester Guardian*, or *The Times Literary Supplement*, along with the date on which it had appeared, was stamped on the square of green paper. All three dates were in December of 1940.

A name on the *Sunday Times* clipping caught my eye. I blinked uncertainly, as though I might have misread it, and looked again. Underneath the headline "New Mysteries" and the subsequent list of four titles and their authors, the reviewer's name stood out boldly and indisputably. It was Willoughby Webb Springer.

My first thought was that it could not possibly be the man I knew. Then I did a quick calculation. If he was in his early seventies now, he would have been in his early twenties in 1940—young, surely, to be a reviewer for a paper like the *Times*, but perhaps not too young. And, unless it was his father, how many other men could there be with that name?

What doubts I had resolved themselves when I read the review itself, which followed the subheading "Sermon on the Mound." I recognized the supercilious tone, which seemed to have remained unchanged in fifty years. His reviews of the three other books in the group gave short summaries of the plots, the names of major characters, and brief descriptions of the settings. His review of *Life Blood*, by contrast, was painfully brief.

One may find sermons in stones, but one does not expect to find them in a mystery story, however leaden. *Life Blood* by Miss J. M. Morrile purports to be a mystery, but it is in reality a homily on loyalty and betrayal sugar-coated with not uninteresting digressions on Druids and burial mounds. Somewhere in all this is a murder to liven the story up when it threatens to become overly didactic.

The plot as a whole suffers from a misguided attempt to harangue the reader into a sense of moral outrage. The characters, occasionally perceived with a fine dry humor, are crudely drawn, and the villain of the piece is a cardboard monster, a creature direct from a "penny dreadful." Although I was never in doubt as to his real identity I did not believe in him for a moment.

Miss Morrile shows some promise as a writer. I can only hope that in her next book she will confine her considerable sermonizing skills to the pulpit.

After a review like that, I thought, who could be surprised that there never was a next book? The unsigned review from the *Times Literary Supplement* was even worse. Here as well, *Life Blood* was reviewed in the company of other novels. It was mentioned last. As in the previous review, this one's only redeeming feature was its brevity.

Miss J. M. Morrile, the author of *Life Blood*, must be congratulated on her ability to transform the spicy stuff of melodrama into half-baked pudding prose, heavy and indigestible. I could no more stomach the style of this novel than I could swallow its improbable plot. If the reader is tempted to persevere through the mistaken belief that a book once begun must be finished, I would recommend that a healthy dose of salts be close at hand.

The third review, in the *Guardian*, was longer—and kinder. So much kinder, in fact, that the reviewer might have been discussing a different book. And with a prickle of excitement I saw that it offered a summary of the plot.

Life Blood by J. M. Morrile is a mystery which aspires to offer more to the intelligent reader than the average yellow-back. It succeeds admirably. It tells the rather familiar story of three friends, young men, idealists all, or so it would appear at first, who vow to work together to promote the brotherhood of man. As in many another such fellowship, greed and betrayal have their destructive, albeit somewhat melodramatic, ways.

Two of the three friends go off to fight in the Spanish Civil War. One of them dies heroically, leaving as his legacy an embittered widow and the manuscript of a novel. The survivor, John Mayhew, comes home from that sorry war to find that the third member of the trio has appropriated the novel, now published and an immediate success, as his own work. The widow of the dead hero, meanwhile, has been killed in her isolated cottage. From the outset of the book, the identity of the murderer is too obvious for suspense. However, the author has sufficient skill to keep the reader interested in the villain's progress.

The portrait of John Mayhew, the main character, is sympathetically drawn. A man of high ideals, he is troubled both by the complex realities of a war whose issues once had seemed clear to him, and by the disillusionment of a friendship betrayed. His conscience determines his course of action. He must reveal the truth, even at the risk of his own life.

J. M. Morrile tackles the vexed issues of socialistic idealism and selfish opportunism with considerable skill. His characters may at times seem somewhat crudely drawn for subtlety but their behavior is invariably interesting. Occasionally his dialogue seems to be a little stiff, but his book never fails to sustain the reader's interest. This is a mystery for those who like their soufflés studded with something they can get their teeth into.

I hoped that this review had eased the pain Nan must have felt when she read the other two. Curiously, the *Guardian* reviewer was under the impression that J. M. Morrile was a man. Willoughby had known better. Had the publishers told him, I wondered, or had someone else?

Restless, I got up and went outside. The sun was warm on the doorstep, drawing up the stiff green shoots of irises that May had planted along the path. Small clouds of bees hummed among the yellow flowers of the boxwood bushes by the door. In the garden, Anna was running circles around Max, who stood tottering, clutching Sophie's leg, laughing at her. Both children were crowned with the buttercups that grew thickly in the grass.

I felt a sudden bitterness, almost an anger. Something, or someone, had cheated Nan and Charles of the chance to stand together in this garden, watching their daughter run with flowers in her hair.

Sophie was staring at me. "What's the matter, Jo? Bad news?"

I shook my head. "Bad reviews. Take a look at these." I gave her the two negative reviews. Max began to pull apart his crown and was looking at it thoughtfully, as though it might be edible. I kept a watchful eye on him while Sophie read.

She winced at the unsigned review in the *Times Literary Supplement.* "Your poor grandmother. 'Pudding prose,' 'dose of salts'! I'd never want to write another word if I got a review like that."

"She never did, as far as I know. The other one's just as bad. Look who wrote it."

Her eyes widened when she saw the name of the reviewer. "Him again!" When she had finished, she stared at me, one eyebrow raised. "If he felt that way about the book, why does he want it *now*?"

"That's what I'd like to know. But the book might not have been as bad as he made out." I handed her the third clipping, then sat down on the stoop with Max on my lap.

Sophie was looking thoughtful. " 'Embittered widow,' it says here. That's Evelyn Allerton, right?"

"That's my guess. Yesterday you said your grandfather was the policeman here when she was killed. Can you remember what he told you about it?"

"Yes, very well." As she sat down beside me on the stoop, a ladybug, prodded by Max, took wing. "Granddad loved to talk about his old cases, especially that one. It was his first real case, you see, and it was such a gruesome one. When Gran was alive, she'd shush him when she thought his stories were scaring me. But of course I'd egg him on, I wanted all the details, the gorier the better." She paused to admire Anna's bouquet of dandelions and buttercups. "That's lovely,

Annakins. Why don't you add some of those violets we saw just now, over by the wall." When Anna had wandered off in search of the violets, she went on. "Granddad was just a young bobby at the time. Never dealt with anything more exciting than the disappearance of the local cricket cup. There'd been a heavy snow, and he noticed her front door was open . . ." She stopped, aware no doubt as I was of the door behind us, its painted oak seemingly so solid and secure. "Look, Jo. Are you sure you really want to hear this?"

"Yes. But it might be easier somewhere else. Let's go for a walk." We decided to walk down to the village shop to buy ice cream for the children. Lulled by the warm sun and the bumpy rhythm of the stroller's wheels, Anna fell asleep almost as soon as we came out into the lane.

"Well," Sophie began, "it was two days after a big snowstorm. It was near the end of March but you can get snow here as late as April. A sudden drop in temperature and a storm blowing in off the wolds. It can bury a place like Shipcote, down in a valley. Seems unthinkable on a day like this, doesn't it?"

It did. As unthinkable in this warm and gentle landscape as violent death. The only sign of passion was the struggle waged over a worm by two robins in the grass below the hedgebank.

"Granddad was going round the village, checking up on all the old people and anyone living alone. He comes up the lane to Longbarrow Cottage and sees the door open. And thinks, Oh-oh. The path to the door is knee-deep in snow and it's obvious no one has gone in or out of the place since the storm. But he hesitates. He's young and she has this reputation, you see, for giving the rough edge of her tongue to anyone she thinks might be poking their nose into her affairs.

"He tells himself he'll come back later. If the door is still open, then he'll know something's wrong. He's about to continue on up the lane to Ashleaze Farm but the wind is skimming the snow off the drifts. No one, not even a daft creature like her, he thinks, would leave their door open on such a day. Besides, there's no smoke coming from the chimney. So he forces himself to go on up to the cottage.

"The door's wide open. Drifts of snow have blown into

the hall. It's bitterly cold inside. Like the grave, he thinks, and he knows something's terribly wrong. He calls out her name, but all the while he's thinking, What's the use? The cold's killed her, he's sure of that now. He's just hoping he'll find her in bed, so she won't be too dreadful to look at. So he starts upstairs and the first thing he sees is clothes strewn about everywhere. Her bedroom is wrecked, but she's not in it. She's nowhere at all upstairs.

"He's quite frightened now and he doesn't want to stay but he knows he has to. So he goes back downstairs and into the living room. And there she is. Lying by the fireplace, blood everywhere. And she's staring at him. He thinks she is anyway, and he runs back outside and is sick in the snow."

We had reached the bottom of the lane. Sophie broke off a small spray of lilac from a bush growing over a garden wall and gave it to me, as though she knew I could almost smell the blood and the vomit. With the scent of lilac sweetening the air, we turned right onto the main road into the village.

"After a while," Sophie continued, "Granddad went back into the cottage and did what he had to. First, he made sure she really was dead. He said the poker had been used to kill her. It was still lying there on the floor. The room was an incredible mess, books pulled off the shelves, crockery smashed. And the kitchen was worse. A window was broken and swinging open, the cupboards all ransacked. Snow had blown in and it was as cold inside as out. Of course, he was bound to think that someone had broken in, killed her, and then turned the place over looking for valuables.

"He was too young and inexperienced to handle the investigation. The police in Wychley did that. But he was involved. It looked like food had been taken from the larder—later, when the snow melted, they found some tins dropped in the lane. Then some of her belongings turned up a couple of months later at a pawnbroker's in Liverpool. So the police figured it had to be a tramp. Even though she had a bit of a reputation for crankiness, there was nothing to prove anyone local had enough against her to do her in."

"Did they figure out a time of death?"

"I remember Granddad saying it was like a refrigerator

in the cottage. That preserved the body longer than usual. But the coroner said she died the night of the storm. Someone had seen her around teatime that day, in the garden. Then one of the local children confessed to throwing snowballs over the garden wall the next day, and noticing the open door then. But he didn't say anything to anyone because he was terrified of her."

"People round here locked their doors for a while after that, Granddad said, 'til the war gave them something else to think about."

Evelyn's murder had occurred on the night Benedict and Charles had planned to visit her. In his letter to Charles, however, Benedict had implied that it had happened sometime later. He had lied.

CHAPTER 22

A dog barking at us from behind a low wall as we passed by startled Anna awake and frightened Max. They fussed until we distracted them by letting them throw stones into the brook that crossed the village green. Nearby was a public telephone in its bright red booth, and while Sophie watched the children, I called British Telecom in an attempt to find out why it was taking so long to connect the cottage phone. An operator informed me that the order was in the computer and that a service van should be around either that day or the next. Only partly reassured, I hung up and joined Sophie and the children watching for minnows in the brook.

On the other side of the green was the village shop and post office, one half of a pair of joined stone cottages. Sophie told me that Shipcote was unusual in having a shop; most villages its size no longer did. Formerly owned by an elderly couple who had been quietly starving to death on its meager income, this one had been all but finished off by the opening of a giant supermarket outside Wychley. A Pakistani family had bought the cottage with its moribund business and post office license.

The place might not have been all things to all customers but it made a valiant effort. Its tiny space was crammed with racks of newspapers and magazines, shelves stacked with staples like flour and sugar or odds and ends like greeting cards, wrapping paper, thread, disks of wax for jam making, penny candy in large glass jars, and a freezer full of ice cream and frozen foods. It smelled good, of spices and chocolate.

A plump, pretty woman in a long blue sweater over a pink sari came smiling out to greet us from behind the post office counter at the back of the shop. Her thick black hair was neatly parted and pinned up on her head. When she saw Sophie, her smile broadened, her teeth strong and white against her dark skin. "Amir," she called out, "come and see who it is here."

Her husband appeared through a curtain that divided the shop from the rest of the downstairs, a thin, rather stooping man with graying dark hair and a gentle face. Both of them made a fuss over Sophie, repeatedly telling her how happy they were to see her again, and over Anna. "We are so glad to meet her at last," Mrs. Hussein said. "Your mother always brings in the photographs you send her."

Sophie inquired after the three Hussein children, who were at school, and introduced Max and me. "Jo lives in Longbarrow Cottage. You know, Miss Armitage's old place. I'm staying with her."

"Ah yes," said Mr. Hussein, "we had heard. We were very sorry to lose Miss Armitage. But"—and here he looked benevolently at Max and Anna—"the dear lady herself would surely have said that to gain such beautiful children is a blessing." Both the Husseins pressed sweets on us for them. I bought more perhaps than I actually needed, but the little shop was as seductive, in its domestic way, as Aladdin's cave.

As we were paying, a tall, middle-aged woman in a quilted jacket and patterned head scarf, with a small white dog clasped to her chest, hurried into the shop. "Ah, there you are, Mr. Hussein," she began loudly, as though he had been attempting to hide from her and she'd had to track him down. She had a high-colored, handsome face with a nose like the beak of some bird of prey.

Beside me, Sophie was showing Anna the pictures in a comic book while we waited as Mrs. Hussein rang up my bill. At the sound of the woman's voice, Sophie's head came up and she swore softly. Mr. Hussein, who was arranging a display of greeting cards in a revolving wire stand, greeted the new customer politely, but without the warmth he had shown Sophie.

"How are you today, Mrs. Fenton?"

"Dreadful. It's one of those tiresome days when everything simply falls apart. My cook is ill and the Pony Club mothers are coming to luncheon. And I've just discovered that my husband has gone off and left me without—" Then she noticed Sophie and interrupted herself. "Why, it's Sophie Dymock. Someone told me you were back."

"Hello, Mrs. Fenton," she said without enthusiasm.

The woman's appraising look took in the black layers, the kohl, and the hennaed hair, and yet somehow managed to avoid resting directly on Anna. "I'd hardly have known you, Sophie."

"I'm carrying a little extra weight these days," Sophie replied dryly. She hoisted Anna higher in her arms.

Mrs. Fenton's embarrassed glance slid past Anna. "Yes. Well. You've been in Paris, I understand."

"That's right." With a look at me that I interpreted as a plea to hurry up, Sophie edged past the woman toward the door. I began stuffing my purchases into the carrier bag I'd brought with me. Mrs. Hussein helped me, gave me my change, and smiled good-bye as I thanked her and followed Sophie.

"As you're back," the woman's voice pursued Sophie, who by this time had the door open, "perhaps you'd like to give me a hand on Friday. We're giving a dinner party, and my husband still talks about your profiteroles . . ."

Sophie paused, turned, and said innocently, "He hasn't left you, then?"

"What?" Mrs. Fenton looked astonished, and also, I thought, a little unnerved. "Where on earth did you—"

"Just now, you said—"

"Oh, that." The woman's laugh was tinged with relief. "No, no, you misunderstood. I was only going to say that Gerald fed the last tin of dog food to Carlyle this morning, and left me without any in the house. Poor Carlyle is absolutely ravenous. That's why I'm here, Mr. Hussein. I'm in a frightful hurry. The Pony Club luncheon, you see."

Mr. Hussein inclined his head courteously. "Certainly, Mrs. Fenton."

The little dog gave a low growl as Mr. Hussein reached past its owner to retrieve a can from the shelf. "Oh, dear" was her response when she saw the brand. "Carlyle is very particular. Well, if it's all you have . . . Oh"—seeing Sophie about to escape—"about the dinner party, Sophie . . ."

"How very kind of you to invite me, Mrs. Fenton," Sophie said sweetly. "But I'm afraid I'll be busy that night." She waved to the Husseins and slipped through the door.

Mrs. Fenton's handsome face expressed a baffled uncertainty. Clutching the dog, she stood there looking at the closing door as though she were trying to make up her mind whether Sophie had been rude or merely ingenuous.

Sophie was waiting for me outside, next to a large black Peugeot blocking access to the pillar box. Seeing my questioning look, she said, half-repentantly, half pleased with herself, "That was naughty, I know. But she looked right through Anna as if she didn't exist."

"It's hard to imagine Gerald Fenton getting enthusiastic about anything," I said as we pushed the strollers back through the village, "let alone profiteroles."

"Oh, he can be very enthusiastic about money. And property. He loves property. He made an offer for the farm once, after my father died. Carl talked Mum out of it—it would have interfered with his own plans. But sometimes I wish my mother had accepted Fenton's offer." She was looking down at the top of Anna's fair head so that I heard but did not see her bitterness. "Carl hates Fenton. Says he's out to own the whole village. Of course, Carl rarely has a good word to say for anyone." She paused, and added in a quiet voice that in her opinion the village was long overdue for another murder.

I glanced at her. "Any victims in mind?"

"I can think of a few." Her voice was mischievous now. "It's too bad we haven't got your grandmother's book. It would be interesting to see how she used the murder."

"I think I know how she used it," I replied. "She used it as revenge."

"Revenge?" Sophie paused and stared at me. "What do you mean?"

I told her about Nan's story of the three brothers and the parallels I was increasingly seeing between it and my grandfather's relationship with Stephen Allerton and Benedict Mallaby. "I'm convinced that she used what she knew, and what she suspected, as the basis for the plot of *Life Blood*."

The explanation seemed to me simultaneously more compelling and increasingly farfetched. It was like a story out of Alice in Wonderland, perfectly logical to the teller, absurd to the listener. "I'm not saying any of it's the truth. Obviously, Benedict did not steal Stephen Allerton's work. The reverse, if anything—he may be why the book survived. But Nan felt compelled to make him the villain."

Sophie helped Anna out of the stroller and watched her run up the lawn toward the front door. She looked at me. "For revenge, you said. Revenge for what?"

"For killing her husband." Then I took the photocopy of Charles's letter out of my purse and handed it to Sophie. "I'm not saying he did, but I think this might be why she believed he did."

When Sophie had read it through, she gave it back to me, saying, "I see what you mean. Your grandfather knew Benedict was planning to see Evelyn the night she was murdered."

"Benedict told him he never got there. Maybe that wasn't the truth. When Charles came back to England he might have found out that Benedict had lied to him. Then confronted him."

As we went into the house, Sophie looked thoughtful. "So the Benedict character kills the Evelyn character. Then he kills the Charles character to cover up the first murder.

But why does he kill the Evelyn character in the first place?" Before I could reply, however, she answered her own question. "To get the manuscript, right?"

"I think so."

"That's a bit extreme, isn't it?"

"Perhaps it was an accident," I said as we went upstairs to the bathroom, where we took turns washing off Max and Anna at the sink. "Maybe she wouldn't give the manuscript up. Even threatened to burn it. You know, that might explain why she was killed beside the fireplace."

"An accident with a poker?" Sophie's voice was incredulous. "To a log maybe, but a human skull?"

"This is all speculation anyway. It's a novel, not necessarily the truth. Oh, Max, you're not supposed to eat that." I removed the cake of soap from his mouth, remembering the allure of the translucent Pears soap from my own childhood. It had always seemed to me as tempting as an oversize fruit jelly. He looked surprised by its flavor, smacking his lips together with a kind of experimental relish.

"If that was her plot, it was libelous, surely?" She handed me a towel for Max.

"Not if she was very careful to disguise the facts. I put two and two together because she told the same story over and over again when I was a child. Maybe nobody else would see the parallel."

"Except Benedict. And anyone who knew them all."

"Which was the point, of course. To let them know she knew." Max pushed the towel away and put his arms around my neck. As the four of us went downstairs, I added, "Part of the satisfaction might have come from believing there was nothing Benedict could do about it. After all, suing for libel only draws attention. But Benedict was lucky—the Germans made sure most people never got to read the book."

"And reviews like Webb Sp;ringer's took care of the rest." She paused, and glanced at me. "What about old Webbed Sphincter? After all, he knew the people involved, and he wrote the review." We were in the kitchen now, preparing the children's lunch. The room smelled of the soup Sophie had made earlier and left to simmer during our walk. She was cutting bread from the loaf we'd bought at the shop, chewing on the heel as we talked.

When I replied that I had been wondering about Willoughby Webb Springer myself, she went on to suggest that perhaps he had written the anonymous review as well. As another thought occurred to her, she grew excited, flourishing the soup ladle in the air. "Benedict may even have put him up to it, to make certain no one read the book. After all, it couldn't have been nearly as bad as he makes out. Not if the favorable review is anything to go by."

"It's an interesting idea." I set the children's bowls of soup on the counter to cool. Eager for their lunch, Max and Anna were banging their spoons on the table. "But why," I asked her over the noise, "would he be so obliging?"

"For all sorts of reasons. To do a favor for his friend Benedict. For money. Because he hated your grandmother. Who knows?" She tied bibs around the children's necks and put their plates in front of them. A silence fell, broken only by the sounds Anna and Max made as they spooned up their soup, the clinking of metal on china, a soft slurping noise from Anna, a louder one from Max.

Nan might have been right about Benedict, Sophie told me. "When Granddad had had a pint or two, he would go on about how he was sure Evelyn Allerton's killer was no tramp at all but someone from the village. But the police never could find a motive to link any one person with the murder. People were afraid of her, some even said she was a witch, but you can hardly arrest someone for that.

"I'll tell you something else," she added. "He thought there might have been two people there that night."

"Two? What made him think that?"

"The open door. The murderer would have closed it, to give himself more time until people began to miss her. Why call attention to the place, after all?"

"Carelessness?"

"Perhaps. But Granddad said he noticed something as he left the cottage. There was a depression in the snow by the front window, the one that looks into the living room. As if someone had been standing there a while, looking in, and packed the snow down. It had filled up again but you could see a difference. The trouble was, by the time he thought to mention it, the others tramping round the place had tramped over it. Then he couldn't be sure."

"Maybe it was the murderer, waiting until she went upstairs."

"Then why not smash that window, instead of the one in the kitchen? It's closer to the ground after all, and larger."

Any further discussion was abruptly halted by Anna telling us to look at Max, who was sitting in his high chair, smiling hugely, with the soup bowl on his head.

CHAPTER 23

Rafe turned up the cottage later that afternoon. The shoulder pouch hung flat against his side. "No Spike?" I asked as I invited him in. He pointed to a bulge in one of the deep pockets of his oversize battle jacket. "He's asleep."

In the living room, Max was sitting on the floor while Sophie and Anna circled him singing "Ring Around the Rosie." Max's contribution to the game was a happy but piercing screech, which grew louder when he saw Rafe. "Poor Spike," I said to Rafe. "He won't be asleep much longer."

Rafe assured me the noise wouldn't bother his pet. "Ferrets sleep so deeply you think they're dead. You can pick them up and they're totally limp. They don't wake up right away either, so you have to be careful not to frighten them. That's when they can be dangerous."

As he spoke, he was gazing at Sophie with mingled admiration and unease, as though she herself were an exotic and slightly dangerous species. She was wearing a long black T-shirt with a fluorescent orange tiger printed on the back, over black tights and knee-high lime-green leg warmers. The ship earring had been replaced by a tiny gold bird cage hanging on a thin gold chain, which had been given to her by an American admirer in Paris. The cage contained what looked like the skull of some tiny creature but was instead, Sophie swore, only the dried husk of a seedpod.

When I introduced them, Rafe seemed to know that they were staying with Max and me, from his father perhaps, for he politely observed that it was nice for Max to have someone to play with. "Even if it's a—" he started to say, then stopped and flushed. The unspoken word, "girl," hung in the air. To prevent Sophie's thinking that he might have meant something more unkind, however, something specific to Anna's paternity, I explained that a new baby sister had given Rafe certain reservations about females.

"Oh, yes?" Sophie glanced up at him as she wiped Anna's nose. "I thought they were educating you kids better these days."

Taking her seriously, Rafe was flustered and began to say that girls were fine, as a rule, it was just sisters. . . . Then he saw the humor in her eyes. With a grin, he added, "Yeah, well, if she hits as hard as the girls at my school do, I guess she'll be okay." He turned back to me, his face mildly accusatory. "I came by yesterday, after school. But you weren't here."

While I was explaining that we had gone to London for the day, I caught Sophie's look of quizzical amusement. She had registered Rafe's slightly possessive tone. I was sorry we had missed him, I told him, but was very glad he was here now. "Sophie and I were just saying that we could use a strong right arm to help us move some furniture." We had decided that the small chest of drawers in the empty downstairs room would provide extra space for Sophie's and Anna's belongings, most of which still remained unpacked in the two suitcases.

Eagerly, Rafe offered to start at once, carefully taking off his jacket and looking around for somewhere to lay it. He shook his head when I suggested the sofa. "Somebody might forget he's there and sit on him." He saw Sophie's puzzlement and explained the jacket's contents, reassuring her that Spike was tame. Then he turned and asked me earnestly if I knew what one of the leading causes of death for pet ferrets was.

"Being sat on?" I hazarded.

"La-Z-Boy chairs."

Sophie and I couldn't help but laugh. I said, "You mean they rock themselves so deeply to sleep that they never wake up?"

His reproving look shamed me. "They like to get inside them and go to sleep. Then someone comes along, sits down in the chair, and—" With an expression of horror, Sophie held up one hand and told him she could imagine the rest.

The wicker basket by the fireplace, which contained a small heap of old newspapers, seemed to be the safest place for Spike. Gently, Rafe laid his jacket down, then helped us shift the chest of drawers upstairs. Afterward, we all sat around the dining room table eating the jam-filled sponge cake Sophie had baked during the children's nap, while she and Rafe discussed the local fauna. He was thrilled when she told him the best places locally to find lobster moth larvae. The formic acid squirted by this aggressive and very unappealing-sounding insect could, he informed me, stun a small bird. As a third piece of cake disappeared into his mouth, Rafe was obviously falling under Sophie's spell.

In the meantime, Spike had waked up and emerged from the jacket pocket. The chink of falling mortar by the fireplace was the first warning we had of his explorations. When we looked around, he was nosing at the crack that had fascinated him the other day. Then, like a metamorphosed Houdini, he seemed to force himself into the stone. In the next instant, he vanished.

"Oh, no," Rafe groaned as he rushed over to the fireplace.

"I can't believe he did that," Sophie said. We stood staring at the spot where the ferret had been only a moment before. A long crevice between the stones lay exposed, but it was little more than an inch wide and it seemed impossible that any animal as big as Spike could squeeze through such a narrow space.

"Ferrets can squeeze through anything. Their heads will flatten." Rafe looked gloomy, pride in his pet's abilities tempered with anxiety. When I asked if Spike would come out on his own, he confessed miserably that the ferret might very well decide to curl up and go back to sleep, possibly for hours. Rather desperately, I asked if there was a way to lure him out.

Rafe's face brightened. "Have you got anything sweet? Honey's the best. He loves honey."

I fetched the jar of honey and a long-handled spoon from the kitchen and gave them to him. He dipped the handle end of the spoon into the honey, twirled off the excess, then squatted down and poked the spoon handle into the opening. Tapping the spoon from side to side on the stone, he made a clucking noise, then held the spoon still. We waited, but there was no response. Either Spike was refusing to be lured out, or he had already gone back to bed, or he was somehow trapped behind the stone. By now, Rafe looked close to tears.

"Maybe we can get the stone out," I said. "The mortar looks like it's loose all the way around." The stone itself was a rough, soot-darkened rectangle about the size of a large loaf of bread. Using a screwdriver and a heavy kitchen knife, Rafe and I scraped at the crumbling mortar. In a few minutes, we had cleared most of it away.

As I tried to prise the stone free with the screwdriver, Rafe pleaded with me to be careful, afraid that Spike had found himself in a space so tight he had no room to maneuver. Gingerly, I wiggled the stone back and forth like a loose tooth until it began to move forward and I was able to lift it out and set it on the hearthstone. It left a gaping, and completely empty, space.

Then, to our left, we suddenly heard a scrabbling noise and a series of excited squeaks coming from behind the cast-iron panel that blocked the opening of the hearth. Somehow, Spike had got into the fireplace.

"I don't think we're going to be able to get that panel off by ourselves," I told Rafe, who was trying to twist the rusty bolts that held the plate to the stone with his fingers. He nodded unhappily and offered to call his father.

Explaining that the telephone was still not connected, I said I would drive over to the farm park. He should stay with Sophie and the children in case Spike reappeared. As I walked out to the car, however, William Ebborn came up the lane in his truck. I waved and called out to him, and he pulled over into the drive. When he heard the story, he gave a short, incredulous laugh but was quick to offer his help, promising to come back as soon as he had collected some tools from Ashleaze Farm.

On his return, he seemed unsurprised to find Sophie and Anna at the cottage, greeting them both with a kindly matter-of-factness. Then he set his canvas bag of tools down on the hearthstone and examined the iron plate and its bolts. It would be a slow job, he told us, for he would not be able to use power tools. "Wouldn't want to hurt the little creature."

As he worked patiently, we could hear Spike rustling and scratching behind the plate. "Do you think he'll go up the chimney?" Rafe asked anxiously.

"He won't get far," William replied. "Not if the damper's closed. There'll be a net across the pots as well, to keep the swifts and starlings out. So he'll not be able to get onto the roof."

After half an hour's hard work, he had the last bolt out. I helped him lift the heavy piece of metal away, and as we did, Spike bounded out into the room. He sat up on his hind legs, chittering happily at us, his coat filthy with the dried leaves, cobwebs, and ancient bird droppings clinging to it. Beaming with relief, Rafe picked him up and scolded him in a crooning voice, cuddling him under his chin, then took him out to the kitchen to clean him off.

"You've a fair mess in that hearth," William said. "There's a lad I know, a chimney sweep. I'll send him over to you, shall I? Now that it's open you might as well use it." He refused my offer of cake, brushed aside my thanks, and when I said that I wished he would let me reciprocate in some way, observed that there would doubtless be plenty of opportunity for that.

Before he left, he told Sophie to bring Anna up to Ashleaze Farm for a visit. "Glad you're back," he added, almost shyly. "The wife was just saying it had been too long." Her smile was affectionate as she promised to come around soon.

William and I carried the plate out to the garden shed to get it out of the way; reinstalling it might be difficult, he said, given the state of the bolts. Then I walked with him to his truck. "Nice girl, Sophie," he said as we went down the path. "Hope she'll stay for a bit. It always seems a pity when the younger ones leave the village. Like seeing life go out of the place. But her stepfather, now ... well, he won't be welcoming her back with open arms. Carl Jope's not a forgiving man." He rubbed the back of his neck with one large hand, his weather-beaten face grave. "Let me know if there's trouble from that direction. I'll do what I can."

Disturbed, I asked if he thought Jope would bother her.

He shrugged as he climbed into the truck. "Take it out on her mother, more like." Then he started the motor, lifted his hand in farewell, and reversed slowly down the drive. I went indoors to find Rafe making a strenuous effort to sweep up some of the dust and dirt with a broom, with Spike tucked into the bag hanging from his shoulder. Rafe's subdued expression suggested that he was feeling responsible for Spike's mischief, and he began to apologize when he saw me. I told him Spike had done us a favor; we could have a fire now.

"It's big enough to roast an ox in," Sophie said, peering into the wide stone space. Suddenly, she leaned forward, her attention caught by something on the right interior side. "There's some sort of recess here."

When Rafe and I looked in, we could see the alcove in the wall of the hearth, about a foot square and two feet off the floor of the inner hearth. "Perhaps it was used for slow-cooking or keeping food warm," I suggested. Rafe stretched out one hand and ran it over the stones. "There's a kind of hole at the back. That must be how Spike got through into the fireplace." He wiped his dirty hand on the leg of his jeans, leaving a long dark smudge on the cloth.

Anna and Max had watched the entire proceedings with fascination, as though it were entertainment laid on especially for them, but Anna now came over to her mother and announced in a soft voice that she wanted her supper. On cue, Max began to fuss. Rafe picked up his coat and said good-bye, politely but firmly refusing my offer of a lift to Summerhays, still obviously downcast despite my efforts to convince him that no one minded Spike's adventure.

Several hours later, when the children were asleep and

the dishes done, I was able at last to take out my sketch pad. Sophie was upstairs transferring the contents of the suitcases to the chest of drawers. I'd had an idea for a new picture book, the glimmer of a scene provoked by the picture of Rafe cradling the rescued Spike. But as I sketched, my thoughts wandered to the irresistible puzzle of Nan's book.

Sophie's description that morning of her grandfather's account of the murder had been so vivid that it seemed immediate, rather than secondhand. *Life Blood* no longer seemed to me a work of fiction. Yet it was hardly fact. It existed, instead, in that undefined and dream-filled territory that lies somewhere between the two, where the imagination spins the stuff of fantasy from the thinnest of threads.

I put the drawing aside and stood up. For the first time, I cursed my imagination. I had come to Shipcote for release from pointless speculation, only to find myself increasingly consumed by an equally futile obsession with someone else's tragedy. I should be working, moving ahead with new ideas, and instead I was becoming mired in a past not even my own.

The knock on the front door sounded at first like the slam of a drawer. When it was repeated, and I recognized it for what it was, I immediately thought of William Ebborn's words that afternoon, before he drove away. I hoped it was not Carl Jope who had come calling.

It was David Cornelius. He looked slightly taken aback by the warmth of my welcome, but not displeased. He had come on behalf of his son, he said, his face apologetic. "I gather he and Spike were over here this afternoon destroying property. He feels pretty bad about it."

"Rafe's conscience works overtime. I tried to tell him it didn't matter."

David had brought a large wire-mesh fire screen with him, in partial restitution, he explained. "Rafe and I knew you would worry about the kids climbing into the open fireplace. You know," he added as he set the screen in place, "I wouldn't blame you if you banned Rafe from the cottage, while it's still in one piece."

"I'd miss the excitement. Besides, Rafe and Spike are

good material. If they get out of hand I'll threaten to put them in a book."

He laughed. "That's not much of a threat. Rafe already sees himself as the hero of his own story. Either Indiana Jones or Oliver Twist, depending on his mood." With a mock-formal air, he added, "To make amends, Rafe invites you and Max to come to dinner tomorrow night with us. To be fair, I have to warn you that Rafe plans to do most of the cooking. But we're both hoping you'll say yes."

I would like to very much, I told him truthfully, but added that if Sophie were free to look after Max I might leave him at home. To David's credit, there was no sign of relief on his face when he replied that whatever suited me was fine with them. He left then, saying that he had promised to help Rafe with his homework.

After he had gone, I was restless with some undefinable emotion, the slight shiver of a pleasure only faintly felt, like the premonition of far-off but steadily approaching happiness. In a burst of energy, I settled down with my sketch pad and finished off the Geraldine drawings, working late into the night. At last, I stood up, ready for bed, and as I did I glanced at the loose stone, which was still sitting beside the fireplace. I should replace it, I thought, before either of the children got hurt.

Idly, I felt with my hand in the empty space for the fissure that had allowed Spike to slither his way into the fireplace. At the back on the left, there was a surprisingly wide gap between the stones. Reaching along it as far as my arm would go, my fingers suddenly touched something metal. Slowly, with my fingertips, I made out the shape and realized with a rush of excitement that it was a small metal box. But it was too tightly wedged in the crevice to pull free.

I withdrew my hand and, ducking my head, stepped into the hearth among the debris. Crouching, I reached back through the alcove into the gap Rafe had noticed. I could feel the other side of the metal box. Groping, my fingers found a small handle. I pulled hard, hoping I was not wedging the box more tightly into its space. But from this side it came free easily.

It was a small, hinged, black container, roughly two

inches deep by six inches square, with a keyhole lock. Dust and soot lay thickly over it. I blew off some of the dust into the fireplace and tried to open it, but it was either locked or rusted shut. I shook it gently. Something inside moved back and forth with a rustling noise.

I took the box into the kitchen, to try to jimmy it open with a knife. But the blade would not fit between the lid and the side, and I was reluctant to damage the box by forcing it in any way. Frustrated, I decided the best thing to do would be to find a locksmith in the morning. With a damp cloth, I wiped the box clean and looked it over. There was nothing to tell me how old it might be, or even what its purpose was. All I knew was that someone had gone to the trouble of hiding the box and that there was, very definitely, something inside it.

Next morning after breakfast, Sophie and I drove with the children to Wychley. While Sophie and Anna did some shopping, Max and I went in search of Timms the locksmith, whose name I had found in the yellow pages. According to the sign over the door of his shop, he was also Timms the ironmonger. The shop was narrow and deep, with the random appeal of any hardware store, its shelves filled with the domestically familiar and the arcane.

A bell tinkled somewhere in the recesses of the shop when I opened the door. In a moment, a wizened old man with the face of a friendly troll appeared. I showed him the box and explained my problem. Silently, he peered at the lock, then shuffled to the back of the shop, motioning for us to follow. He went behind a counter and squirted some sort of oil onto the hinges, and another sort of oil into the keyhole, wiping the excess away with a cloth. Then he took out a collection of tools, selected one that looked like something a dentist would use on a recalcitrant tooth, and bent frowning over the box.

His hands worked deftly on the lock for a few moments and then he gave a small sigh of satisfaction. Tactfully, he refrained from lifting the lid himself but instead handed the box back to me. "It should open easily enough now."

The temptation to lift the lid was strong, but I waited until Max and I were in the churchyard by the river, alone and unobserved. The lid resisted for only the briefest instant be-

fore it gave way with a rasp of metal on metal. An odd
twist of fear spiked my excitement.

Inside was a piece of paper folded into three; it had the
weight and grain of handmade paper, thick and slightly
stiff. Carefully, I unfolded it. A small woodcut at the top of
the page showed a mound with a clump of trees on top, immediately recognizable as Goody Ridler's Tump. Below
this was printed, on a single line, "Longbarrow Press,
Shipcote, 1937." The striking typeface was very clear and
black against the creamy paper. Two paragraphs in the
same type followed.

Whereas we believe that each man's work has equal
value, that each man's voice cries out to be heard, and
that all men ought to share in a common good, we, the
undersigned, pledge our lives and our talents to one another and to our fellow men. We no longer stand alone
as individuals striving selfishly for our own ends. Instead, we bind ourselves together in a fellowship which
shall be known as The Longbarrow Brotherhood. The
chief purpose of its labours, the inspiration for its crea-
tions, shall be the betterment of man's lot on this earth.

We establish Longbarrow Press as the instrument
whereby our work and our beliefs may reach others. It
shall publish, among various writings, a long work of fiction by The Longbarrow Brotherhood entitled *This Sad
Ceremonial*, upon completion of the manuscript. Any
profits derived from works produced by the undersigned
shall be the property of The Longbarrow Brotherhood, to
be used to further its work.

Underneath were three signatures in black ink: Stephen
Allerton, Benedict Mallaby, and Charles Lorimer.

Slowly, I folded the document back up and replaced it in
the box, which I returned to the carryall. While Max
watched the ducks on the river, I thought about my find.

The document was an idealistic credo and a manifesto,
and a very interesting business contract besides. It was also,
apart from everything else, a puzzle. While it made one
thing clear to me, the strength of Charles Lorimer's relationship not only with his cousin Benedict but with Stephen

Allerton as well, it obscured another: the authorship of *This Sad Ceremonial*.

Whether the work was that of one man or three, however, the document explicitly gave my grandfather a share in the rights to *This Sad Ceremonial*.

Two years after Stephen's death, and only a few months after Charles's disappearance, Mallaby's had published the novel. Had Benedict waited to see whether Nan would come forward with Charles's copy of the agreement, the copy that surely was now in my hands? And when she failed to, had he believed that he and Clarissa were free to enjoy the undivided profits from its success? Or had he worried that Charles might someday return to produce the document and claim his third?

I was sure that Benedict had not worried. He knew that Charles was dead, because he had killed him.

This Sad Ceremonial had been a best-seller in its own day and had continued to sell steadily ever since. Its success laid the foundations for Mallaby and Company's future; the income from its sales had also enabled Clarissa and Benedict to reclaim Summerhays for their own and to restore it. All this had happened, however, after my grandfather's disappearance. No one could have foretold the book's huge success. It was absurd to believe that Benedict killed Charles to avoid sharing in the uncertain income from an as yet unpublished book.

No, I thought, Benedict had killed him to prevent him from going to the police with his knowledge of Benedict's presence in Shipcote on the night of Evelyn Allerton's murder. The financial success of *This Sad Ceremonial* was simply good luck. The same good luck that had come to Benedict when the German bombing destroyed so many copies of *Life Blood*.

With a sudden revulsion of feeling, I stood up, brushing the grass from my clothes. I was speculating again, making a murderer out of someone who might have been guilty merely of greed and sharp practice. Benedict had almost certainly cheated Nan of her portion. That did not mean, however, that he had killed her husband.

Men disappear, I told myself as I pushed Max's stroller toward the center of town. Some open a door and walk out toward another life, others choose to go sailing in bad weather. For all I knew, my grandfather was living still, an old man with the occasional bad dream to trouble his sleep. Or perhaps, on that long-ago summer's day, he had taken my own husband's path to oblivion.

CHAPTER 24

On the way back to the cottage, I told Sophie about my discovery. "Who do you think hid it?" she asked me. "Charles?"

"Possibly. Although if he did, why didn't he tell Nan about it? She couldn't have known—she would never have left it there. No, it seems more likely that Stephen or Evelyn Allerton hid it."

"Why?"

"I don't know. Maybe we'll never know."

She was quick to see the document's implications, both for the past and for the present. "It's a time bomb. What will you do with it?"

But I had no answer to that either, yet.

The postman brought a brief note from Robin Mallaby later that afternoon. In it, he explained that he was forced to excuse himself from his promised tour of the neighborhood the next day. He blamed the pressure of work, but went on to write that he hoped to come down to Shipcote someday soon. In the meantime, if I made any decision about selling the cottage, would I please let him know through Tony Munnings.

When I came downstairs, dressed for my dinner with Rafe and David Cornelius, Sophie was sitting cross-legged on the sofa, reading the biography of Stephen Allerton. She glanced up from the book and gave me the once-over.

"Very nice. Terrific dress. Eye shadow, too, I see. Rafe should be impressed." Her face was innocent of irony. "I've been looking through this," she continued, riffling the pages of the biography. "I can see why the Mallabys called old Webbed Sphincter The Constant Nymph. He was mad about Stephen Allerton, wasn't he?"

"You think so?"

"Well, it's the way he never has anything bad to say about his subject. He makes him out to be quite the lad. Poet, hero, martyr. Not to mention gorgeous. No wonder poor Evelyn was a nervous wreck." Then her voice grew serious. "I see what you mean about Willoughby deliberately keeping your grandfather out of the book. I mean, there're a lot of places where it would make sense to mention him, but Willoughby just glosses over them."

I said that when I had lunch with him on Monday I hoped to find out why. Tonight, however, I intended to put the whole business out of my mind. "Max is finally asleep," I went on. "If he wakes up, there's a bottle in the fridge. His diapers are dry now but sometimes if he dirties them it wakes him. I put the cream for his diaper rash beside—" I stopped; I had gone through all this with her an hour before. "Sorry. I don't know why I'm telling you this again."

"That's okay," she said, straight-faced. "Eleven-year-old boys have that effect on me, too." Then she laughed and told me to have a good time.

Rafe was sitting in the evening sun on the low stone wall in front of Summerhays, waiting for me, as I drove up. He was wearing a pair of pressed navy trousers with a white polo shirt, and his hair was neatly combed; I was glad I had made a similar effort for the occasion.

Opening the high wooden door in the stone wall, he led me along a narrow flagstone path into a large vegetable garden, which was neatly quartered by paths lined with low boxwood hedges. Rows of green-netted currant and gooseberry bushes filled one of the sections, broad beds of asparagus another, the third held tripods for runner beans and sweet peas, and in the fourth the new green shoots of various young vegetables were pushing through the loamy earth. It was, Rafe assured me, a great place for finding toads.

A high stone wall bordered three sides of the garden, but on the fourth was the long facade of Oldbarn, where Rafe and his father were living. Before its conversion, the massive building must have looked very like the medieval barn at Ashleaze Farm, with the addition of a pigeon roost in its large gabled stone porch. The birds' small rectangular nest holes, underlined by wooden perching timbers set into the stone, formed a pyramid above a pair of modern French doors that opened onto a small, raised terrace.

At the far end of the barn, a flight of stone steps led up to another door; it was the entrance, Rafe explained, to a small apartment used by Mela whenever she came back to Shipcote.

As we went onto the terrace, the smell of roasting meat and herbs drifted out to meet us, and from somewhere in the house came the music of Grieg's "Peer Gynt Suite." Through the open French doors lay a long, cream-painted living room with a dining area at one end where a pine table was laid for three. The room was decorated with tenants in mind, with sturdy modern furniture in bland fabrics and neutral colors that wear well and make no special demands on the eye, a tweedy beige carpeting, and pleasant rural prints on the walls. It showed the signs of recent, unnatural tidying, stacks of newspapers and magazines pushed haphazardly into bookshelves, part of a Lego construction sticking out from under a chair, and a half-finished game of Chinese checkers on a card table in front of the fireplace. Rafe asked me if I would like to play a game after supper. His look was so eager that I could only say yes, adding that he would have to remind me of the rules. "They're easy," he told me as he pushed open a swinging door.

The kitchen had a cheerful squalor that consisted of exuberant disorder rather than grime, for it was actually quite clean. Certain things about the room sent the fairly unambiguous message that it was the preserve of males. In the midst of typical kitchen clutter were extraneous items like fishing rods, various tools, and spread out on the tabletop beside a chopping board, the workings of some kind of small motor.

Whistling along with the Grieg, whose source was a small stereo on a countertop, David Cornelius was taking a roasting pan with a leg of lamb out of the oven. When he heard us come in, he looked up and smiled. "Perfect timing. I think this is done, Rafe."

Even as my own smile irresistibly responded to his, an awkwardness, slight but pronounced, made me turn my gaze toward the roast lamb. "That looks good. And it smells wonderful."

"Rafe's the chef. I'm just the timekeeper." He lifted the meat from the pan to a china platter, then rolled down the sleeves of his shirt and buttoned the cuffs. Like Rafe, he had dressed for dinner, in a pair of khaki slacks and a white shirt. He picked up the navy blazer that was lying over the back of a chair and put it on. As I watched him, each of these trivial domestic actions seemed to carry a peculiar resonance; in my eyes, they were almost beautiful. Perhaps simply because it seemed a long time since I had seen a man do any of them.

I knew, however, that it was more than that. David himself seemed beautiful. The observation, I told myself, was a dispassionate judgment, a simple matter of aesthetics, the result of light and color and a certain lucky conjunction of angles, curves, and lines. Physical beauty always moved me; by now I ought to know that the emotion it aroused in me was inevitable, disturbing but transient. And best translated onto paper.

Rafe showed me the salad he had made. When I congratulated him on making the dinner by himself, he admitted that all he'd really had to do was put the lamb and the potatoes in the oven. "The only hard part was the salad. Dad made me wash the lettuce. It takes forever to get it dry again."

"Not everyone would be as easily consoled as you are, Rafe," his father said, "for the discovery of a snail in their salad by its interesting trail of slime." He held up a bottle of red wine. "Médoc all right, Jo? We've got the usual alternatives if you'd prefer something else." The red was fine, I said, and he poured some out for himself as well. With a tumbler of Coke in one hand, Rafe insisted that we all clink glasses. "Cheers," he said, looking shyly pleased.

As we sat down at the dining table, I asked Rafe how school was going. Pretty good, he replied; he was in the middle of a project on long barrows that was turning out to be interesting.

David laid slices of lamb on each plate beside a baked potato. He looked at his son and smiled. "You're getting to be an expert, aren't you, Rafe?"

Rafe emphatically denied this. "But I have found out a lot of great stuff." Without much prompting, he went on to tell us the various theories about barrows that had been held at one time or another, from the medieval belief that they were the burial places of saints to the twentieth-century conviction that many of them were deliberately laid out by astronomer-priests in alignment with standing stones, the most famous of which was Stonehenge, and had astronomical significance. Those who were buried in them were most likely from the ruling or priestly class, he told us earnestly, or were some sort of sacrifice.

He looked up from his plate at his father with an innocent expression. "Did you know that they might even have sacrificed babies? We could learn a lot from them."

David gave me a dry look. "I've tried to tell Rafe that it's a sign of civilization and maturity when the strong protect the weak, instead of sacrificing them. But he's at the age when the survival of the fittest is more appealing."

When I asked Rafe if he had ever been inside a long barrow himself, he nodded vigorously, his mouth full of food. "Humblebee Barrow," he said after he had swallowed. "It's been excavated. You can go partway in." It was a giant long barrow high on a hill in the western Cotswolds, he added, half an hour's drive from Shipcote. When I remarked casually that in that case I would have to go and see it, he at once volunteered himself and his father as guides. David seemed to accept this good-humoredly and, when pressed by Rafe, proposed Sunday afternoon, and a picnic, if the weather held. When I asked if we could invite Sophie and Anna, he suggested including Val Lenthall as well.

As the meal progressed, I began to see how skillful David was with his son, effacing himself in order to let Rafe play the host, tactfully guiding the conversation so that

Rafe felt himself included but did not dominate it. He had a gently humorous way with the boy, but took him seriously as well, discussing his theories with him as though he were another adult. The pleasure each took in the other was visible, and moving.

When we had finished our second helpings, Rafe carried the empty plates into the kitchen. In a moment, he returned, looking stricken. "Dad! We forgot to put the pie in the oven. It'll take forever."

"It just needs warming up. The oven'll still be hot. Why don't you show Jo your project while I take care of it?"

Rafe led me out into a hallway with the front door and a staircase. His room was on the second floor, directly opposite the top of the stairs. It contained a narrow, rumpled bed, a desk, and a set of shelves filled with a jumble of books, comic books, various Lego constructions, and rows of tiny plastic soldiers, as well as odd bits of the natural world and an elaborate-looking jar for catching bugs. One corner of the room was taken up by Spike's large wire cage, which had several levels, a small piece of sheepskin, a tube lined with shag carpeting for him to sleep in, and a hammock. Spike himself was invisible, asleep, Rafe said, in the tube. The smell in the room was an overwhelming but for the most part inoffensive combination of ferret and boy.

On the desk was Rafe's project, a large poster propped against the wall with several drawings, some paragraphs of writing, and a number of photographs pasted to it. He and his father had taken the photos when they visited Humblebee Barrow. Some were shot from a distance and showed a huge, smoothly grassy mound rising like a swelling from the earth. In one, Rafe was crouching at the entrance, half in shadow, beneath a low overhang of gray stone, with the green curve of the mound above and darkness behind him. Beneath the mound, Rafe told me, was a long passage with three chambers, one on either side of the passage and another at its far end.

One of the drawings showed the barrow as though seen from above with the layer of covering earth sliced away to expose the passage and the chambers. Oriented north-south, it was long and vaguely trapezoidal in shape, with the northern end the wider of the two.

"See this?" Rafe pointed to a photograph that showed what appeared to be the main entrance to the barrow, a portal deeply recessed between two convex horns of drywall masonry. It was a false entrance, Rafe told me. "There's a long tunnel but it doesn't lead anywhere. Maybe it was to fool grave robbers or invading tribes who might try to wreck the place. There was a skull set into the entrance, like a warning. Or maybe it was where some sort of sacred rite happened." He gave a small sigh of frustration. "You know, Goody Ridler's Tump could have something like it. I'd give anything to find out."

Some children in Rafe's situation, faced with the breakup of their home, might have resorted to endless hours with video games or computers. Rafe's particular refuge, it occurred to me as I listened to him, was information. He burrowed into theories the way he longed to burrow into Goody Ridler's Tump.

Spike, of course, was another consolation. Rafe opened the door of the cage and began gently calling to the ferret, trying to wake it up. Meanwhile, downstairs, the doorbell rang and we heard almost simultaneously the sound of the front door opening and a woman's voice calling out David's name.

Rafe stiffened as he bent over Spike's cage. "Mela," he said, his voice glum.

I said that we had better go down. He turned back to the door of the cage. "Just one more minute. I want to get Spike."

Below, I could hear David come out into the hall to greet Mela. Their voices carried clearly up the stairs; hers sounded upset. "You know Benedict's turned down Gerald's offer," she was saying accusingly.

"Yes, I knew." David's voice was quieter but still audible. "I'm not surprised."

"Well, I am," Mela retorted. "It was a lot of money."

"Benedict and Clarissa see Shipcote Farm Park as Phil's memorial. It's very hard for them to sell their share."

"I hope you haven't been encouraging them in that." Mela's voice was heated. "If you're not prepared to buy the family out, I don't think you should stand in the way of someone who is."

"That's not what you would have said a year ago."

"That was a year ago. This is now."

Rafe, intent on waking up Spike, seemed not to be listening, but I felt uneasy, an eavesdropper. I was about to leave without him when the ferret sleepily poked its head out of the tube and allowed Rafe to pick it up. He draped it over his shoulder and together we went into the hall.

"They're living in the past," Mela was saying as we came out of Rafe's room. "Benedict thinks you can run a publishing company today the way he used to. He doesn't realize—" She stopped abruptly as she caught sight of us at the top of the stairs. Several expressions passed briefly over her face, the last an amused wariness. "Jo. I had wondered if that was your car."

She was standing under the glare of the ceiling light, which only served to emphasize the perfection of her skin and features, and that cool radiance that always seemed a part of her. The long shining hair was caught loosely back by a scarf, with soft tendrils escaping around her face. She was wearing a black leather trouser suit, so perversely mannish that it seemed the perfect foil for her femininity. It gave her the look of a Botticelli nymph dressed by Karl Lagerfeld. In her own way, I thought, she was as much a visual tease as Sophie.

"Rafe invited me to dinner," I said as we came downstairs. It seemed important to stress that my presence was the result of Rafe's invitation rather than his father's. "He's a very good cook."

"Rafe is full of surprises." She turned her cool, amused gaze on David. "Like his father."

"What happened to your plans?" David asked her as the four of us went into the living room. "I thought you were going to the Craddocks' for the weekend."

"I canceled." She threw her leather jacket over the back of a chair. Underneath it, she had on a plain white blouse buttoned to the neck, very prim above the tight black pants. "As you wouldn't leave your beloved sheep, I'd have been the extra woman. A thankless role." She turned to me. "David's very loyal to his sheep. It's quite touching, I suppose, but it does make arranging a social life rather difficult. People don't understand when you tell them dinner's off on account of frothy bloat or fly-strike."

David gave a tolerant smile. "My refusal had nothing to do with the sheep and everything to do with the host. Craddock thinks a conversation consists of him talking and everybody else nodding."

"You could have gone fishing. All that private stretch of river to yourself. You could have been as solitary as you like. David's the original Trappist," she said to me confidingly, almost as if it were a warning. "He's happiest alone."

The pie was ready, David said smoothly. Would she join us for dessert? She shook her head, but said she would like a drink. "Some white wine, if you have any."

We ate our apple pie in the living room. Mela did most of the talking, sitting at first, then moving restlessly around the room as she drank her wine, apparently unable to settle. She seemed to glitter, filled with a nervous energy that threw off little sparks, like a Catherine wheel, in the form of malicious jokes about people she and David knew, colleagues, the writers she worked with, the London scene. David's face was unreadable; but there was a wariness, I thought, in the way he watched her, as though he were in some way afraid of her or of what she might do. Rafe doggedly ate his way through piece after piece of pie while Spike slept on his shoulder.

Abruptly, Mela sat down beside me on the sofa and said, apropos of nothing that I could make out, "I hear Sophie Dymock and her child are living with you. It's terribly kind of you to take them in."

"Not really. It's an arrangement that suits us all. Sophie's good with Max. I'm managing to get some work done, and Max has Anna to fascinate him."

"I see. Well, it all sounds very cozy and domestic. I should imagine a man would be quite de trop, wouldn't he?"

I stared at her, not quite sure if she meant what I thought she did. She gave her angelic smile, and then I knew she intended me to understand her in just that particular way. For the first time I began to see a resemblance between Mela and her aunt Cece. There was something in the eyes and in the intonation of their voices, a hint of a malice that went beyond simple mischief making, wanted to wound. Mela's gaze was softened by thick lashes but it could be just as cold as Cece Breakspear's.

"But I should warn you," she continued with an air of mild concern, leaning forward to tap her cigarette ash into her glass, "if you haven't already discovered it for yourself, that Sophie is rather a gypsy. She was constantly running away from home as a child. Not the most reliable girl around." With a shell-pink fingernail, she flicked a strand of silvery hair back from her cheek. "Do you leave Max alone with her?"

"Mela—" David began, warningly.

"Well, I simply don't think it's wise to leave someone you care for with a woman you don't know very well." She gave me a level look. "You never can tell what will happen when your back is turned." Her meaning was plain, and it had nothing, I knew, to do with Sophie.

David rose to his feet and said he would make coffee. I caught Rafe's wistful glance at the Chinese checkers board. Grateful for the excuse to evade further conversation with Mela, I reminded Rafe that he had promised to play me a game after supper. At that, his eyes lit up and he put aside his plate of half-eaten pie. Miming a yawn, Mela said that she would give David a hand with the coffee.

Rafe sat across the table from me with Spike draped over his shoulder, one hand supporting the ferret's body, much as I had held Max as an infant to burp him. The animal might have been dead, and I remembered Rafe's description of the way it slept, so deeply that is seemed comatose. Once he had reminded me of the rules, Rafe and I settled down to play, and for a little while the only sound in the room was the clicking of the marbles against the round tin board as we moved them in small bumps from hole to hole along the lines.

In a few minutes, David came back into the room with Mela, carrying a tray with a coffeepot and some mugs. As she passed Rafe, Mela wrinkled her nose. "Are you bathing that animal, Rafe?" More teasing than critical, this nevertheless brought a polite defense of his pet from Rafe, who observed that Spike was descented and had a bath once a week; more frequent washing, he stated firmly, would dry out Spike's skin. "Anyway, I think Spike's smell is a lot nicer than the perfumes some ladies wear."

With a small shrug, Mela accepted the mug of coffee David was holding out to her. She took only a sip before setting it down on the mantelpiece and lighting another cigarette. Then, as though continuing a conversation she and David had been having while they were in the kitchen, she said, "You know, it's very tiresome of you, David, to be so stubborn."

"My Scots blood coming out." His voice was good-humored. He asked what I would like in my coffee, then brought the mug over to me and placed it on the table. Our eyes met briefly. He gave a small smile, the equivalent almost of a shrug.

"All the same," Mela went on, "you might try to understand the situation from my point of view."

"Maybe I could, if the viewpoint didn't keep changing. Anyway, I'd like to keep out of something that's really your family's affair." He placed the slightest emphasis on the "your," as though his patience were wearing thin.

"It's a little late to take that particular line, isn't it?"

"This must be boring for Jo," David observed quietly. Reluctant to meet his eyes, I glanced instead at Rafe. His forehead was furrowed as he concentrated on his moves; I suspected he was happy to be able to ignore the grown-ups.

"*Are* you bored, Jo?" Mela asked me. I gave her a meaningless smile and shook my head. Impatiently, she walked over to stand at Rafe's side, facing me. Her movements were abrupt now, the fluid grace so habitual to her seemed momentarily to have vanished. The hand with the cigarette moved jerkily to her mouth. "I think Jo's become very interested in the Mallabys. And in our belongings. Am I right, Jo?"

"Sorry?" I pretended to have been concentrating on the game. "Look at this. Rafe's blocked all my moves."

"You don't strike me as the type to give up so easily." Abruptly, with the hand holding the cigarette, she reached past Rafe's arm as though to move one of the marbles. Perhaps the jerky movement or the lighted cigarette startled the sleepy ferret, for all at once the small head suddenly lunged out at Mela's hand.

She screamed and snatched her hand away. The cigarette fell to the carpet. Drops of bright red blood beaded up on the back of the hand and then began to run across the white skin. "Oh, God," she said with a little moan.

While I scooped up the cigarette, which left a small burn mark in the rug, David grabbed a clean napkin from beside the coffeepot and wrapped it around Mela's hand. "There's disinfectant in the kitchen," he said. Over his shoulder, he calmly told Rafe to take Spike back upstairs and put him in his cage.

"I just hope there's no danger of blood poisoning," Mela was saying as David led her away, one arm around her shoulders.

Under his breath, Rafe muttered, "Spike's more likely to get blood poisoning than she is." Then he looked up at me miserably. "He didn't mean to do it. It's just that she frightened him."

The ferret seemed far from frightened now, skittering around the room, literally bouncing off the walls, with his fur fluffed out so that he looked twice his natural width. I almost expected him to break out, like Rikki-tikki-tavi, into a little chant of triumph. Rafe captured him and went slowly up the stairs.

When David and Mela came back into the living room, her hand was bandaged. Oddly, the bite seemed to have stilled that febrile restlessness. Pale and subdued, she appeared composed, shrugging off commiseration. She ought to have been more careful, she said; it was her own fault. One of their neighbors was a doctor who worked in the cottage hospital in Wychley, David told me; he had telephoned her and would drive Mela over to her house now, so that she could take a look at the bite.

As he was helping Mela on with her coat, Rafe came slowly down the stairs. "I'm sorry Spike hurt you, Mela."

"He must have been dreaming of rabbits," she said dryly. Rafe looked surprised at this sign of forgiveness and gave her a tentative, apologetic smile, which she returned. His father seemed relieved at this sign of a rapprochement. They shouldn't be long, he told me; would I wait? There was the undertone of an appeal in his voice. I nodded. When the front door had closed behind them, I suggested to

Rafe that we do the dishes, then finish our game. David returned in less than an hour, alone.

"I'm really sorry, Dad," Rafe said as we stood up from the checkers board. "Is Mela okay?"

"She'll live." His voice was laconic. "But for the next few days I think you'd better keep Spike out of her sight." Then, "Bedtime, okay?"

"Okay. Good night, Jo."

"Good night, Rafe. Thank you for dinner, it was wonderful. Bring the Chinese checkers over to Longbarrow Cottage sometime. You owe me my revenge."

He looked at me doubtfully. "Promise you didn't let me win."

"I wouldn't do that. I hate losing."

He grinned. "Me too."

After he had left the room, David gave a philosophical smile. "I'm told that not all eleven-year-olds are like Rafe. There's hope for Max."

"Rafe reminds me of how I felt at that age. Wanting to be grown up but somehow knowing it was better to be a kid. It was very confusing." I looked around for my coat. "I'd better be going."

He didn't move. "I can't imagine you ever feeling confused. You always seem as though you're very sure of what you're doing."

Surprised, I told him that it seemed to me a better description of himself than of me.

"I am very sure of myself, about some things. There are others, though . . ." He let a beat go by. Then, with what sounded like a sudden determination, he said, "There's something I want to clear up. I've been meaning to tell—" At that moment, the telephone rang. "Damn," he muttered. He went to the doorway into the hall and called up the stairs to Rafe, but the sound of water running meant Rafe was probably in the bath. The phone went on ringing, insistent.

I put my coat on. "I really should get back. You go ahead. I'll let myself out." As I left him there and went out through the French doors onto the terrace, I knew with a vague sense of failure, and cowardice, that I was escaping from something. What it was precisely, I left undefined.

CHAPTER 25

The next morning, I left Max with Sophie and drove to Oxford to visit the Bodleian Library and the secondhand book dealers' fair. During the night, clouds and cool moist air had moved in, giving both fields and sky the soft, uncertain look of damp blotting paper. On Sophie's advice, I parked the car on a residential side street about half a mile from the city center and took a minibus the rest of the way into town. Packed tight with shoppers and foreign students, it sped down the road past hanging flower baskets, red-brick Victorian villas, and medieval stone facades, swerving out to pass a scarlet double-decker like an impudent schoolboy mocking a cardinal.

Near the center, I got off the bus and turned left into Broad Street. A row of narrow shops painted ocher, mauve, or cream faced the smooth fronts of gated college walls across the wide street. Lanky, jeans-clad students with sweaters past their hips, bored French teenagers, and tourists draped in cameras with belt bags strapped around their stomachs loitered on the sidewalk, speaking a polyglot of languages.

At the far end of the street was the handsome cluster of university buildings—pedimented, columned, and decorated with statues—that contained the Bodleian Library. The library was guarded by a high iron railing crowned with a row of giant bearded stone heads that gazed down with an air of jaundiced solemnity, as though long exposure to the ways of students had taught them to be watchful.

In the library admissions office, a number of people were waiting to be interviewed by a woman in an academic gown. When my turn came, she listened politely to the explanation Sophie had suggested I use, that I was researching a book and wanted to consult the library's holdings, a partial if not the literal truth, and then asked me several questions. Seemingly satisfied with my answers, she gave me a form to fill out, then motioned the next person forward.

Glancing over the piece of paper, I saw that while the admission requirements were liberal enough, there was a single stumbling block. The form itself had to be signed by a recommender, someone official who had known me for a certain length of time and could attest to my good character. Anyone I would ordinarily ask, however, was living on the other side of the Atlantic Ocean. Momentarily balked, I took the form away with me, consoling myself with the thought that I could fax it to Paulina, my editor, in Toronto.

I played the tourist for a little while, wandering haphazardly along narrow streets in the ancient heart of academic Oxford, forbidden to most cars but thick with bicycles and pigeons. There was the smell of fish and chips and pipe smoke in the cool air, and the chill of damp stone. Facelifts were under way everywhere. Scaffolding and green netting cloaked a pinnacled facade like a veil on a beautiful woman; beneath an archway, a mason worked on a wall, cutting away the blackened and rotting blocks.

At last, after several wrong turns, I came out onto the High Street. Spires, towers, and domes rose into the air along the length of its gently sloping curve, an intricate fretwork of gray and yellow stone against the sky. The public library was housed in a modern shopping center a few minutes' walk away. In the main reading room, I checked the computer printout of catalog listings for *Life Blood* but found no entry under either J. M. Morrile or Joanna Margaret Lorimer. It occurred to me that Nan's publisher could still be in existence and might own a copy of her novel, which I could have photocopied. Surely publishers kept one copy at least of each of their books? After consulting several reference books, however, the young librarian behind the information desk informed me that the publisher had gone out of business in the late fifties. It had been a long shot anyway, I told myself as I left. And there was still the second hand bookdealers' fair.

The book fair was held at the Randolph Hotel, a massive

yellow-brick hybrid between a French château and a Gothic cathedral. A sign directed book fair visitors through a small parking area to an entrance at the back, where I paid a fee and was given a guide to the bookstalls set up in rows in three large and rather gloomy rooms.

There were close to a hundred stalls, representing booksellers from all over the country, each one indexed by specialty in the guide. The general heading of "Twentieth-Century Literature" listed ten that looked promising. Unfortunately, none seemed to specialize in mysteries. At the back of the guide was a map of the fair, with the stalls numbered.

It was eleven o'clock and the place was already crowded; largely, it seemed to me, by men. They called to one another in loud cheerful voices, proposing coffee breaks, hailing old friends. Like the books themselves, they appeared a little worn around the edges, comfortably shabby, possibly interesting, smelling of old cigarette smoke and musty cloth. A few had the easygoing, contented look of people who have chosen their calling for love rather than money.

With my pen, I circled the stands on the map that seemed most likely to yield results, then headed for the nearest. Two men were deep in conversation beside it. They paused to listen to my request, glanced at each other, shook their heads in unison, and turned back to their talk. The next four stands were equally discouraging.

For a short while, I was sidetracked by a display of illustrated children's books, all tempting but all too expensive. Eventually, I went on to the fifth stand, where a rumpled-looking man with a drooping mustache was sitting on a chair, reading a newspaper. He looked mildly interested when I explained my search but told me he carried only the better-known writers.

"There may be a copy lurking in someone's attic somewhere. But the odds are against it. During the war so many books were pulped, you see, because of the paper shortage. A book may have survived the critics, only to perish at the hands of the vandals in Whitehall." He seemed to take almost a lugubrious pleasure in the thought. Then he advised me to try his colleagues over at Desmond Clitheroe Books. "Des and Sylvia pick up the occasional oddity."

Des wasn't there, but Sylvia was. She was something of an oddity herself, at least in the context of the book fair, with the brassy, extravagantly made-up good looks and bold manner of a prototypical barmaid, and the voice to match. She must have been in her fifties, but she was dressed like a twenty-year-old from the sixties, in a short Op Art–patterned dress of black semicircles on a white background, and white leather boots. The fit of the dress and its curvy pattern emphasized her remarkable figure. Several men were clustered around her, bursts of their laughter punctuating whatever story she was telling. "Here, I've got a customer," she said cheerfully when she saw me. "You lads push off now." Obediently, they drifted away to other stalls. She smiled at me. "What can I do for you, my love."

I finished my explanation by saying that most book dealers seemed to think I was on a wild-goose chase. She gave a snort of derision. "Rubbish. Lazy buggers, some of them. Don't want to move their arses if they can help it. As for me, I like a challenge. Give me the details and I'll see what I can do for you. No promises, mind. Keep looking yourself."

"Sylvia will find it for you, if anyone can," a voice to my right said smoothly and very suddenly. "She's a positive ferret for books." Startled, I turned to find Willoughby Webb Springer standing at my side. He inclined his head in greeting, a small smile on his thin lips. Dressed in a navy pin-striped suit with a red waistcoat and matching silk tie, his longish crinkly gray hair meticulously parted, he had the air of a superannuated dandy and was easily, Sylvia apart, the most dressed-up person in the room.

Sylvia bridled at his remark. "That's not a very nice way to put it, Willoughby."

"Mrs. Treleven will tell you that ferrets are very fashionable in some circles these days," Willoughby replied blandly. He gazed at her appraisingly. "You are even more delectable today than usual, Sylvia."

"Des likes me to look my best at these affairs." With a mock-modest fluttering of very thick and patently false lashes, she ran a plump hand freighted with rings over the tight skirt of her dress.

"Where is Des?"

"Off in North Oxford. An old lady there just turned up her toes. Had quite a library. The son's asked Des to take a look at it and make an offer."

"Be sure to put any treasures away for me, Sylvia."

"I put all my treasures on display, Willoughby, as you well know." She winked at him, an outrageous, extravagant wink, guying herself.

"I only know that they don't come cheaply, my dear."

Far from offended, she seemed highly amused by this. "If you weren't such a skinflint, more might come your way." Another customer was browsing among the books, a thin little man with bicycle clips on his gray flannel trousers, who interrupted to ask the price of a book. Before she moved away to check, I gave her the piece of paper on which I had written my name and address and the details of *Life Blood*. With a breezy confidence I found oddly hopeful, she told me she would send the book off to me as soon as she found it. She then turned her charm on the man, who stared at her with the unblinking fascination of a mesmerized rabbit.

As we walked away together, Willoughby said quietly, "Des was an English don at Merton. Drank himself into a breakdown. Sylvia cured him, set him up in business, and made him a very happy man. He's the one who knows the books themselves, but Sylvia knows how to sell them. Among other things." He adjusted the cuffs of his shirt. Then, in a casual voice, asked, "Are you after something special?"

The truth, I was tempted to reply.

I knew what he really meant, of course; the suggestion of a more sinister interpretation was simply a product of my imagination, fed with Sophie's account of the man and my own speculations. There was so much I wanted to confront him with—that cruel review of *Life Blood*, his own hidden interest in the book, the deliberate exclusion of my grandfather from Stephen Allerton's biography—but I preferred to choose my moment, not have it forced upon me by a man who kept his own secrets.

"A novel called *Life Blood*," I said, trying to match his own bland tones, "written by my grandmother." If this aroused a response in him, he did not show it. His heavy-lidded eyes were opaque, and his only comment was a non-committal sound in his throat. Tentatively, I went on to say that I was not having much luck, and explained my difficulty in gaining admission to the Bodleian Library.

This seemed to interest him. "Do you have the form with you, by any chance? Good. Then, if I may . . . ?" He held out one hand, and when I gave him the piece of paper, took out his little gold pen from his breast pocket, placed the form on a tabletop, and to my surprise signed his name in the required place. As he returned it to me, he said, "I believe we have an affinity, my dear. When such is the case, mere length of acquaintance seems an irrelevancy." He added that he was looking forward to our lunch on Monday, and then, before I had a chance to say a word, turned and walked away through the crowds.

I stood there with the inexplicable conviction that, by doing me the favor of signing the admission form, he intended to manipulate me. Obviously, for some reason, he wanted to make certain that I read *Life Blood*. That letter from Goddard Grant Ltd. had been no more than a teaser designed to provoke my interest in the book, just as his signature now ensured my access to it. Yet fifty years ago he had done his best to discourage anyone from reading the novel. Why had he changed his mind?

I glanced at my wristwatch. The Bodleian admissions office closed at twelve-thirty on Saturdays, in less than an hour, the library itself at one o'clock. I would have to hurry.

As I was leaving, I passed by a stall specializing in local history and archaeology, where a book on display caught my eye. "Long Barrows of the Cotswolds: A Description of Long Barrows, Stone Circles and other Megalithic Remains" was stamped on its dark green cover. Handsomely printed on deckle-edged paper, with photographs, maps, and illustrations, it was a lovely piece of work. Seeing my interest, the woman who ran the stall told me it had some slight damage from damp, and for that reason was not expensive. "Still, it's a nice bit of printing. The illustrations are particularly fine." On impulse, thinking of Rafe, I told the woman I would take it.

At the admissions office, I handed in the form, paid a small fee, had my picture taken, swore an oath not to kindle fire in the library, and emerged with my reader's ticket in hand. Now the barriers seemed to fall easily enough. The guard standing by the entrance to a worn stone staircase smiled and waved me past. No one challenged my right to enter the silent, light-filled room that held the catalog volumes. Gradually, with the help of a booklet on how to use the Bodleian, I was able to make the antique system of leather-bound catalogs give up its secrets. And at last, triumphant, I found a slip of paper printed with Nan's pseudonym, *Life Blood*, and a call number. With rising excitement, I filled out a book order form and took it over to one of the librarians sitting at the main desk.

There was no book-retrieval service on Saturdays, she told me as she dropped the form into a basket with a pile of others. I would have to come back on Monday morning. I swallowed various words of vulgar regret, thanked her, and left.

My work, and Max, had taught me to be patient, for all that it went against the grain, but a return to the book fair to visit the dealers I'd missed was out of the question. I could not face another disappointment or one more uninterested shake of the head. A letter or phone call would have to do. For the moment at least, the romance of old books had lost its glamour.

Still, the morning had been so frustrating that I needed to feel I was making some sort of progress. Sophie had told me to take as long as I liked, and so instead of leaving the highway at the Shipcote turning, I drove on to Wychley. I wanted to check the library's old newspaper files.

The librarian told me that back issues of the local paper, *The Wychley Clarion*, were on microfilm. She found the reels for 1938 and showed me how to work the reader-printer, which would make copies. I scrolled forward to the first issue to appear after Evelyn Allerton's murder. Both the murder and the snowstorm were front-page news, but violent death had the edge over violent nature by several columns of print.

The newspaper account of the murder contained little that I did not already know from Sophie and from Willoughby's description in the biography. At the end of the article, however, was a paragraph that appeared to confirm my grandfather's claim that he had let Benedict off on the high road late that afternoon. "A man was seen getting out of a blue Rover at the Withyford turn, shortly after six o'clock in the evening. He was wearing a hat and a long overcoat. The same person was next seen some fifteen minutes later on the footpath beyond Withyford church. The police would like to talk to the driver of the car or to anyone who might have knowledge of this individual."

I made a copy of this and then scanned the rest of the issue. On an inside page, I came across a short item that made me catch my breath. "An MG automobile belonging to an Oxford University undergraduate, Mr. Willoughby Webb Springer, was extracted by a team of horses from beneath the branches of a great oak yesterday morning in Shipcote. Both automobile and tree were victims of the snowstorm. It is thought that the venerable tree fell during the blizzard owing to the great weight of snow on its branches, thus trapping the automobile. Mr. Webb Springer, who was not in the vehicle at the time, is staying with friends in the village."

Willoughby had been in Shipcote at the time of Evelyn Allerton's murder.

As I considered the implications of this fact, I remembered my reaction to his description of the murder, that it had been so vivid as to seem firsthand. Had he heard it from the murderer himself? If that were so, if Willoughby, the lover of secrets, possessed such knowledge, how had he gained it? And what had it gained him? Had he used it to blackmail Benedict all these years? I thought back to the Sunday lunch at Summerhays. The relationship between the two men had seemed friendly enough; in fact, Willoughby had been treated as part of the family. Murderer or not, would a man like Benedict allow a blackmailer that close to people he loved? Perhaps, if he had no choice.

I copied the page and moved on through subsequent issues of the paper. There was nothing useful until a piece a month later on the recovery of Evelyn Allerton's locket from a pawnshop in Liverpool that had seemed to confirm the police theory of a tramp as the murderer. The article went on to say that several items taken from the cottage were still missing, among them a pair of pearl-and-amethyst earrings that had once belonged to the victim's mother-in-law and a gold pocket watch that had been her husband's. These were identified as missing by Clarissa Allerton, the dead woman's sister-in-law. I made a copy of this page as well. By now, it was close to two and I was tired and very hungry.

When I got back to Longbarrow Cottage, there were two vehicles already parked in the drive, a Land Rover and a pickup truck behind it. Sophie, Anna, and Max were in the living room with Val Lenthall and a skinny, sooty-faced man dressed all in black. A rolled-up canvas and some brushes were stacked by the hearth. As I hugged Max and said hi to Anna and Val, Sophie introduced the man in black. He was, of course, the chimney sweep sent by William Ebborn. His job done, he was just packing up his equipment to leave. "Should draw nicely now," he promised as I paid him. "Must've been a fire in the chimney once. Left a right mess, I can tell you."

After he had gone, Sophie said that she and the children had met Val when they were out walking and he had given them a lift home. "Lucky he did, or we'd have missed the sweep." There was soup in a pot on the cooker for my lunch, she added.

They all kept me company at the dining table while I ate. Max sat on my lap, chewing on a crust of Sophie's bread, while I tried not to drip soup on him. Sophie had guessed that I did not want to discuss the morning while Val was there, and so we talked about other things. Despite their brief acquaintance, Sophie and Val had an obviously strong rapport, an easy teasing way with each other that was appealing to watch.

Afterward, Val offered to collect and cut up the fallen apple boughs for the fireplace. If we had a saw, he said, it would save him the trip back to the farm park to fetch one of theirs. On inspection, the garden shed behind the cottage turned up a rusty saw and an ancient but working wheelbarrow. While I put Max and Anna down for their afternoon naps, Sophie and Val went around the garden gathering up the branches. I watched them from the window by Anna's bed with a small pang of what I was surprised to recognize as envy.

I sat down on the sofa to work on some half-finished drawings, but as I took them out of the portfolio I found a sketch I had made earlier of the murder scene as Sophie had described it. I stared at it for a while, and as I did another picture began to grow in my mind, simultaneously taking shape on a fresh piece of paper. A picture of the front of Longbarrow Cottage in the darkness and the storm, light falling on the snow from an uncurtained window. A figure in a hat and long overcoat crept into the drawing, back turned, peering in through the living room window. He seemed to have a life of his own, a strange independence that controlled my fingers.

The sound of the back door opening, followed by voices, startled me as though I'd been asleep. I shoved the drawing back into the portfolio as Sophie and Val came into the room.

"There," Sophie said, pointing proudly to the stack of applewood in Val's arms. "We can have a fire tonight."

Val set the wood carefully down on the hearthstone. "Applewood smells good. But you'll want a slower-burning wood as well. I'll see what I can bring over from the farm park tomorrow, before the picnic." Saying he had errands to run in Wychley before the shops closed, he took himself off, with a piece of Sophie's cake in one hand as a thank-you. There was a small silence after he left. Sophie tidied up the wood by the fireplace.

"What was that expression again?" I asked her. "A casserole? Boeuf bourguignon, if you ask me."

Surprisingly, for Sophie, she blushed.

Later, after we had talked over the events of my morning and I had shown her the copies from the newspaper, I asked her if she knew anyone with the police in Wychley. I wanted to find out whether Benedict had come forward to identify himself to the police as the man getting out of the car at the Withyford turn. I wanted to know, too, about that gold pocket watch, and if it had ever been found.

There was a sergeant who had been a young friend of her

grandfather's, she said. He was now a detective inspector. She could ask him. Whether he would be willing or able to find out the answers was another matter. Neither of us knew if the records for a fifty-year-old murder would still be available, but the fact that it had never been solved might mean they would have to be kept.

CHAPTER 26

The sun shone down from a cloudless sky on Sunday morning, the air smelled sweet, birds sang. It was perfect picnic weather. When I went downstairs with Max, Sophie was already in the kitchen with Anna making the shortcrust for small turnovers. Some would be filled with the mixture of finely ground lamb, potatoes, onions, and herbs that was cooking in a frying pan on the stove, others, for dessert, with jam or sliced apples and sugar. While Sophie rolled out the pastry, Anna sat at the table eating curlings of apple peel. We were going on a picnic, she told me gravely.

"She's talked about nothing else since she got up," Sophie said, giving Anna a quick hug, careful not to touch her with floury hands. "Thank goodness the weather's fine."

After breakfast, Sophie organized the picnic while I took Max and Anna in the car to the Husseins' shop for the Sunday papers and a box of sugar. Mr. Hussein and I chatted for a few minutes about Toronto, where he had relatives, and then the children and I left with our purchases. As we came out into the sunshine, a silver-gray Jaguar pulled up behind my car.

Benedict Mallaby had filled my thoughts during the past week. In my imagination, he had become not only larger than life but a much younger man, as though I had forgotten what he really looked like. It was a shock to see him now, as he got out of the Jaguar, smaller and indisputably older than his image in my mind. Like a glimpse of someone famous in the flesh, the sight of him provoked a confused response: surprise that he was human after all, and a vague suspicion that somehow there had been a sleight of hand, some trick to palm off the ordinary in place of the exceptional. But reality has a way of mocking the wilder flights of fantasy.

All the same, I would have liked to avoid him. But he saw me at once and called out hello as he came across the road. With Max on my hip and Anna gripping one hand, I was tethered there, forced to pretend a friendliness in response to his own smiling affability. He asked about the children and life at Longbarrow Cottage; if he knew about Sophie's presence, he was sufficiently well-bred to avoid a direct question. Slowly, I began to relax. It was hard to reconcile the murderer of my imagination with this urbane, somehow melancholic man. His skin seemed less pinkly healthy than the last time I had seen him and there were yellow pouches under his eyes, as though he were sleeping badly. He looked almost unwell.

Clarissa would be pleased we had run into each other, he said; she wanted to invite me around for tea. I murmured some sort of polite acquiescence. The sunlight glinted off the gold chain across his vest, and a faint bulge of cream wool marked where the pocket watch lay hidden against his chest. Suddenly, the words of the inscription in their thin curling script seemed to waver before my eyes, like a message or a warning. I thought of life blood and time, mingled, beating together, then thickening and slowing until at last the pulse was stilled.

"Would Tuesday suit you?" Benedict's voice seemed very loud, the measured cadence like the slow stroke of a clock. "Three-thirty, shall we say?"

Max squirmed, complaining against my side. I said Tuesday was fine, thank you, and now before Max disturbed the Sunday silence I really should get him and Anna home. A kind of babbling desperation took hold of me, but he seemed not to notice, said good-bye, and went on into the shop. On the way back to Longbarrow Cottage, the multiple images of

Benedict Mallaby fanned out like a spread pack of cards in my mind. Idealist, loyal friend, loving husband, paterfamilias, local squire, greedy businessman, betrayer, murderer. Take your pick, the faces on the cards announced, but don't be too sure you'll get it right.

Around eleven-thirty, a car drove up outside the cottage. From the living room window, I saw David, Rafe, and Val getting out of the green Range Rover. David turned to help someone else emerge. It was Mela.

"Is that them?" Sophie stood in the doorway of the kitchen, screwing the top back on a jar of mustard.

I nodded. "Mela Mallaby's with them."

"In that case, count me out," Sophie said firmly, her face tight. "Anna and I'll stay here."

Surprised, I protested that she mustn't do that. "All the work you've put into making the picnic. And we'd miss you. She's really not that bad," I finished lamely.

"Yes, she is." Sophie turned on her heel and disappeared back into the kitchen. With a small sigh, I went to open the front door.

"I've invited myself along, you see," Mela said as everyone came inside. "Your picnic sounded irresistible." She gave me one of her angelic smiles. Dressed in a pale green wool jacket over linen trousers of a darker green, with her hair piled loosely up on her head à la Alphonse Mucha, she looked like a long-stemmed flower. There was a small bandage on her right hand. Behind her, as he said hello, David's face was unreadable, but Rafe rolled his eyes dramatically, then went to squat on the living room floor in front of Max, who beamed gummily up at him.

"Sophie's in the kitchen," I told Val. "She's getting cold feet about coming. I think all the cooking she's done for the picnic may have worn her out." Disappointment plain on his freckled face, he said he would try his luck at persuading her to change her mind, and pushed open the kitchen door.

While Mela looked around the living room, taking in my sketches and the changes Sophie and I had made to the place, I gathered up the carryall that contained Max's belongings as well as the book for Rafe, and an old blanket I'd found in the airing cupboard.

At that moment, Val emerged from the kitchen with Sophie and Anna, carrying the various plastic bags that, for lack of a hamper, held the picnic food. He gave me a pleased, mildly triumphant look. I wondered what he'd done to persuade her. Sophie smiled and said hello to David and Rafe. Then, holding Anna's hand in hers, she turned to Mela.

"It's time you met my daughter. This is Anna." Her manner was very cold, almost defiant. She stared at the other woman with undisguised dislike.

"What a little beauty she is," Mela said with enthusiasm, or the perfect imitation of it. "Quite ravishing." She seemed unaffected by Sophie's reaction to her, standing there with her hands in the pockets of the long, loose jacket, smiling at Anna, who stared back solemnly. Given Sophie's dramatic reaction to her, Mela's aplomb was in its way remarkable.

Anna eased the situation by announcing in worried tones that Max would cry if we didn't have the picnic soon. "Tum, Mama," she pleaded. "Now." Sophie suddenly grinned, and lifted her up into her arms. "Right, then. Shall we go?"

Sophie and Anna came with Max and me, the others went in the Range Rover. At the last moment, Rafe came running up to ask if there was room for him as well. "Long as you don't mind squeezing in back with Anna and me," Sophie told him, opening the door.

"I'd like that a lot more than having to ride with her," he announced darkly as he climbed in. He went on to say that Mela had dropped by Oldbarn and found his father and himself putting together their picnic. "He had to ask her," he explained. "Spike's not allowed to come, but she is." His voice made it plain that he thought this arrangement very unfair. Sophie asked why Spike had been left behind.

"Because of Mela." He told her what Spike had done.

"I can see why you're so fond of Spike." Sophie's voice was very dry.

Rafe's resentment of Mela was easy enough to understand, given the various threats she might represent to him, but Sophie's reaction to Mela seemed more than a childhood dislike that had hardened with age. There was some sort of history between the two women, and I would have given a lot to know what it was. All I said now, however, was that I was glad Sophie had changed her mind about coming.

"Anna had her heart set on it," she replied. "I decided I wasn't going to let anyone spoil it for her."

Although David had given me a map with the way to Humblebee Barrow marked on it, I followed his car. For half the journey we took a main road, then turned off onto lanes that wound through little wooded valleys or climbed over hills that gradually grew steeper, with vistas of distant uplands tilted against the sun. A midday Sunday quiet held the countryside in its drowsy grip.

During the drive, Rafe and Sophie discussed long barrows. She seemed to know a certain amount about them herself, much to Rafe's delight. He asked her if she had ever tried to explore Goody Ridler's Tump.

"It was always made fairly clear to us when we were kids that it was off-limits," she replied. "Anyway, I had heard too many stories to want to go near it."

"What sort of stories?"

"Oh, the usual. That a giant's buried in it standing upright. And of course the one about Goody Ridler and those poor—" She paused, and I could imagine her downward glance at Anna. "Once a group of us climbed up onto it after dark, for a dare. But it seemed wrong somehow. Not the trespassing bit. That I liked." There was a grin in her voice.

"Why, then?" Rafe asked her.

"I felt sacrilegious. As if I'd been knocking over tombstones in a churchyard."

For some time the winding, narrow road we were on had been climbing steadily along the edge of a hill. Now, up ahead, the Range Rover signaled, slowed, and pulled off into a lay-by. I parked behind it. On our right, the land fell away to a wide valley of patchworked green fields, spinneys and hedgerows cradled by smoothly sloping hills of lush pasture, with the gray roofs of some large estate and the spire of a church just visible through a thick plantation of trees.

Across the road, a black-and-white sign pointed the way to "Humblebee Barrow, Ancient Monument," up a steep,

tree-clad hill. Clutching picnic paraphernalia, with Max in
the carrier, on David's back, and Anna perched astride Val's
shoulders, we followed the footpath through the green
wood of young beech. After a few minutes the path
emerged from the wood to skirt a wide field of long grass
ruffled by the wind. Far below us was the wide green bowl
of the distant valley, vivid in the midday sun.

"Come on," Rafe urged as we neared the top, and began
to run. Sophie took up the challenge and raced off after
him. Max and Anna, excited, began to bounce up and down
in sympathy; their bearers quickened their pace, jogging, so
that the two children crowed happily.

With a hand on my arm, Mela held me back. "Has
Sophie told you who Anna's father is?"

The question was so abrupt that I was startled into an answer. "No," I replied, "she hasn't." But I did not want to
discuss Sophie behind her back, least of all with Mela.
Coldly, I added, "And it's none of my business anyway."

The tone of my voice failed to discourage her. "She
claims it's my brother."

"Robin?" Because I was shocked, I said the name without thinking.

"Yes." Her sideways glance was surprised. "I didn't
think you knew him."

"We met once in the village." Then, before she could go
on, I added, "If Sophie wants to talk about it, she can. But
I'd rather it be her decision."

"I'm telling you so that you'll understand that Sophie's
not very reasonable on the subject of our family. She's angry with us. Don't believe everything she tells you about
us."

I stopped and faced her. "I'm only interested in the truth
about your family as it relates to mine."

The blue eyes narrowed. "What do you mean?"

"Your grandfather's relationship to my grandparents. Not
just that he and my grandfather were cousins. Beyond that."

"There wasn't anything beyond that," she said blandly.

I began to walk again. "Have you ever heard of something called The Longbarrow Brotherhood?"

"Oh, that." Her laugh was dismissive. "A lot of romantic

thirties nonsense that fizzled out fairly quickly. Nothing came of it."

We had caught up to the others by this time, which put an end to the discussion. As we all walked on together, I reflected that although Mela was involved in the family publishing company it did not necessarily mean she knew anything about its origins or the document that might be a threat to it. The only person who could answer my questions was Benedict himself.

At the top of the climb we came through a gate in a hawthorn hedge onto a wide plateau, a meadow filled with the white-puffed and yellow heads of thousands of dandelions. Several hundred feet away to our left, Humblebee Barrow rose in a smooth green hump like some enormous beached whale. Around it was a drystone wall, a barrier protecting it from larger animals. There was a general consensus, loudly opposed by Rafe, that we should eat before exploring. The majority ruled and we spread the blankets in the lee of the hedge. Rafe was consoled by the sight of the feast as it emerged from its various packages: loaves of bread, wedges of white and yellow cheeses, Sophie's turnovers, their crimped tops baked golden, salads in plastic bowls, and for dessert, grapes and a round, white-iced cake studded with cherries.

Conversation at first was minimal, as though the undercurrents were too strong to let us be easy with one another. But, for whatever reason, Mela laid herself out to charm, and to a degree succeeded, her good humor eventually infecting us all. Even Sophie seemed to relax. A companionable, lazy atmosphere grew, helped by the good food and wine, and the warm sun. Rafe was the first to finish and went off to clamber over the barrow on his own. At my side, Max lay on the blanket sucking on his bottle, his eyes slowly growing heavy and unfocused until at last the bottle dropped from his hand and he was asleep. Anna crawled into her mother's lap while Sophie and Val fashioned the dandelions that grew about us into chains for her.

Mela was wearing sunglasses, so it was impossible to know what she was looking at. But something, a stillness in the way she held herself and the slight turn of her head in their direction, suggested that she was absorbed in watching

Sophie and Anna. Sophie's "claim" might well be true, I thought. At certain angles, Anna had a look of Robin Mallaby in the curve of her cheek and the slope of her eyebrows.

Abruptly, Mela stood up, brushing crumbs from her skirt. "All that food. I need some exercise. David?" Her voice had a rough, sensuous edge; it held an invitation as well as a question. Slowly, she removed the sunglasses, revealing the blue gaze. Val glanced up at her, then across at Sophie, who lifted an eyebrow.

Half-raised on one elbow, David was stretched out on the blanket next to Val, a long stalk of bearded barley between his teeth. He looked up at her, his eyes narrowed against the sun, then took the grass out and threw it away. "Maybe later. It's very pleasant sitting here."

"Don't be lazy." She held out her left hand to him. It was the closest, I thought, that she would ever come to a direct appeal. To refuse it would seem loutish.

He gave her a long look, and then, ignoring the proffered hand, got to his feet. "That's better," she said in her clear, silvery voice. She glanced at me slantwise before they walked off, her hand tucked into his arm.

There was a small silence. Softly, Val began to whistle. After a few notes, I recognized the Triumphal March from *Aïda*. Sophie and I looked at each other and burst out laughing. Anna glanced up at us from her dandelions, surprised. Just then, Rafe came running back. "Are there any more of those turnovers with the apples?" He polished off the last three, and announced it was time for my tour. Sophie was content to admire the barrow from a distance, she told us, and would stay with Max. Val, in turn, said he would stay with Sophie and the children. Adjusting Max's sun hat to cover his face, I stood up and followed Rafe across the field.

The barrow seemed to swell from the ground, its long green flank sprawling hugely across the field like the thigh of some indolent, lymphatic goddess. We went through the gate and along the low stone ditch that ringed the barrow, to the entrance at the northeast end. Like the earth's bones, thin pieces of pale stone littered the ground. Framed by narrow uprights supporting the thick slab of lintel stone, the dark crevice of the portal lay deeply recessed between two long sloping green horns of earth. As we faced it, the body of the barrow, spread-legged, rose in front of us.

Rafe described how the mound's builders had ensured that at a certain moment during the winter solstice, the rays of the rising sun would penetrate the passage through the portal. In mid-explanation, a toad hopped out of the grass onto a flange of layered stone projecting from the turf by the entrance. Rafe hunkered down to get a better look at it.

I peered into the entrance. The daylight lit up only a few feet of the passage before it was absorbed by the rock. I asked Rafe if he had brought a flashlight with him.

He looked up from the toad. "I forgot. It's in my jacket. Hold on, I'll go get it." He ran off toward the picnic blankets, passing Mela and his father on the way. They were walking toward the barrow, obviously deep in conversation.

I stooped and entered the barrow. The stone roof was low enough to make crouching necessary at first, but within a yard or two grew higher until at last I could stand upright. I could not see, but when I stretched out my arms, the touch of damp stone walls on either side served as a guide. Slowly feeling my way along, I went farther down the passage. The floor seemed to descend, and after a few yards I stopped, reluctant to go deeper in without Rafe's flashlight. Gradually, the blackness shifted into a gray fog that dimly revealed the drystone walls and wide roofing slabs overhead. The yeasty smell of sour earth rose from the floor.

I shut my eyes, leaving the palms of my hands pressed against the moist stone. Against my closed eyelids moved the shadows of the unknown people who had waited here for that ancient sign of rebirth, their symbol of the ripening year. A profound silence, filtered of all sound by the stone and the enclosing mound of earth, held the darkness. Void of light, time seemed suspended or distorted, simultaneously lengthened and compressed. Disoriented, increasingly breathless, I began to feel an obscure pressure thickening the air, as though the earth were a muscle slowly contracting around me. A trickle of liquid ran over my hand.

I whirled around and stumbled for the entrance, suddenly desperate for the open day.

A dark mass outlined in light filled the end of the passage. After the first shock of fear, I recognized David. Desperately, as if he were my only connection to the light, I stretched out one hand to him. His own was warm against mine as he drew me forward.

"It's bloody dark in here," a voice said loudly behind David. Then the crouching figure of a man bumped up against him, jostling us both. "Crikey! I didn't see you people."

The man pressed himself against the passage wall to let us by. As we emerged, blinking, into the light, a woman in hiking gear stood by the entrance. She gave an exaggerated shiver. "Ooh, you look like you've seen a ghost," she told me. With a laugh, she bent down and called out to the man, "You still alive in there, Tim?" Giggling, she stooped and followed him inside.

Rafe ran up with the flashlight. "Max is crying," he told me breathlessly. "Sophie says please come."

Max had been stung on the leg by some sort of insect. The bite seemed minor, with very little actual swelling, but it took some time before he could be comforted. When Mela appeared, walking slowly across the field, and announced that she would like to be back at Summerhays in time for tea, we began to gather up the picnic things. To assuage Rafe's disappointment at not being able to show me the interior of the barrow, I told him that I had explored a little of it on my own and was curious to know more about the parts I'd missed. He discoursed on these in great detail all the way back to the car.

At his father's request, perhaps to spare us further information, Rafe rode back with the others in the Range Rover. Before he climbed into it, I called him over and gave him the book on barrows I'd bought for him. "Maybe you'll write one of your own on the subject someday," I told him with a smile. The idea, and the gift, seemed to please him.

For the first few miles, Sophie and I talked carefully around the issue of Mela. Finally, when Anna had fallen asleep, she said without preamble, "Did she tell you?"

I didn't pretend not to understand. "She said you claimed that Robin Mallaby is Anna's father. That was how she put it. I wouldn't let her say any more."

"It's true."

"I believe you. I can see the resemblance."

"You know Robin?"

"I've met him." Then I remembered the phone call to Mela I had overheard at Summerhays, the one in which she urged him not to miss his plane flight, and told Sophie about that.

"She sent him away," Sophie said flatly. "I'm sure of it. She can be very possessive, even when she doesn't care tuppence for whatever she's decided to hold on to."

She had called Robin from Paris, Sophie said, and announced she was coming to Shipcote. It was time they discussed Anna. They had arranged that he would pick her up in Wychley, but when she called Summerhays to let him know she'd arrived, Mela had told her that he was in New York on business. I had overheard Sophie's angry response, when she had called Mela a bitch, and thought she might have been speaking to her mother.

"He's as weak as watered milk," Sophie said. "I always knew it, even when we were little. But I thought university had changed him. It hadn't." They had grown up in the same village without really knowing each other, as Robin was usually away at school, then met again when Sophie came to Martyrs Hall, where Robin was a student in his final year. Anna was the result of their brief affair.

"His sister wants him to marry money. That's his mission in life. He used to make a joke of it, but now I think he agrees with her. Anyway, I don't want to marry him. I just want him to acknowledge Anna."

She sighed. "I was very stiff-necked in the beginning. Told myself I didn't want anything from him. I can see now, that's ridiculous. It's not just me, it's Anna. If something happens to me, he has to be responsible. He's not a bad person, but he has no imagination. So it's easy for him to avoid accepting the facts. Once he sees her, though, he'll feel differently."

Yes, I thought, remembering how he had been with Max, he probably would.

"Mela's afraid of that. That's probably why she arranged for him to go off. As long as I'm in Shipcote, she won't let him come near the place."

"What about Benedict and Clarissa?"

"Mela says they don't believe me." There was a silence. "So you can see," Sophie said after a moment, her voice uninflected, "why I don't like the Mallabys."

CHAPTER 27

I went up the worn steps in the Bodleian Library on Monday morning to claim *Life Blood*. Tweedy backs were bent over books at the long tables marching down the room in rows. A skinny boy with a tatty green sweater hanging past his hips stood behind the reserve desk sorting slips of paper. When I gave him my name, he took a small book with a mustard-yellow cloth cover from a shelf beside the desk, checked the slip tucked inside it, and handed it to me. "Life Blood" was printed in gold letters on the spine, and below it, "J. M. Morrile." The book felt properly heavy in my hand. As I quickly riffled through the pages, I saw with relief that the copy was intact. This time, it seemed, I was in luck.

I opened the book wider to look at the title page. The spine gave a loud crack, and the boy behind the desk glanced up. "Nobody's read that in a while," he said with a smile. But I hardly heard him. Instead of "Life Blood," the title read "Storm in Oxford." And the author was not J. M. Morrile, but someone named E. Tangye Lean.

Dismayed, I leafed hurriedly through the book, scanning the title printed at the top of each left-hand page. On page after page, right to the end, the same three words, "Storm in Oxford," appeared again and again. The contents of the book I was holding had nothing whatever to do with the title printed on the spine. At that point, like an actor doffing his mask, the entire body of the book came away in one piece from the cover. As I stood there staring helplessly at the clump of pages in my hand, the boy left his filing and came over to see what the matter was. With a sinking heart, I showed him the discrepancy between the title on the cover and that of the imposter inside.

"How very odd," he said. Just then a man with shoulder-length white hair and an extremely large belly barely contained by his buttoned tweed jacket came out of a door behind the reserve desk. Raising one hand, the boy motioned him over. "Mr. Belston, would you have a look at this, please."

The man accepted both cover and contents from me and examined them carefully, his face grave. "Someone has obviously cut away the original and glued this"—he held up the bundle of pages—"in its place. How very odd."

"Just what I said," the boy assured him.

"It's deliberate, then," I asked, "and not a printing mistake?"

"No, no, quite deliberate. No doubt about it whatsoever. Someone sliced very neatly along here"—he pointed to the hinges of paper glued on the inside front and back covers—"and then rather inadequately stuck the replacement to the spine. From the look of the glue I'd say it was done some time ago. You must be the first person to ask for the book since then. It was bound to come apart like this as soon as it was opened." He placed the contents back inside the cover. "Any idea what the original was about?"

I shook my head. "That's what I was hoping to find out. All I know is that it was a mystery."

"Someone obviously wanted to make a mystery out of a mystery," the boy said cheerfully. "A deconstructionist, from the look of it." A quelling glance from the librarian set him to sorting slips again.

"Well, I'm very sorry," Mr. Belston continued. "Perhaps the two books were switched as some sort of prank. Students, you know." He cast a dark look in the direction of the skinny assistant. But the gutted copy at the British Museum was sufficient proof, for me, that the Bodleian Library's substitution was no spur-of-the-moment student prank. Whoever was responsible had taken the trouble to find a novel of the same size and length as the original, so that it would fit properly between the covers. Unable to steal the book outright, he had come prepared with replacement pages. That argued a certain amount of planning.

The librarian told me that they would try to obtain another copy for me on interlibrary loan, and scribbled down a telephone number where I could reach him the next day to find out if the pages of *Life Blood* turned up in the Bodleian's copy of *Storm in Oxford.*

"Don't bother to try the British Museum Reading Room," I said as I filled out the interlibrary loan form. When I explained what had happened to the copy there, he looked astonished. In that case, he replied, the only likely alternative was the university library in Cambridge or the British Library in Yorkshire.

I suspected, however, that their copies would already have suffered a similar fate.

As I walked through the streets to Martyrs Hall for my lunch with Willoughby Webb Springer, I found that of all my emotions anger was the strongest. Stronger, even, than my disappointment. The German bombs that had destroyed so many copies of *Life Blood* had not been aimed specifically at Nan. These two separate acts of vandalism were. One alone might have been an unlucky chance; two could only be deliberate.

The person who had struck at *Life Blood* had done so, I believed now, out of fear. Fear that it would be read. Fear, perhaps, that it told the truth.

On a cobblestone back street where no building seemed later than the seventeenth century, the huge crenellated tower of Martyrs Hall loomed up, dominating its neighbors. Gargoyles and grotesques with outstretched tongues peered rudely down from their stony perches, leering at those who passed below. On a stone rosette by the gate was the secretive face of a Green Man half-smothered in leaves, sprouting vines from his open mouth. A voyeur's face.

A burly man in a long dark coat and a bowler hat stood with folded arms at the gate, his own face as intimidating as any of those carved above him. I began to understand why Sophie had felt like an interloper here, even as a student. Before I could give Willoughby's name as my password, the man himself appeared, hurrying toward me across the green quadrangle that lay beyond the gate. As always, he was nattily dressed, today in a pale gray tweed suit with a plum-colored waistcoat. His tie, a gray silk, was held in place with a pearl stickpin.

"Such a pity," he began, after we had said hello, "my friend is unable to join us after all. Sciatica, you see. It plagues him. But that will give us a chance to have a little talk all to ourselves." Behind him, crouched on a drainpipe, a dwarf was biting its tongue.

I doubted that Willoughby's friend had ever been invited. For reasons of his own, he was clearly as eager as I was for our "little talk." Whether our subjects would coincide remained to be seen.

"I thought we would lunch in my rooms," Willoughby told me as we walked across the quad past a tumbling fountain. "It's not done, you understand, to talk to your own guest over lunch in the fellows' dining room. Conversation must be general. That would hardly suit us, would it?"

Before I could reply, he launched into an anecdotal history of the college, its founding by Henry the Eighth after a bad meal at Christ Church, its "flexibility" during the Civil War years, when a careful watch for the winds of change preserved it from the retaliation of Royalists and Parliamentarians alike. Thanks to a succession of canny bursars, he said, Martyrs Hall became one of the richest colleges, with farms in Devon and vineyards in Portugal, famous for its specially blended port. "Cardinal Newman once jibed unkindly that the only martyrs here were those martyred by gout." He gave his dry little laugh.

As he led me down a little passageway beside a cloistered garden, he told me that his set of rooms was in the Victorian addition to the college, which unfortunately happened to be under renovation at the moment. With a certain amount of banging and crashing, some workmen were erecting a scaffolding against a wall. "They're making life quite impossible," Willoughby said in a peevish voice. We went up a flight of narrow stone steps to a small arched door, which he unlocked and held open for me.

The large and very beautiful living room on the other side of the door was a bibliophile's dream. Willoughby had obviously taken to heart the dictum that books do furnish a room. Leather-bound, gold-tooled, jacketed, cloth-backed, antiquarian or modern, they filled the many bookshelves, sat in piles on tabletops, and in the case of a William Morris, *The Wood Beyond the World*, lay open under glass to display the work of the Kelmscott Press.

"As you can see," Willoughby said with a self-satisfied smile, "books are very precious to me."

" 'The precious life blood of a master spirit,' " I quoted automatically. When he looked surprised, I reminded him that I had seen the words on Benedict Mallaby's pocket watch. "Don't you think the title of my grandmother's book refers to those words?" The question came to my lips and was asked before I considered its possible consequences.

But Willoughby chose not to answer it directly. Gazing into the middle distance, he recited from memory: " 'Who kills a man kills a reasonable creature, God's image: but he who destroys a good book, kills reason itself, kills the image of God, as it were, in the eye. Many a man lives a burden to the earth; but a good book is the precious life blood of a master spirit.' " He turned his deceptively mild sheep's eyes on me. "Milton was defending the freedom of the press, but one might use such an argument to claim the precedence of a masterpiece over a human life."

"That would be a perversion of its meaning, wouldn't it?"

He spread his hands wide. "Some might reply that no sacrifice is too great for an enduring work of literature."

"The word 'sacrifice' always makes me think of the story of Abraham and Isaac. Sacrifices often cause the innocent pain. And in the end you may find out they weren't required anyway."

He merely smiled, and invited me to appreciate the view from a pair of tall windows recessed beneath a pointed Gothic arch. The windows looked over walled college gardens to a meadow where cows grazed and had their pictures taken by passing tourists. The pastoral scene seemed utterly divorced from the modern city beyond the gates.

When I had duly admired the view, and the room itself, Willoughby said, "These rooms are much coveted by the other fellows here. By rights, I ought to have relinquished them to a younger man some years ago. But the prospect of acquiring my collection after my death has persuaded the powers that be to let me remain." Fondly, he gazed around the shelves. "I owe a great deal to my books." He spoke of them almost as though they were his children, the support of his old age.

At Willoughby's request, I had brought copies of two of my own books, which he now asked to see. He professed himself "charmed" by them, asked intelligent questions about technique and printing methods, and was interested in the stories, which in both instances were based on Canadian legends, as well as the illustrations. He showed such a sympathy for my work, in fact, that inevitably I began to like him better. I was sure, however, that my books were not the reason why he had invited me to lunch. But I could wait.

Near the windows, a small round table was set with china and silver, a bowl of apples, and a bottle of uncorked red wine. On a trolley a spirit lamp burned beneath a silver chafing dish, and beside it were a quiche on a china plate, a green salad, and a napkin-covered basket of rolls, all prepared, he said, by the Hall kitchens. He invited me to sit down in one of the handsome scroll-backed chairs drawn up to the table.

As we ate, I began to take in the details around me. Apart from the books and the handsome, unobtrusive furniture, the objects in the room had been chosen with an eye to a quiet and almost diminutive beauty. Among these were a dozen miniature eighteenth-century silhouettes in silver frames, a collection of cameos hung on blue felt, and on a table three tiny, exquisite models of nineteenth-century printing presses, salesman's models, Willoughby told me, for connoisseurs. There was no grand dramatic statement, but the cumulative effect of his possessions was of a discriminating luxury free of ostentation. Anyone who lived in such a room, with its books and its view of meadow and river, ought by rights to be contented. And yet something about Willoughby, that waspish humor perhaps, suggested he was not.

"Now tell me," he said, "did you have any luck at the Bodleian?"

If anyone could give me information about *Life Blood* it was this man, whatever his motivation might be for satisfying my curiosity. I doubted I would learn anything from him, however, unless I satisfied his own curiosity at the same time. And so as I described the results of my visits to the British Museum Reading Room and the Bodleian Library, I tried to make a little drama out of the sorry business, to whet his appetite, in a sense, for more. At first, his face was pleasantly bemused, seemingly uninvolved, but gradually a flicker of interest grew in his eyes. Whether that interest was in the results of the search itself or in the manner of narration was difficult to say. For all that he claimed to be appalled by the books' destruction in both libraries, he did not seem surprised, as though it only confirmed some suspicion of his.

"I'm not sure where to go from here," I said when I finished. "I don't have much faith that interlibrary loan is going to be any more successful. I'm willing to bet whoever did it to these copies will have been careful to destroy any other library copies. They've probably been buying up the few secondhand copies as well."

This observation provoked a sharp look from Willoughby, but his response was merely to observe that I must not give up hope. He might have been encouraging a student with some knotty problem of interpretation, interested in a detached fashion to see where the research would take her. "Over the years, there have been one or two rare books others gave up for lost. In the end, they came to me because I pursued them unrelentingly."

"You think the book's worth pursuing, then? Despite your review when it was published?" This was a calculated risk. I did not want to make him angry, but somehow I had to resolve the contradiction between the review and his interest in the book.

Unperturbed, he lifted the lid off the silver chafing dish. Inside were thin slices of veal with sage, which he placed on fresh plates. "How our old sins come back to haunt us. Now that I'm older, I must admit I am often shamed by the violent language of my youth." The expression on his face mimed repentance, but he sounded more amused than ashamed. "I was too harsh."

"Then it was a better book than you implied in your review?" I was trying to keep my own voice as detached as his.

"Let's just say there were elements that deserved a readership."

I tried to push matters forward a little. "I'd be very grateful if you'd tell me what you remember of the book."

But he was not to be forced to a pace quicker than his own. "No, I don't think I shall do that," he replied smoothly. "That would spoil the surprise. I'm a great believer in coming to the text fresh."

As I struggled to conceal my frustration, I felt a sudden sympathy for the generations of students who had come to these rooms, papers in hand, for help. Their mental wrigglings must have afforded Willoughby hours of entertainment. I looked around at the rows of books. "You don't happen to have a copy yourself, do you?"

His smile was ambiguous. "Unfortunately not. I did, some years ago. I seem to have mislaid it, however."

We ate our veal in silence. After a minute or two, determined to learn something useful from him, I mentioned that I had been reading his biography of Stephen Allerton and finding it very interesting, not least because of where I was living.

"A little disconcerting, I should think, if you've reached the chapter dealing with Evelyn's murder. When I finish my memoirs I really must revise the book. New material has come to light since it was first published."

I glanced up from my plate in surprise. "About the murder?"

"I was thinking more of the life."

"My grandfather's, for instance?"

It was his turn to look surprised. "Yes," he conceded, drinking his wine. "Among others."

"It did strike me as strange that you never mention him. After all, he owned Longbarrow Cottage while the Allertons were living there. He even turns up in one of the photographs taken in the cottage, unidentified."

Willoughby poured more water in my glass; I had refused the wine. "You noticed that, did you?"

"Among other things. What really made me wonder, though, was finding out he'd been one of the Longbarrow Brotherhood. That made his absence from the biography seem deliberate."

Willoughby's response was evasive. "Brotherhood has a somewhat dated ring to it, doesn't it? It's rather out of fashion now. But you know in those days it was all the rage. The General Strike and the Depression gave people a certain sympathy with the working class. Unfortunately, Stephen carried it to an extreme. Benedict was essentially a pragmatist. And Charles . . . ? Well, I suspect he was the fulcrum that balanced the two of them."

"Why didn't you say that in the book?"

"Let's say I misunderstood the true nature of the relationship at the time. I believe I did mention your grandfather once or twice, but as I say, the book needs to be revised. He should have his due." He stood up, as though to put an end to the conversation, and gathered up the empty plates, stacking them neatly on the bottom shelf of the trolley. Suddenly, there was a startlingly loud banging from the stairwell on the other side of the door. Willoughby looked annoyed. Just as abruptly, the noise ceased.

"At Summerhays," I said, "when we met, I mentioned my grandfather. No one seemed very eager to talk about him—"

"You must understand that Clarissa and Benedict are quite sensitive on the subject of your grandfather. Originally, Charles was very close to both of them. To be truthful, he was a little in love with Clarissa at one time." The banging began again, forcing Willoughby to raise his voice. "Everyone was, of course. Benedict was cordially hated when he married her." As the banging grew louder, Willoughby's face darkened. "Oh, really, this is intolerable. If you'll excuse me, I'll just go and have a word with them."

He opened the door and went out into the stairwell. While he was gone, I got up to have a look at his various collections. Above the case containing the Kelmscott Morris was one of the dozen or so Victorian bookcases built into the walls around the room, their lancetlike doors decorated with traceries of wood against the glass. This particular bookcase appeared to contain twentieth-century novels, most still in their jackets, arranged alphabetically by author.

Idly, without hope, because after all Willoughby had said his copy was missing, I scanned the shelves through the patches of glass, looking in the *M*'s. And there it was, in a faded cream-colored jacket whose spine was printed with black letters.

Life Blood by J. M. Morrile.

After the shock receded, I reached out to the handle of the bookcase door. But of course it was locked. Outside in the hallway, the hammering suddenly stopped. With my heart beating furiously, I walked quickly over to the windows. Willoughby had lied, yet he had made no effort to hide the book, had deliberately left it in plain sight. Why?

Desperately, I tried to think what to do. To confront him with the lie seemed a risk. If I lost my temper, I might also lose any chance of learning more from him. But if I were patient, playing the game his way, my reward eventually might be the book itself. And his copy could well be the only one left.

The banging started up again as Willoughby came back into the room. "I'm informed that hideous noise will persist. I suggest we continue our conversation outdoors. I generally take a constitutional after lunch anyway." A walk would be very pleasant, I said truthfully. Anything to be out in the open air, away from the book, which would inevitably draw my eye back to it.

Downstairs, we came out through a door in a wall that opened onto the broad sandy path between the college gardens and the meadow. Willoughby suggested we follow the path down to the river and around. Once again, as we walked, he played the tour guide, describing the various colleges whose backs lined the meadow, pointing out the cottage where Auden had spent his last years. When we reached the river, a long scull swept past with a tiny coxswain screaming at the brawny rowers facing him. After all that nagging, it's no wonder they throw him in the water when they win a race, Willoughby observed tartly. Across the river, on the opposite bank, the coach paralleled the boat's progress on his bicycle.

A punt came drifting by, close to the bank. The boy who stood on the flat stern handled the long, unwieldy punt pole clumsily, and his passengers, two girls in jeans and bright sweatshirts, watched with giggling dismay as the pole stuck for a moment in the river bottom. At the last possible moment, the boy dragged it free from the mud but, in recovering it, overbalanced and, loudly cursing, fell forward into the punt amid the girls' shrieks of laughter.

Beside me, Willoughby gave a shudder of distaste. "Damn silly fool. He might have gone into the river."

"Is it deep?"

"Deep enough to drown in. The real danger is the weeds." He shivered again. "I'm afraid I have never been convinced of the pleasures to be gained from simply messing about in a boat."

I said that my husband had drowned when he was out sailing. As soon as the words were out, I wondered what had possessed me to tell him.

He looked shocked. "How perfectly dreadful. I am so very sorry, my dear." This was the first show of a genuine emotion I'd had from Willoughby. Was that why I had told him, to provoke it, to gain some advantage by making him sorry for me? I was ashamed of myself.

The path now ran along the third side of the rectangle, between the meadow and the tributary brook, through a thicket of trees and bushes. Two children and their mother were feeding the ducks, throwing bread into the quacking melee. More ducks splashed down from above to join the throng. The youngest child, a round-faced little boy with merry eyes, reminded me of Max. Both children stood perilously close to the edge of the bank.

Willoughby asked me if I had ever read *The Water Babies*. I replied that it was one of my favorite childhood books.

"And mine. Although I hate the very idea of being underwater." It struck me as an odd phobia for a man with such a watery name. "You know," he continued, "I sometimes wonder how many children's deaths Kingsley may have caused with that book." Startled, I asked him what on earth he meant. He gave a grim smile. "Weren't you ever tempted after reading it to leap into a river, confident the water babies would save you?"

No, I replied, but it was an interesting theory. "Books can have such power over us."

"Your grandmother certainly thought so. She intended hers to be a very powerful weapon indeed."

For a moment I was so shocked, both by the words and the admission, that I wasn't sure at first I had heard him properly.

"Against Benedict Mallaby? Is that what you mean?"

"You've worked that much out, have you, without having read the book?" He made it sound as though I were a clever student. "Yes, against Benedict."

"Did he ask you to write that review? And the other, the anonymous one in *The Times Literary Supplement*?"

"Now you're leaping to conclusions. Just like your grandmother." There was disapproval in his voice. "As a matter of fact, he did not. Clarissa did. As she saw it, your grandmother used her novel to tell lies about Benedict. Therefore she deserved to be treated equally harshly in print."

Bleakly, I said, "You must have hated Nan, too, then."

He paused to gaze at me in astonishment. "How naive you are, my dear. Every day reviews far more cruel than mine are written by those who may have genuinely friendly feelings for the author and cannot understand why he or she snubs them at the next literary luncheon. I hardly knew your grandmother, and certainly did not hate her. It was simply that I was under an obligation, and the review was my way of fulfilling it. A knightly duty, so to speak."

"Hardly chivalrous."

"On the contrary. In the best tradition of the Redcrosse Knight dealing with Duessa."

"I don't know who you mean."

His tongue clicked against the roof of his mouth in disapproval of my ignorance. "Duessa is a villain in Spenser's *Faerie Queen*. She is falsehood personified. It was Clarissa's name for your grandmother."

I had barely absorbed this when a woman's voice hailed Willoughby. Coming toward us along the path was the Mallabys' daughter, Cece Breakspear, and a short, balding man with a round face and a protruding lower lip, giving him the look of a pouting baby. Cece was dressed dramatically in a sweeping blue cloak that emphasized her size. She dwarfed her companion. "Such a lovely day," she was saying loudly as they approached. "George and I felt we simply must come down to the river, didn't we, George?"

"Cece! What a delightful surprise," Willoughby said. "George, my dear fellow, how are you?" Without waiting for a reply, he introduced me to George Breakspear, who blinked unsmilingly at me in response. Cece looked surprised to find me with Willoughby, nodded curtly, and then proceeded to direct all her comments at him. Apparently the river was no longer quite so compelling, for she announced they would walk back with us. Linking her arm in Willoughby's, she moved ahead with him in tow, rather like a great barge pulling a trim little dinghy. George Breakspear and I fell into step behind them. As he merely grunted in response to my admittedly not very brilliant remarks, conversation between us soon flagged. I remembered Mela's description of him as the most silent man in England.

Cece was eager to tell Willoughby some gossip or other about mutual friends. Her voice shrilled with the confidence of someone on her own turf. Once or twice she turned to her husband for confirmation of some point, and each time he seemed utterly oblivious, like a child who has shut out the grown-ups to concentrate on his own thoughts.

In front of us, Cece's voice rose into the air, loudly confiding. "You're coming down to Summerhays tomorrow, Mother tells me."

"Yes, for a week or two," Willoughby replied. "Your mother has very generously offered me the use of the garden house. I shall work on my memoirs in rural peace. It will be a relief to escape the hammering."

Willoughby in Shipcote. It was not a wholly appealing prospect. He was less threatening here in Oxford, safely at a remove. On the other hand, when the Breakspears had so frustratingly interrupted us, he had seemed on the verge of further revelations. In Shipcote, perhaps, there might be opportunities to learn more from him.

By now, we had made our circuit of the meadow and were back at the arch that led to Willoughby's staircase. Cece said, "George has a tutorial, poor dear, but there's something I simply must talk over with you, Willoughby."

Willoughby glanced at me and began to make polite noises. Quickly, I said that it was time I got back to Max, and thanked him for the delicious lunch. "Perhaps when you're in Shipcote—"

"Then we will certainly continue our most interesting conversation." Willoughby's smile held out the promise of those future disclosures. A sixteen-year-old tease could have learned a lot from it, I thought.

I said good-bye to the three of them. Cece gave me a strange, almost triumphant look, the look of someone who has routed an enemy. Her husband merely looked startled, like a man waking up from a deep sleep to find a stranger staring at him.

CHAPTER 28

When I called Mr. Belston at the Bodleian the next day from the pay phone on the green, he told me that their copy of *Storm in Oxford* was intact, containing only its rightful pages. He went on to say that he had phoned a colleague at Cambridge University library on other business and had thought to ask about Cambridge's copy of *Life Blood*. That one, too, was mutilated, the pages as neatly removed as those in the copy in the British Museum Reading Room.

"Someone certainly seems to have taken against the book," he said, bafflement as well as curiosity audible in his voice. "We'll see what we can do to replace it. But in the meantime, I should try secondhand book dealers if I were you."

Angry and discouraged, I went on to Summerhays for my tea with Clarissa. I was determined to question her about Charles and, if she was willing to discuss a woman she had hated, about Nan as well. My experience with Willoughby, however, had taught me to be pessimistic. None of the three people still alive who had known both Nan and Charles was a trustworthy narrator when it came to the story of their common past.

Mrs. Blackwell, the housekeeper, brought me to Clarissa in the garden behind the house. Flagstone paths sunk in grass wound their way among great tufts of lavender and thickly planted flower beds. On one side, the garden was sheltered from north winds by a high stone wall covered with the vines of wisteria and climbing roses. To the east and south, however, there were open views across the fields or down to the river and the low, enfolding hills beyond.

Erect and graceful, Clarissa sat on a bench under a trellis, gazing toward the river, which ran at the bottom of the garden some hundred feet away. One hand rested on the top of her cane, and in the other, lying on her lap, she held a pair of secateurs. Around her, laburnum hung from the latticework like golden rain, its scent sweet as honey.

Staring forward with a fierce concentration, she seemed at first oblivious to our approach. When Mrs. Blackwell spoke her name, however, she turned and the stern look vanished at once. With a smile of welcome, she invited me to join her on the bench. "We'll have our tea in the garden house, Blackie," she said to the housekeeper in her leisurely voice. "If it's not too much trouble."

None at all, Mrs. Blackwell replied, her good-tempered face equable; she would bring it out to us now. When I remarked on the beauty of the garden, Clarissa looked around with an air of tranquil pleasure. "Yes, it is lovely, isn't it. This garden is my refuge. As it was when I was a child. I had strings of governesses, you see, and I used to escape from them here. Once, when I was older, I asked my mother why I had so many. D'you know what she said? 'Well, they didn't like you, darling. You were a tiresome child.' " She shrugged, and gave a low chuckle. "I suppose I was. Stephen was the one they all adored. I made life difficult for them, I'm afraid. I would persuade Stephen to run away from them with me. He and I were like twins. Each wanting only to be with the other. The governess of the moment would search for us while we hid from her over there, in the garden house."

She gestured with the secateurs to a tiny stone building with a steeply pitched roof that stood in a far corner of the garden, backed by the stone wall, a short distance from the riverbank. Like some oversize child's playhouse, it sat on a grassy mound, approached by a short flight of stone steps, with a beautiful shell-headed porch over the small front door. "It's the family bolt hole," she said. "A private place for Greta Garbo moods. I've promised it to Willoughby, in order that he may write his memoirs in peace. Poor Willoughby, he's easily disturbed."

"It looks like the perfect place for writing." The only sounds to disturb him would be the river lapping at its banks and the waterfowl that swam among the reeds.

Clarissa lifted the secateurs from her lap and placed them on the bench beside her. "I only wish he were writing something other than his memoirs. The temptation to dwell in the past is so powerful, particularly at our age. One shouldn't give way to it. I never think of the past, myself. I prefer the present."

The deaths of three of her four children would make her past a painful place to visit; no wonder she preferred the present. I preferred it myself. Leading her back to the subject of Willoughby's memoirs, I said, "Perhaps he thinks his memories will interest other people?"

The large violet eyes regarded me, amused. "Oh, I daresay Willoughby's memories will arouse interest. Whether healthy or morbid is another matter entirely. As is the issue of their accuracy." Her voice was astringent, not quite disapproving but mildly disparaging, as though commenting on some tabloid's dubious journalism. "Memory so often plays us false."

"The trick," I said deliberately, "is to decide whose memory to trust."

If she read into this everything that I intended her to understand, her face did not show it. Serenely, she replied, "Trust no one's, my dear. For every event there will be a dozen different stories. Each, in its own way, the truth. You must be the judge." Was this the general "you," I wondered, or the specific?

With the aid of the cane, she stood up, shaking her head at my offer of help. "Pride goes before a fall, Blackie is fond of telling me. But as long as I am able, I prefer to manage on my own."

Slowly, she led me around the garden, using the secateurs to point out roses with the names of dead queens, columbines, a wide swath of lily of the valley under a whitebeam, the fat pink and white buds of peonies sprinkled with ants. "Blowsy flowers, peonies," she said. "I prefer flowers that surprise you, that keep something of themselves hidden. Irises now, or tulips." She paused to clip some straying tendrils of a honeysuckle vine that grew around a stone statue so worn by the weather that its features had vanished. "I like to prune. It's an art, you know. Knowing where to cut. One has to be bold, even ruthless. There is no place in a garden for the faint of heart." Beneath the tranquil observation, disturbingly, was the glint of a formidable, even implacable, will. I would not, I thought, want to be a weed in Clarissa's garden. When I bent to pick up the fallen pieces, she told me not to bother; the gardener would go around later collecting up the clippings.

"I spoke with Cece this morning on the telephone. I understand that she met you yesterday at Martyrs Hall with Willoughby." The hint of a question was implicit in her voice. I explained that he had invited me to lunch. "Oh, yes? Obviously, you've made an impression. Willoughby never bothers with people unless he finds them interesting."

Carefully, I replied, "I'm not sure what sort of an impression. But he strikes me as someone who likes to study people. Almost like a collector."

She glanced at me. "That's very astute of you, my dear. A collector is precisely what Willoughby is. Thank you, Blackie," she said to the housekeeper, who had come to tell her that everything was now ready for us in the garden house. As we walked slowly in that direction, Clarissa added, "The children always liked to pretend that Willoughby was in love with me. Not in the least. Oh, he's fond of me, I know that, but it was Stephen, my brother, whom he loved. He is devoted to me only because I am a relic of the person he loved. In some ways, Willoughby is very old-fashioned."

The tip of her cane struck the flagstones with a repeated crack as we progressed through the garden. Instead of making her seem weak or doddery, the cane gave her a distinguished look, perhaps because she wielded it as though it were decorative rather than buttressing. "Naturally," she continued, "he loathed Evelyn. Hated her with a passion. I remember how he used to rail against her when she was alive. He was convinced she was destroying Stephen. Well, of course, in many ways he was right. Stephen, however, was quite capable of destroying himself. But Willoughby was unreasonable on the subject of Evelyn."

So Willoughby had loved Stephen. That would explain the odd tone of the biography, its suggestion of repressed emotion. Although far from hagiography, it was written by a biographer who was under his subject's spell and eager to persuade the reader into an equal admiration. It would explain, too, why Evelyn came off so badly in the book. No wonder the description of her murder seemed so vivid; Willoughby must have enjoyed the writing of it. Might even, or so Clarissa seemed to be implying, have enjoyed the doing of it.

Slowly, Clarissa and I mounted the short flight of steps and went through the open door of the garden house into a pretty room cluttered with objects. A small round table next to a window was laid with a silver tea service and a plate of cakes, with two straight-backed chairs drawn up to it. Indicating that I was to take the other chair, Clarissa sat down and began to pour the tea. The secateurs lay like a peculiar cake knife beside the other silverware. Through the window I could see the back of the main house, its stone like clotted cream in the afternoon sun.

"I have never lived anywhere but here," Clarissa told me when I made some comment about the beauty of Summerhays. "Never wanted to. Unfortunately, my grandchildren feel differently. Mela prefers London, as does Robin. Their brother, Phil, was different. He was happiest here." She handed me a cup. "If a place is in your blood, you leave it at your peril. You will never be happy anywhere else. Of that I am certain."

As though the rituals of welcome were now accomplished and the real matter at hand could be introduced, Clarissa said calmly, "But if you will forgive an old woman's curiosity, tell me, my dear, why you have left your own home to come here."

I tried to make my voice casual and open, without overtones. "I came simply because I inherited Longbarrow Cottage and needed to make up my mind about the place. But

I'm beginning to realize that it must be more than that. That I wanted to know more about my own family's past." I took a cake from the plate she held out to me. "More about my grandparents."

The violet eyes considered me. "Do you want to hear the truth? I shouldn't, if I were you. After all, there's not a thing you can do about the past. Much better to let it rest."

Mela, too, had said something along these lines to me. The Mallaby women seemed very eager for me to leave the past alone. It's too late, I almost said to Clarissa; I know too much, and too little, to let it rest.

For an instant, I was tempted to tell her about that curious document from the past, the Longbarrow Brotherhood's contract, with its potential power to alter her family's present, and even my own. But it was a threat of last resort, the only negotiating weapon I possessed, however questionable its power might prove to be, to persuade the Mallabys to tell me the truth. It gave me, however, enough confidence to pursue Clarissa now.

I said, "The truth might help me understand certain things about my family. It certainly can't disillusion me about my grandfather. He wasn't held up to me as a shining light."

Her look was speculative. "What were you told about him?"

"Very little. I understood that he left my grandmother before my mother was born. You may know more about that than I do."

She inclined her head. "Perhaps I do. I remember the day he left Shipcote very well. It was memorable for quite another reason. It was the day war was declared." Careful not to scatter crumbs, she took one of the little cakes and broke it apart. As though some momentary greed had passed, she merely contemplated the pieces on the plate, pink and white icing around a dry biscuit heart. In a moment, she continued: "Charles came to me very upset. He'd had enough of war, he said, and he wasn't going to fight in this one simply because the politicians had made a fearful mess of everything and now expected ordinary people to clean up after them.

"He was right, I suppose. And yet I believed then, and

believe now, that you must fight to protect what is yours. You don't simply hand it over to those who wish to take it from you." The words were fierce enough, but the voice, that weary, leisured voice, made it difficult to believe that she had ever had to fight for anything. She might have read my thoughts, for she smiled and said, "Looking at me now, you wouldn't think I'd be up to much, would you? It's this tiresome heart of mine. Lets me down every now and then. But I was very strong when I was young. And I had courage. I'd have made a good soldier." She smiled at the thought, then picked up the silver teapot. "More tea?"

"Yes, please." We were dancing a minuet over the tea-cups, I thought, this elderly enigmatic woman and I.

"Charles told me he was in love with me," she said suddenly, shockingly, as she poured the tea into my cup. "Said that he had always been in love with me. That he had gone off to Spain to forget me, married Nan and almost at once regretted it. He wanted me to run away with him. To Kenya, I think it was. Well, of course I said no. The idea horrified me. I was in love with Benedict. Sugar?" I shook my head. She shifted slightly, maintaining the small distance between herself and the chair's back as though its touch might weaken her.

"Poor Charles was distraught. He said dreadful things. Even threatened to kill himself. I thought it all melodrama at the time. I'm afraid I told him to behave like a man. I think I must have been rather harsh." Repentance was bright, like unshed tears, in her beautiful eyes. "I was very young and I don't believe I handled it at all well. I ought to have been kinder."

"You think he killed himself?" I sipped a little tea, and wondered whether to believe her.

"Perhaps. Oh, not because of me. But he seemed genuinely fearful of the war. His experiences in Spain had harmed him in some way. Then, too, he was very remorseful for having married your grandmother without loving her."

How plausible it all sounded. And Peter's suicide made it easy enough for me to accept that my grandfather, too, might have chosen that path.

"When I was young the idea of suicide was anathema,"

she said. "Unthinkable. Now, I'm not so sure. Occasionally, I find myself thinking that it would be quite a good thing to opt out before you get too creaky. There are hooks that hold you on to life, however, even at my age. And of course," she added with a little laugh, leaning toward me across the table, her face momentarily very like Mela's, "most of the time you simply forget you're so ancient. I'll catch a glimpse of myself in a looking glass and think, 'Oh, who's that old woman?' "

It must once have been very seductive, that confiding air combined with the beauty whose remnants had a lingering power to disturb; it was seductive now. I wanted to say to her with a lover's reassurance, You are still lovely, you still have power over others. The memory of Willoughby's review, of the mutilated books, rose up in my mind, giving me the strength to resist her charm. I asked her coldly if Benedict had known of his cousin's attempt to run off with his wife.

She registered the tone. Although her face did not change, she withdrew slightly, folding her long, thin hands together on her lap. "I had to tell him after Charles disappeared. Naturally, he felt betrayed. He was very hurt, and very angry. Charles had been like a brother. Charles's name was never mentioned in this house. Until you came."

"You'd think his body would have been found. If he'd killed himself." I was musing out loud, more to myself than to her.

"Yes, you would," she replied slowly. "I sometimes wondered if he went back to London that night and drowned himself in the Thames. His body might have washed out to sea."

"Back to London? Weren't he and Nan living in Long-barrow Cottage?"

"No, they were living in London at the time. Charles had come down to do some work on the cottage. I believe they were planning to move into it shortly. If memory serves."

I hardly heard her. My head was aching now, and my mouth tasted of tannin and sugar. The room seemed stifling. I longed to throw open a window, to let fresh air blow away the smell of potpourri and perfume. Abruptly, I said that it was time I went back to the cottage. As she stood up with me, the cane, which was lying against her chair, fell to the floor. I bent over to pick it up. The curved top of yellowed ivory was cool and smooth to the touch, threaded by faint, hairline cracks of age.

"It's a nuisance sometimes, this cane," she said as I gave it back to her, "perpetually falling over. Still, it can be very useful. And I suppose I should be grateful to it for helping me get around."

She came to the door of the garden house with me. On impulse, I said, "I'm told you hated my grandmother. Why was that?" As soon as the words were spoken, I recognized their futility.

"I should like us to be friends, my dear, but you force me to unpleasant truths." Her face now was as weary as her voice, and she rested both hands on the cane. Still, the body remained straight, as though the will even more than the spine held her upright. "Your grandmother was an unhappy woman who turned that unhappiness against others. She told lies. Her book was a terrible lie. But I think you know this already."

"I don't know anything. I'm just trying to find out."

She said a strange thing, then, before she turned away to go back inside the garden house. She said, "You may discover what it is you want to know, but I don't believe you will ever understand it. And you may regret your curiosity." She sounded almost sorry for me.

CHAPTER 29

Defeated, I walked back to Longbarrow Cottage. Clarissa had been very skillful with me. I could not complain that she had refused to tell me what I wanted to know, and yet I felt no closer to the truth. She was like the stone that lay everywhere around me, beautiful, changeable, and utterly impenetrable. In their various ways and for various reasons, she, Mela, and Willoughby used a facade of well-bred cordiality to create a spurious intimacy. They were, in a sense, emotional teasers who tried to evoke revelation from others while simultaneously evading or mimicking a reciprocal disclosure. Uninitiates, like myself, who did not know the rules of the social game, would be subtly led astray by their counterfeit offers of friendship. The upper hand in any relationship would undoubtedly always belong to someone like Clarissa.

All the same, I thought, looking at a layered garden wall fissured with moss and tiny wildflowers, tenacity and a gradual persistence might find a way through the barrier to the truth. If those three elderly witnesses to the past, Clarissa, Benedict, and Willoughby, only lived long enough.

When I got back to the house, Sophie told me that her mother had come by earlier. "Carl's had to go up to Nottingham unexpectedly. He'll be there overnight. And this time it's certain he'll stay. She wants Anna and me to be with her while he's away, until tomorrow. Would you mind? I know you're not comfortable here when it's just you and Max on your own."

Despite my reassurances, she was reluctant to leave. Only when I told her not to be absurd, that she mustn't miss this chance to be alone with her mother, did she finally go upstairs to pack a change of clothes for the two of them in her knapsack. To distract the children, and myself, I picked up the folder of drawings that I had been working on for Nan's tale of the bell tower mouse. Because Anna was curious, asking questions about the pictures, I began to tell them the story.

"Once upon a time, there was a little village with an ancient church named St. Sebastian's, which had a very beautiful bell tower. At the top of this tower hung a set of bells and at the bottom lived a small gray mouse. The people of the village were poor, but they loved the music of the bells. However, no one loved it quite so much as the mouse, Matilda. Matilda was very proud of her church, and proud most of all of her bell tower. From her mousehole, she could watch the feet of the bell ringers dancing as the bells rang out.

"The vicar of St. Sebastian's was a kindly old man who was careful always to leave a few crumbs from his supper by Matilda's mousehole. Matilda was as happy as a mouse can be. She had the vicar's crumbs to feed her body and his sermons to feed her mind, when she remembered to wake up for them. The only threat to her peaceful life was the vicar's fat ginger tomcat. He was very lazy and spent most of his time sleeping on the gravestones in the sunshine.

"One day, the bell tower of St. Sebastian's, which was very old, was found to be unsafe. Until it was repaired, the people were told, the bells could not be rung. But there was no money for the work. A sad silence fell upon the little village, and the people found their poverty harder to bear.

"When the vicar called a meeting, the whole village crowded into the church, filling the pews. Matilda crouched under a pew, where she could listen unnoticed. Eagerly, the villagers suggested ways to raise money for their bell tower, a church fête, a bring-and-buy, a bake sale. But they knew that none of these would come close to meeting the cost of the repairs.

"At last, the vicar said that they must have faith. The Lord would find a way. 'Let us hope He finds the church treasure instead,' said one old lady, who was known for her plain speaking. This treasure, which included a jeweled Bible of great value, had been hidden for safekeeping during a war by a previous vicar, a very forgetful man who could not remember where he had put it.

"Despairing, the people returned to their homes. Matilda was saddest of all. She went back to her mousehole with a heavy heart and no appetite for the vicar's crumbs, which lay untouched. All night, she rustled restlessly in her nest as she tried to think of some way to help the village. Next morning, she scampered out again, no wiser but very hungry. Intent on her breakfast, she did not notice that the church door was open. Nor did she the vicar's ginger tomcat creeping through it.

"The ginger tom pounced. But because he was so fat, he was too slow. At the last moment, Matilda saw him out of the corner of her eye and jumped aside just in time. But now he was between her and her mousehole.

"Frantically searching for a refuge, Matilda raced along below the pews. Swiftly, the ginger tom pursued her, his toenails clicking angrily on the flagstones. Matilda could feel his hot breath on her back. Just as it seemed she was about to become his breakfast, she noticed a small crack in the flagstones below the altar, a hole big enough only for a small mouse. As the ginger tom opened his mouth, she vanished into the hole. He bit into the empty air, and his tongue. With a yowl of fury and pain, he leaped straight up, then crouched down by the hole to wait.

"Under the flagstone was a cool, dark space partly filled with lumpy objects. Trembling at her narrow escape, Matilda sat among them with her forepaws tucked up under her chin. When her nose stopped twitching with fear, she looked about, wondering if there was some other way out. Something gleamed in the darkness. With a squeak of excitement, Matilda saw that it was a silver cup. Beside it was a parcel wrapped in oiled cloth. Matilda nibbled away at a corner of the cloth and poked her head through. Inside was the jeweled Bible.

"She had found the church treasure!

"The ginger tom soon got bored with his vigil and went in search of easier prey. When Matilda smelled that he had gone, she crept cautiously out again. Now she was safe enough, but she had another problem. How was she to tell the vicar about her discovery? Who would listen to a little mouse?

"As she sat there thinking, the morning sun shone through the east window. The stained glass showed St. Sebastian clutching some arrows in one hand. The sight gave Matilda a brilliant idea.

"The untouched crumbs lay scattered around her mousehole. One by one, she carried them to the floor in front of the altar and arranged them carefully. Although she was very hungry, she did not eat a single crumb, for she knew she would need each one. Finally, when her work was done, she hid below the altar cloth and waited.

"At five o'clock, the vicar arrived to conduct evensong. The afternoon sun streamed in, falling on the altar and on the flagstones below. As the vicar bowed his head before the altar, his gaze fell on a strange sight. There on the flagstones, lit by the late afternoon light, was an arrow.

"Wonderingly, the vicar saw that the tip of the arrow was pointing to a crack in the flagstones. He knelt down and put his fingers into the space, then lifted. From below the altar cloth, Matilda watched him with joy in her heart.

"Allelujah!" the vicar cried when he saw what lay beneath the stone. 'A miracle! St. Sebastian has saved his church.' There beside the altar, he and Matilda each gave a little dance of happiness.

'That night, in celebration, the vicar left a large lump of cheese by Matilda's mousehole. And it was not long before Matilda, and all the villagers, heard the music of the bells once more."

Max twisted off the sofa and crawled over to his toys before the story was finished, but Anna listened to the end, her face creasing with worry when the cat seemed about to catch Matilda, smiling up at me at the treasure's discovery. I might never find *Life Blood*, I told myself, but I had Nan's stories. Something of her endured.

Sophie came back downstairs as the story was ending. There was a casserole in the larder, she said, which she had made for our dinner. "You have it, will you? Then I won't feel so guilty about deserting you."

"Wouldn't you like to take it to your mother?"

She shook her head. "I'll make something from scratch. It'll give me a chance to show off a bit."

On the way to Crookfield Farm, I described my conversation with Clarissa, ending with her account of my grandfather's disappearance. From the backseat, when I finished, came a low whistle. "What a brilliant story. It would make a terrific film." Sophie's voice was heavily ironic. "You don't believe her, do you?"

"I'm not sure. It seems to make sense. Until I remember the letter he wrote to Nan."

"And if she's lying?"

"Then it must be to protect her husband. And she wouldn't need to do that unless . . ."

"Precisely."

"Sophie, do you think I'm crazy? Here I am, suspecting

an old man and his wife of the most terrible things all because of a few stories from my childhood and some parallells with real life. I mean, look at the Mallabys. They seem so respectable."

" 'Seem' being absolutely the right word," she responded, her voice very dry. "And no, you're not crazy. Except maybe in believing that respectability has anything at all to do with morality."

We had reached the turning for Crookfield Farm, a graveled lane running between hedgedrows patched with bits of rusty corrugated iron. Surrounded by trees, the farm itself stood in a small bowl of land with the wide fields sloping gently up from it. The house had a disheveled beauty, cluttered by too many ramshackly sheds, the hulks of rusting farm equipment, and bashed-in oil drums draped in strips of blue plastic sheeting. Only the garden beside the house, her mother's pride, Sophie said, showed evidence of careful tending.

The front door of the farmhouse opened. I half-expected Carl Jope to materialize, but it was Sophie's mother who came out to meet us. Small and slender, with finely made features and black eyes, she looked, like her house, in need of loving care, her own beauty disguised by unhappiness and the droop of her shoulders. But her smile for Sophie and Anna transformed her face and made the resemblance to her daughter immediately visible.

Shyly, she said hello when Sophie introduced us. I had thought to leave right away, knowing they would want to be alone, but she asked me to come inside with Max. She had something for him. "And for you as well, my love," she told Anna gently. Her voice was very soft, with a faint echo of Sophie's warmth.

We went in through a dingy hall to a room that might have been pretty once but was drab now. Dirt was not the problem, it was perfectly clean; hopelessness was. Everything was worn into a weary shapelessness and no effort had been made to brighten things up with fresh paint or even the flowers that grew in the garden. Mrs. Jope took two packages wrapped in tissue paper from a shelf and gave one to me. I could open it now, if I liked, she told me. Or later. Whichever suited me. Her diffidence was almost painful. She was disturbingly like a Sophie with all the spirit and energy crushed out of her.

"Go on, Jo," Sophie urged. "Don't wait for Anna. She always likes to take her time." Anna had sat down on the floor with her package and was contemplating it as it lay on her lap.

Inside Max's present was a Noah's ark knitted entirely out of bright wools. It contained eight pairs of animals wearing swimsuits, a Mrs. Noah holding an umbrella, and Noah himself in a large black rain hat with an upturned brim. Four pockets knitted into each side of the ark held the animal pairs. Max immediately fell for the elephants, whose gray trunks curled perfectly around his small fingers. It was a wonderful piece of work, intricately detailed, a true labor of love. Mrs. Jope flushed with pleasure, ducking her head like a child, when I said as much, and thanked her.

On the floor, Anna was intently studying her Noah's ark, which had a completely different set of animals from Max's. Sophie told her mother that the Flood story was one of Anna's favorites.

Quietly, Mrs. Jope said, "I sometimes think that anyone who has a child is a bit like Noah."

Sophie, who was squatting down beside Anna, looked up. "How's that, Mum?"

"We send our children out on the waters of the world and all we can do is pray they find dry land." Her look rested on her daughter. "And come back to us with an olive branch."

"Now, Mum, you're going all soppy on us." Sophie's voice was teasing, but she stood up and kissed her mother's cheek.

When I said it was time I took Max home for his supper, Mrs. Jope invited us to join them, and was seconded by Sophie. I thanked her but refused, firm in my intention to let them have their time together. As I drove away from the farm, however, I thought how pleasant it would be to sit talking with the two of them, listening to them find their way back to each other.

At bedtime, Max clung to wakefulness like a sailor skirting the regions once marked on ancient maps with the warning "Here be monsters." At last, during "Wynken,

Blynken and Nod," his eyes glassed over and his lower lip began to quiver. He drifted out into the vast sea of sleep holding his breath until it seemed he might never breathe again. When the exhalation came, in a long sighing breath, his hand suddenly opened like a sea anemone, the small tentacles of his fingers releasing mine. I'm safely there, was the message of his peaceful body, you can go now. I tiptoed from the darkened room.

As I ate, the silence in the cottage swelled around me, oppressive, dense with loneliness. The warmth of the day was ebbing away, absorbed by shadows and stone. I shivered, and drained the wine in my glass. All at once, I felt utterly bereft of human comfort. My usual amulet against the loneliness was fast asleep upstairs, powerless now to solace me. Slowly the self-pity that always snuffled in the corners of my solitude crept toward me like some ingratiating mongrel hoping for a home. To shake it off, I went outside for a walk in the garden before the last of the day disappeared.

In the west, the sun was slowly dissolving into hills rimmed with a line of mauve-gray cloud. Somewhere a thrush sang, the sweetness of its song mingling with the scent of lilac from the bushes by the gate. A trick of the dying light gave a peculiar, Rackhamesque life to bush and shadow, sketched in a gnomish face, the teasing glimpse of a half-turned head that laughed and vanished. In the far corner of the garden, the cluster of stunted apple trees bent their mob-capped heads of white blossom toward one another like a group of gossiping old women. The wind that moved over the long grass might have been the soft susurration of their thin voices whispering secrets.

I stared, half-dreaming, at the apple trees, at the soft white mass floating like snow above the twisted trunks. A leafless branch hanging from a dead limb wagged slowly in the wind like the gnarled and monitory finger of a witch. Beneath it, a figure seemed to gather shape among the shadows on the grass, the wraithlike image of a woman, ghostly in the twilight.

Ice thickened my blood. I took a step toward the apple trees. Go away, I screamed at the pale figure, you don't belong here, but my mouth was too cold for sound and the words blew away as silently as snow. A flicker of light passed through the long grass, and was gone. Trembling, I walked down the sloping garden to the apple trees. All that glimmered there now was a sifting of blossoms across the grass. The swaying branch seemed to mock me for my foolishness.

I turned away, shivering. To the north, across the field beyond the garden wall, lay the long barrow. It looked now like a great ship sailing into the darkness of the woods, its stern lit by the setting sun, the green trees on the summit like sails bellying in the breeze that rises with the dusk. A full moon, translucent as a disk of honesty, hung above it in a pale blue sky. The silence was broken only by lambs calling in the distance, and from the lane the sound of a car passing slowly by.

The car pulled into the drive and a man got out. For what seemed a long suspended moment he stood beside the open door of the car, staring up at the house, while I, unseen, gazed at him from among the apple trees like the ghost of the woman in the grass. Frozen with an old grief, old fears.

The sun wheeled over in the west and in a last great blaze of fire, its rays touched the man, turning him to gold. He seemed incandescent. And like any wraith chilled in the shadows, I yearned with all of my being toward that glowing promise of life and heat. When he turned to get back in the car, something in me broke through the ice.

Calling David's name like a cry for help, I stepped out from the circle of trees. He raised his head then, and saw me. With the last of the light from the west falling on him, he came to me across the grass, on fire, his face so bright it blinded me. My own face must have given back that image of desire, for his arms came around me and his mouth sought mine. His touch sent a shiver of flame over my skin.

"You were leaving," I whispered, my face in the hollow of his neck. "I couldn't bear it."

He held me away from him a little and looked down at me, his eyes questioning. "I was afraid you would think . . . Well, the truth—that I had come for this." He bent his head, and his mouth drifted down across my face like the soft fall of apple blossoms. "And this," he murmured, his breath like cool fire on my flesh. He drew back, his eyes searching my face. "Jo, I should tell you—"

I put my hand to his lips. "Later. Tell me later. Can you stay a little?"

He nodded. "Rafe's in London with his mother. He won't be back for a day or two."

I said that Sophie and Anna, too, were away for the night. "I don't want to be alone." Gravely, he replied that I had no need to be, he would stay with me.

Hand in hand, we went indoors and up the narrow staircase. Together, in the growing darkness, we put fresh sheets on Sophie's bed. The moon shone into the room from a sky of steadily deepening blue, its light a silvery path to the bed. I put my hand to David's face, touching the contours of his mouth, the hollow at his temple, studying him with my fingertips. I was a student again, eager to relearn the lessons of the body, to learn happiness now, instead of pain.

Gently, he pulled me to him, brushing the hair away from my face. Like good children, we knew by heart the new catechism of the age, asked each other the sad questions, obediently following the rituals of safety that hedge modern love. Then we lay down together on the narrow mattress, palm to palm, like naked lovers in old manuscripts, their long pale bodies awkward with the newness of an unfamiliar passion. Ravenous, I moved my mouth across his skin, tasting at first only the past, the bitter salt of half-forgotten sorrows. But his body was as sweet and hard as the flesh of an apple, ripe with the present tense. A windfall, golden as any from the garden of the Hesperides. And gradually the old memories melted away like the snow.

Later, as I lay in his arms, content, David said quietly, "That first time I saw you, in London, I thought, Yes, there she is at last. I think that every time we meet." He ran his hand down my arm, weaving his fingers through mine. "I've wanted you so badly. But you always seemed out of reach."

"There were other people in the way," I said. One, a ghost. "I couldn't see past them."

He was silent for a moment before he spoke. The moon had moved in the sky, leaving the room in shadows, so that he was a warm darkness beside me, like the first stirring of new life. He said, "I wanted to tell you that things weren't what they seemed. But how do you say that without sounding disloyal? Or arrogant?"

"Mela and you . . . I thought . . ."

"Yes, I know." His voice was somber. "But it was over before you came."

When Mela's brother Phil had died, he told me, she had turned to him. Phil's death had hurt him, too. David and Phil had been good friends, had worked together, had plans for the farm park. He and Mela had helped each other through a rough time. "But she's never stuck with anyone for very long, and I was no exception. I don't think either of us expected it to last." He shifted on the bed, half-turning, with his head propped on one hand so that he could look at me. His face was grave. "She has someone else now, but when she's unhappy . . ."

She would go to him. I remembered what Sophie had said, that even when Mela had grown tired of a possession she would not relinquish it. And I knew the power another's unhappiness could have over us.

I told him, then, about Peter. Not everything, but enough. He listened silently and when I finished took me in his arms and kissed me with great tenderness. As though he could heal me with his mouth, his hands, could minister to my spirit with his body. And as he moved against me, deliberate, insistent, he urged me forward into the future, away from the past.

Max woke us long before six in the morning. David got up with me and made coffee while I fed Max his bottle. As Max sat on my lap, sucking his milk, his eyes followed David around the kitchen. David put my cup in front of me and sat down across the table from us. He watched Max, amused by the grunts of pleasure Max was making as he drank the milk. "I've bottle-fed lambs who made that noise," he said. "I don't think I realized human babies sound that way, too."

With regret in his voice, he told me that he had very few memories of Rafe at Max's age. "I was almost never at home when Rafe was awake. I saw him at breakfast and sometimes on the weekend, and that was about it. His mother and I had an unspoken agreement—I would make enough money to get her the kind of life she wanted and in return she would take care of the domestic side of things. She was very good at that." He cradled the mug of coffee in his hands, his eyes fixed on its contents. "It took us eight years to realize it was a lousy arrangement for all three of us."

"Rafe seems to have come out of it amazingly well," I said, wiping Max's chin.

"Thanks to his mother. I had very little do with it."

He judged himself too harshly, I thought. Whatever his failing had been as a father, he had given Rafe enough love to build his sturdy character on.

He said, "That book you gave Rafe? It meant a lot to him, your taking him seriously."

"When I saw it, of course I thought of him. I hoped he'd like it."

"He said you found it at a secondhand book fair in Oxford. Were you looking for something of your own?"

I smiled. "Metaphorically or literally?"

He smiled back at me. "Either way."

I let the smile fade and looked straight into his eyes. "The metaphorical doesn't seem to matter anymore. After last night . . ."

His own eyes held mine, held them until I felt the blood beating through me. Then he looked at Max, who lay drowsy with the milk, his head warm on my breast.

"Will he fall asleep again?"

"I hope so."

Obligingly, Max did. And so we went back to bed ourselves.

Later, as he was leaving, David said that he would be in London until the following day, but would come to the cottage when he and Rafe returned. Watching him walk down to his car, I wanted to call him back, to tell him about *Life Blood* and all that it meant to me. But inevitably, whether or not he believed I was right, the knowledge would color his relationship with the Mallabys. He had to work with them, had been their grandson's friend, lived in their house.

Eventually, I might have to tell him. But not yet.

CHAPTER 30

Sophie and Anna came back from their night's stay at Crookfield Farm after lunch. Max crowed with pleasure at the sight of them. Sophie told me that she and her mother had spent most of the night talking, assuaging some of the pain of the two years' separation with the ordinary details of their lives, tentatively exploring a future together. Her face glowed with a weary happiness.

In our different fashions, we had each found a reason to hope, Sophie and I. My own happiness was the simple thought of David, which, with the memory of our night, filled my imagination with images of light.

"I'm dead tired," Sophie said, yawning widely. "But it's a good feeling." If the skin below her eyes was stained with weariness, the look in the dark eyes themselves was triumphant. "Mum's going to finish with Carl. She's wanted to for a long time now. Seeing me again, and Anna, helped her decide." Sophie had told her mother she would come back to Crookfield Farm to live once Carl was gone. "I loved the place when my father was alive. But Carl spoilt it for me."

Her mother intended to sell off a large part of the farm, keeping the farmhouse and enough land for privacy and a garden. Some of the proceeds would go to Carl, to persuade him not to contest the divorce. Sophie sounded resigned, rather than approving, as she described her mother's plans. "I told her she doesn't have to give Carl a thing. What with his women and all, a good lawyer would make mincemeat of him. But she says she wants to be fair." They would use the rest of the money to start up a farmhouse bed-and-breakfast, offering dinners as well, with Sophie as chef.

Eventually, if it was successful, they planned to develop it into a proper restaurant, Sophie's dream.

"Val thinks it's a brilliant idea."

I glanced at her. "He does, does he? And that matters?"

"Yes, I rather think it does." She explained that she had told him about it when he had met the pair of them, Anna and herself, at Crookfield Farm, to give them a lift back to the cottage.

She gave another enormous yawn, and I told her to go have a nap. When she woke up three hours later, we cooked an early supper together and afterward decided to take a walk down to The Mason's Arms. It was a lovely evening, warm as summer, with a golden haze over the horizon. The children could feed the swans on the river, and Sophie and I would have a drink to celebrate her mother's decision.

As we left the house, Val drove up. When she saw him, Sophie's face made it clear that he was as much the source of her sudden happiness as her mother's plan to separate from Carl Jope. She gave me a grateful look when I invited him to join us.

At the pub, we went down to the riverbank to let the children feed the ducks the crusts of bread we'd brought. With thin, wild cries, swallows darted through the clouds of gnats that hovered above the river. Supported by my grip on his trousers' straps, Max ate the crusts meant for the ducks and watched a family of swans forage for food along the bank. Val was showing Anna how to tear up the bread into pieces small enough for the ducks. He struck just the right note with her, gradually drawing her out with a gentle playfulness that elicited the occasional shy sideways smile. And once, as he squatted by her side, a whispered confidence too low for any ear but his.

When the last of the bread had disappeared into Max and the ducks, we walked back to the empty forecourt of the pub. I sat down at a table with the children while Sophie and Val went inside to get our drinks. A few minutes later, Sophie returned alone with her shandy and mine. Val was talking to some friends inside the pub. "You'll never guess who else is in there," she said as she set the glass mugs down on the table. "Willoughby Webb Springer, dressed to kill. I'd forgotten what a dandy he is."

The words were barely out of her mouth when the man himself came out of the pub. He was wearing a peacock-blue paisley waistcoat with a green silk cravat, and carried a bottle tucked under one arm. When he saw us, he came over to the table, greeting both Sophie and me with such voluble enthusiasm that I wondered if he'd bought more than the bottle. Out of politeness rather than any real wish for his company, I invited him to join us, counting on the children's presence to act as a deterrent. To my surprise, he accepted.

As Willoughby sat down, Val rejoined us. He saw that Willoughby had no glass, and asked if he could get him something to drink. Willoughby shook his head. "Nothing, thank you. I should like to begin work with a clear head. If inspiration does fail, this will revive it." He set the bottle down on the table. "An aide-mémoire, so to speak. Madeleines may work for some, but I find Laphroaig infinitely preferable to dry biscuit. Tomorrow I shall settle down to work with a vengeance." He gave a little laugh, as though pleased with his choice of words. The smell of whiskey came in a gust toward me. "One's autobiography is, after all, a form of revenge on the past. I shall spare no detail, however unpleasant."

Words seemed to spill out of him on a wave of whiskey breath. He was excitable, almost feverish, as he told us stories about various famous memoirists of the past and the discomfort they had given to those whose confidences and secrets they revealed. His smile was too frequent, almost gleeful, as though this was all somehow self-referential, but only he knew how. At one point, Sophie glanced across at me, an eyebrow raised. I remembered what she'd told me about him: and he did, in fact, seem like someone harboring a delicious, scandalous secret.

Later, when I was asked to describe the quarter hour or so he spent with us, I thought of a phrase: On the verge. That's how, in retrospect, he seemed to me. On the verge of what, exactly, was harder to say. Perhaps on the verge of telling, if only in the writing that was to commence the next day.

Seeing that glasses were empty, Val went back inside for another round. Just then a pickup truck came thundering over the little bridge, driven far too fast. As it rattled past the pub, Carl Jope looked over at us from the driver's seat. When he saw Sophie, he scowled. The truck disappeared around the corner. We could hear it turn with a screech of brakes into the small parking lot at the side of the pub.

Sophie stared at me, her face grave. "He's stopping. There's bound to be a row." Willoughby looked across at her. The expression of bright interest on his own face was almost avid; unwholesome, like a voyeur's.

She would take Anna inside, Sophie told me, to find Val. But before she could do more than unstrap Anna from the stroller, Jope strode around the corner, his unbuttoned jacket flapping open to reveal his sagging beige-shirted paunch. Under the thatch of curling gray hair, his face was dark with anger. Resigned, Sophie stood her ground, holding Anna. I assumed she preferred to have the inevitable scene outside rather than inside the pub, where there would be a larger audience.

Jope came into the tiny forecourt and stopped just inside the gate, effectively blocking it. Without acknowledging the presence of anyone else, without even seeming to see us, he launched a furious attack on Sophie, angrily accusing her of coming between her mother and himself.

"You're doing your bloody best to turn her against me!" he shouted.

"I've been listening to her, if that's what you mean," Sophie replied coolly, shifting Anna in her arms so that the child's head was tucked against her neck. "It's time someone did."

From his chair, Willoughby was watching Sophie and Jope with patent fascination. His glance flicked back and forth between the two of them as if he were an onlooker at a tennis match. The faintest of smiles was on his thin lips and his tongue came out once, licking the corner of his mouth.

"If you think you can come back here and make trouble," Jope was saying, his face twisted with rage, "just you bloody think again. Hear that, you interfering bitch?"

"Go away, Carl," Sophie said. "You'll frighten the children." Her voice was calm, flat, the voice you would use on a bully, refusing to be intimidated.

I had taken Max up into my arms and was about to go into the pub to get Val when Willoughby rose from his chair, perhaps deciding that this was not a spectator sport after all. At the same moment, Jope moved forward to get around the table and at Sophie. The two men collided. The bottle of Laphroaig slipped from Willoughby's arm and smashed on the paving stones, its contents splashing up onto Jope's trousers.

Jope blinked, and stared at Willoughby as though he were only now taking him in. Then he looked down at his trouser legs, stained with the liquor. "Bloody hell! What's that, for crissake?"

"That," said Willoughby icily, "is a fortune in good whiskey watering the pavement."

"You want your eyes tested, Gramps," Jope said furiously. "Going around getting in people's way."

Willoughby's face mottled with anger. "If I were a younger man—"

At that, Carl Jope looked Willoughby up and down, deliberately registering the waistcoat, the carefully arranged cravat. "I'd say you're trying hard enough to be. Mutton dressed as lamb, that's what you are." His voice was sneering.

All at once, Willoughby's urbanity deserted him. "This is outrageous. I'm not prepared to stand here and be insulted by a latter-day Snopes. A man who plays with matches—"

"What did you say?" Jope's voice cut roughly across Willoughby's. The reference to Snopes had meant nothing to him, but at the word "matches" his eyes narrowed. He took a step toward Willoughby.

"I'm going inside to get help," I told Sophie. "Let me take Anna." But as I turned with the children I found the door blocked by a couple who were just emerging. Behind them was Val with our drinks. Obviously aware that something unpleasant was happening, the man told the woman to get the pubkeeper. Val handed the drinks to the woman as she passed and stepped out into the forecourt.

Meanwhile, Jope had penned Willoughby between a table and the stone wall, fencing him in with the bulk of his large body. At Jope's back, Sophie was pleading with him to leave Willoughby alone. He whipped around, his face savage. "Shut your face," he said furiously. The pouchy eyes flickered with a dangerous light.

Then he turned back to Willoughby. "You want to be a bit more careful about your health. Loose talk costs lives, and all that." With one thick finger, he reached out and flipped Willoughby's cravat loose from the waistcoat.

Before he could do more, Val had his wrist in a grip that forced him to step back, releasing Willoughby. When Willoughby was beyond Jope's reach, Val let go of Jope, who swore violently at him while he nursed his bruised wrist. At the same moment, the pubkeeper and several other men appeared. The pubkeeper swiftly assessed the scene and moved in to deal with it, as he must have dealt with others like it in the past, his loud jolly voice overriding Jope's, defusing his anger. Sullenly, Carl Jope allowed himself to be moved along back to his truck.

Visibly shaken, Willoughby looked around the little group gathered in the forecourt. "Did you hear him threaten me?" he asked us. He looked ashen-faced now that the flush of anger had faded, and much older. In fact, he seemed so unsteady that I persuaded him to sit down while the pubkeeper brought him coffee and a brandy. "On the house," he told Willoughby. He stooped to sweep up the broken glass.

Ignoring the coffee, Willoughby raised the brandy to his lips and downed it at a gulp. Then, somewhat shakily, he stood up, adjusting his cravat. He looked so crumpled, so shaken out of his habitual sangfroid, that I felt a pang of pity. When Val said that he would walk back with him to Summerhays, Willoughby shook his head. "Thank you. I can manage." He barely looked at us, and with a curt good-evening, went off up the road.

CHAPTER 31

That night the full moon hung low over the long barrow, heavy with silver. From the kitchen window, the dark shapes of the trees looked like cloaked figures standing in a row, staring down across the field toward the cottage. They seemed to be waiting, or watching.

While Sophie and the children slept, I wandered restlessly about the silent house, folding laundry, picking up toys, thinking of David.

At last I settled on the sofa, sketch pad in hand. The ugly scene at the pub nagged at me. Although the anger on Carl Jope's face had been frightening enough, it was a straightforward emotion I could identify and name. Willoughby's face was more disturbing. It was the face of a voyeur, a man with secrets to keep or tell, someone damaged who would do damage in turn. But there was something else implicit in his eyes, almost an appeal. And I felt as though I had deliberately failed to understand it.

Like automatic writing, I let the pencil go where it would on the paper. A vine gradually grew under my fingers, the branching tendrils curling thickly over the surface of the page. From its leaves, a gargoyle face peered out at me, Willoughby as the Green Man, but a Green Man with withered leaves, dying on the vine. Dead leaves veiled his face as they fell from their stems.

Other faces took shape among the leaves, Carl Jope, Benedict, Clarissa, Mela, May, Nan, Charles, Evelyn and Stephen Allerton, each face caricatured by my pencil into a grotesque version of the original. From the features of beasts or birds, demons or angels, their eyes gazed at me with anger or distress, with wary curiosity, amusement, affection, or in mournful warning.

There was another pair of eyes as well. Narrowed, malevolent, in a face whose features were entirely invisible in the dense thicket of leaves, they stared out at me with an implacable hatred. They were both threat and warning. A threat from someone whose identity I could only guess at, and a warning to myself. I was meddling with a past that might be more dangerous to me than I knew.

Shaken, I put away the sketch pad and went upstairs. Still dressed, I lay down on my bed, looking into the darkness, trying to make sense of it all. From the garden, the shrill screech of some nocturnal animal came through the partly open window by my bed. The sound dropped through the deep silence of the night into my sleep, became a woman's scream. In a dream, an indistinct figure was bludgeoning Evelyn Allerton again and again with a book. When at last she collapsed to the floor, the murderer threw the book onto the fire. Smoke billowed out in choking gray clouds, filling the dream.

I sat up, the smoke from my dream sharp in the air. Suddenly, violently, awake, I scrambled off the bed. The smell seemed to be drifting in through the open windows, growing stronger. I ran into the hall. And thanked God that here at least the frightening smell was absent.

Desperately, I shook Sophie awake. She sat up groggily, her face dazed and creased with sleep. But when she heard the word "fire," she leaped to her feet, grabbing the long sweater she used as a dressing gown. As she thrust her arms into the sleeves, I said I thought the fire was outside, not in. "But I think we should get Max and Anna out of the cottage. Just in case."

Hurriedly, we wrapped both children in blankets and carried them downstairs, switching on lights along the way. There was still no smell of smoke in the house but when we opened the front door it was pungent on the air. Sophie laid Anna on the backseat of the car, then climbed in beside her and took Max from me. They stirred, eyes flickering open briefly, then settled back to sleep again.

I put the keys in the ignition and told Sophie I was going to have a look around, to see if I could find out where the smoke was coming from. "If there's anything serious, we'll drive up to the Ebborns and call the fire department."

"Be careful," Sophie said, her face blanched white in the moonlight.

The acrid smell grew stronger as I came around to the back of the cottage. Smoke was pouring out in thin streams from around the badly fitting door of the garden shed. Covering my nose and mouth with my sweatered arm, I reached out gingerly to the handle of the door. The metal was still cool. I wrenched the door open and jumped back as a great choking cloud of smoke billowed out. Once it had cleared away I could see the small fire burning in the heap of burlap sacking at the back of the shed, its flames licking hungrily up toward the wooden shelves above it on the wall.

Several lidless paint cans and an open tin of turpentine stood dangerously close to the fire. Gleaming with a slick of yellow oil, liquid white paint sloshed in the bottom of the cans as I carried them outside. I grabbed a spade and dug a shovelful of earth from the ground just outside the door, dumped it on the fire, smothering it, added several more spadefuls for good measure, and ran indoors for a bucket of water to pour over the heap of earth. The resulting muddy mess of charred sacking smelled vile but was reassuringly beyond flammability.

Once the children were tucked back in their beds, Sophie and I went to look at the dead remnants of the fire. "The burlap sacks were already here," I said, "but I don't remember the paint tins or the turpentine. Did you see them when you and Val worked in the garden on Saturday afternoon?"

She thought for a moment, her arms wrapped tightly around her waist, hands tucked into the sleeves of the sweater. Then she shook her head. "I don't think so. But I can't be sure." In a moment, she said, "How could a fire start on its own like that, Jo?"

Our eyes met. Each of us knew the answer. Sophie's gaze faltered and she whispered, "I'm sorry, Jo. It's my fault. If I weren't here . . ." For a moment, she seemed so like her mother that I couldn't bear it.

I put my arms around her. She felt too small and fragile

to take on Carl Jope, her bones like a child's beneath the thin stuff of the dressing gown. "I'm glad you've been here, Sophie," I told her. "Nothing could make me sorry for that."

We set the paint cans and the turpentine on a high shelf in the pantry, unwilling to leave them outdoors where they might be used again. Before we touched them, we put on gardening gloves, an almost certainly futile gesture aimed at preserving fingerprints. Afterward, I drove up to Ashleaze Farm to call the police. A sleepy-eyed William answered my knock as Pat came down the stairs behind him, knotting the cord on her dressing gown. Apologizing for waking them up, I explained what had happened. They glanced at each other, grim-faced.

While Pat called the police, William returned to the cottage with me, overriding my protest that we would be fine. "A bad business," he said somberly as he stood contemplating the interior of the garden shed. "Still and all, even if the shed had gone up, the house itself was probably in no danger. That's the beauty of stone and slate. Take a lot more than this to burn it down from the outside."

"How did those other fires start?" I asked him. "The ones in the empty cottages."

"In builders' rubble. Outside. But as no one was there to notice, they had time to do real damage."

Sophie told him about the incident at the pub and Carl Jope's behavior. "He did this," she said flatly. On his own, I wondered, or was he paid for it by someone who was interested in buying up property in Shipcote, someone like Gerald Fenton? William merely grunted in reply to Sophie, but he did not refute her. Several minutes later, a police car pulled into the drive. The young constable who got out examined the shed and made a thorough search of the garden. He was annoyed that I had moved the paint cans, but grudgingly conceded I'd had no choice. The arson experts would visit us in the morning, he told us before he left, and in the meantime we were to leave everything else as it was.

When William, too, had gone, Sophie and I sat in the kitchen, drinking the last of a bottle of wine. We were silent, preoccupied with our own thoughts. With the flare of a match, Carl Jope had destroyed the tentative hope for the future that had begun to grow in both of us.

"I can't stop here now," Sophie said dully. "We can't risk Carl trying again. It's me he wants out, after all."

"Me as well, perhaps. The way he feels about outsiders . . . I don't think we should take any risks. For Max and Anna's sake."

She nodded, her face bleak. "Yes, I know."

"Max and I'll go to a hotel until I make arrangements about the cottage. What will you do?"

"Go up to London, I suppose. Stay with my friends." Then, very savagely, "That's what he wants, of course. To drive us both away. I hate to give him the satisfaction." I didn't bother to ask who she meant. And I knew she was right.

Too dispirited to talk any longer, we checked that all the downstairs windows were locked, placed chairs against the front and back doors, then went upstairs, leaving the lights on. Sophie said a muted goodnight before she disappeared into her room. Roiled by fears and anger, I turned restlessly on my bed in the fitful half-sleep that hovers between bad dreams and wakefulness. When Max woke shortly after five, I dressed him, warmed his bottle, and left a note on the kitchen table for Sophie, should she wake up, saying that we had gone for a walk.

Gritty-eyed, I pushed the stroller down the lane toward the village, while Max, a blanket tucked around him, sucked peacefully on his bottle. Pools of darkness lingered in the early light as the rising sun touched the treetops, glanced off shining slate roofs, warmed the ridges of the hills. In the hedgerows, birds stirred and sang, welcoming the new day. The fresh spring air held the ripe promise of beginnings. That promise would be made to someone else, however, not to me. I would go back to Toronto and build on the old life. It was safer.

Carl Jope's vicious act seemed emblematic. I had been playing with fire myself. Even at fifty years' distance, murder was dangerous. I had no right to risk Max in order to satisfy my curiosity and vindicate Nan. The living should always take precedence over the dead.

I flinched away from the thought of David. I had been

naive to believe we could have any sort of relationship, or
that I could make a life in Shipcote, so long as Benedict
Mallaby lived in the village. In a city, it might be different;
Benedict could easily be avoided. But here he was as inimical to my happiness as Carl Jope was to my safety.

There was the whole other issue of my work as well.
Like Max, I thrived on a schedule, did my best work when
there was order and tranquillity in my life. It seemed unlikely I would achieve these in Shipcote now.

As these thoughts whirled around in my brain, I wondered
if the thin-skinned susceptibility to worry that had come with
Max's birth was making me overreact now. Was I sacrificing
a possible future to an unfounded fear of the past?

We went through the sleeping village, past the church. I
decided that I would turn back at the bridge, but as I came
around the corner of The Mason's Arms I saw two police
cars drawn up in front of the pub. An ambulance stood by
the bridge, its rear doors wide open. Two men were lifting
a white-sheeted figure on a gurney into the back.

CHAPTER 32

A group of men stood on the riverbank, just beyond the
pub, where the children had fed the ducks the evening before. One, a photographer, was packing away his equipment; another was staking out a patch of ground with ropes.
In one of the patrol cars a young policeman in uniform was
speaking into his police radio. I recognized the constable
who had come to Longbarrow Cottage only hours earlier.
Through the open car window came the crackle of an answering voice, unintelligible.

Near the ambulance, the owner of the pub was talking to
a tall, middle-aged man with pale red hair, who was taking

notes as he listened. When the publican glanced up and saw me, he said something to the other man that made him turn and look in my direction. He closed the notebook and walked toward me. He had a lean, amiable face and an un-hurried air. A reassuring figure, in other circumstances.

"Miss Treleven?" When I acknowledged I was, he intro-duced himself as Detective Inspector Terrant and showed me the ID clipped to his notebook.

"What's going on?" I asked him.

"A body's been found in the river. A Mr. Willoughby Webb Springer. Harry Shankman over there, the publican, says you knew him."

Too shocked to speak, I could only nod my head.

"Was he a friend of yours?"

I swallowed; my throat seemed filled with dust. "No, not a friend. An acquaintance. I've known him less than two weeks." Almost against my will, I asked him what had hap-pened. "I mean, I realize he must have drowned. But how?"

He replied that they were not sure yet. "It would help us if you'd answer a few questions. Would you mind stepping into the pub for a moment?" His manner was courteous, al-most friendly; he might have been inviting me to join him for a drink.

"Yes, I mean no. Of course I will."

Doors slammed. In a moment, the ambulance drove off over the bridge. Something terrible had happened, yet the green-and-gold fields stretched placidly away to the hills, the peaceful river flowed quietly beneath the little bridge, and back around the bend in the road, the village slept, oblivious.

At that moment, the young constable who had been speaking on the police radio got out of the car and came over to us. We said hello, and the constable, whose name was Skeffington, explained the circumstances of our previ-ous meeting to Terrant. The older man listened with an im-passive face.

"Have the arson people taken a look at it?" he asked the constable.

"Not yet, sir."

"See that they're sent over now. Tell them it's a priority."

"Right." The constable nodded to me and returned to his car.

"Any coffee going, Harry?" Inspector Terrant asked the pub owner, who was standing in the forecourt beside the table at which Willoughby had joined us the evening before. The other man raised a hand in answer and disappeared inside. Following the inspector, I pushed the stroller over the threshold to the saloon bar, a small, cream-painted room with an uneven ceiling and wide-planked floor. The room felt very cold. Max was warm enough, but I tucked the blanket more tightly around him.

We sat down at a table close to one wall, against which stood a worm-eaten grandfather clock. Inspector Terrant took out his notebook and wrote down the details of my own identification first. Then, after some preliminary questions concerning how and where I had first met Willoughby, he asked me about last night's scene at the pub.

"I understand there was a bit of a blowup between Mr. Webb Springer and Carl Jope. Some words passed between them, of a not very friendly nature. Could you tell me about it?"

Neutrally, I described the encounter between Carl Jope and Willoughby, trying to minimize Sophie's role in the confrontation as much as I could. Inspector Terrant was pleasant but persistent, and his questions were thorough. In the midst of them, Harry Shankman set two cups of coffee down on the table. The inspector thanked him. "What about the young fellow there?" he asked me, indicating Max with his head.

I glanced at the pubkeeper. "Do you have a roll or a piece of bread and some cheese? That would keep him happy."

"Of course," he replied. "Won't be a minute." As he left the room, I wondered idly how much a pubkeeper would know about people in a village this size. Everything, probably.

After I had drunk a little of the coffee, I began to feel warmer. I finished my account of the confrontation.

"You would say that Mr. Jope was the aggressor, then?" Terrant asked me.

"Absolutely. He was very rude to Mr. Webb Springer, in-sulting."

He asked me to be specific about the insults, writing down each epithet. Afterward, he asked me to describe Willoughby's response once more, listening carefully as I repeated what I had told him. "Did you have the impression they knew each other, Miss Treleven?"

I thought back to the Mallaby's lunch, when Carl Jope's name had come up. Although Willoughby had mentioned Sophie, I was almost certain he had not contributed to the brief discussion of Jope himself. "I don't think they did. But I can't say for sure. The Mallabys would know." A thought occurred to me. "He was staying with them. Do they know what's happened?"

Smoothly, he replied that they would certainly be in-formed. The pub owner reappeared with a plate of French bread and cheese. Max had begun to fidget in the stroller but cheered up when I gave him the bread to gnaw on.

"About Mr. Jope's stepdaughter, Sophie Dymock," the inspector continued. "You say Carl Jope stopped to talk with her and then got involved in the argument with Mr. Webb Springer?" I nodded. "Was their conversation friendly, Miss Dymock's and Mr. Jope's?"

"I haven't heard Carl Jope have a friendly conversation with anyone." Terrant looked up from his notebook and gave a small smile. Pale lashes fringed light blue eyes of a disconcerting shrewdness. I went on: "She just wanted him to leave her alone. We both did. You could ask her about their conversation. She's staying with me."

"I will. But at the moment I'm interested in what you heard."

"They didn't really say all that much to each other. He accused her of trying to persuade her mother to leave him. And he called her names." Dutifully, I recited the names I remembered.

Terrant said, "Mr. Webb Springer claimed that Carl Jope had threatened him. Did he?" I assumed the pub owner had told him this. I replied that Carl Jope had certainly made threats against Mr. Webb Springer. "And even if he hadn't used the words themselves, his behavior was threatening enough."

"Could you describe it?"

"He was furiously angry. Frightening. I think we were all concerned for Mr. Webb Springer. That Mr. Jope might attack him physically." I described how Val Lenthall had been forced to come to Willoughby's aid. "Afterwards, when Mr. Jope drove off, Val offered to see Willoughby safely back to Summerhays. But he refused." I offered Max the cheese, but he turned his head away. "Do they know when he died?"

"Not yet. Only that he was in the river all night. Now, about these threats, can you remember the exact words?"

I thought for a moment. "He told Mr. Webb Springer he ought to be careful about his health. And something about loose talk costing lives."

Terrant lifted one sandy eyebrow. "Loose talk? What did you understand him to mean by that."

"Willoughby—Mr. Webb Springer—said something about Carl Jope's playing with matches. I assumed that was a reference to arson. That he was implying Mr. Jope was the arsonist. Mr. Jope took offense at that, to put it mildly." While Terrant made his notes, I went on. "I understand there've been a couple of unexplained fires in Shipcote. Like the one at my place. In cottages owned by weekenders. I thought that maybe, as I'm sort of an outsider myself . . ."

"That whoever set the other fires might have done yours as well?" Terrant finished for me.

"It seems the obvious conclusion. Do the police have any suspects for the other fires?"

"You could say so." There was a small silence. The tick of the clock seemed very loud in the room.

"Carl Jope?"

Terrant replied, pleasantly enough, "We're not at liberty to say, Miss Treleven."

Constable Skeffington came into the room and asked to speak to the inspector in private. Excusing himself, the older man got up from the table. While he was gone, I let Max stretch his legs, holding his hands as he navigated his way among the tables. All the while, I kept seeing Willoughby's face as he stood by the riverbank, confessing his fear of the water.

After a few minutes, Inspector Terrant came back into the room. "I'd like to talk to Miss Dymock now. If you're ready." His courtesy was unnerving; it suggested the velvet glove, and the iron beneath.

Constable Skeffington drove us to Longbarrow Cottage in his police car. The inspector sat beside him in the front seat, Max and I in back. Max waved his bottle about, enjoying this unexpected freedom from a car seat. During the drive, the inspector asked me about Willoughby's relationship with the Mallabys. I replied that I knew they'd been friends since the thirties, and that he had written a biography of Mrs. Mallaby's brother, Stephen Allerton. "Mr. Webb Springer was staying in their garden house. He was going to write his memoirs."

Cautiously, I added, "I don't know how to say this . . ."

The inspector glanced back at me. "Go ahead."

"Well, it's only that he was behaving oddly at the pub. Willoughby, I mean. Compared to the way I'd seen him act before."

"But you'd only known him a short time, you said."

"Yes, but . . . Well, it's probably nothing. Just that he seemed keyed up. As though he were on the verge of something. That's the way he struck me anyway."

"On the verge of what?"

"He was about to write his memoirs. I think he intended to do some harm with them."

The two men in the front seat glanced at each other. Terrant said quietly, "Are you saying that he might have known something about Carl Jope that he was going to reveal?"

I hadn't thought of this. "No, not at all. I really don't think they'd met before. I'm sorry, it was just an impression."

Skeffington remained in the patrol car while Terrant went into the cottage with Max and me. When Sophie heard us, she came out from the kitchen. And gave a broad smile at the sight of Inspector Terrant. "Hallo, Terry. You're on the arson squad now, are you?" She turned to me. "Terry was Granddad's friend, the one I told you about. If anyone can find out who set the fire, he can."

"He's not here about the fire, Sophie. It's about Willoughby."

"Oh?" Uncertainly, she looked from me to him. In a few succinct words, he told her what had happened to Willoughby. Her hand went to her mouth. "Oh, God, how horrible."

Terrant said, "I have to ask you some questions, Sophie. About last night, at the pub."

"Yes, of course." Her face was sober. "Look, I've got the kids' breakfasts ready. Could we talk in the kitchen?" That was fine with him, he said. Anna was already sitting at the kitchen table, eating toast. I put Max in his high chair and pulled a chair up to it, to feed him his cereal. Sophie poured tea for Terrant and me, then stood with her back against the counter while Terrant asked his questions.

He took her over the same ground that he and I had crossed together. She repeated much of what I had already told him, expanding only on her own responses to her stepfather. "You know how he is, Terry," she said simply. He nodded. Then she added, "It wasn't an accidental drowning, was it? You wouldn't be involved if it was."

"He was hit on the back of the head before he went into the water. That's sufficient to get us involved. Maybe it was an accident, but the forensic pathologist doesn't think so."

She asked him point-blank if the police suspected Carl Jope of being responsible for Willoughby's death.

He gave a tolerant smile. "You should know I can't answer that, Sophie."

"Look, Terry, my mum's alone with him. I can't go to her, it would only set him off. But if he's—"

Quietly, he interrupted. "Carl's been taken in for questioning. That much I can say. And your mum's fine. She was calling your uncle when I left. To get him to come stay at the farm." As he stood up, he said, "By the way, that information you wanted? About the Evelyn Allerton murder? It seems the driver of the car never came forward. Or the passenger. You wanted to know about the watch that was taken from the cottage as well. It never turned up."

Sophie glanced at me. "Was there a description of the watch?" I asked him.

He looked at me, curious. "It was inscribed. I wrote

down the words." He riffled through the back pages of his notebook. "Here it is. 'A good book is the precious life blood of a master spirit.' "

Benedict's watch. Through the weariness I felt a small hot flame of vindication. I asked Terrant how the police had known the watch was taken.

"The district nurse had seen it the day before the murder. She'd been to the cottage. Evelyn Allerton had been ill. The watch had been lying on a table by the bed, and she said the dead woman had shown it to her." He stared at me. "Why are you so interested in this case?"

"Living in this cottage, it's hard not to be." Then, prompted perhaps by Willoughby's death, I said, "But there's another reason. My grandfather owned the cottage at the time of the murder. The Allertons were his tenants. He disappeared a year and a half later. I think the two events were connected."

He was too polite to look openly skeptical, and anyway was probably too busy with Willoughby's death to care about a fifty-year-old murder, but before he could respond in words there was a knock at the front door. The arson squad had arrived, two men in canvas coveralls, carrying equipment. Leaving Sophie with the children, he and I went around to the shed with them. They took the paint cans and the tin of turpentine from the larder shelf, asked me a series of questions, photographed the shed, and poked about in what seemed to me a random fashion. Inspector Terrant drew one of the men aside and they talked together intently for some moments. Then he and Constable Skeffington left. Finally, I was allowed to go back indoors.

Sophie was sitting with the children on the living room floor. She looked up at me wonderingly as I came into the living room. "They think Carl killed him. I wish I could believe he did. . . . Poor old Webbed Sphincter. When I remember what you told me, about him being so afraid of the water, I almost feel sorry for him. Drowning. It must be a terrible way to die."

I picked Max up from the floor and sat down on the sofa with him on my lap. At that moment, I needed to feel him in my arms. Then, suddenly, I could see Peter's face, for the first time since his death. All at once the tears were rolling down my cheeks, unstoppable.

Sophie, occupied with arranging puzzle pieces for Anna, was speculating on the possibility of Jope's guilt; careful, on Anna's account, to be elliptical. After a moment, registering my silence, she glanced up. "Jo! What's the matter? It's not because of old Willoughby, is it?"

I shook my head, unable to speak. Max was playing with a spoon, banging it against my knee. I leaned my head back against the sofa cushions, my eyes closed. But still the tears poured out.

"I'll take the children into the garden for a little while," Sophie said. Holding Anna by one hand, with Max on her hip, she went out of the room. And I cried all the tears I had never shed for Peter.

Finally, exhausted, I got up and splashed cold water on my face, then went out to join Sophie in the front garden. She and the children were looking for violets in the grass. I sat on the stoop, watching them. After a little, Sophie left the children and came over to sit by me.

"Better now?"

I nodded.

"Want to talk about it? You don't have to."

"I was crying for Max's father. He drowned, like Willoughby." Sophie put her arm around my shoulders. "Only it wasn't really like Willoughby at all." I told her how he had taken the boat out. "I know he killed himself."

Sophie looked shocked. "What a shitty thing to do!" Then, contrite, she immediately started to apologize. "I'm sorry, Jo, I shouldn't have said that—"

"No, no, it's okay. You're right. It was exactly that."

It was as though a great gassy bubble of sentiment had burst in my mind. Until now, I had recognized only Peter's unhappiness. All-consuming, it had blocked out and devoured everything else until at last it had destroyed our marriage and his joy in his son. All other emotions, even love, had seemed too weak to withstand it. And after his death, the ghost of that unhappiness had continued to claim so much from me that it had left no room for anger. At him, anyway. Anger at myself, yes; and at his parents or anyone I thought had failed him. But never with him, until now.

I knew now that, if I let it, the anger would coil its tendrils around me and like the Green Man's vine I would someday find my mouth full of it, choking me. I thought of Nan, living out her life unable to break free of it. My only defense was forgiveness. If I could forgive Peter, I might be free.

Sophie said, "You look exhausted. Did you sleep at all last night?" When I shook my head, she insisted I go to bed at once.

"But your mother," I protested. "You should be with her."

"I will be. But I want you to get some sleep first."

Although I tried to argue, she made it plain she would not give in on this. Obediently, I climbed the stairs, stripped off my clothes, which smelled faintly of smoke, and slipped between the cool sheets. My head felt swollen with sorrow. After a little, I slept.

The sound of a car in the drive woke me at last. I glanced at the clock by the bed. It was past three. When I came downstairs, Sophie greeted me with a triumphant smile on her face.

"That was Terry. He came by to tell me the police are holding Carl. They've charged him with arson."

Two witnesses had come forward, she said. One had seen Jope shout from his truck at Willoughby, who was walking past the church, shortly after the pub incident. The other, a villager coming back along Blacksmith's Lane around midnight after visiting some friends at a nearby farm, had seen Carl Jope's truck parked off the lane on the track that led to the barrow.

Armed with a search warrant, the police had combed Crookfield Farm. They had found no evidence to prove Carl Jope had murdered Willoughby, but had uncovered, literally, a cache of paint cans and solvents hidden under some sacks of fertilizer. Traces of paint matching that in the cans set near the fire in the shed were found under Jope's fingernails and in his truck. Confronted, he had admitted to the arson attempt on Longbarrow Cottage, but continued to claim that he had nothing to do with Willoughby's death.

"But he's where he can't bother anyone," Sophie said happily. "That means you don't have to leave the cottage." Not immediately, at any rate, I thought. She went on to say that her mother had driven over from Crookfield Farm earlier, while I was sleeping. "My uncle's come from Bristol to stay with her for a few days. To help with the farm work." She grimaced. "He would never come near the place so long as Carl was there. We agreed, she and I, that as Uncle Robert's here, I would stay with you."

Terrant had told her something else, she added. Willoughby had died before his body went into the water, struck on the back of his head by some blunt instrument. The police were treating his death as murder.

CHAPTER 33

For the rest of the afternoon and into the evening, as Sophie and I tended to the children and chores, I looked for David to come by the cottage. More than the physical ache for his touch, I longed for the future his body had offered, that promise of happiness. The past seemed to hold only death and the revelation of evil. It was not until dusk, however, that I knew he and Rafe had returned.

Sophie and I were washing dishes in the kitchen when a sound distinct from the clatter of plates made us pause and look up. The window near the sink was open, and through it came a desperate voice shouting my name. Startled, we glanced at each other. "That sounds like Rafe," I said.

We rushed to the back door to see him running full tilt down the field toward the cottage, a small figure in the fading light with windmill arms that seemed too long for his body. Once he stumbled and fell but staggered up again immediately. He scrambled over the garden wall and I ran to-

ward him and caught him as he collapsed, gasping for
breath, into my arms.

"Rafe! What is it? What's happened?"

He struggled free and looked up at me with an anguished
face. "It's Spike," he blurted out. "He's hurt and it's all my
fault. I took him there, and I knew I wasn't supposed to."
A cramp doubled him over momentarily, one hand clutching his side.

"Where? To the barrow?"

He nodded, trying to catch his breath. He smelled of
sweat and earth, and his hands and arms were covered with
dirt, as though he had been digging with them.

"Come inside and tell us about it."

"No, no," he said wildly, shaking his head, "I can't leave
him for long. Please, I need a shovel or something. Can
you come, too?" His glasses were smudged with dirt and
there were twigs and leaves in his hair. A long bloody
scratch ran down one cheek.

"Of course. Wait, I'll tell Sophie."

But Sophie was there behind us on the doorstep and had
heard it all. She ran for the shovel while Rafe calmed down
just enough to explain that the ferret was trapped in Goody
Ridler's Tump behind a collapsed wall. Even as he talked,
he worked himself up again into the frenzy of worry. Grabbing the shovel from Sophie with a breathless thanks, he
seemed about to rush back on his own, but I held on to his
arm, insisting he wait while I fetched a flashlight.

Sophie stayed behind at the cottage to be with the children as I ran at a dogtrot with Rafe across the field to the
long barrow. Daylight was swiftly ebbing away, leaving
the side of the barrow that faced us deep in shadow. In the
woods, the rooks were settling into their nests with a rustling of wings like dry leaves in the trees.

The barbed-wire fence that ringed the barrow looked un-
broken. In fact, it had been neatly cut open, the section with
the severed strands hidden by the twisted branches of a
shrubby elder tree. As Rafe held the wire back so that I
could pass through it, a thought occurred to me.

"Rafe, are you the one who's been cutting the fences?"
Wordlessly, he nodded, not meeting my eyes. "But why?"

"So we'd have to leave," he said simply. "I didn't want to stay here."

I was bewildered. "Why would it mean you'd have to leave?"

"Dad would get fed up. Try something else, move somewhere else."

"Do you really think your father gives up so easily?"

"He did with my mom, and their marriage and everything." I bit my lip, searching for the right words, but he went on: "That's what I used to think, anyway. I guess I don't anymore. Anyway, I've changed my mind about leaving. It's not so bad here." I wondered if this change of heart had anything to do with his recognition that David was not involved with Mela in the way he had feared. He gave me no time to think about it, however, urging me to hurry.

On the other side of the fence, a thicket of bushes roughly fifteen feet deep and as high as my head screened the base of the barrow. Bramble, rockrose, hawthorn, privet, and spindle, their branches were woven together to form a far more effective fence than the barbed wire. Sleeping Beauty in her castle could not have been more securely defended by the thorny hedge than was Goody Ridler's Tump by this prickly barrier dense with leaf and vegetation. Or so it seemed.

Rafe asked for the flashlight. He switched it on, then dropped to his knees and pulled aside some branches to reveal a low tunnel carved through the undergrowth. He had made it himself, he told me proudly, as he turned to crawl into it.

On hands and knees, I followed behind him along the dark corridor toward the barrow's flank. The beam of the flashlight moved jerkily ahead of us down the passage, lighting up the mass of tangled branch and vine that writhed around us. Mindful of a Rackham drawing of a witch trapped in a blackberry bush by the long skeins of her hair, I kept my head low. Through the rich compost smell of rotting leaves came the sickly scent of privet flower and the musk of some animal.

After ten feet or so, the tunnel reached the edge of the barrow. Here, Rafe had cleared away the brambles and the bushes to make a little semicircle of space where we could stand upright. On the great flank of the long barrow, the jungle of greenery seemed like the matted coat of some sleeping animal. Overhead in the sky, the first stars shone pale and very far away. The silence, apart from the occasional rustle as some night creature moved through the undergrowth, was profound.

"Look," Rafe told me in a whisper. He turned the flashlight's beam on the mound.

Directly ahead, the thick ravel of vegetation had been shorn away to reveal a large patch of drystone walling roughly four feet high and three feet wide, most of which was enclosed by two stone uprights supporting a lintel stone. This was his discovery, Rafe said. During the past months he had worked his way from east to west along the flank, cutting away the undergrowth until he found what he had always suspected was there. The portal of a side chamber.

He had hacked out the passage through which we had just crawled in order to come and go easily, and to work in secrecy. On either side of the portal, he had cleared away the turf cover to expose the thin layers of stone that formed part of what was probably the main wall of the barrow. These stones seemed far more tightly and smoothly laid than those that blocked the portal, which had the appearance of being stuck in higgledy-piggledy, as though someone had closed up the entrance in a hurry.

A few hours earlier, on his return from London, Rafe had begun to remove the top layer of the stones sealing the portal. "That's when it happened," he said somberly. "I thought I'd tied Spike's leash tight, but he got free. I only had time to grab the end of the leash before he disappeared inside through the opening I'd made. I tried to pull him back, but the leash was caught on something. Then some of the stones fell in." His face was deep in shadow but I heard the wince in his voice.

I saw then that one of the supporting uprights, the one on the right or eastern side, was shorter than its mate. The difference between the two had been made up with drystone layers. These had caved inward, causing the lintel stone to sink down slightly on that side. With the lintel weakened, it was perfectly possible that the whole wall might collapse.

Rafe was lucky, I thought, not to have been hurt, or even killed.

He had wound the end of the leash around the trunk of a sapling growing by the portal. From it, the thin yellow nylon ran like a snake up the wall to disappear through the narrow hole that he had opened up just below the lintel stone. Now, he leaned his head close to this opening. He listened for a moment, then made a loud chirruping noise, very like Spike's. Then listened again, and again repeated the sound.

This time there was a response, very faint but audible. Rafe's face blazed with joy. "He's alive!"

The shovel we had brought was useless, for we could neither dig nor batter our way in. To try to remove the other stones without some sort of support for the lintel stone would almost certainly lead to further collapse. What was needed were wooden props to hold it in place while the drystone wall below was carefully taken out stone by stone. We could not do that alone, however. But when I said as much to Rafe, he begged me not to tell anyone.

"I'm not supposed to be here. If they find out I've been doing all this—" Hunched and miserable, he stood there with his face turned away from me, picking at some moss growing on the wall.

"They" were undoubtedly the Mallabys and his father. Of the two, I could make a fair guess as to who would be the more angry. It was a measure of Rafe's discontent, and the powerful appeal of the barrow's mystery, that he had been prepared to risk that anger by disobeying the Mallabys' injunction. Anyway, what chance could the threat of some unnamed and perhaps avoidable punishment have against the lure of a highwayman's treasure? If I were eleven again, I would be digging with Rafe.

As gently as I could, I said that I didn't think we had much choice but to tell his father. "If we're going to save Spike."

Gnawing on his lower lip, he thought this over but could suggest no workable alternative. At last, reluctantly, he acknowledged that I was right. "Okay," he said glumly, "you can tell Dad." Then, pleadingly, "But you won't tell him that I cut the fences, will you?"

"No. But I hope you will. Okay?"

His eyes met mine, and then he nodded. "Okay."

I pointed to the tunnel. "Will you lead the way?"

He shook his head. "I can't leave Spike." It was a flat statement, not a plea.

"I know how you feel, but after all, he can't go any-where—"

"You don't understand." His voice was urgent again. "He could be hurt. Maybe some other animal will try to get at him. Like a fox or a badger. I have to protect him." Above the flashlight, his shadowed face was obstinate. There was no point arguing, and although I did not like to leave him alone, I supposed he was safe enough.

All right, I conceded; he could stay, so long as he promised not to try to rescue Spike on his own. I tried to impress on him the danger of the wall's collapsing, for himself as well as for Spike, and promised to bring his father back as quickly as I could. "Is he at home, Rafe?"

"I think so." His voice was doubtful. Then in a rush, "Well, maybe he's at Mela's. She came over when we got back from London. She said she had something she wanted to talk about. He went to see her after dinner. That's when I came here."

"Okay." I gave him a swift hug and turned to go.

He put a hand on my arm. "Jo?"

"Yes?"

"He doesn't like her anymore."

Not knowing how to reply to this, I merely nodded, then crawled back along the tunnel under the brambles and ran down the field to the cottage. Sophie was waiting by the kitchen door. Briefly, I described what had happened and told her I was going over to Summerhays to fetch David. There was nothing she could do, I said, except listen out for Rafe. I had told him to come straight to her if he got nervous.

When I reached Oldbarn, the lights were out on David's side, but on Mela's they shone from an upstairs window and from the glass double doors that opened onto her terrace, a smaller version of David's. As I lifted my hand to rap on the glass, Mela entered the room.

She looked up, startled, at my knock. For a moment, she

simply stared toward the doors, as though irresolute, before coming swiftly over to open them. "Jo," she said, both voice and face wary and unwelcoming. "What are you doing here?" In a green silk kimono and slippers, with her hair tumbled about her flushed face, she looked as though she had just come from her bed. She had the indefinable air of a woman who had not been there alone.

"I'm looking for David," I said.

"I'm sure you are." She stretched languorously, raising one hand to push the hair off her neck. The green silk parted sufficiently to declare that she wore nothing underneath. "He *was* here," she acknowledged, her voice heavy with implication.

I could feel the impatience rising in me, but tried to suppress it. "Do you know where he is now? Rafe needs him."

"And you're Rafe's messenger? How obliging of you." She yawned and smiled at me through half-closed eyes. "They say the way to a man's heart is through his stomach, but I suppose if one can't cook—you did say you hated to cook, didn't you?—then his child is a good alternate route."

A confusion of feelings made me feel stupidly slow and I could only stare at her, unable to think of any response. It took the image of Rafe waiting alone in the darkness to spur me on to repeat my question.

"Why do you need him so badly?" she asked, her smile overtly malicious. "Apart from the obvious reason."

Before I could answer, a man's voice called out from somewhere behind her in the house. "Mela, I've changed my mind about the Drambuie. It's time I was going." Gerald Fenton came into the room, knotting his tie. He stopped abruptly when he saw me. With his mouth open, the handsome face looked almost foolish.

"You remember Jo Treleven, don't you, Gerald?" Mela said. "She has an unfortunate habit of turning up at inconvenient times."

Looking as uncomfortable as any man would in the situation, he simply nodded his head.

I turned to Mela. "So you haven't seen David, then?"

"He's with Benedict, in the library," Fenton said curtly. "Or was an hour ago anyway. I left them together."

"Thank you." Then, because I was suddenly happy, I

found it easy to smile at Mela. "And thank you, too. I see some things more clearly now."

"It's a pity," she said as I turned away. "We might have been friends."

Perhaps, I thought; but I doubted it.

When I went up the walk to the front door of Summerhays, the full moon was falling whitely on the smooth stone facade. Beneath its cold light, the gables stood out in sharp relief, with black shadows in the intervening valleys. On the roof, the row of chimneys looked like stubby fingers raised in admonition, or warning. Hoping against reason that Mrs. Blackwell would answer, I rang the doorbell. The last person I wanted to see now was Benedict Mallaby.

From the thick vine that gripped the stone around the door like a long and sinewy muscle came the minute sounds of nocturnal life, beetles and moths moving among the leaves, and some scurrying creature whose nails rasped against the stone. At last, as I was about to ring again, the door opened.

Benedict stood on the other side of the threshold.

For the briefest of moments, he and I were equally at a loss. He seemed disconcerted by the sight of me; his eyes blinked rapidly, as though adjusting to the darkness beyond. For my part, I was startled into silence by his appearance. Willoughby's death had left a visible mark on him. He looked old and inexpressibly weary, with the stooping, humbled air of a man who has been dealt a terrible blow. Like a straw man, he gave me the feeling that any strong wind might blow him apart.

I recovered first, explaining that I had been told I might find David at Summerhays. In an abstracted voice, he replied that David was in the library. Then, instead of asking me to come in, he moved toward me. Instinctively, I moved back, stumbling over the step. When he reached out one hand to my arm, presumably to steady me, I gasped and pulled away. Something in my reaction, and perhaps in my face, registered with him. An angry life came back into the gray face.

"Don't be ridiculous!" he snapped. "You have nothing to

fear from me." Then, with a sharp look, he added, "You've read that deluded book, have you?"

Mustering some semblance of self-control, I replied evasively that if I had, it was no thanks to him. "You tried hard enough to destroy it."

He seemed not to be listening. Wearily, he rubbed at his face. "She was wrong, you know. Your grandmother. Very wrong. Her lies might have done terrible damage. . . ." The words, and the way he said them, held the faintest hint of an appeal, seemed almost intended as a justification.

They only served to enrage me. Bitterly, I said that she had spent the rest of her life suffering. "Because of you. Because of what you did."

He made a gesture of impatience or denial, almost as though he could ward off the reproach with his hand. I might have gone on to accuse him of everything, all the crimes, petty and great, I harbored against him, if it hadn't been for the thought of Rafe, waiting for his father.

Suddenly David was there in the hallway. "Benedict? Look, I'm sorry to interrupt but we'll have to continue this tomorrow. I'd better get back. Rafe will—" Seeing me, he broke off in surprise. "Jo!"

"Rafe sent me," I said quickly. "He's okay, but he needs you right away." I glanced at Benedict, nervously hoping that David would not press me for reasons, but at that moment Clarissa's languid voice came floating down the stairs, calling to her husband.

Dressed in a long dressing gown of deep purple, she stood on the landing below the enormous portrait of Josiah Allerton, her Victorian forebear. In her own way, she looked at that moment as formidable as he, with the same unyielding steel implicit in that ramrod back, the tilt of the head. "What's going on?" she asked. Without waiting for his answer, she began to make her way downstairs, one hand clutching the banister, the other her cane.

His face suddenly anxious, Benedict went back into the house, crossing the hall to her. "It's nothing to trouble yourself about. You should be in bed."

"I don't understand. Why is she here?" A querulous note appeared in her voice, so unlike her that it seemed to belong to some other woman. "Haven't we been through enough . . . ?"

In a low voice, David asked me what had happened to Rafe. When I told him about Spike, he swore under his breath. "The number of times I've told him to stay away from the barrow." Taking my arm, he moved toward the door. "What do you think we'll need?"

Behind us, Clarissa called out, "Is the boy all right, David?"

David turned to her. "He's fine. He's gotten himself into some trouble, but it's nothing serious."

"In trouble? What kind? Where?" The questions came out staccato, the voice suddenly anxious. And now, with the light of the hall full on her, I could see that she looked as ravaged as her husband, as though Willoughby's death had taken the same physical toll of her. She was very pale and her left lid drooped heavily, almost obscuring the eye.

Calmly, David said, "I'm afraid he's been trespassing. On the long barrow."

There was a small silence. Clarissa and Benedict held themselves so still they might have been turned to stone. Benedict cleared his throat. "Might I ask what has happened?"

"His ferret got trapped somehow. He wants us to rescue it."

"On, or in, the barrow?" Clarissa asked quietly.

"In."

Benedict's face mottled. "I forbid you to dig there. Absolutely." His voice grew louder and, ignoring Clarissa's remonstrations, he came back to the door, trembling all over with what seemed to be rage. "You realize you could disturb important archaeological material? And for the sake of a ferret? No, the idea's preposterous!"

David said quietly, "Let me take a look at what's happened—perhaps we can get Spike out without damaging anything. But Rafe's there alone. We need to go." He spoke to the older man with respect, but his tone made it firmly unequivocal that he would do what was necessary for Rafe.

Wordlessly, Benedict conceded defeat. His face seemed carved by shadows, so deeply hollowed that it might have been a death mask. Bowing his head, he turned away and went back to his wife. As David and I went through the door, I glanced back at them. They stood beside each other at the bottom of the stairs, clasping hands like figures on a tomb, with the chill white look of alabaster in their faces. In spite of myself, in spite of everything, I felt a pang of pity for them.

From Oldbarn, David called Val Lenthall, who was on night duty at Shipcote Farm Park. He described what had happened and asked him to meet us at the cottage with the equipment we thought we would need, struts of wood of various lengths, the longest about four feet, a pair of heavy-duty cutters for any roots that might be in the way, work gloves, and a couple of powerful battery-run torches. He also asked Val to bring their first aid kit and the small animal carrier, in case Spike was hurt.

We drove back to Longbarrow Cottage in separate cars. Sophie came out when she heard the engines. "Thank God you're back. I thought you'd never get here." There had been no sign from Rafe, she said, and she hated the idea of him up there, alone.

As she was speaking, Val drove in behind us in the Land Rover. Quickly, I described the location of Rafe's tunnel and then, while the two men carried the equipment up to the barrow, went inside with Sophie to collect the food and hot cocoa she had put together for Rafe. When I came across the field, I could see the glow of the electric torches at the barrow, glimmering like a fire in the brush. By the time I joined the three of them, they had begun the work of bracing the lintel stone. With grateful murmurings, Rafe devoured the food and cocoa and then joined me in carrying away the stones as David and Val removed them, stacking them where they would not be in the way.

We said very little to one another, each of us conscious perhaps that what we were doing verged on desecration, both spiritual and archaeological. Conscious, too, of a suppressed, almost furtive excitement at the thought of what might lie behind the portal seal. Moving in and out of the torchlight, from eye-blinding brightness to darkness, we worked in a well of silence, the thicket around us muffling all sound. The saplings and the snarled complex of branch and tendril cast weird, attenuated shadows against the barrow, their slender limbs like thin and bony arms entwined in some strange dance.

As we peeled away the middle layers of stone, Val suddenly stopped and stepped back to study the portal wall, shining a flashlight over the surface. When he spoke, his voice was mildly puzzled. "I'd swear someone's been here before us. Fairly recently, too. In terms of the barrow's age, that is."

David, who was occupied in adding another strut, stood up, brushing the dirt from his hands. "I was thinking that myself. The stones seem so badly placed, compared to the work on the other side of the uprights. Just crammed in any which way."

"Maybe I'm right," Rafe said excitedly, forgetting for a moment his anxiety for Spike. "Maybe Dick the Handless did use the barrow as his hideout." Behind his glasses, his eyes grew wide. I could almost read his thoughts, the sudden bright vision of the highwayman's treasure hidden here in the barrow's flank and never discovered. Until now.

"Maybe," Val replied, smiling a little. "But someone's been here more recently that that. In this century, I'd say. You'd expect more of a root system established if these stones had been left undisturbed since the eighteenth century. We're having too easy a time of it, getting them out."

Rafe's face fell as the vision receded. If someone had dug into the chamber before us, they would almost certainly have stripped it of anything valuable. Gallantly, he said, "I don't care that much about the treasure anyway. I only care about Spike."

We went back to work, and at last had made an opening large enough to peer inside. As Val was standing closest, David gave him one of the small flashlights and asked him to take a look. Val crouched down and put his right arm, the one holding the flashlight, into the hole. The light cast a dim glow back. There was a dry rustle from inside. Careful to avoid the sharp edges of the protruding stones, Val squeezed the upper half of his body into the crevice.

Then flinched back as if he'd been shoved in the face.

"Bloody hell!"

He rubbed vigorously at his forehead, at the thick thatch of hair that flopped over it, as though trying to rid it of some substance clinging there. "Something touched me," he said in a harshly unnatural voice. "Brushed against my hair. Ugh." However, he refused David's offer to have a look himself and cautiously moved forward again. This time, he directed the beam of light up, instead of down. In a moment, he gave a sheepish laugh. "Roots hanging down. That's what it must have been. God, they felt like fingers."

"I think this place is getting to us all," David said. "The sooner we're out of here, the happier I'll be."

In a soft voice partly muffled by the stone, Val said that he could see Spike. "His eyes are open. The leash is twisted around a root, poor fellow. No wonder he can't move. But he looks okay, Rafe." He withdrew, turning to look up at us. "We'll need to make the opening bigger in order to reach him."

It took us another twenty minutes of patient, careful work to clear away the stones for an opening large enough to allow a body to squeeze through. We had to work slowly, changing the position of the bracing struts when needed, checking that the remaining wall was secure.

As we worked, a strange oppression grew, a thickening of the atmosphere, like a fog, although the night was clear. And the sense of being watched. I think we all felt it, for I was not the only one to look around from time to time. The night sky was bright with stars, a vast velvety expanse brushed with light, which seemed only to accentuate our own dwarfed and darkened state and the dense, jungly blackness that enclosed us. The barrow's shadowed bulk was like some enormous, wounded animal crouching in the bushes, waiting to spring on those who tormented it. It gave off the rank spoor of death, the feral presence of a hidden evil. We were four, and yet all at once I felt alone and vulnerable.

At last, David said the entrance was large enough. He put on a pair of heavy gloves. "Talk to Spike, Rafe. He needs to hear the sound of your voice." While Rafe made soothing noises, David took the flashlight from Val, knelt, and edged himself on bent knees into the narrow opening.

With a kind of dread, I watched as he vanished. The urge to call him back took hold of me, sharp as a visceral pain, and I had to bite my lip to keep from crying out.

From within, his voice came to us as he murmured reassurances to the ferret. In a few moments, to my unspeakable relief, he began to ease himself back out again, to reappear with Spike held lengthwise, cradled in his two hands.

Relief and joy mingled in his face, Rafe took his pet, placed a cheek against its fur, then gently laid the little creature in the carrier among the clean rags, stroking it with a loving hand. Then he turned and hugged us all.

While Rafe and Val looked Spike over to make certain he was unharmed, David disappeared back into the chamber, to give a proper look around, he said. For all his dreams of treasure, Rafe was so involved with Spike's welfare that he failed to notice his father's return into the barrow. There was a long silence, during which I said a silent prayer.

After what seemed to me an eternity, David emerged, his face grim.

CHAPTER 34

Val happened to look up. When he saw David's face, starkly lit by the glare of torchlight, he opened his mouth to speak. But David quickly shook his head as a warning, glancing at Rafe. Occupied with the ferret, Rafe had noticed nothing. Then David stood up, brushing the dirt from his clothes and arms, and in an ordinary voice asked me to take Rafe and Spike back to the cottage while he and Val finished up.

"But I want to help," Rafe protested, glancing around at his father. "And besides, I want to look inside—"

"Do as you're told, Rafe!" David said sharply. Rafe blinked, and hung his head. More gently, David added that they would not be long. When I said that Spike could probably do with some water, Rafe nodded mutely and after arranging the rags around Spike, obediently closed up the carrier.

We left the two men there and went back to the cottage, neither of us saying very much on the way. A small wind had risen, whispering through the long grass, bringing clouds from the east to shadow the moon. Faces tumbled through my mind like the swiftly shifting pieces in a kaleidoscope, flashes of light and dark, superimposed one upon the other. Mutable, often unreadable, the expressions on the faces seemed as fluid as water. Among them, however, was a single expression common to all. Passing over each face in various forms and for differing reasons was the same fear: the fear of revelation, the fear of the hidden emerging into the light. For Rafe, revelation might mean nothing more than the end of his treasure hunt; but for Benedict, and perhaps for all the Mallabys, it would mean something far more devastating.

Just before we got to the cottage, Rafe stopped and turned to me. "I want you to have something," he said. His head bent, he dug in his jeans pocket with one hand. When it emerged, the flint tool was lying on his palm. He held it out to me. "That's for what you did tonight. And everything else."

I knew it must cost him a pang to give it up, and tried to refuse it. But he would not let me. As I tucked it away in my own pocket, I said that we would consider it a loan he could claim back someday.

While Rafe gave water to Spike, who seemed to have survived his adventure with his curiosity intact, I took Sophie into the living room. We sat down together on the sofa, and I told her about David's reaction at the long barrow. With a grimace of distaste, she said that perhaps the stories about Goody Ridler were true after all.

"Maybe," I replied. "But I think it's something else."

I was going to mention Benedict's reaction to the news that we might have to dig into the barrow when Rafe entered the room with Spike fast asleep in his arms. He settled down on the rug in front of the fireplace. His delight at finding his pet alive had subsided sufficiently to allow the worry about possible punishments to grow. He contemplated his fate with a stoical resignation and a certain air of drama, observing fiercely that however terrible his punishment might be, Spike's rescue had made it worthwhile.

"Your father doesn't strike me as a hanging judge," I said, suppressing a smile at his rhetoric.

He looked up at me with eyes that were suddenly anxious, for all his bravado. "It's the Mallabys I'm scared of."

Sophie, who had greeted Spike's return with a genuine pleasure that had clearly won Rafe's heart, told him to cheer up. "If they give you a hard time, we'll run away together, you and me. I'm an expert at running away."

This provoked a pleased, if half-embarrassed, grin from Rafe, who looked as though the idea of taking off with Sophie might have its appeal. The back door opened and we heard David and Val come into the kitchen. When we joined them, they were washing up at the kitchen sink. Sophie uncovered the plate of sandwiches she had put together and we sat around the kitchen table while they wolfed them down.

"You've certainly made the archaeologists' job easier, Rafe," Val observed solemnly between large bites of bread. "That tunnel of yours, now, I could see a lot of work went into that. And the way you cut those wires? Neat as you please. Your father and I were saying we could use your talents up at the farm park. Isn't that right, David?"

While Rafe looked uncertainly at Val, as if not quite sure of his meaning, David translated for him. "Two weeks' hard labor after school at the farm park. That's your punishment, Rafe. Mucking out the loose boxes, cleaning up the litter, generally helping us out. Okay?"

"That's it?" Rafe looked from one man to the other, as though not quite daring to believe in his good luck.

His father nodded, but added warningly, "Of course, Benedict may have his own ideas on the subject." He then told Rafe to take Spike and wait for him in the car. Rafe gave me a quick, shy hug, thanked Sophie for the food she had sent him at the barrow, and went out through the back door looking considerably happier than he had almost three hours earlier.

When he had gone, David told us what he had found: a

man's body, arms folded over its chest, placed in the center of the small drystone chamber under Goody Ridler's Tump. "Judging by what's left of the clothing, he's twentieth-century. Not prehistoric."

A cold finger seemed to touch my spine. Our eyes met, Sophie's and mine.

"Not even eighteenth-century," Val was saying. He was straddling the seat of a kitchen chair, resting his arms on the back. "No treasure, either, that we could see. I'm sorry for Rafe. All that work for nothing."

David's smile was dryly amused. "I suspect a dead body will have its compensations." Then his face grew serious again. "I don't want him to hear about it tonight, though. He's had enough excitement for one day. I haven't even told him about Webb Springer's death yet. A murder so close to home . . ." When Sophie asked him if he thought the body in the long barrow might be that of another murder victim, he replied that he did not see what else it could be. "Someone had to wall him in, after all. And why go to the trouble, unless you were afraid of him being found? But if it is a murder, it's one that shouldn't affect us. It must have happened years ago."

I was certain that he was wrong, that the body in Goody Ridler's Tump was going to have a profound effect on all of us, in some form or other. I was equally certain of something else. The body could be that of only one man: my grandfather, Charles Lorimer. Benedict's reaction tonight made me certain of that.

Val was arguing that we should wait until morning to call the police. "That way we'll all get a night's sleep. If they come now, God knows when we'd have the chance. They'll want to talk to Rafe, too. Much better tomorrow than to-night. After all, whoever the poor fellow is, he's lain there long enough that one more night's not going to worry him." Sophie and David agreed that his suggestion made sense.

I turned away from the others. Those words, "poor fel-low," made the body a person, a man I might have known, someone whose blood ran in my veins. They filled me with a terrible sadness. Looking out through the kitchen window across the fields to the dark barrow, I was standing now where Nan must so often have stood in those long months of hopeless waiting for her husband's return. And he had lain there all the time, walled into his tomb beneath the mound, within her sight.

Stretching, David stood up. "I'd better get Rafe home." He went on to say that he would call the police first thing in the morning, and warned Sophie and me to expect their early arrival. He would join us as soon as he could.

The four of us walked outside together. The moon was hidden by the house and the black immensity of the sky stretched over us like a cover for the earth, pierced with the light of the stars. It seemed both shroud and comforter, its starry softness sheltering sleep and death. Somewhere a night bird's sudden song poured from its throat, spilling a flood of music into the silence.

While Sophie and Val lingered talking on the doorstep I went with David down the path to his car. Rafe was asleep in the front seat, his head slumped sideways, with Spike's carrying case on his lap. Sleep had softened his features into those of a much younger child, made him defenseless in a way that reminded me of Max. I felt the same yearning to protect him, as though he were my own, and the same poignant knowledge that I could never, should never, entirely shelter him from the sorrows of life.

"You won't let the Mallabys be too hard on him?" I said.

David smiled, and shook his head. "Anyway, they've got more important things to think about."

Assuming he meant Willoughby's murder, I said it had obviously come as a terrible shock. "Clarissa and Benedict both looked ill."

"It couldn't have happened at a worse time for them." He heard himself and gave a grim smile of atonement to Willoughby's shade for the words. "They'd just had some other bad news. And the two, taken together—" He broke off. After a long silence, he said, "I missed you, Jo."

"I missed you, too."

We stood there facing each other while the rising wind stirred the trees and the night flowed around us like a dark river alive with hidden currents. As he moved toward me, I saw with the desperate hope of a woman who believes she is drowning the lifeline of light in his face. His mouth on mine was the rescuer's act.

When we heard Val's footsteps on the path we broke apart like guilty children. "Storm coming," he said as he went past us to the Land Rover. Sophie remained on the doorstep, watching him go, a bright figure in the light from the hall. She turned to go inside when the Land Rover disappeared down the lane. Rafe stirred at the noise from the engine but did not wake up.

David took his keys from his pocket. Turning them over in his hand, he said, "I wanted to come to you this afternoon, Jo. When Rafe and I got back from London. But Benedict and Clarissa needed me."

His words chilled me. Was the Mallabys' need always so compelling, so seductive, that anyone around them would inevitably want to assuage it? Did they, like Mela, have that power over him?

When I asked him what had happened, he replied that the publishing house was in trouble. "Serious financial trouble. Has been for a while, apparently. But it was only recently that Benedict began to suspect something was up. He's furious it was kept from him this long." Mallaby's had overextended itself, he said. An overoptimistic expansion followed by poor sales had weakened it. Rising production costs and interest rates had made the resulting collapse inevitable. "Things looked good on the surface but they weren't plowing enough back in. It's not an untypical situation these days. Especially for an independent publisher like Mallaby's."

"Did Mela know?"

"Apparently so. She's really been running things for a while, and she insisted he be protected. I'm not sure her motives were entirely pure. She's been arguing for some time that Mallaby's was an awkward size, that they should look for a partner. A successful big brother, so to speak. She's proposing they adopt Gerald Fenton into the family." His voice was very dry, as though he knew as well as I that Fenton's relationship with Mela was far from brotherly. "Benedict flatly refuses to consider selling. But he might not have any choice, if Mallaby's is going to survive. And if he and Clarissa want to keep Summerhays."

"Things are that bad?"

He nodded. "In fact, he just offered to sell the family interest in Shipcote Farm Park to me. To raise some cash. That's what we were talking about when you arrived. Mela's been after me to buy them out. Now I know why."

"What will you do?"

"That depends on a number of things." He seemed about to say more, paused, and let four or five seconds pass. In a voice that held the whisper of an appeal, he said quietly, "Will you stay . . . ?"

I wanted to walk into his arms and tell him that of course I would stay. But I could not. So long as Benedict Mallaby was alive there was no home for Max and me in Shipcote. If the body in the barrow was my grandfather's, I would know beyond any doubt that Benedict had killed him. How could I hear that his business was failing, that he might lose his home, with anything but an angry sense of retribution? Yet to say as much to David was impossible. I could not let my anger and my suspicion spoil what he had built here, any more than I could build something of my own with him while keeping the truth from him.

After Peter's death, I had vowed that never again would I live a life composed of evasions and well-meaning lies for the sake of someone else. The beginning that David and I seemed to have made was a false start. A single night, the simple act of physical love, was not the future. And if the body seemed to promise that it was, well, the body often lied.

David took my silence for another kind of uncertainty. Softly, he said, "Tonight's not the time to talk about this. Tomorrow, when you're rested." He held me in his arms and gently kissed my mouth before he drove away with Rafe. As I watched him go, the old sense of loss crept back into my heart.

When I came into the cottage, Sophie appeared at the top of the stairs in her nightclothes, toothbrush in hand. She said, "It could be the tramp, you know."

I stared up at her, not understanding.

"The body in Goody Ridler's Tump," she explained as I came upstairs. "It could be the tramp. He might have gone up there after he killed Evelyn Allerton to shelter from the blizzard and then frozen to death."

Perhaps the police had been right all along, I thought.

Then I remembered the gold locket found in the Liverpool pawnshop. I reminded her of it, and of the fact that someone had walled the body into the chamber.

She made a rueful face. "My brain's already asleep. The rest of me should be, too. You'd better go to bed as well. You look all in." Then, seeing something in my face, perhaps, she hugged me and, in the voice she sometimes used to comfort Anna, said, "It'll be all right, Jo. You'll see."

A brief but violent storm raged over the cottage that night, throwing rain against the windows, battering windily at the house. In the morning, the world glittered with the brightness that had fallen with the rain. Shortly after breakfast, David and the police drove up one behind the other. In the hectic time that followed, he and I managed only a few brief words together. He said that Rafe had taken the news of the barrow's contents with the sangfroid of an eleven-year-old boy, eager for details, eager, even, to watch the police at work. David had flatly refused to permit this. As for Willoughby's murder, the old man had made his dislike of Spike too obvious for Rafe to feel more than a mild shock at his death, as well as relief that the murderer was already safely in jail.

David walked across the field to the long barrow with the police to show them the chamber, a procession of half a dozen men and one woman carrying various bits of equipment on their shoulders. I thought of going with them, to stand as a long-overdue mourner at my grandfather's tomb. But I could not face that grim vigil.

Sophie called out that she was making scones and would we like to help. Later, as we removed the scones from the oven, the serviceman from British Telecom arrived. By tacit consent, as a revenge for his taking so long to get to us, Sophie and I refused to satisfy his obvious curiosity about the police presence. "You know," she told him sternly as he set to work on the telephone in the front hall, "this place could've burned down the other night 'cause you lot have been so slow."

He muttered something about a computer snafu that kept registering the job as completed. "Happens every now and then. Not our fault, you know. But," he added apologetically, "sorry for any inconvenience." He gave a sideways glance at the plate of scones in Sophie's hand. She took pity on him and gave him one with a cup of tea.

As soon as he had finished and departed, Sophie inaugurated the telephone with a call to her mother. While she was on the phone, Inspector Terrant knocked on the door. There was nothing new to tell us, he said, but he wondered if he might speak with me for a moment or two. He raised a hand in greeting to Sophie as I took him into the living room, where Max and Anna were playing.

He sat down on the sofa. "You've come to a quiet little village, haven't you?"

"The body count does seem to be rising." I settled on the floor beside the children, stacking plastic cups with Anna for Max to knock down.

He was here, he said, because he remembered my telling him about Charles Lorimer's disappearance. "I'd like to hear what you know about it. Let's start with your grandparents' full names, ages, backgrounds, that sort of thing." After I had given him the details I could remember, he asked if I knew the precise date of Charles's disappearance.

"It was the day Britain declared war with Germany. I know that for a fact because Clarissa Mallaby recently told me so." I went on to describe her story of the reasons for my grandfather's disappearance. He wrote all this down in his notebook without comment, interrupting once or twice to have me repeat something.

While this was going on, David came back from the barrow. Seeing that I was busy with the inspector, he simply said that he was going home with one of the sergeants, who wanted to question Rafe now. He would come back later. Wistfully, I watched him go; the distance between us already seemed to be growing.

"You don't happen to have a picture of your grandfather, do you?" Inspector Terrant asked me.

"I do. Not a very good one, though." Taking Willoughby's biography of Stephen Allerton from the bookshelf, I opened it to the page with the group photograph that showed Charles half-hidden by Benedict and Clarissa. He asked if he might take it with him. It was a library book, I explained. With a smile, he promised it would come to no harm.

All the while Inspector Terrant and I were talking, I could feel a pressure building inside me, a compulsion. When Sophie finished her phone call, I asked if she would mind taking the children outside for a moment.

"There's a story I want to tell you," I said when he and I were alone. "It's about Evelyn Allerton's murder and the way it might be connected to my grandfather's disappearance. You may not believe me, and even if you do, there may be nothing you can do about it, but I have to tell somebody." Someone unconnected to the Mallabys, with the power to investigate, if enough evidence came to light. I was leaving Shipcote, but I wanted the truth to stay behind.

I told him everything I knew, everything I suspected. Although it seemed to take a long time, he listened patiently, his face impassive. When I finished, I felt as though a weight had shifted from me. He was silent for a moment, and then asked me if I had told this to anyone else.

"Sophie knows some of it. Not all." For Anna's sake, I was sorry now I'd told her as much as I had. Someday, Robin Mallaby might accept his responsibilities, might try to be a father to Anna. How could Sophie ever have a rapprochement with the Mallabys, knowing and suspecting all that she did?

"I see. Well, I shouldn't mention it to anybody else if I were you." His voice was cautionary, although his face expressed nothing more than the hint of concern. "Now, as far as I understand it, the only substantial facts to make Benedict Mallaby a suspect in Evelyn Mallaby's death are the watch and your grandfather's letter, which puts him in Shipcote the night of the murder. The rest is speculation and assumptions." He ran a hand through his hair and gave me a long, considering look. "To be honest, I'd have a tough time making any sort of case out of what you've told me. And after fifty years . . ."

"I know. I didn't think there was much you'd be able to do about it." I thanked him for listening.

He stood up. "I'm not saying it's all wrong. Just that most of it's circumstantial. You can't accuse a man with stories."

There was a hint of reproof in his voice, the barest emphasis on that last word. Yet I did not feel he entirely disbelieved me. Something came through the official facade, a flicker of interest or wonder. A door had been opened, and he had not completely closed it.

Just then the telephone rang. So unfamiliar was the sound that I jumped. As I picked up the receiver, Inspector Terrant said that he would find his own way out. He wanted to have a word with Sophie anyway.

"Hello?"

"Is that Jo Treleven? This is Sylvia Clitheroe. I ran one of the stalls at the book fair last week, Desmond Clitheroe Books. Remember?"

How could I forget? I was tempted to say. Over the wire, her voice sounded as earthily jovial as her person had been. "Of course I remember," I said. "I asked you to find a book for me." She could only be calling to say she now had a copy of *Life Blood* to sell me. I tried to control my rising excitement.

"I just saw the paper. Shocking news that, about Willoughby. Poor old sod. I think the milk of human kindness ran a bit thin in his veins, but he knew books, I'll give him that much. Well, I really rang to say I got hold of that book you wanted. The thing is, I gave it to Willoughby. I just wanted to check that you got it because of ... well, you know."

With a sinking heart, I replied that I did not have the book. "Willoughby never even mentioned it."

"Oh, Gawd. I should have known better than to trust the crafty bugger."

"Where did you find a copy?"

"Well, it's a coincidence really. That old lady up in North Oxford, she had a copy in her library. I found it when I was sorting through the fiction with Des. That's my husband. Then I ran into Willoughby and told him our bit of good luck. He said as he was going down to Shipcote that afternoon, he'd bring it along to you. I tried to ring you, to tell you it was on the way, but you've been having a spot of trouble with your phone, haven't you?"

Yes, I said, we had. "Maybe the book's with Willoughby's belongings. You're sure he actually brought it here?"

"Sure as I can be. He was in his car, just leaving, when he came by the shop. Said he was going straight to Shipcote."

"I see. Well, I'll try to find out what's happened to it. In the meantime, let me send you a check for what I owe you."

"You don't have to do that. Not if you never got it."

I insisted; the book would surely turn up, I said with more optimism than I was able to feel. Well, all right, then, Sylvia Clitheroe replied; five pounds, that was the price. "Are you certain that's enough?" I asked her, surprised, remembering Willoughby's anonymous offer. But she assured me that five pounds was all it was worth. "It's in good shape, mind. Even got the original jacket."

After I had thanked her and hung up, I stood cursing Willoughby's memory with every expletive I knew. His neglecting to tell me about the copy of *Life Blood* when we met at the pub had not been the forgetfulness of age; the look that had been on his face assured me of that. "Crafty," Sylvia Clitheroe had called him, and "crafty" was as good a word as any to describe his expression that night.

I might never know how long Willoughby had intended to dangle *Life Blood* in front of me, or his motives for doing so. But I was certain of one thing, that he had used the book, as he had undoubtedly used other secrets, to tantalize and control. His manipulation of me must have given him a thrill as powerful as any drug. And if he had played that game with me, he had surely been playing it with the Mallabys as well.

There was a shout from the garden. Sophie, calling my name. "Look at Max," she cried happily as I ran to the door. There he was, coming toward me over the grass, arms outstretched, with triumph and surprise on his face. All by himself on his own two feet. I came down off the doorstep, knelt, and waited for him. He took three more tottering steps and pitched forward into my arms with a wild cry of delight. Then pushed me away and staggered off again.

For the next fifteen minutes, as Max gained confidence, cheered on by the acclaim of his fans, I sat in the grass and forgot everything but the pleasure of watching my child, forgot even to draw this singular rite of passage. Like a balm to the soul, the sight of Max making the most of his moment of glory mended something inside me that had seemed to be breaking.

CHAPTER 35

Sophie wanted to go over to Crookfield Farm, to visit her mother. I suggested that we drive there now, and then I would continue on to Wychley with Max to do the shopping. While she sat on the stoop with Anna making up a grocery list, I took Max indoors to change him.

During the few minutes that I was upstairs with Max, a car pulled into the drive. I assumed it was someone come to help out with the work up at the barrow. Through the open window drifted voices, Sophie's and a man's. With a start of surprise, I recognized the male voice as Robin Mallaby's. He seemed to be doing most of the talking, but the words were indistinct. Reluctant to interrupt, I sat on the bed looking at a picture book with Max, letting my own voice muffle those below the window. As I remembered the appeal of Robin's looks and charm, I felt a pang of concern for Val.

After ten minutes or so, Sophie's voice called up to me. "Jo? Are you there?"

I looked out of the window to see her standing below with Anna in her arms. Robin's car was backing into the lane. "All clear?" I asked her.

"Less muddy, anyway. You can come down now."

When I met her outside, I tried to keep my expression impassive, free of questions, but she simply laughed at me. "What a poker face! Go on, admit it, you're dying to know what he said."

"Every word." Then, with dignity, "But you don't have to tell me."

"Course I do," she said with a grin. "Who else *can* I tell?" She seemed so cheerful that my worry for Val grew. On the drive to Crookfield Farm, she gave me an account of the conversation, which had been brief and necessarily elliptical. Concerned that Anna might understand some of it and be upset, she had not allowed Robin to say all that he'd wanted to. "It didn't matter. I got his drift."

As I had guessed he might be, he was taken with Anna, Sophie said, and seemed to be contrite, wanting to make up for his neglect. "D'you know what he told me? That when he tried to buy Longbarrow Cottage from you, it was so that we could live there together, he and I and Anna."

"I suppose that's why he wanted to keep the offer a secret from his family."

"Typical Robin behavior," Sophie said, with the same humorously exasperated intonation some parents use in speaking of their teenagers. "Impulsive, well-meaning and absolutely self-centered. No thought to whether I'd agree, just the assumption that I'd fall all over him with gratitude." After a moment, she added, "Still, at least it shows he was thinking about Anna."

We were approaching the turn for Crookfield Farm. I glanced quickly back at her. "I may have to sell, you know. If the idea of living there with Robin—"

"No fear. I scotched it at once." She said this so firmly that my hopes for Val rose again. "But I'm glad he came, because as soon as I saw him I knew it was over. He's not my future, but I'm happy he wants to be a part of Anna's. Mind you," she went on, "he gave me the impression his own future's just a bit shaky at the moment. Apparently, there's some sort of upset at Summerhays. That's one of the reasons he's here. Family conference, he said."

"Their firm's in trouble, according to David."

"Ah. Poor Robin." There was genuine sympathy in her voice, but she added tartly that, in that case, it was just as well she hadn't counted on him for child support. "Looks like it's time I got a proper job, Annakins. Made us some money."

"Honey?" Anna echoed, puzzled.

Sophie laughed. "You look after the honey, Anna love, and I'll take care of the money." She would, I thought; Sophie was a survivor.

When we got to Crookfield Farm, Sophie suggested I leave Max with her while I did the shopping. She and her mother would give the children lunch. Mrs. Jope seconded the idea. For a woman whose husband was in jail accused of arson and suspected of murder, she seemed remarkably calm. In fact, she looked like someone given a new lease on life. Already, that wispy, uncertain manner seemed marginally less pronounced and her smile came more readily. As I left, she and Sophie were carrying the children off to the henhouse to visit some newly hatched chicks.

The shopping took less time than it might have done with Max along to help me. Shortly after one, I was driving back through the village when I saw the Jaguar pull out of Summerhays and drive off in the other direction. Benedict was at the wheel, with Mela beside him and Robin in the backseat.

At the sight of Benedict, I felt my anger flare into life again, fueled by the thought of that body lying in the long barrow. He had robbed Nan of so much. One thing, however, I could, and would, reclaim. On impulse, I turned into the Summerhays drive.

My search for Nan's book had taught me certain lessons about myself and about my past. More importantly, it had taught me that no one has the right utterly to obliterate the creation of another. Peter's self-portraits might wound me, might make others believe that I had wounded him, but I could not destroy his paintings simply because other people might interpret them wrongly or to my disadvantage. His work should be seen, just as Nan's should have been read. When Max and I returned to Toronto, I would organize a show of his work that included the self-portraits.

And, if I salvaged nothing else from the past, I would rescue *Life Blood*.

That Benedict and Clarissa had the book seemed irrefutable. Willoughby had brought it with him; if it was not among his things, then one of them had taken it. Almost certainly, Clarissa would refuse to give it up to me, but when that happened, I would use the Longbarrow Brotherhood agreement to persuade her. If the Mallabys were forced to sell part of their publishing company to Gerald Fenton in order to save it, they would certainly not want a possible claim on the company to complicate the sale. I had almost no interest in pursuing that claim through the courts, unless they forced me to it. All I wanted was the book.

Mrs. Blackwell answered the door. She seemed subdued, as though she knew or sensed the family troubles, and her manner to me was a shade less welcoming than before, as if she suspected I might have something to do with those troubles. As she asked me to come in, she told me gravely that Mrs. Mallaby might not be up to seeing visitors this morning, but she would let her know I was here.

Ten minutes passed by before Mrs. Blackwell returned. She said that Clarissa would see me now, in the library. "Be sure you don't tire her," she admonished me. "She's had a bad night."

I replied that my business with Mrs. Mallaby should take only a few minutes. Something in the tone of my own voice made her glance at me questioningly, but she merely opened the door to the library and let me pass through.

Clarissa was sitting in a straight-backed chair near the fireplace. A log fire was briskly burning and there was an odd smell, acrid and unpleasant, as though the burning wood had been treated with some chemical. Although the room seemed too warm, she was wrapped in a white mohair shawl, sitting as always very upright, with her cane resting against her legs. She looked much older, however, almost shrunken, and the sagging left eyelid seemed worse this morning. I felt a sudden distaste for what I had come to do. It was Benedict I should be confronting, not this frail old woman.

"Sit down, my dear." She motioned to the leather sofa opposite her chair. "This has been a shocking time for all of us." Despite its weariness, her voice still held that note of quiet authority.

"In all sorts of ways," I replied. Deliberately ignoring her invitation, I remained standing, nervously fingering Rafe's flint tool in my pocket, wanting simply to come to the point as quickly as possible, take the book, and leave. "I want my grandmother's book," I said bluntly. "I know Willoughby brought it here."

She did not pretend surprise or seem to take offense at the implicit accusation, but only inclined her head. "It tells such lies."

"It is fiction, after all." My voice made it plain I thought otherwise.

She compressed her lips and folded her hands in her lap. "Your grandmother set out to destroy Benedict's peace of mind and his reputation with that book. She was very clever, there was no hint of slander, but anyone who knew us would see the similarities and make their mistaken assumptions. To allow her imagination to destroy a man's good name was inexcusable."

"Not if she believed Benedict killed her husband," I blurted out angrily.

She glanced up at me with cool contempt. "Do tell me why you think this. You won't shock me, I promise you. There is nothing now that can shock me."

"Least of all the identity of that man buried in Goody Ridler's Tump."

"You're convinced it's Charles, aren't you? I believe you'd be quite disappointed to learn otherwise." She seemed almost amused, and I began to feel uneasy. "Oh, do sit down. It wearies me to look up."

"There's no reason to tire yourself looking at me. Give me *Life Blood* and I'll go."

"And if I should refuse?"

"I have the Longbarrow Brotherhood agreement. I'll take it to a lawyer." My answer came so quickly and with such a powerful sense of release that I might have felt some taste of revenge for Nan's wrongs—if I had been talking to Charles's murderer instead of the murderer's wife.

As I spoke, I watched Clarissa carefully, trusting her to understand the implication. She did. For the first time, I saw fear in her face. The sagging lid trembled uncontrollably, blurring the beautiful violet gaze.

"But I—" she began. Then she halted, and looked down at the clasped hands in her lap. She turned them over, twisting the gold wedding band around her finger, before leaving one hand in the folds of the shawl and placing the other on the head of the cane. I could feel my impatience rising. After a moment, she glanced up at me again, observing me with a clinical interest, as though I had undergone some unexpected metamorphosis. "It seems you are capable of surprising me, after all."

I ignored that. "I don't want to have to use the agreement, unless you force me to. I simply want what's indisputably mine. Willoughby was bringing the book to me."

"Before I give it to you, I want to tell you a story. A true story." She registered my disbelief and raised one eyebrow. "Or are you not interested in the truth?"

Grudgingly, I sat down on the sofa, at the end farthest from the fire, taking the flint tool from my pocket. While she spoke, I turned it over and over between my hands, as though it were some sort of touchstone capable of detecting the lies.

"You are wrong about the man who is buried in the long barrow," Clarissa began calmly. "He was not your grandfather, but my brother. The police examination will bear that out."

I gaped at her. "But I thought Stephen Allerton was killed in Spain?"

"So did we all, at first. We were assured he was dead. His body was never found, but then many were not, so we had no reason to think he had survived." The words came out slowly, with apparent difficulty. She grasped the cane handle, smoothing its ivory curve with restless fingers. "Instead, it seems he ran away." There was a small silence. She looked at me almost defiantly, as though expecting some reaction. "I suppose your generation would find nothing shameful in that. But I promise you ours thought quite otherwise.

"He was captured, however, and imprisoned. Eventually, he managed to escape, and made his way back to us. But he was desperately ill by then and he arrived in Shipcote the night of a terrible storm . . . the night Evelyn died. In those days, I lived in a little cottage in the village. Summerhays had been sold, of course."

"Your brother came to you? Not to his wife?"

"Of course." The expression on her face was tranquil, reminiscent, and there was a faint smile on her thin lips.

"As I once told you, Stephen and I might have been twins, we were so close, so alike in our thoughts. Evelyn was merely an aberration, symptomatic of his weakness for waifs and strays. He saw his mistake almost immediately after they married, although he was too honorable to abandon her. But it was I he wanted to be with at the end." Pride was so strong in her voice that it was virtually triumph.

"Stephen was very ill, but he refused to see a doctor. He had come home to die, he said, and wished to do so in peace. And he did not want anyone to know of his cowardice." I wondered if it had been Clarissa herself who had felt this way, rather than Stephen. "But he became delirious and in his delirium called for the manuscript of *This Sad Ceremonial*, wanting reassurance that it was safe. Well, of course Evelyn had it. Mercifully, Willoughby happened to be staying with me at the time and at last he said he would go up to Longbarrow Cottage and do his best to persuade her to give it to him. She would never have given it up to me. She hated me."

The fire made the room too warm. I wanted to hurry her through her story, to force her to an end. Impatiently, I said, "You're implying that Willoughby killed Evelyn?"

"I assume he must have. We never spoke of it, however. He returned with the manuscript, and Stephen was able to die knowing it was safe. That was all that mattered to me. When I heard later that Evelyn was dead, I was perfectly content to accept the police explanation."

"And to tell them that Willoughby had spent the evening with you?"

"Yes." Her eyes held mine. The look in them was neither remorseful nor defiant; she might have been acknowledging some minor social lie, not a perjury in order to protect a murderer. "Stephen died two days later," she continued. "It had been a childhood wish of ours to be buried together in the long barrow. When the snow had melted sufficiently, I took his body up there by horseback. Obviously, if he'd had a proper funeral, there would have been questions. We did not want that."

"Questions about Evelyn's murder, you mean?"

"That, and about Stephen. In people's minds, he had died

a hero. Willoughby and I wished to leave it that way." To the extent that they had not even called a doctor in to treat him, I thought. "Later, when I married Benedict, I told him, in order that he understand why there must never be any excavation at the barrow."

"But Benedict already knew. He was with you that night."

"Was he, indeed?" The sagging lid fluttered, but Clarissa's face betrayed only a bemused curiosity.

"My grandfather and your husband drove up from London the same night that Evelyn was killed. I know this from a letter written by my grandfather. Charles was going north, to Liverpool, to say good-bye to his mother before setting out for Spain. Benedict was after the manuscript of *This Sad Ceremonial*. He intended to visit Evelyn to try to get her to part with it. My grandfather says that in his letter."

"Do go on." Her voice was even wearier. Both hands rested on the handle of the cane, which she held upright now, to one side of her knees. Her body was leaning forward slightly, as though the rigid bar that held her upright had begun to weaken.

"They ran into the blizzard," I continued. "Charles was afraid he'd get stuck in the valley by drifts, so he dropped Benedict off on the main road. Benedict used the track past Withyford church to approach the cottage. Walking, it would be faster than the road. When he got to Longbarrow Cottage, I think he and Evelyn quarreled and when she threatened to destroy the manuscript, he killed her. Accidentally, perhaps."

"Kind of you to give him the benefit of the doubt," Clarissa said, her voice very dry.

"At first I thought he covered it up himself, but I think the shock was so great that he ran from the cottage with the manuscript. Not knowing that someone else had seen him kill her."

"Willoughby?"

"Willoughby. I think he covered up for Benedict and then blackmailed him. Charles went to Spain not knowing Evelyn was dead. It was only when he came back that he learned the details and realized their significance. I think that finally he went to Benedict and confronted him. And Benedict killed him."

Clarissa looked across at me for a long moment. "Most ingenious. And as much a slanderous fiction as your grandmother's work was."

"There is some proof. Your brother's watch, given to him by my grandfather. The police reported it stolen and never recovered, but Benedict has it now. He must have taken it on the night of the murder."

"You are wrong. Stephen gave it to my husband before he went to Spain."

I stared at her. The lie was so blatant and so careless that it seemed to say she had given up caring whether I believed her or not.

"And my grandfather?" I asked her, with irony heavy in my voice. "Did Willoughby kill *him*, too?"

Clarissa's shrug seemed to imply that it hardly mattered if he had. "Perhaps. Charles and Willoughby never really got on terribly well. Charles was rather stuffy about Willoughby's feelings for Stephen, disapproved of them. I've always believed that what we most dislike in others is what we fear in ourselves." She gave a malicious smile. "Perhaps Charles suspected Willoughby of Evelyn's murder, and confronted him."

At this moment, the door of the library opened and Mrs. Blackwell came in. She began to say that Clarissa really must rest now, and would I please come back another time, but Clarissa lifted one hand to stop the flow. "I'm perfectly well, Blackie," she said firmly. "Do leave us alone." It was a command, not a request. Reluctantly, Mrs. Blackwell acquiesced, retreating back through the door with mutterings that if Mr. Mallaby were here he would insist she lie down. The door closed behind her.

I said, "Willoughby seemed to want me to read *Life Blood*, but at the same time kept it from me. Do you have a theory about that, too?"

She smiled faintly. "Willoughby always liked to set the cat among the pigeons. It amused him to disconcert people. He may have enjoyed watching you delude yourself with the book."

"Even if I caused his friends pain in the process?"

She brushed aside the issue with a dismissive wave of one hand. "That wouldn't have troubled him. On the contrary, I'm quite certain that for him it was part of the pleasure. The older and lonelier he got, the worse he became. I think at the last the sight of someone else's happiness caused him actual physical distress. That may be why he and Cece got on so well—the poor child has never been happy." A spasm of sorrow or pain passed over her face, but vanished almost at once. "Willoughby was used to tormenting civilized people, people who had no way to defend themselves. Perhaps that made him careless with Carl Jope. A man who had no such inhibitions."

"If you felt that way about him, why did you keep up your friendship?"

"Well, of course I was in his debt. And he was a charming man when he was younger. Very amusing, very witty." She saw my reaction. "It's possible to forgive someone a great deal if he makes you laugh. And then, one falls into habits as one ages, learns to accept what to others might seem unacceptable."

I was weary and confused, no longer sure of what to believe. The fire made the room too hot, thickened the air already dense with the smell of age and that peculiar odor from the burning wood. Books rose up around me, shelf after shelf of cloth and calf, backs turned, concealing, perhaps, the one I sought. I half-expected to see them suddenly tumble from the shelves, flying at me through the air like the playing cards in *Alice's Adventures in Wonderland*, defending their owners. I needed to get out of this room, I needed air.

I stood up. "You said you had Nan's book. Please give it to me now."

She simply smiled at me for a long moment. And this time her smile was full of malice. "We've been enjoying it, you and I, for some time."

"What do you mean?" Through the confusion, I felt a flicker of fear.

Still smiling, she looked toward the fire. Even as I turned with horror in the direction of her gaze, I was thinking that Mela and Cece had inherited that smile.

"It was an inflammatory book. A single match sufficed."

But I hardly heard her. I was already on my knees, grabbing for the poker, pushing aside the burning logs. Sparks flew, the heat from the flames scorched my face. In the ashes beneath the collapsed heap of logs were the charred and smoldering remains of *Life Blood*. Burned beyond redemption.

Fury at the thought of all that the Mallabys had destroyed seared my heart. My vision seemed clouded by the heat. I looked around, murderously, at Clarissa, my hand still clenched around the handle of the poker.

She was standing right behind me, with the cane raised high in both hands.

CHAPTER 36

"Clarissa! No!"

Benedict stood in the doorway. His shout caused her momentarily to falter, and her aim to skew. At the same moment that she struck at me with the cane, I raised my left arm to ward off the blow. My hand still held the flint tool, which grazed the knuckles of her clenched fists as the cane glanced off my shoulder. With a cry of pain, Clarissa dropped the cane to the rug, then collapsed onto the seat, one hand held against her chest. Benedict was already at her side as I got unsteadily to my feet.

The poker was in my right hand. Carefully, I set it back in its place among the fire irons, slipped the flint tool into my pocket, and then, automatically, picked up the cane from the floor. When my hand grasped the ivory head, I felt an unfamiliar roughness on its surface. The ivory was badly chipped. In addition to the hairline fissures, there was now a long crack running down the curve of the handle. The crack had not been made by the blow against my shoulder,

I was certain, because in it, and in the thinner fissures, was a peculiar rusty-looking substance, as though some liquid had seeped in and dried there. It looked like blood.

With a sudden certainty I knew that the cane had served as a weapon once before, had struck at another's head from behind. I stared at Clarissa. "You killed Willoughby!"

"Don't say anything!" Benedict told her fiercely.

But her voice overrode his. Weary no longer, it was filled with a violent strength. "Of course I killed him," she shouted at me. "He would have destroyed us. His damned memoirs! Vile lies and innuendo! They all told lies. Evelyn, Charles, Willoughby. They tried to harm us, but I stopped their mouths for them." Glaring up at me in triumph, her face was like some small shriveled monkey's, the violet eyes wicked. All her beauty had vanished. She was trembling uncontrollably, with the shawl lying in a white pool at her feet.

"I put Charles in the river after I killed him," she said with malevolent pleasure, "weighted him down with stones. It always made me laugh to hear the fisherman talk about the size of their catch after that. I tried to kill your grandmother as well, burn her up for the witch she was."

"That's enough!" Benedict gripped her arms. "For God's sake, Clarissa, don't say any more!" But she was unstoppable, ranting now almost incoherently, saying how she had killed Evelyn to save Stephen's book, that Evelyn deserved to die, that anyone who threatened her family deserved to die. The virulent words burst from her as though she were emptying herself of some long-pent-up poison.

My shoulder ached, bruised by Clarissa's blow. I was chilled with a deadly cold, which the heat from the fire could not warm, a cold that seemed almost to come from the cane in my hands. I should throw it onto the fire, I thought, let it burn with the book.

While Clarissa was shouting, three people had come through the door, only to be stopped short by her confession. I half-saw them, half-knew they were there, but in her collapse Clarissa seemed to suck the energy of the room toward her, like a black hole, absorbing us all. We could see only her, hear only her.

Then David walked away from Mela and Robin and

crossed the room to me. Wordlessly, he put one arm around me. And the simple act somehow broke her power.

Clarissa sagged back against the chair, her eyes cloudy, veiled by the heavy lids. "I don't feel well. I want her to go." Her voice was suddenly as plaintive as a tired child's, a weary whisper in the silence of the room.

"Yes, my darling." Benedict stooped over and picked up the shawl. His own hands were shaking now as he wrapped it tenderly about her. Then he turned toward his grandchildren. "Robin!" he said harshly. Robin Mallaby was staring with uncomprehending horror at Clarissa, his boy's face shocked into adulthood. At the sound of his name, he started, turning dazed eyes to his grandfather. "Pay attention," Benedict told him. "Call Dr. O'Brien. Ask her to come at once. And tell Blackie that Clarissa's not well and needs to go to bed." Mutely, Robin nodded.

"She's to blame, isn't she?" said Mela angrily as her brother left the room. She was looking accusingly at me. Some of her seemingly unquenchable radiance had faded. Her face was colorless, the lips unpainted, the bright hair dragged harshly back and twisted tightly into a knot. "What did you do to her?" she demanded, taking a step toward me.

Before I could speak, Benedict roughly told her to be quiet. "All that can wait. Your grandmother needs you. Help me get her to her room."

Mela bit her lip, then came forward to put her arm around Clarissa, to help her up from the chair. "That's it," she said in a gentle voice. "Slowly, now." On the other side, Benedict cupped one hand under Clarissa's elbow, guiding her.

"Where's my cane?" Clarissa demanded querulously as she rose from the chair. "I need my cane."

Benedict and Mela both glanced at me. Unable to speak, I could only shake my head and grip the cane tightly in both hands. Evil seemed to linger in the room. I felt sickened by it, and by an unwilling pity. The devastation wrought by this old woman had turned, at last, on herself and on those she loved.

As if she could read my thoughts, Clarissa raised her head and stared at me. "You've never seen someone you loved taken from you, possessed by another, destroyed. Or you would understand. But I was punished. My children . . ." Her voice cracked, and she looked piteously up at her husband. "Oh, Benedict, our lovely children . . ." Pain twisted his features while he soothed her, murmuring some words against her hair, his eyes closed as though in prayer.

Before he took her away, he said, almost humbly, that he would be very grateful if I would wait for him to return. Then he and Mela slowly led Clarissa from the room. Her back, that proud, straight back, was bent like a bow.

Turning to David, I rested my head against his chest, listening to the steady rhythm of his heart. Gradually, I felt the violent beating of my own heart slacken and grow steady, the sickness in my throat recede, until the semblance of calm crept over me. At last I stepped back, looking up at him. "Did you hear her?" I asked him anxiously. "What she said?"

He nodded, his face grave. "You'd better tell me what's happened."

I said that I would, but that I wanted to call Sophie first. More than anything else, I needed to know that Max did not miss me, was not crying for me, as though the reassurance of his tranquillity might help me through this. There was a telephone on Benedict's desk. When Sophie came on the line, I explained that I had been held up at Summerhays and that it might be a while before I could get away. Take as long as you like, she replied cheerfully; Max was perfectly content. "He's scarfing up beans on toast like a long-distance lorry driver." Then, "Are you all right? You sound odd."

"Yes, I'm fine now. And David's here." Our eyes met, his and mine, and we smiled. Ah, was Sophie's light reply, then she knew she needn't worry.

As we said good-bye, Mrs. Blackwell came into the library bearing a tray with sandwiches and cups of soup. "Mr. Mallaby thought you might be hungry," she told David as she set the tray down on a table. She refused to look at me. "The doctor's just come. But Mrs. Mallaby's in a bad way. Her heart is not strong. And then all these troubles ... She should have been allowed to rest." Before she left the library, she gave me a single baleful glance.

Set against his wife's confession and his own duplicity, this display of courtesy on Benedict's part seemed grotesque. All the same, at the sight of the food, I found I was suddenly ravenous. David and I sat together on the leather sofa, and while I ate, I told him everything. He listened quietly, interrupting to ask the occasional question when the story became complicated. Once or twice, he swore softly, the only sign he gave of shock or dismay. Never once did he say "Are you sure?" or betray by any other sign that he doubted me, although much of what he heard must have seemed incredible. For this, and for his simple presence, I felt an overwhelming gratitude.

"I didn't tell you any of this before," I said, when I had finished, "because it seemed unfair to put you in the middle that way. They're your friends, you have to live here. And then there was your work, the fact that you were involved with them at the farm park. . . ."

"Not any longer. Val and I bought them out this morning. Barring some legal work that needs to be completed, he and I are co-owners now." For the first time, he smiled.

"So Benedict and Mela will be able to save Mallaby's?"

He shrugged. "They'll probably have to come to some arrangement with Fenton. Unless he backs out now." He took my hand, weaving his fingers through mine. After a moment, he said musingly, "I always wondered where it came from, that single-minded ruthlessness of Mela's. Phil didn't have it, neither does Robin. Benedict's determined, but he's not ruthless."

"Except at blinding himself to the truth."

He looked at me. "He's going to ask you what you intend to do. You know that, don't you?" I nodded. "Whatever happens, you aren't alone. I'm here. I heard what Clarissa said."

"I can't let Carl Jope be accused of a murder he didn't commit. No matter how loathsome he is. That much I'm sure of. As for the rest . . ." I stared at the fireplace, at the glowing embers of the book. An idea was coming to me, a way of salvaging something from the ashes. Before I could tell David, however, Benedict came into the room, quietly closing the door behind him. He was gray with fatigue, the faded blue eyes dull and vague. David was about to stand up, but Benedict motioned to him to stay where he was and sat down himself in the armchair opposite.

"Clarissa . . . ?" David began.

"The doctor's with her. Thinks she ought to be in hospital. An ambulance is on its way." For a long moment, he sat there, whistling tunelessly under his breath. He looked like a man devastated of all he has carefully built up over a lifetime, standing amid the smoldering remains, mourning what had been. But I had the distinct impression that all the while another part of him was busy assessing the damage to determine what might be saved.

He raised his head and looked toward me, his eyes not quite meeting mine, and confirmed that impression. "You have every right to hate us, to want to punish us. And I have no right to ask you to be generous. But I am asking."

I stared at him. "I don't understand. Do you mean, not to say anything? But Carl Jope—"

Benedict brushed this aside. "The police haven't enough evidence to hold him for Willoughby's murder. They've told me that."

"I see." For the moment, however, I wanted to ignore Willoughby's death and Benedict's implicit plea to remain silent. There was another death that mattered more to me. Intently, I leaned forward, toward him. "Why did Clarissa kill my grandfather? Do you know?"

"I asked her, before the doctor came. It was partly because Charles refused to allow us to publish *This Sad Ceremonial* under Stephen's name alone. He said we must abide by the agreement we'd made and use any money from the book for our original purpose. That otherwise Stephen's sacrifice was pointless. He had his copy of the contract with him. He showed it to Clarissa, telling her he'd see it was enforced.

"But Clarissa wanted Stephen to have the credit for his work. She'd always had faith in the book, was sure it would be a success. And she'd dreamed of someday buying back Summerhays because of it. She thought she could persuade Charles to change his mind, but he dug in his heels. They argued, and then somehow it came out that he believed I'd killed Evelyn. Clarissa was frightened and angry. She lost her head."

"How did she kill him?" I asked.

"She shot him. She liked to hunt, and kept a gun—"

"Loaded?" I said, incredulous. The loaded gun surely meant that Clarissa had expected Charles's visit and had been prepared for things not to go her way.

"And the contract," I asked Benedict, "did she destroy that?" He nodded. The one I had found, then, must have been Stephen Allerton's copy, perhaps sent to Evelyn along with the manuscript and his other effects on his supposed death in Spain, and hidden by her.

"Did you suspect she'd killed him?"

He shook his head. "Like everyone else, I assumed he disappeared to avoid the war. And then, there was something else. . . ."

I remembered Clarissa's story about Charles's attempt to persuade her to leave Shipcote with him. "She told you he asked her to go away with him, didn't she?"

"Yes. It was easy enough to credit. He had cared for her in that way, once."

"How can I believe you?" I asked him bitterly. "You knew she killed Evelyn, and yet you've protected her all these years."

"I had no choice." His eyes would not meet mine. "I loved her."

"Is that why you cheated Nan? Out of love for Clarissa?"

The contempt in my voice reached him, made his own voice angry when he replied. "I tried to give your grandmother a share in the profits. She refused it. And after she wrote that damnable book, got it all so wrong . . . Well, it seemed to me she'd had her pound of flesh."

"I thought you were a murderer, too," I said simply. "Who's to blame for that? Nan or Clarissa?"

For the first time, he looked straight at me. "We were certain you came here because of what you suspected. To make trouble. But you had no idea at all at first, did you?" He gave a short, mirthless laugh. "That's the terrible irony in all this. If we'd left you alone . . ."

"Willoughby would have made sure I found out."

"Of course. Absurd of me to forget." He began to whis-

tle between his teeth again. As I watched him, I had the
strangest sense that here was a man who had trained himself to forget, had become so adept at it that he was even
now in the process of forgetting, in order to go on loving
his wife.

Beside me, David stirred. He had listened to our exchange, Benedict's and mine, without comment, all the
while keeping my hand in his. Now he asked Benedict if he
knew why Clarissa had killed Willoughby.

"To protect Stephen. Or, rather, his memory. It's not an
exaggeration to say that Willoughby had worshiped
Stephen. He was devoted to him alive, and to his memory
after he died. I think he persuaded himself that his love was
returned. However, about six months ago, some letters
came up for auction, letters Stephen wrote from Spain to a
friend. Willoughby bought them on Clarissa's behalf. Unfortunately, he read them before she did. In one, Stephen
mocked Willoughby rather cruelly. Called him 'The Constant Nymph.' It was a family joke, I'm afraid. But coming
as it did from Stephen . . . Clarissa thought she'd persuaded
him to forgive Stephen. It seems now she hadn't. When he
came here on Wednesday, he told us he intended to revise
the biography. We knew what he meant. He would expose
Stephen as a coward, destroy his reputation, perhaps even
reveal that Clarissa had killed Evelyn."

I saw Willoughby's face as it had looked that evening at
the pub, anticipatory, on the verge of revelation. The look
of a man who would go too far.

"But who would publish a book like that?" I asked him.
"Wouldn't publishers be afraid of a lawsuit?"

"Willoughby was clever. He would have found a way to
phrase things . . . But in any event, publication was almost
irrelevant. It was enough to know others would read the
manuscript." Haltingly, Benedict went on to say that on the
evening of his death, two days ago, Willoughby had been
walking with Clarissa in the garden at Summerhays, by the
river. "He began to taunt her, in his way, with what he
knew. What he might say. When he told her he had a copy
of your grandmother's book and that he was tempted to
give it to you, she was frightened. She let her shawl fall

onto the riverbank. He leaned over to retrieve it. She hit him. And he fell in."

The terrible words, which had the simple rhythm of some childish recitation, seemed dragged out of Benedict, were slurred and uncertain.

Like Evelyn, I thought, and like Charles, Willoughby had made the mistake of threatening Clarissa's being, her family. And had been too certain of her seeming impotence.

I knew Benedict was going to ask me again to keep silent, to give up the cane, the proof that she was guilty of the only murder it was likely she could be prosecuted for. But how could I? How could I conspire to deny Nan and Charles their justice at last?

Before anyone could speak, however, the library door opened. Mrs. Blackwell stood on the threshold, her face stricken, tears on her cheeks. "Oh, Mr. Benedict," she began despairingly, "I can't bear to tell you . . ."

With a cry, Benedict was on his feet. "What is it? Is she—?" He checked himself, as though the words might make the fear true. But the housekeeper's face, and the way she looked at him, must already have confirmed that fear.

"It was her heart," Mrs. Blackwell moaned. "It just stopped."

Benedict moved toward the door with stumbling, uncertain steps, almost blindly. Muttering that he would be back, David went after him.

All I could feel at that moment was an immense, overwhelming relief. Clarissa's death absolved me of revenge, freed me from hatred. Exhausted, I sat on the sofa, staring at the fire, thoughts swirling without pattern in my head.

I was not alone long, however. Mela appeared, inimical, accusatory. I stood up to face her. "She's dead," she told me flatly. "You killed her." She had the pale fury of some avenging fallen angel, using a falsely righteous anger to suppress her own knowledge of the truth.

"Your grandmother murdered three people," I said, deliberately brutal. "You should be thankful your grandfather will be spared the pain of her trial." Relentlessly, pressing my advantage, I went on, "You can save yourself another kind of trial as well."

She had seemed about to retort, but this brought her up

short. The blue eyes narrowed. "What on earth do you mean?"

While she listened, moving impatiently about the room, rarely looking at me, I described the Longbarrow Brotherhood agreement and the claim I might have on the family publishing house because of it. "It might make Gerald Fenton nervous. Just when you're trying to get him interested in Mallaby's."

She stopped pacing and coldly stared at me. "I doubt it. Gerald's used to dealing with threats like that." From a box on Benedict's desk, she took out a cigarette and matches. She lit the cigarette, then came over to the fireplace and flicked the spent match onto the embers, as if to demonstrate her indifference.

I called her bluff. "I'm sure I won't have any trouble finding a good lawyer willing to take the case. The press would probably find it all very interesting, too. . . ." With a pang of self-disgust, I thought of Willoughby, and hesitated.

But Mela was convinced. She had her own brand of ruthlessness, David had said; perhaps it recognized mine. "Do you want money?" she said with contempt as she blew a thin stream of smoke upward. "Is that it?"

At that moment, I wanted very much to hit her. Sometimes it must be easier to be a man, I thought, to lash out with a fist. Instead, I did what mothers always tell their toddlers to do: I used words. I said, "No, not money. Restitution. I want Mallaby's, or whatever it will become, to publish *Life Blood*, my grandmother's novel."

She must have known something at least of this part of her family history, for she said uncertainly, "But there aren't any copies left, are there? I understood they were all destroyed."

"Willoughby had a copy. I saw it in one of his bookcases at Martyrs Hall. I'm sure you or Benedict could persuade the college to let you have it. It's not worth anything to them. If you'll publish it, and promote it, I'll sign an agreement not to pursue any claim against Mallaby's."

She stared at me through the plume of cigarette smoke. "Benedict told me you would cause us trouble. It seems he was right."

"He told you about that old agreement?"

"That something like it had once existed. I thought it might be in the file Tony Munnings had, but it wasn't. Where did you find it?"

"Hidden in the cottage. So you took the file, did you?"

She nodded, dismissive. "I saw it lying on Tony Munnings's desk when Benedict and I were in his office one day." It might account for a certain amount of Munnings's discomfiture, I thought, if he realized that the file had disappeared around the time of the Mallabys' visit and suspected them of taking it.

"There was nothing interesting in the file," Mela went on, as though that somehow made her theft less culpable.

"To you, anyway. I'd like it back, all the same."

She ignored this. "Is that all you want, then? That Mallaby's should publish the book?"

"That's all. You have to make it a part of whatever deal you work out with Fenton."

She considered this. Perhaps she saw that it made sense to accept my offer, that she had nothing to bargain with. "Very well," she said evenly. Clarissa had been wrong, I thought; we can do something about the past, after all. "And you'll keep silent about everything else as well?" Mela continued.

"I can't do that. Willoughby's death doesn't involve just your family and mine."

"If you mean Carl Jope, well, that can be arranged. A word to the right person. None of this has to come out."

Stubbornly, I said that I would only agree to give up my claim to Mallaby's; as for the rest, the police had to be told. After that, the Mallabys could keep it as quiet as they were able to. I certainly wasn't going to talk about it, and I didn't imagine David would want to, either. I glanced at him. Unnoticed by Mela, he had come through the doorway and was standing a little way behind her.

Her smile was not pleasant. "Ah yes. David. I wish you joy of him." It was like her, that implicit hint of something ambiguous, a parting shaft meant to unsettle.

But it had no effect, and my own smile was unforced. "Thank you. I think 'joy' is just the word."

I went past her, then, to David. Together, we left Summerhays and walked out into the sunshine. Neither of us spoke until we were well away from the place, driving down the lane toward Crookfield Farm. As we neared a gateway set into the hedge, David asked me to pull over. Hands clasped, we stood by the gate, looking across the fields to the river and the hills beyond. We struggled to make sense of all that we had heard and seen in that room at Summerhays, but nothing we could say seemed adequate. At last, we turned toward each other, and for a time words became irrelevant.

When our mouths moved apart, he whispered against my hair, "I asked you once before if you would stay. You said you didn't know. This time it's not a question, it's a plea. I want you to stay, Jo. Do you think you can, in spite of everything?"

Before I lifted my mouth to his again, I gave him his answer. It came free of doubt, with a promise of the future, the beginning of a new and happier story.

"Yes," I told him. "Yes."